THRACE

Bisanthe Perinthos Selymbria Chrysopolis
Byzantium Chalcedon

PROPONTIS

BITHYNIA

CHERSONESE P.

Lysimachia

Pactye

SEA

Aegospotami R.

Sestos

Lampsakus

Hellespont

Cyzicus

Daskylon

Abydos

Cape Helles

Ilium

PHRYGIA

LESBOS

Mitylene

Arginussae Is.

LYDIA

AEGEAN

Phocaea

Magnesia

Sardis

CHIOS

Clazomenae

Ephesus

ANDROS

SAMOS

SEA

Miletus

IONIA

KARIA

PAROS

NAXOS

Halicarnassus

COS

# THE
# FLOWERS OF ADONIS

*by*

*Rosemary Sutcliff*

**HODDER AND STOUGHTON**

Copyright © 1969 by Rosemary Sutcliff
First Printed 1969

SBN 340 10665 4

Printed in Great Britain for Hodder and Stoughton Limited
St. Paul's House, Warwick Lane, London, E.C.4,
by Cox & Wyman Ltd, London, Fakenham and Reading

# HISTORICAL NOTE

In writing *The Flowers of Adonis*, I have followed the historical accounts as closely as in me lies—allowing for the fact that no two historical accounts of the same events ever exactly tally. But being an historical novelist rather than a historian, I have felt free to "fill in the gaps" and tidy up a little here and there.

I have provided a possible explanation for Antiochus's insane foolhardiness when left in command of the Athenian Fleet, because Thucidides's bald account is so unbelievable (unless one assumes that both Antiochus and Alkibiades were mentally defective) that any explanation seems more likely than none. I have departed from Xenophon in making Timandra the companion of Alkibiades's escape from Sardis.

Alkibiades himself is an enigma. Even allowing that no man is all black and all white, few men can ever have been more wildly and magnificently piebald. Like another strange and contradictory character Sir Walter Ralegh, he casts a glamour that comes clean down the centuries, a dazzle of personal magnetism that makes it hard to see the man behind it. I have tried to see. I have tried to fit the pieces together into a coherent whole; I don't know whether I have been successful or not; but I do not think that I have anywhere falsified the portrait.

I admit, before anyone accuses me of theft, that the lament for Adonis, which I have used in the first and last chapters of this book, is in fact a lament for Tammuz the Babylonian original of the same God, as anyone may see, who reads *The Golden Bough*.

It remains only to thank Richard Nelson for his kindness in checking the naval side of my Peloponnesian War for mistakes; and to point out that any mistakes remaining in that department are therefore his and not mine!

R. S.

# LIST OF CHARACTERS

*Athenians*

| | | |
|---|---|---|
| Kymon | Timotheus | Tekla |
| Vasso | Myrrhine | Eudorus |
| Gaulites | Konon | Theron |
| Pericles | Kritias | Arkadius |
| Lamachus | Nikias | Nikomedes |
| Socrates | Antiochus | Teucer |
| Androcles | Diocleides | Demosthenes |
| Corylas | Astur | Cleomenes |
| Hipparite | Strombichides | Phrynichus |
| Paesander | Charminius | Thrassylus |
| Ariston | Thrasybulus | Callias |
| Theramenes | Episthenes | Telamon |
| Cleontius | Myron | Tydius |
| Thasos | Menander | Heraklides |
| Adeimantus | Dexippus | |

*Sicilians*

| | | |
|---|---|---|
| Archagorus | Aristarchus | Menaethius |
| Pharysatis | Basius | Demetrios |
| Alexandros | | |

*Spartans*

| | | |
|---|---|---|
| Endius | King Agis | Lysander |
| Gylippos | Queen Timea | Dionyssa |
| King Pausanius | Gorgo | Eurynomae |
| Panthea | Leotichides | Alkmenes |
| Chalcidius | Kalitikades | Clearchus |

*Persians*

| | | |
|---|---|---|
| Artaxerxes II | Cyrus | Tissaphernes |
| Pharnobazus | Megaus | Sousamitras |

*Bithynians*
Timandra                    Seitelkas

*Syrian*
Polytion

*Chersonese Thracians*
Seuthes                     Medacus

## FOR RUPERT

Cyrano: *Si nouveau . . . mais oui . . . d'être sincère:*
   *La peur d'être raillé, toujours, au coeur me serre . . .*
Roxane: *Raillé de quoi?*
Cyrano: *Mais de . . . d'un élan! . . . Oui, mon coeur,*
   *Toujours, de mon esprit s'habille, par pudeur:*
   *Je pars pour décrocher l'étoile, et je m'arrête*
   *Par peur du ridicule, à cueillir la fleurette!*

                                             Cyrano de Bergerac

# 1

## The Citizen

If I had not fallen out of an olive tree and broken my leg when I was ten years old, or if it hadn't been badly set so that it mended short, I should in all likelihood not be remembering now—unless the dead remember—the day that our Army sailed for Syracuse.

Not being fit for soldiering, I had to stay behind and go on helping my father in the shop. But I was out in the street, close down by the Piraeus Gate with everyone else, to watch them go. More than five thousand heavy-armed hoplites beside the light spearmen, and the archers and slingers. They came, company by company, tribe by tribe, swinging along, the round shields clanging on their shoulders at every step: a bronze sound in the fading torchlight before dawn. The ground under our feet felt the tramp of their footsteps, like a great ragged pulse beating; one heart beating in all of us, those who went and those who stayed behind. The sun was up before the last companies went by, though the street was still full of shadows. And we began to see their faces . . .

Some were seasoned fighting men, for the Council had called up several of the senior classes; but others were my own age; men who had been Ephebes doing their national service training only last year, and their faces under the curved bronze crests were alight and purposeful with Alkibiades' dreams that they thought—that we all thought—were our own. Friends and kinsfolk hurried and jostled alongside the marching columns, as they would do all the way to the ships, carrying baskets of last moment provisions, calling out messages from others who could not come.

They passed out through the Gate and away down the broad straight road between the Long Walls, to Piraeus and the waiting ships. And the dust cloud of early summer rose behind their rearmost ranks, hiding them from our sight. The throbbing in the ground died away, and we heard the cheering run on, rippling ahead of them down the Long Walls.

Behind them, the street in the emptiness and early sunlight was splashed and spattered with blood!

For the one instant, before the truth that my mind already knew could reach my body, the hair crawled on the back of my neck. Then the moment passed. It was the day when the women mourn for Adonis; when at every street corner one meets little companies of them carrying clay figurines of the dead God laid out as though for burial, in their midst; and all over the city, now here, now there, one hears them lamenting against the wail of the flutes. My own mother and Tekla my sister had loosened their hair and gone out to wail for him long before first light, with baskets of the little dark red roses, that are his flowers in the summer as the crimson anemones are his flowers in the waking spring, to scatter before his bier. Many such little mourning companies must have passed through the streets before the marching columns that morning; the scattered flowers, dark-bruised and smashed beneath the armies' feet, were as though they left the street spattered with blood behind them.

There was a sudden quiet; only the cheering growing fainter in the distance, and somewhere down a side street, still the thin wailing of the flutes.

"At his vanishing away she lifts up a lament,
    'Oh my child.' At his vanishing away she lifts up a lament.
Her lament is for the herb that grows not in the bed,
    Her lament is for the corn that grows not in the ear—"

"It's a pity the delay should have brought the fleet's sailing to this particular day," said an old man beside me in the crowd.

His younger companion laughed. "You and your omens! You're as bad as our valiant General Nikias who goes back to bed for the day if a fly settles on his big toe, and consults his soothsayers every morning as to the meaning of his last night's dreams."

But I thought the laughter sounded a little overhearty.

I am not one to trouble much about omens, either. But Athens is noticeably empty of men of my own generation, even today . . .

The fleet had been nearly ready to sail when the thing happened that delayed it for two days; and excitement was mounting in the city like the heat mounting in the body of a man with fever, who is wild with the exultation of it yet screams out at shadows. Maybe that was why it took such a nightmare hold on our most evil fears.

12

A few dogs barked in the night, but that was all. Even now I cannot imagine how the work was done so silently; but in the morning, going out early to open the shop (we lived behind and over the shop, as I still do) I saw that the face of the guardian Herm before our door had been hacked to pieces, and the phallus on his column smashed away.

I can remember now, standing before it like a fool, shaking and sick, and making the sign against ill-luck with my fingers, and wondering what we could have done to make the Gods so angry with our house.

But it was not our house alone. Almost every Herm in the city had had the same treatment, even the ones that were made of stone.

We purified the house with seawater and hyssop, and opened the shop very late. I do not think we have ever had so many customers, before or since, as we had that day. Not customers exactly, for many of them did not even make pretence of having come to buy; people always gather to the barbers or the armourers or the perfume shops to meet their friends and talk, as an alternative to the palaestra colonnades; and there was plenty to talk about in Athens at that time. For months past, the men who came to my father's shop to buy iris perfume and oil of rosemary had been drawing each other maps of Sicily with their long walking-sticks on the floor, and arguing endlessly about the coming campaign. Ever since the envoys had arrived from Segesta begging for help in the name of the old alliance, against Syracuse who had already swallowed up their neighbour-town Leontini and was well on the way to controlling all Sicily. And what could Athens do, in honour, when an old ally cried for aid? (We conveniently forgot Plataea and other occasions on which our honour had been less sensitive; but on those occasions, of course, it had not had Alkibiades' dream to prick it on.)

But today our customers had left their maps of Sicily, and talked startle-faced, as I suppose all Athens was talking, of nothing but the mutilated Herms.

One of the first-comers, Eudorus, a small devout man, plump as a partridge and with a mouth pursed in perpetual disapproval, began telling everyone that it was a sign the Gods were against the Sicily campaign. "Socrates has been against the whole insane business from the first," he said.

And another, sniffing rose oil from the inside of his wrist, said, "Since when have you been a follower of Socrates, Eudorus?"

"I? My dear Gaulites, I'm not a green boy to go mooning after

13

that creature; but there's no denying he has an uncanny way of being right at times."

"Ah, that Daemon of his— Myself, I'd say more likely there were human hands responsible for last night's work."

"The Corinthians," said a third man. "They're generally at the bottom of anything unsavoury; and after all, Syracuse is a Corinthian colony."

Gaulites nodded to my father that he would take the rose oil. "Come to that, the Spartans would have good enough reason to try scaring us off the expedition; both Corinth and Syracuse are allies of theirs."

"But we are at truce with Sparta," Eudorus objected.

"For the moment a somewhat brittle truce. A Syracuse that had gobbled up the rest of Sicily, wealth and manpower and all, would be in a good position to help Sparta break it."

The latest-comer, who had been standing unnoticed for the past few moments in the doorway, said, "This wasn't foreign work. It was done by somebody who knows the city like their own after-deck."

"*Somebody!* My dear Konon. It would have taken a couple of hundred men at least to get through last night's work!"

Konon, the young Trirarch of the *Thetis*, came forward and sat down on the cushioned bench. His square, heavy-browed face was thoughtful, and he seemed to be studying his finger-nails as though he had never seen them before. "Every city has its traitors; its men who have their price," he said. "I dare say there might be two hundred to be found in Athens, given one man to set the thing moving."

"You're all leaving out the Gods," Eudorus said fretfully. "That's the trouble with the world today. I dare say I'm old-fashioned, but—"

"Never mind," said Gaulites kindly, "it suits you, Eudorus dear."

My father looked round from replacing some flasks of rubbing oil. "If you'll forgive me saying so, gentlemen, there's something else you're leaving out— Oh I admit I was shaken when I saw my own Herm this morning, but I'm wondering now if there's need to look further than one God, and that one Dionysus. The young of today mix too little water with their wine, and they have no more respect for the Gods than they have for their own fathers. You're right there, sir—especially those of them that have listened to Socrates."

That was meant for me, because I did not always agree with him about certain things; but one of the growing company pounced on quite another meaning that he read into my father's words. "Well, we all know who *that* description fits."

For a silent moment they all looked at each other with raised brows. Then someone said, "He wouldn't! Not with Syracuse at stake!"

"Some people find playing with fire amusing," Gaulites said. "When most other forms of amusement have palled, with frequent usage. And we all know how he likes to give the city something to talk about."

"There's a difference between cutting off his dog's tail and committing sacrilege," Eudorus said primly.

No one actually spoke Alkibiades' name; but nevertheless, that was the first time I heard him connected with the mutilation of the Herms. Then my father saw me goggling, and bade me go down to the storeroom and check the new consignment of sesame oil; and when I came back, the unspoken name had come out into the open, and they were all talking about the scandalous things that Alkibiades had done since he could crawl.

People always talked about Alkibiades, with love or loathing or laughter, or a kind of shocked delight. But this time I think they were talking to convince themselves that he was the kind of man who might have committed the outrage; because it was better for one's peace of mind to believe that he and his friends and followers had done it in a drunken revel than to believe that the Gods or the Corinthians had done it.

"There was that time he bit his opponent in a wrestling bout, and when the trainer called him to account for fighting like a woman, he said, 'Not I, I fight like a lion!' He can't have been more than ten or eleven."

"He was younger than that when I saw him myself playing knucklebones in the street, and a wagon came along, so he bade the wagoner pull up while he finished his throw. And when the man would not, and the other boys scattered out of the way, what does my young Lord do but lie down under the mules' noses and dare the wagoner to drive over him!"

Then they fell to talking about all the lovers he had had trailing after him for his beauty when he was a boy, and how shamefully he had treated them all. I only heard snatches of that, because my father kept me busy; but anyhow I know most of the stories by heart. They said how strange it was that the good and noble Cleinias should have had such a son, and Pericles, who reared him after his father was killed at Coronaia, such a fosterling. Someone

15

said with a snort, "Pericles may have virtually ruled Athens for fifteen years, but he could never control that young devil for a day."

"Nobody has ever been able to control him except Socrates."

"There you are then: a man who rejects the guidance of Pericles to follow at the heels of that creature with a face like a satyr's mask, who has taught half the youth of Athens his own disrespect for the Gods—"

In another moment they would be back to the mutilated Herms, but Konon the Trirarch, who had taken little part in the conversation, put in quietly, "They were old tenting companions on the Potidea campaign, you know."

"Oh yes, we all know that, and saved each others' lives in the best tradition of true love—without even being lovers."

"That wasn't for want of trying on Alkibiades' part. Did you ever hear him tell the story of how he tried to seduce Socrates? I nearly laughed myself sick."

('Gods!' I thought, 'and they say women are the gossips!')

Konon got to his feet. "Yes," he said. "I was at that dinner party too, but maybe you have forgotten. It *was* funny. It doesn't seem so funny since they broke up." He strolled towards the doorway, then checked and looked back. "It's odd, you know, we were talking just now about his lovers. Of them all, Socrates was the only one who was ever able to hold him to the best in himself— even strip the shine of other men's flattery from him and make him look at himself naked for the good of his soul. That must have been extremely unpleasant for the likes of Alkibiades; and yet if he ever gave any man love in return for love, it was Socrates. Incidentally, Socrates seldom wastes his time on men not worth the expenditure."

He turned with a swirl of his light summer mantle and disappeared down the street.

The others looked after him for a moment in silence. Then Eudorus said, "Really, that was in extremely bad taste."

"It was faulty logic, which is worse, since even Socrates had to admit himself beaten, and slip the leash and let him go his own wild way in the end."

"Socrates, for all his disrespect for the Gods, would never have countenanced this bad business with the Herms."

"We still don't know that it *was* Alkibiades."

"By the Dog! Who else could it have been?"

And then they really were back where they had started; back to the damaged Herms.

The Corinthians, the Gods, a drunken debauch with Alkibiades' name generally cropping up somewhere. Other customers came and went, bringing the same theories over and over again, and stayed to argue them. But as the day went on, people seemed to be coming more and more to a new belief: that it was part of some plot to cause civil unrest and overthrow the government and bring in the Oligarchs again. I did not follow that line of reasoning myself, especially when, yet again, Alkibiades' name started coming into it— His democratic sympathies were chief among the things that his own kind, the old ruling families, held against him.

Then somebody said, "But he would not risk the Syracuse expedition— He dreamed it up himself."

And somebody else said, "He might think it worth exchanging for a Tyrant's diadem."

We Athenians have been afraid of finding ourselves again bridled and bitted by a Tyrant, ever since Pisistratus. If Alkibiades was really playing for that, with or without the help of Corinth . . .

But even then I did not understand the really dangerous thing: that most of the men who came into our shop that day—most of Athens—were afraid. It is when an animal is afraid that it turns vicious.

That evening we heard that the Council had offered a reward, together with a promise of immunity, to anyone giving information about the mutilating of the Herms, or indeed of any other act of impiety that had lately taken place in the city.

Nothing more was forthcoming about the Herms—not at that time—but suddenly the rumour was running wild through Athens, that a slave who had been overlooked and so remained in a room where he had no business to be, had sworn to a mock celebration of the Eleusinian Mysteries after a riotous supper party in a private house. The slave was uninitiated and so free to speak, and gave an account of the whole ceremony, the Washing, the Invocation in the dark, and those other parts concerning the Showing of Demeter in the reaped ear of corn, of which the initiate may not speak. He gave place and time and names. The mock ceremony had been held at the house of one Polytion, a rich Syrian merchant, who had himself taken the part of the Herald, while the part of the High Priest had been played by Alkibiades, son of Cleinias.

It was an almost perfect opportunity for his enemies. He was a man who burns too insufferably bright not to have enemies, and they were always alert for a chance to pull him down. The accusation broke on the very day that the fleet was ready for sea. Alkibiades was the youngest by far of the three appointed leaders, but the only one who counted for anything; and I remember thinking at the time it was odd that men should be prepared to wreck the Sicily expedition for the sake of ruining Alkibiades. I said as much to my father, but he told me I was only a boy and did not understand politics.

True I did not understand politics; but it was three years since I had dedicated my boy's long hair to Apollo, and I had the rights of a man and a citizen; and so I was on the Pnyx with the rest when Alkibiades stood up before the Council and the Citizens Assembly to deny the charges that had been made against him. I remember how his lazy blue gaze flickered over the Council then dropped them as a man might drop a dead mouse. It was little wonder, when one comes to think of it, that so many of his fellow nobles hated him, especially those such as Kritias, who had the itch for power themselves and knew that they looked small and mean when Alkibiades' shadow fell across them. He demanded to stand his trial then and there while the fleet waited. He demanded that if they found him innocent, his innocence should be declared before the world, and his command restored to him without a fly-speck on the burnish of his name. He demanded death if he was found guilty, as a man demanding his rights. Then when he had said all that he wished to say (and he was one that could always sway a crowd with his tongue; even the lisp which made him pronounce his Rs as Ls, which any other orator might have found a disadvantage, was a distinction in him. I have sometimes thought that he could have carried off a short leg like mine and had half the young men of Athens limping, just as he had half of them lisping in those days) . . . but I'm wandering from the point; that's because I'm growing old. When he had said all that he wished to say, and left his hearers feeling as though they had one skin less than when he started on them, he strolled down from the Speaker's Rostrum and departed, trailing one corner of his big violet-coloured mantle through the dust behind him. He was not under arrest, so far, and so the Scythian archers of the police force made no attempt to stop him.

The Council sat constantly in the next three days; and news of their debates drifted out to us in the city. At first it was all confused and contradictory; then it began to seem as though they would put Alkibiades on trial as he demanded.

I had a friend in the fleet, a rower in the *Halkyone*. Generally only resident aliens and the lowest class of citizens take to the rowing benches; but they get their half drachmas a day, and no equipment to find except their own leather rowing cushions; and

18

his father, who was a merchant shopkeeper like mine, had suffered shipwreck and died in debt. While the fleet waited, some of the rowers were given dawn-to-dusk leave; and he came up from Piraeus to have another glimpse of his family, and then came on to me. We went out and sat under a white oleander among the tombs beyond the Dipylon Gate, with a handful of honeycakes between us. And we talked, as everybody was talking, of whether Alkibiades would get his trial, and if so, whether it would be rigged.

Theron was quite determined that there would be no trial. "Not yet, anyway," he said.

And I said, "I suppose the people would forgive him almost anything just now, with all our dreams hung round his shoulders. They're frightened, of course, but I don't believe they're frightened enough to find him guilty."

"And an acquittal wouldn't suit Kritias and his party. Also", he took the grass stalk he had been chewing from between his teeth and squinted at it, "they do say that the Argives and the rest of the allied troops are threatening to desert and go home. They say they came to follow Alkibiades and they won't fight if he doesn't lead them."

I nodded. "I heard that, too. Theron, what does the fleet feel about it?"

"I'm not the Admiral."

"You might have a better idea than the Admiral does."

"Well then, from where *I* sit, third bench starboard side *Halkyone*, I'd say the fleet was getting in a nasty temper with waiting. And, at a guess, the Army will be going much the way of the fleet." He lay back with his hands behind his head, looking up with narrowed eyes into the white-flowered sprays hanging low above us. "If they try Alkibiades now, I'd not be all that surprised if they have a mutiny on their hands."

"Then there's not much they can do to him."

I remember he didn't answer at once, just went on squinting up into the oleander sprays. Then he said, "Not just now, no."

When I asked him what he meant he wouldn't explain, and showed signs of turning sour, as he always did if one pressed him with a question he didn't want to answer. So I had to let it go, and we talked of other things until it was time for him to be getting back to the ship.

Next day there was a surprise change, when certain orators began to get up in the Council and protest that now, with the expedition ready and waiting to sail, was not the moment to be trying one of its generals for blasphemy. No doubt, they said,

Alkibiades had a perfectly good defence, so why not let him sail at once, in his original command; and doubtless the whole matter would be cleared up when he returned.

Fool that I was, I thought the news was good; that when he returned triumphant everyone would have forgotten about the trial; and I could not really see why Alkibiades himself protested so furiously at the decision of the Council.

As my father told me, I did not understand politics.

There was a clatter of horses' hooves, and someone shouted, "It's the Generals! Give them a cheer, lads!"

It was two of the Generals. Old Lamachus, very grim and upright on his borrowed horse, his faded cloak hunched round him as though he were riding a night patrol. Poor old Lamachus, he was a good enough soldier once, so the men of my father's generation used to say, and had a dash of the fire-eater about him still, but so ridiculously short of cash that he was like a character out of one of Aristophanes' comedies! A General who indented for his own shoe leather! All Athens had rocked with laughter when that story got about! We gave him a cheer, all the same; especially the old soldiers in the crowd, and he put up his hand briefly in reply, but never looked to right or left of him. Then he was past, and his bitter-faced son Tydius riding with his staff officers behind him; and Nikias came clattering by, with his staff at his heels and his tame soothsayer riding beside him with the tripod and sacrificial knives. He must have just been sacrificing, for the wreath of golden laurel was still on his head. One could see over the top of it how bald he was getting, and his sickish look and yellow colour showed clear enough that his kidneys (which were as much public property as Lamachus' boot leather) had turned sour again.

"*Not* in good condition for leading an army," said the younger of my two neighbours in the crowd. "Ah well, he's only there to keep the curb on Alkibiades."

Nikias looked so noble under the priestly wreath, that one forgot that he made *his* money as a contractor supplying slaves to the Laurian silver mines, where the strongest sometimes last three years and the weaker as many months. So we cheered him too; and he was more gracious about it than Lamachus, bending a little to the left and right as he rode, and making again and again the same stately gesture of acknowledgement with one thin yellow hand.

Then they had gone clattering by, their escorts behind them, and once again the street was empty, with its dark stain of trampled

Adonis flowers. And again I heard from the side street, the women's voices wailing against the flutes.

"Her lament is for a field where corn and herbs grow not,
Her lament is for a thicket of reeds where no reeds grow,
Her lament is for woods where the tamarisks grow not."

And then, far up in the heart of the city where the street turns from the Panathenic Way, we heard the cheering. It came roaring towards us like the autumn spate down a dry river bed, and we heard the shining shout of Alkibiades' name.

It was so exactly like him to leave that stretch of empty, waiting street between himself and his fellow Generals, making of himself the final flowering of all that had gone before.

He had no escort with him, save for a mounted groom to carry his shield; as though he would say, 'Why should I need an escort? For splendour? I am Alkibiades, that is splendour enough! For safety? Are you not my own people? My own city?' It was one of the most superb pieces of arrogance, I think, that I have ever seen.

There is no need to speak of the horse he rode; he always rode horses of his own breeding, and with Thessalian stallions he bred the finest horses in Attica. His chlamys, of the deep violet colour he so often wore, was flung back from one shoulder as though by accident, but no accident could have set the straight folds falling with such perfection. The sunlight splintered on the fine gold inlay of his thorax, and on his famous gilded shield, with its blazon of Eros wielding a thunderbolt, that the groom carried behind him. His helmet, with its high stallion crest of dark blue enamel, was the open kind, so that one could see his face as he looked about him. And we knew that it was for us that he cocked his golden beard and made his eyes wide and lazy-dancing, as a woman puts on her best chiton and her fairest face for the man she would rather please than any other.

He was not smiling; indeed rather grave about the mouth, but with a kind of delight like a bloom upon him, and we knew, all of us crowded along the sides of the street, that it was us he delighted in, as we delighted in him.

And I thought suddenly, 'We're in love with him; all Athens is in love with him, and he with us; but it isn't a good love, not on either side—it isn't trustworthy—like a tame leopard that plays with the dogs, and one day turns and tears you . . .'

As he came opposite to where I stood, he turned his head, and just for a breath of time he looked full at me.

It was not easy to be young, and to watch the young men march away to the war that was to gather so much glory (I was still so near to being a boy that war seemed to me a fine and valiant thing) and that passing glance made it no easier. In that moment, if I could have known what waited for our troops in Sicily, I think that with Alkibiades' blazing blue glance upon me, I would still have asked nothing more of life than to follow him.

Then he was past, and the gold-dust fell from my eyes; and I saw again the empty street between its long hedges of craning people, and the bruise-dark stains of the trampled Adonis flowers. Men broke forward to follow him; some would run at his horse's heels all the way to Piraeus.

The younger of the two men beside me said, "The Gods help him if ever he betrays us."

And the old man said, "And may they help both him and us if ever we betray him."

In the empty street it was as though the sun had gone behind a cloud; and somewhere the women were still wailing for the dead Adonis.

"Oh my Enchanter and Priest! At his vanishing away she lifts up a lament.
Like the lament that a house lifts up for its master, lifts she up a lament.
Like the lament that a city lifts up for its Lord, lifts she up a lament.
The lament for a herb that grows not in the bed,
The lament for the corn that grows not in the ear . . ."

I knew it was time to be going home.

# 2

## The Soldier

I was on the young side for a lieutenant of marines, especially aboard the flagship (one of the flagships. Officially there were two more, each carrying an antique general on board, but in practice the *Icarus* was the only one that counted.) But it always used to be said that Alkibiades was a young man's Commander; he promoted for skill at the job, not for seniority; so much so that some of our elders and betters didn't like it.

We were quartered in barracks behind the arsenal at Zea the main war harbour, but the increased fleet had meant heavy recruiting from the hoplites into the marines, and so we had spilled over on top of the first-year Ephebes in the Munychian Fort. Even so, it was close quarters. But at any rate, for us, there was no long march down from Athens that morning, only a few steep stades past the temple of Artemis and down through the main market-place of Piraeus to the Great Harbour for embarkation. We had made the same march every morning, through the angry days of waiting; but now we knew that there would be no marching back to barracks, no more days spent in drill and weapon-practice and cleaning equipment that was clean already. No more evenings in the wine shops, telling each other what we would do to the Council and the Archons if they laid a finger on him. The orders had come at last; the wind was for Syracuse.

It was the day of the Adonia, which was a pity. We had heard the flutes and the women wailing even before first light, and all up and down the narrow ways between Fort and Arsenal, where the shipwrights lived, among the warehouses of the foreign merchants, even along the water-front itself, the dead Adonis had passed, and the little red roses that the women scatter before his bier lay bright on the ground. We trampled on them as we marched. Some of my dozen didn't like it much; sailors are notoriously a superstitious lot, and the marines catch it from them. One or two made the sign against ill-luck, when they thought I wasn't looking. So I made them sing. There's nothing like a good quick marching song for blowing away that kind of cobweb. Other companies took it up from us, and we went swinging down from the market-place and along the quayside roaring at the tops of our voices. It was "Simaetha Sweet, come kiss me now." Men very seldom sing of war when they are marching out to it. They sing about girls or drinking or beautiful boys; or rude catches about their officers. It's the old men, remembering, who sing the soldier songs.

The crowds were gathering already, lining the streets, hanging out of windows, fringing the flat roofs of warehouses. The gay ladies of the port had done with mourning for Adonis and bound up their hair again. A girl I'd rounded off several pleasant nights with leaned out from her doorway and pulled her veil half aside as we passed. I blew her a kiss; then we swung left-handed down towards the jetty where the *Icarus'* boats lay ready for us, and the bright boys of Alkibiades' staff already stood waiting for his coming.

The store ships and big transports had sailed for the gathering at Korkyra, before the trouble about the Herms blew up; and only the fighting ships, brought round from Zea and Munychia remained; a hundred and twenty of them; the slim fierce triremes of the fleet, made fast alongside wharves and jetties or riding at single anchor out in the harbour. Their newly vermilioned flanks stained the water with their reflections; the painted masks of their bows, boars' heads, dolphins' heads, leopards' heads, tossed a little in the swell lifting the bronze rams at times almost clear of the water, staring back at the sun with hard-painted eyes. The masts were already stepped, with the sails close furled at the yards; the rowers were in their places.

The boats took us out to the *Icarus*, and we took up our cere- monial positions on the fore-deck, standing easy with probably a long wait before us. All the harbour was full of picket-boats ferrying men out to their ships. Around us, as we stood resting on our spears, was the ordered bustle of the flagship making ready for sea. The rowers waited, arms on knees, their oars lying inboard; the seamen were busy with the tackle; on the after-deck Antiochus, our sailing-master, stood talking to his second and the bo's'n, and playing, in the way that he had, with one of the great silver and coral ornaments he wore, like any barbarian, in his ears.

Then we heard the cheering begin, far up between the Long Walls, rolling down to the harbour and out across the water. And suddenly between the masts of the fleet, the waterfront was dark with men.

"Close quarters, with that lot, until we can make Korkyra and turn them over to the transports," said Corylas, my second.

I nodded. "But not for us. *We*'re the flagship."

"It has its advantages."

The troops were embarking, swarming across the gangplanks onto galleys alongside wharves and jetties; while the small boats had grown busy again, scuttling to and fro like water-beetles as they ferried their loads of hoplites out to those offshore. The embarkation was still going on when a fresh wave of cheering told us that the Generals must have come on the scene.

Corylas listened with his head cocked, and said, "Only Lamachus and Nikias by the sound of it." There was anxiety in his tone.

Antiochus who had come from the stern heard him and looked round, grinning all over his wind-burned face. "Did you think Alkibiades would ride with that pair of beauties? He'll be following on last, a clear field and no one to steal his sunlight!"

And a flicker of laughter ran from one to another along deck and rowing benches. But it was a long wait, all the same. At the sterns of the *Lion* and the *Penelope* the Commanders' pennants fluttered out and the trumpets sounded as first Lamachus and then Nikias came aboard. Lamachus would be sniffing the wind like an old warhorse; but I wondered what Nikias made of it all. He had tried to persuade the people against the expedition from the first, telling them it was a thing beyond their powers: an Athenian Empire supreme from the Black Sea corn lands to the Pillar of Heracles—as though anything was beyond our powers, with Alkibiades who had given us the dream, to lead us!

"Arkadius," Corylas said suddenly.

My true name is Hagnon, but if anyone calls me by it they generally have to call three times before I remember and answer to it. My father was an Arkadian merchant, and I was born in Arkadia and bred there till he died when I was five years old and my mother brought me back to her own people in Athens. When she married again, her second husband adopted me for his own (even in these more easy-going days it is probably owing to him, good dull old man, that I have the rights and duties, including military service, of an Athenian citizen) but Arkadius or "The Arkadian" I have been all my life, none the less.

"What?"

Corylas laughed a little uneasily. "I was just thinking—you know, this is a subject for Aristophanes to put into a play. Here's the greatest fighting force Athens has ever sent overseas, setting off with her blessing and—we are told—the blessing of the Gods, under the command of a man with a blasphemy charge hanging over his head."

I said, "I wonder if he knows he's sailing under death's shadow." I had not known I was going to say that. I had not even thought it, until the moment it was spoken.

"Don't we all, setting out for war?" Corylas said.

But death seemed very far away from us, that morning of our sailing. We felt immortal. The Gods never like that.

And then at last, far over the water and up through Piraeus, we heard the cheering again, and this time a new note in it that there was no mistaking. "Alkibiades!"

Then we saw the boat coming, and the figure in the stern. You can always pick out Alkibiades even at a distance among a hundred other men. It is something to do with the way he carries his head.

The *Icarus* sprang to attention; Antiochus came straddling forward again, the ship's trumpeter at his side. Out of the tail of my eye I could see that my lads were standing steady as though they, like the mast, were stepped through the deck planks into the keel. It takes time to learn to stand like that on the deck of a galley except in a flat calm; but most of them had been at it longer than I had.

The boat came alongside. The trumpet crowed, the purple and gold Commander's pennant went fluttering up at the stern; and Alkibiades, with his gilded young men behind him, came over the side.

Antiochus had snapped to attention in the formal salute that the occasion demanded, but his seaman's bonnet was tipped far back on his head, and he grinned like the veriest dockside urchin. And Alkibiades, receiving the salute with graceful formality, had the laughter dancing like devils behind his eyes, for all the gravity of his mouth.

"Behold, I am here—blasphemy charge and all," said our Commander sweetly. But there was something behind the raillery —a defiance. I saw then that he did know he was sailing under death's shadow, and that he was enjoying the knowledge.

"Blasphemy charge and all, sir," Antiochus said. "There was a time when I doubted you'd make it."

"There was a time when I doubted it myself—a little," Alkibiades said. "Well, we've only to take Syracuse for them and they'll forget the whole affair."

"In any case, you've always got the fleet if you should happen to be needing one," Antiochus said meaningly.

Alkibiades gave a shout of laughter and clapped him on the shoulder. "You old pirate!" But they looked at each other an instant, eye into eye, all the same; and I noticed for the first time, in the way that one does notice unimportant things at important moments, that their eyes were exactly on a level.

Alkibiades turned his head and sent one hard appraising glance along our dressed line, then walked aft, Antiochus at his shoulder and his staff officers following. There was one among them I had not seen before. He was very young, I should have said scarcely old enough to be through his Ephebes' training. A very dark boy with one of those grave quick faces that one knows instinctively will break easily into laughter, and become grave again as soon as the laughter is over. I found later that he was a distant kinsman of Alkibiades, and that his name was Astur.

Almost at once after that, across the water from Nikias' flagship, we heard a single trumpet, and all through the fleet, and on shore, all sounds fell away into a quiet filled with the slap of water along the triremes' sides, and the crying of the gulls. And into the waiting silence, small and clear with distance, came the voice of the Herald raised in the Invocation. It was taken up from ship to ship, and on ship after ship smoke rose from the altars set up in the stern. On our after-deck Alkibiades laid his helmet aside and set the sacrificial wreath on his head, took the golden libation cup that the youngest of his staff officers held ready for him, and raised it high; the altar smoke fronded across his face and the scent of frankincense trailed down the length of the *Icarus* on the light breeze. He made the Invocation for Victory, turning shoreward to Athene of the Citadel, whose upraised spear, four miles away, made a flake of brightness on the blue air. Then crossing to the seaward side, to Blue Haired Poseidon, for the safety of the fleet. And standing there with one foot on the mounting of the rail, poured the meal and the wine into the lapping water.

And at full pitch of his lungs, he raised the Paean. For a heart-beat of time his voice hung alone; then we caught it up from him, rowers and seamen, and fighting men alike; and the next ship took it from us, and the next, until from the whole fleet the Paean was ringing upward.

As the last note died, Antiochus shouted the orders to up-anchor and stand by to set sail. The great bronze-bound anchor came dripping in over the side; and all round us was the shrilling of flutes and the shouted orders of the pilots as the fleet up-anchored and cast off for sea. The rowers began to sing at their oars, taking their time from the bo's'n's flute as we came round and headed for the harbour mouth. Once past the mole, the topmen sprang into action and sails, brilliant with coloured suns and stars and dolphins, broke out from masts that had been bare stalks before. The canvas filled with the north-west wind that was rising as usual towards noon and we spread out and made a race of it till we were past Aegina, then fell into the proper stations of a fleet at sea.

## The Seaman

We makes the gathering at Korkyra and turns the troops over to the transports, and picks up the storeships—which besides corn and supplies, carries stone-masons and carpenters with the tools of their trade for building war machines and raising siege walls and Poseidon knows what-all beside. And we sails the long haul across to Italy. It's not all Hymettus honey, making that crossing direct—two nights at sea is well enough for pot-bellied trading vessels, but a warship isn't built for sleeping in like a floating barracks. It's not too bad for the marines, they can bed down snug enough under the awnings forward, and the Commander has his sleeping space aft and can spread as wide as he chooses, so long as he doesn't foul the steersman's feet; but for the rest of the ship's company from the rowers to the pilot . . .

Name of the Dog! It's times like that, especially in anything like dirty weather, you begin to wonder why you didn't hamstring yourself in infancy and take to street begging instead!

That particular crossing goes off smooth enough, though, with no one lost overboard and no rammings in the dark. But we were none of us sorry when we rounded Cape Heraklea the third morning out from Korkyra, and saw Etna trailing smoke to the north.

That night we lies at Rhegium on the toe of the mainland, the storeships as close inshore as we can get them, the war-craft, except for a few scouts, hauled up on the beach. The locals allows us harbourage and a market for supplies, but "no entrance" says they; so we makes camp above where the ships are beached, in the precincts of the old Temple of Achaea just outside the city, with the tents of the Generals close under the Goddess's own stone-pines.

At Rhegium the scouting vessels we sent on ahead rejoined us with news to make a man sit down and weep or curse his own grandmother. The Generals called a Council of War, and seemingly came to some sort of agreement, though a drunk man can see with one eye it doesn't make them love each other any the more. And that evening Alkibiades himself comes down to my quarters—a spare sail rigged out from the side of the galley—and orders me to have the *Icarus* ready to sail for Messana at first light. And when I asks the reason, he smiles as soft as mother's milk, and, says he, "to make the Messanians love us, Pilot."

So at first light next morning, we sails for Messana. But my bonny lad, pacing the after-deck with his great cloak dragged round him against the chill that blows up off the water at that hour, doesn't look, for my money, as though he's going to make anyone love him. I'd taken over the steering oar myself—I'd a good second, well up to handling the *Icarus* even in the tricky currents of the Strait, and ordinarily I'd have left it to him, but I've a feeling that what's coming may be the kind of thing best not said with a third pair of ears to hear it.

Astern of us there's these few lights burning in the camp; and ahead, there's the mountains of Sicily. No wind to fill the sail, but the sea's choppy with the meeting of cross currents; short irregular seas that make it hard for the rowers to keep time, and give the steersman plenty to keep him occupied; but even so, I begins to feel the silence stretch out long and thin between him and me, and it's not the companionable kind of silence, either. To break it, I says, "What for your chances with the Messanians?"

"The Lordship of Athens, a matched chariot team, an outworn sandal strap. How should I know?" says Alkibiades, still pacing. "I am Alkibiades and there is no other Alkibiades but me; but alas! owing to some oversight, I am not numbered among the Gods. It's inconvenient, and I feel the lack of Godhead from time to time." He passes me in his pacing, and flings the words over his shoulder. "I'll tell you one thing, Antiochus mine: if I were a God I'd blast that old fire-eater Lamachus with a thunderbolt, and send our devout Nikias such a spiritual ecstasy he'd never come out of it again but sit smiling harmlessly into the white eye of the moon and picking bits out of his navel for the rest of his life."

"I'll not have that kind of talk aboard my ship," says I, "it's unlucky."

He swings round on me. "Apart from the fact that she's *my* ship, who are you to be so careful about pleasing or displeasing the Gods? You raised the hymn to Demeter and Kore as loud as any of us

29

that night after supper. You invented a new version to the second strophe that was—unorthodox to say the least of it."

Well, it's true enough, but I don't care to be reminded of it just then, so I says, "What I do ashore is one thing, and what I do at sea is another thing. Nobody takes liberties with the Gods at sea. Not if they're wise, they don't."

We looks at each other an instant in the growing light. I hears the dip and thrust of the oars and the slap of water along the sides, and the faint creak and play of the whole trireme under way. And I knows Alkibiades pretty well; I ought to, by that time. "It was a stormy Council, was it?" I says.

The little waves slaps against the oars and sends the spindrift flying in my face. And he turns his back on it and leans on the dipping gunwale. "Stormy enough. Old Daddy Nikias was for trying to settle everything with treaties and agreements—*more* treaties and agreements that aren't worth the papyrus they're written on—and then sail round the coast making a show of Athenian power, like a Persian gamecock showing off his tail at mating time. Then off home to Athens with 'no waste of manpower or resources'—and nothing to show for having come on this jaunt at all!"

"And that wouldn't do much to help on the plans of the Lord Alkibiades. I'm thinking they don't include a peaceful settling of Sicily's affairs."

"We need a victory, and a bloody one, in Syracuse," says he, "not a cobbled-up peace that leaves all as it was before."

"Lamachus will have been with you in that, at all events."

"Our aged fire-eater? Oh he'd have had us beating on the walls of Syracuse by now. Very full of the advantages—including booty —of surprise; very vocal as to advisability of attacking while the enemy are still wetting themselves with fright at the size of the Athenian fleet."

"He might be right at that," I says. "An invading enemy never seems so dangerous or so big as he does at first sight, before you've had time to get his measure."

"Do you think I don't know that?"

"Then why—" I begins; but he flings off from the gunwale and laughs, soft and a bit ugly.

"The Sicils promised us, if we came to their aid, the money to pay and victual our troops and keep our ships in trim. Yes? And now the scouts have come back and we know that the Sicils haven't the price of a new cloak between them! It's quite beautiful, when one comes to think of it; they must have kept our embassage in a golden haze of the grape from the first moment they stepped ashore, so that everywhere they looked, they saw gold; a Midas touch behind their eyes and in their fuddled heads— Gods! And all the wine drunk from the same fine gold and silver cups passed round ahead of them to every table they feasted at." His voice was soft and purring—a panther might have that voice if it spoke with a man's tongue, lying out on a warm rock. Then between one word and the next it turns quick and hard with exasperation. "By the Dog! Antiochus, do you think I like counselling a middle course? I, Alkibiades? What have I to do with middle courses? But look at the other two! For Athens to send out an expedition such as this, and then receive it home with nothing to show for ever having sent it— Can you think what that would do to our place among the allies? Even to what hold we still have in the Aegean? And lacking the Sicils' gold to feed our men and buy mercenaries from the rest of the island, how in Typhon's name can we launch an attack on Syracuse? Without even a base. We have got to gain allies among the other cities; kindle the Sicils to revolt for themselves against the power of Syracuse—men in revolt fight without pay. But before all else we must win over Messana. Safe harbourage, lying in the entrance to the Straits and covering the main approaches to Sicily. Strategically it's the perfect base. *Then* we can spring at the throat of Syracuse!"

"It's not *me* you have to convince; and seemingly you have convinced your fellow Generals— Leastwise, here we are with the *Icarus'* prow set towards Messana."

"I won over Lamachus," says he, briefly. "He's slightly more open to reason than Nikias, because his ears aren't so waxed up with his religion; he can actually hear what's said to him from time to time, if it's shouted loud enough. Then we were two to one."

We comes in to Messana harbour in early sunlight, and drops anchor in the roadstead, a cable's length offshore. There's quite a stir, along the waterfront, at sight of the scarlet sun on our sail; and presently, out comes the state penteconta, to know our business. The Commander and Alkibiades talks together for a while, and then Alkibiades goes ashore in our boat.

We sits on our backsides and waits, while the day goes by and the *Icarus* swings three-quarter circle to her anchor rope. Arkadius, our lieutenant of marines, sets his men to cleaning their equipment from the salt of our passage, and the rowers crawl into the shade under the benches and sleep like dogs on a dunghill. When the

31

shadows of the mountains are beginning to lengthen across the harbour, and the smells of the day's heat, good and bad, come wafting out to us across the water, My Lord comes wafting out with them.

"He's wearing his silken look," says Arkadius, out of the side of his mouth, even before the boat comes alongside. "Now I wonder what that means."

As soon as I gets the chance, I asks him what has happened.

"We had a beautifully civilized Council meeting," says he.

"And?"

"And it was very hot, my dear, and a fly kept on walking about on the Chief Archon's bald head. Messana is largely populated by cautious old men, and young men with cautious old men's heads on their shoulders."

"Then we don't get the base?"

"They'll allow us exactly what Rhegium allows us: a market, and leave to camp outside the city. And nothing I could say . . . Gods! I reasoned with them, I turned the full blaze of my sunshine on them, I even hurled a few thunderbolts—I tell you, Antiochus, I descended to courtship. I *wooed* that Council till I felt like an ageing hetaira. All to no purpose. Syracuse is nearer and has more to offer than we have."

"And more to threaten?"

"To be of most use to us, we need Messana as a friend, not a conquered enemy."

"So, that's it then. Do we sail for Rhegium at once?"

Alkibiades stops his prowling up and down and sits himself down on an armour barrel and smiles at me. "Oh no! Never let it be said that Messana is lacking in courtesy. We are bidden to a supper party in the house of the Chief Archon."

"We?" Sailing-masters don't usually get invited to supper in the houses of the great. On the deck of a trireme with dirty weather blowing up, or when the spears are flying and it's time to manœuvre the ship to ram, then we count as any man's equal and a bit to spare, but on shore we're not gentlemen. Oh yes I've supped with more than one of Alkibiades' friends in Athens, but then all the world knows that a disgraceful number of Alkibiades' friends aren't gentlemen either, and you're as likely to meet a ship's master or a rich merchant with too many rings and a twang of Corinth at the back of his nose, as you are to meet some bright sprig of the older nobility at his table. Most people are more careful of the company they keep.

"You and I," says Alkibiades. "Small and select."

32

"Did you tell them my father made his living gutting fish?"
says I. I'm interested.

"I told them I intended to bring my sailing-master with me,
because if it was anything like as good a party as I expected, I
should require his professional skill to get me back to the *Icarus*.
With the help of the wine and the stephanotis garlands they may
not notice the smell of fish guts."

"There's times," I says, "when I wonder why I've stuck to you
all these years! And if you say 'because I'd not be master of the
*Icarus* now, if I hadn't', you can sail her back to Rhegium yourself
when this bloody supper party is over!"

He turns himself round a bit on the armour cask, and looks at
me. "But I was not going to say that," he says; and he sounds
amused, and in a queer way he sounds puzzled . . .

I shall never understand him and I might as well make up my
mind to it. I've had time enough, if ever I was going to, the Gods
know that! I had scarcely parted with my boy's long hair, the day
that he and I first came to hailing distance, nor had he, come to
that. I had got myself taken on by a kinsman of my mother's who
owned a half share in a fishing-boat at Phalaron (that was a step up
in the world for me!) and my master had sent me on an errand into
Athens. I carried out the errand, whatever it was, and went back
a roundabout way that would take me through the Agora. All boys
like to see a bit of life. The Agora was even more crowded and full
of life than usual. And there seemed to be something special going
on before the Temple of Zeus. I edged up closer, to see what it
might be, and found that it was one of those days the Government
decree when they need to meet a special expense or find themselves
short of obols, for public spirited citizens to make free gifts to the
state. Nobles and rich merchants were outdoing each other at the
receiving tables, and from time to time an ordinary citizen coming
up with his smaller contribution. Me, I'm not in the least public
spirited, and I'd a much better use for the obol in my pouch; but
I dawdled to a standstill to watch, and in the few moments I'm
stood there watching, Alkibiades comes by.

I knew him by sight, of course; all Athens did. Even then, he
was the kind that only has to walk through a crowded place for all
eyes to follow him. He was simply strolling by, when I first saw
him, but suddenly he seemed to wake to what was going on. His
brows flew up, and I saw the idea and the casual amusement come
into his face together. He turned towards the receiving tables,
everyone parting to let him through as though he walked on winged
sandals, and brought out a crimson silk bag from the breast of his

tunic and tossed it down, jingling, among the money already piled there. No one would have guessed, seeing him standing there that Pericles kept him rather short, and the money had been meant to pay a few of his pressing bills. Everyone crowds round to watch the counting, exclaiming in admiration at his generosity, and the public spirit of one so young. And in the general excitement, somehow a fighting quail that he had under his mantle gets free. I've a fair idea he let the thing escape on purpose, just for a little amusement in passing; but that's as may be. It was the time when quail fighting was forbidden, anyway.

Everyone in the Agora, it seemed, dropped whatever they were doing to try to catch it for him as it hopped and fluttered away on its clipped wings. And I—I was the one to get it (it left a few tail feathers in the hands of a master baker)—and brought it back to him where he stood looking on as though at the antics of a troop of tumblers, and doing nothing about it himself, whatever.

I had joined the scramble simply for the sport of the passing moment. But when I stands there before him, holding out the quail with its angry head sticking out like a feathered snake between my fingers, suddenly it's not sport any more. And there's me with my heart drumming right up in my throat, looking down at the quail as he took it from me, and afraid to look up into his face because I knows that when I do, something's going to happen, and afterwards nothing's ever again going to be just the same as it was before. So I looks up, and there's that cool blue gaze of his waiting for me; and the thing happens.

Oh not love, not what men mostly mean by love, anyway. He'd had plenty of men in love with *him*; but we were both of us even then, ones for the women, and the more women the better.

A new fear came to me, that he was going to offer me money, if he had any left, for having caught his quail; but he was only tucking the bird under his arm again. He said, "It's bleak work thanking a man without a name to thank him by. What do they call you, Catcher-of-Quails?"

"I am Antiochus, son of Andros," I says.

And he says, "I am Alkibiades, son of Cleinias."

He must have known I was well aware of that; but maybe he also knew, as I did, that I was his man from then on, and there are rituals to be observed in these things. Even two dogs know that, when they cock their legs in the same spot as a sign that they accept each other.

Then he says, "It's hot. Let's go and find something to drink, Antiochus, son of Andros."

34

No one less noble or less arrogant than Alkibiades would have been seen drinking with a fisher lad at a public wine booth; and no fisher lad with any sense of the fitness of things would have gone happily, without thought of the honour done him, to drink at a public wine booth with Alkibiades.

I never thought of that until I went home and told my parents what had happened. At first they did not believe me; and when they did, my father, who was of a hopeful disposition, kept telling me that my fortune was made. "He'll be the making of you—the *making* of you, boy!"

Until my mother, who took a darker view of life, some said as the result of having married my father, said, "Or the death of you, if all I hear of that one be true."

Well, my father has proved right so far, but there's still time enough for my mother's turn to come.

Alkibiades on the deck of the *Icarus*, says presently, "Not curious as to the real reason that you come with me tonight?"

"There's another reason?"

"There is. Someone jostled against me as I came down the steps from the Council Chamber, and left this in my hand." He fishes a folded strip of papyrus from the breast of his tunic and holds it out to me. I have never found reading come easy; it's a thing you need to learn young, but I can spell out the few words on it with some trouble. "Athens has better friends in Messana than you have found among the Council. Trust the messenger who comes to you at Archagorus' house this evening."

"Archagorus being the Chief Archon? Can you smell a trap?"

Alkibiades shrugs. "Quite possibly. Quite possibly not. In either case I may be needing a friend to cover my back." He gets up from the barrel and stretches until the small muscles crack behind his shoulders. "Go and make yourself beautiful, Pilot."

# 3

## The Seaman

That's a good supper party.

The Chief Archon of Messana was a man who knew how to treat his guests; and the wine, cooled with snow from the mountains inland, was some of the best that has ever gone down my thirsty throat. Just my luck that it should come my way on an evening when it was about as much use to me as vinegar.

"Remember," says Alkibiades to me while we were making ready, "the Gods alone know what hornets' nest we may be running our heads into this evening; and so, my dear, you will keep within reason sober, this one shore-going night, if you never did it before and if you never do it again."

"You've never known me too drunk to have my wits about me," says I.

And he grins, settling the shoulder folds of his mantle. "I've known you with the vine-leaves dripping out of your ears, and the breath of you enough to set them twining up the mast and turn any self-respecting pirate crew to dolphins. And that's when you go looking round for someone to start a fight with for the sheer murderous fun of the thing." And then suddenly he looks at me straight, with the grin wiped off his face, and says, "That's an order, Pilot."

So I curses inwardly and smiles my most gentleman-like, with a thirst on me like a lime pit; and lets the boy pass with the wine krater more often than I holds up my cup to be refilled. And truth to tell, as time goes on, it seems that Alkibiades is drinking more than I am. And 'there's no justice in this world for poor sailor-men,' thinks I.

Very well it becomes him, I must say. And lounging there among the piled cushions, with his mantle slipping half off one shoulder, and his smile and his lisp honeyed enough to make you bilious, he looks like a man without a thought in the world beyond

36

a pleasant evening spent among pleasant strangers. But I wonders if he's as sharp-aware as I am of the bright hardness of the dagger belted under his mantle against his bare skin.

There was good talk round the table in Archagorus' andron that evening. Some of it was above my head, and then I amused myself with the frescoes of nymphs and gambolling kids and slant-eyed satyrs on the walls—they were finer and more lewd than anything I'd seen in Athens, outside Alkibiades' private supper room.

But when the talk turned on the plays of Euripides, I grew interested again; for though taking it all in all I'd sooner have a comedy, I like a good tragedy as well as the next; the kind that gives you something to chew on, and maybe tugs at your heart-strings a bit. (They say most sailors are sentimental.) It seemed that Messana, like the other cities of Sicily, set great store by his work, and Aristarchus and his cronies were eager to hear details of his latest play, presented at the Dionysia that spring. Now that was the year that Euripides presented *The Trojan Women*—a piece of very uncomfortable anti-war propaganda, which could hardly be expected to find much favour in a city just about to launch the greatest attack of its history. (Old Euripides had the courage of his convictions, I'll say that for him!) And it wasn't surprising that the prize that year went to a satyr play.

Remembering Alkibiades storming out of the theatre, and sweeping half the front benches after him, I wondered what he would answer to their questions. He put the tips of his fingers together in the manner of Nikias at his most judicial, and looked at them consideringly. "Euripides is not a young man, and reputedly he is a sick one. I think possibly his powers begin to fail."

It was a damnable slander, and he knew it as well as I did. But it did Euripides no harm.

They shook their heads and said they were grieved to hear it, but pressed for details all the same; and Alkibiades told them how the play opened in the camp before fallen Troy; and how, after the Gods had had their say, it concerned nothing but the portioning out of the captured women among the conquerors, and the slaying of Hector's infant son. "It's scarcely a play at all," he says, "no plot, no shape; just one damned misery after another, with some passable lyrics in between."

And that's not true either. Only maybe it's better to pretend, even to yourself, that it is. I remembers, sudden and too clear for comfort (I didn't know I'd listened that closely), a rag of one of Cassandra's mad speeches, about the Greeks who died in the siege,

far from their homes, fighting a people that hadn't threatened their
walls nor overset their landmarks.

> "And they whom Ares took,
> Had never seen their children: no wife came
> With gentle arms to shroud the limbs of them
> For buried, in a strange and angry earth
> Laid dead. And there at home, the same long dearth;
> Women that lonely died, and aged men
> Waiting for sons that ne'er should turn again,
> Nor know their graves, nor pour drink-offerings
> To the unslakéd dust. These be the things
> The conquering Greek hath won!"

No, it's not much wonder that Athens has hated him ever since.
Playwrights with a message are first cousins to Hades himself.
I has to get my cup filled the next time the boy comes round, to
wash the taste of that wretched play out of my mouth.

But it was not all talk. Archagorus knew how to keep his guests
from going to sleep once their bellies were full. And when the main
part of supper was over, while the slaves were bringing in fruit and
little honey cakes, and fresh garlands to replace those that had
withered in the heat, there was a sudden shrilling of flute music
from the dark courtyard, and into the torchlight came running a
little troop of light-foot Syrian dancing girls led by three flute girls
to play for them.

All evening I had been waiting, questioning in my head every
guest at the table, every slave who entered out of the shadows,
wondering if this, or this, or this, was our messenger. But for some
reason it never occurred to me to look for him—or her—in such
company. I was merely pleased that here was something more to
my taste than after-supper talk, however good; and sat up to enjoy
myself.

It was pretty to watch; all tiny mouse-quick footwork, and arms
swaying like palm fronds, and the chiming of little bright spangles
on swinging skirts of blue and violet and crimson gauzes that you
could almost see through but never quite as much as you'd like to.
You can see much the same thing in any seaport if you know where
to go, though this was better done, more classy.

But when the figs and honey cakes were on the table and the
slaves had departed, the dancing grew wilder and more worth
watching; the flutes made little trills of notes and from their
pretty, commonplace dancing, the girls began to turn acrobat,

38

weaving coloured patterns of themselves in the air, one after another like a shoal of dolphins, going down and over and up, flying heels over head in a whirl of spangled gauzes. One girl in particular seemed to have not a bone in her body but be all fire and whipcord; and every time she came upright from a flying somersault or from some fantastic upside-down trick of skill and balance, she did it with a toss of the head and a flash of a smile that was not just the trained smile of the other girls but seemed to sparkle up from inside her with the pleasure of what she did. There was a hardiness about her, under the paint; she looked as if she could have swarmed up a mast like any of my topmen, to furl sail in a squall of wind. And I says to myself, 'Pilot, if there's one for the taking later, that's the one for you.'

But Alkibiades also was looking that way; and she—every time she spun past him she gave him a flick with her gold-painted eyes; and I saw that if she were for anybody's taking it wouldn't be mine. I wasn't breaking my heart. The other dancers were pretty and gay and any one of them would likely be just as good under the bushes. And failing any of them, I reckoned there'd be plenty more girls in Messana. I'd forgotten with the chief part of my head, that unless something had gone wrong with somebody's plans, we should have other things to do that night than tumble in some dark corner with a girl.

The performance was drawing to an end, the dancers spinning faster and faster, the flute notes flying like sparks from a windy fire; and then—it was so swift that in the coloured whirl of arms and legs and intermingling skirts and flying hair I never saw quite what happened—the girl seemed to slip or maybe turn giddy, and the force of her own spinning carried her into our midst and flung her in a tangle of twisted gauzes across the low couch on which Alkibiades half lay. He caught her on the instant, casual and laughing, like a boy catching a ball at play; the flutes fell silent between note and note, and the dance wavered into nothing. And the girl's thin brown arms flashed up and were round his neck! I never saw a girl so shameless—nor a man for that matter. He simply scooped her into his mantle, swung his feet to the floor and got up, holding her high against his breast and shoulder. She seemed, as far as I could make out, to be biting his ear.

Then she begins to kick and squeal a bit, for form's sake, but not much; and Alkibiades stands there smiling pleasantly round at the rest of us, and at our kind host, who's sitting bolt upright on his couch, his face rigid with startled displeasure.

"See what the Gods have sent me!" says he, and bows a little.

"Archagorus, you are the very prince of hosts! Even I never thought of a more charming way to end a social evening!"

He gives me a quick look under the banquet wreath of stephanotis rapidly sliding over the ear that the dancing girl wasn't using; and I understands.

"I—I—" was all Archagorus could say, and his eyes bulging in his head, and the others weren't in much better case. I never yet found a Greek-speaking port where My Lord's name for outrageous behaviour wasn't known, but it looked as though the chief men of Messana hadn't been prepared for anything quite like this. At sight of their faces the laughter rose in my throat, only as I made ready to move, the touch of the dagger against my bare skin sobered me.

Alkibiades blew a kiss to the other girls who had drawn together in a startled knot, and turns and strides a little unsteadily from the andron, the girl still giggling across his shoulder.

I got up and lurched after him, turning in the doorway to favour the company with a shrug and a grave shake of the head, which they can take for insolence or apology, whichever best pleases them. Then I follows Alkibiades.

The door-slave, also somewhat goggle-eyed, was opening the street door for him as I got there, and Alkibiades says to him with grave courtesy, "A beautiful evening, is it not? And as warm as milk. Can you direct me to the nearest place where there is some grass to lie on and a leaf or two overhead?"

I goes after him up the street, keeping a pace or two in the rear. And after a few steps he bursts into song. An old nursery rhyme, of all things.

> "Gay girl, myrtle tree,
> Little flowering myrtle tree,
> Come away and dance with me.
> And a bird flew out of the myrtle tree."

But as soon as we gets to the end of the street, out of earshot of the Chief Archon's house, he falls silent.


## The Dead

May the dead take their part in the telling of this story? There are many dead because of Alkibiades.

The tyranny of Syracuse lay heavy on Messana, as on the other cities of the Straits. And when word reached us that Athens was sending a great war-expedition against her, it sounded to us as the distant trumpets of a relief force must sound in the ears of a beleaguered garrison. To some of us, that is: ah, not to the Syracusian party who held all power in the city; but to us lesser folk with little power or none. At first it was only that we glanced at each other in the street or the market-place or the gymnasium; and then quickly away again, for fear of making too clear the thought that each man carried behind his eyes.

Later, word came that the Athenian fleet was actually at Rhegium. And then Menaethius, the Olympic victor, gave a supper party to a few friends, at which, when the meal was over and the slaves sent to their quarters, we talked of matters best not overheard by the city in general. We made plans, we few in the summer colonnade of Menaethius' house, with the moon casting the shadows of the vine leaves across the table to confuse the lamplight, and the soft-edged night moths blundering out of the dark to whirl about the flames. Plans to rise against our overlords and hand the city over to the Athenians' protection.

It was a hard choice to make in the first place, not that we owed any loyalty to Syracuse, but we were not the stuff that makes and breaks the patterns of empires; we were merchants, small land-owners, a goldsmith, a couple of ship masters. But we nerved ourselves; we felt ourselves eager and alive, and those of us who were no longer young, felt ourselves young men again.

Then we went our ways, each to make contact with others of like mind.

So the thing spread, quietly under the surface, and presently we knew our strength, and our plans were made, so far as they could be made at that stage. The Athenian fleet was still at Rhegium. "They will need this harbour," Menaethius said. "Soon they will come seeking it."

One morning the Athenian flagship sailed into the harbour, and the news went racing through Messana that Alkibiades himself had come; that the Archons had summoned a meeting and he was with them in the Council Chamber even then.

We had certain eyes and ears in the Council Chamber, and so we knew what passed—but we might have guessed that easily enough in any case. We knew also that the Chief Archon had made plans for feasting the unwelcome visitor. All that morning, little groups met in the perfume shops, in the gymnasium, in the Agora, and exchanged a word or two and moved on.

I was the one who jostled against him in the crowd as he made his way back to the ships, and thrust a note into his hand. There would be no time for a spoken message in the open street, and we dared not commit such things as time and place to paper. So it did no more than let him know (as the Syracusian party knew well enough already), that there were friends of Athens in the city, and alert him for the coming of our actual messenger.

The rest must be for Pharysatis to accomplish.

By that time our ranks had opened to include one woman. Courtesans are quick to hear news and can be quick to pass it on. They have more wit and daring than a good woman who has led a good woman's sheltered life. And the best of them can be trusted to the death when once their faith is given. Pharysatis of old Gorgo's dancing troupe was Menaethius' girl whenever he could afford her, and had already done good work for us in passing messages and the like. Menaethius arranged matters somehow with our fat Chief Archon, so that the troupe was engaged for that evening's supper party, and got word to Pharysatis of what she was to do.

It had been a full and anxious day, and the summer dusk was deepening into the dark, when the three of us appointed to act for the rest came together in Menaethius' garden. Menaethius himself, and I, and Basius, the master of the *Dolphin*. We had chosen the meeting-place because it was easy of access from some waste ground just within the city walls; and being a long garden we could keep well away from the house and all chance that some sound of a late arrival might reach anyone awake in the slaves' attic or the women's quarters.

We waited a long time, while the sky beyond the old temple to Poseidon brightened slowly with the silver fore-wash of the rising moon; but I do not doubt that it seemed longer than it was. I remember how the darkness of the garden began to be watered with moonlight, and that I looked down at my own hand resting on the head of a sculptured gazelle, and saw it like a hand carved from the same marble, every vein and tendon lightly shadowed in, but without colour and without life . . .

And I moved it quickly, to break the spell, and said, because suddenly anything seemed better than the silence, "He should be here by now."

"Soon, anyway," Menaethius said, tranquilly. He was always a very tranquil-seeming man, I suppose all his stresses found their outlet in his running, and he wasted no energy on things that did not call for it.

"Pharysatis may not have been able to get word to him," said

Basius; like me, he was getting edgy. "Or he may have thought it a trap."

Menaethius said, "From what I saw of him at Olympia—unless he has greatly changed in these past few years—I do not think that would hold him back."

And we were silent again.

And Menaethius was right.

He came out of the black shadow of the city wall, wildcat striped and dappled with the shadows of bramble and arbutus branches, and walking with a long light stride that had something of the wild cat in it too. And behind him followed another, not Pharysatis; her task, once she had brought him to the meeting-place, was to keep watch, but a big loose-limbed man who's walk had the unmistakable roll of one used to the deck of a ship under foot. Basius has something of that walk himself.

We came together in the little clearing watched over by the marble gazelle, a small white lake of moonlight among the dark tangle of roses and cistus and sweetbay that hid it both from the house and the temple precincts; and he said to Menaethius, who had moved out a little ahead of Basius and myself, "May I felicitate you on your choice of messenger?"

"I am glad that she finds favour in your eyes," said Menaethius; and then, "May we know who comes with you?"

In watching Alkibiades I had almost forgotten the other; but he answered himself in a rough-textured voice that was made pleasant by the note of humour in it. "Antiochus, pilot of the *Icarus*, come to see the play runs fair." I looked at him with interest; this man who the great Alkibiades had taken out of the fish markets of Piraeus to become the chief sailing-master of his fleet. By the white light of the moon, I saw a man with a drunkard's nose in a dissolute face, with the same humour in the mouth that I had heard in his voice, a dark head curly as a ram's fleece that might have been red in the daylight. He wore heavy swinging ornaments in his ears like a barbarian, and indeed there was something of the barbarian, the Outlander, about his whole bearing. It was not the mark of the Piraeus fish market, it was something in himself that would have been there if he had been born into the ranks of the Eupatridae. He was one of those who make their own laws as they go along, and he would care not a feather in the wind for any other law, and not overmuch for any right or wrong save the will of the man he followed.

"You must forgive me if I seem discourteous," Alkibiades was saying, "but since I have no proof that in coming to this meeting-place I am not walking into a trap, it did occur to me that I should feel more comfortable between the shoulders if I brought a friend to cover my back. It also appeared to me that it would be still more discourteous to come seemingly alone and leave him to hover unseen in the dark behind me." Even in the moonlight we could see the faint smile that barely lifted the corners of his lips. "You may regard him as a statue or a myrtle tree. He will be just as silent as to what he hears."

There was a moment's silence. Antiochus, who had dropped back a pace or two, gazing at the moon with absorbed interest; Alkibiades looking from one to another of us with brows a little raised and still that faint smile on his lips.

Then Menaethius began, "We have no right to expect that you should trust us."

"No, you have not, have you," Alkibiades agreed. "And while we are on the subject, may I point out while I stand here with the moon full on my face, you all have your backs to it?"

It had been quite unintentional, and we all moved, and Menaethius presented Basius and myself as formally as though he had been bringing up friends in the palaestra to be made known to each other; and was just about to introduce himself, when Alkibiades said, "I know you, do I not? Now where—"

"The last Olympic Festival," Menaethius said.

Alkibiades' smile suddenly warmed. "Menaethius! Of course! You won the Diaulos."

"And you the chariot race."

"*And* carried off third and fourth places. That's the advantage of entering seven teams," Alkibiades said. "A runner can only enter himself . . . You, I take it, are the 'better friends to Athens than I found in the Council Chamber'?"

"We are."

"All three of you?" said Alkibiades in a voice as silken as a crocus petal.

"There are—others," Menaethius said. "We three are chosen to represent them, and to put our lives in your hands as surety for the good faith of us all."

Alkibiades looked at us each in turn. I have seen a man look so at a matched chariot team, judging the mettle of the horses. Then he said with quick gravity, "A good choice, I think, and I accept the surety. Now tell me your purpose in sending to me."

Menaethius held the spokesman's place among us by common consent. "Today you sought to persuade the Council to open the city and harbour to you, for a base and repair yard in your attack

44

on Syracuse. We know well enough that you could take without asking; but for the successful breaking of Syracuse, the Sicilian cities must come over to you of their own will. We know that the Council refused."

"It seems that you know many things."

"In one form or another, the thing is being talked of all over Messana. But we have our eyes and ears in the Council Chamber also."

"You? That is, the Athenian faction?"

"Yes."

"How strong is it, this faction?"

"Not strong as yet, but growing among those who do not love the tyranny of Syracuse."

"Growing how quickly?" he demanded; and I felt his mind leap forward, sniffing the wind like a hound.

"Fairly quickly, but there is a way to go yet. It seems unlikely we shall ever be strong enough to take *and hold* Messana; but if we can count on an Athenian force standing by to receive the city from us immediately on its revolt—then give us two months and we will give Messana into your hands."

There was a long silence; and I remember, Oh I remember, that somewhere in the arbutus trees a nightingale began to sing, as though the bright fierce moonlight had been gathered and transmuted into singing. They are fools who say the dead forget . . .

Then Alkibiades whistled as clear and full as the nightingale. "This begins to grow interesting. Give me further details, and I may quite possibly believe you."

"We scarcely supposed that you would take such a matter as this without the details," Basius said.

And so we laid all plain before him, our plans for rounding up the Syracuse party; for capturing the arsenal; the carefully worked out timing, the names of our key men. We set our lives and our hopes of freedom in his hands. And he listened; making a comment, a suggestion now and then; but for the most part simply listened.

When it was all told, he stood for a few minutes, his face turned from the moonlight, so that we could not guess the run of his thoughts. And then he glanced over his shoulder at Antiochus, who had brought his gaze down from the moon. And then he gave his attention back to us. "On the tenth night of Pyanopaion my own squadron will pass up the straits as though for Megara. Light a flare on the headland when you are ready for your guests, and we will put in to join the party."

# 4

## The Seaman

We pulls out for Rhegium at noon: and as soon as we rejoins the main force, Alkibiades goes into action. And by the Dog! how the man can stir when he chooses! Like a God—or a Devil! Within a few days he has a force of sixty triremes manned and victualled and we stands away for Naxos under full pressure of oars and sail, on this business of making allies.

Naxos shows friendly, so we spends only enough time there to sweeten the friendship a little further, and then stands away for Catana. We comes up against another strong Syracusian party there, and in the natural way of things, they've nothing to say to us. So Alkibiades orders us to stand off for a time, while a flying squadron including one of our fast Rhodian pentecontas goes off to reconnoitre Syracuse itself and look for any signs of enemy fleet movements. They brings back word that the Syracusians, expecting, seemingly, that we shall make a landing farther up the coast, are too busy making secure their land defences to be worrying much as yet about the sea approach, and so their ships are still on the slipways.

"So—now we know that we are secure from interruption, in we go again," says Alkibiades; and in we goes again, the whole force, and sits there in the harbour with our ram heads smiling in the sun and our fighting men on deck—not doing nothing, just on deck. And Alkibiades sends off a herald under the olive branch (we'd sent a boat ashore the night before, to cut it in one of the olive gardens just outside the city) to ask, oh very polite and affable, that 'Since his earlier request has not reached the main body of the people of Catana, he may be given a public opportunity of making it again before the full Assembly.' And adding that he cannot imagine that they will refuse him, they being a daughter state to Euboa, where, as in Athens, it's not the custom for such decisions to be taken without the verdict of the people.

"That should draw them, Pilot," says he, "and the sight of the fleet will make a powerful backing to the argument."

And sure enough, back comes our herald bearing pretty speeches—a bit cool, but pretty—inviting Alkibiades to come ashore and address the Assembly next day.

We spends a busy night; first with the scouts coming and going —we uses men from the pentecontas for that; the Rhodians can all swim like dolphins and so one doesn't have to send in boats to put them ashore. But when they've brought in their reports, there's boat work enough; all the business of getting the boats away quietly before moonrise, with a detachment of marines, and an anxious wait until the word comes back that they were safely landed.

But next morning—a dry hot end-of-summer day, with the mistral blowing cold and dusty through the heat of it—off goes My Lord in full glory with his staff behind him. I'm not one of the party that time, and I've affairs of my own to see to, what with the mistral chopping up the harbour water, and half my topmen taken off their proper duties and sprawling around the fore-deck trying to look like marines in place of those that goes ashore in the night. So I sees nothing of what goes forward in the Agora, but I hears about it later from them that does, and they says it's beautiful, quite beautiful.

Alkibiades addresses the Assembly from the Speaker's rostrum; he harangues them fit to bring tears to the eyes, on the subject of their duty to Athens (no one seems very clear how he makes that one out, but he does), he woos them with his most silken and fiery charm, he scourges them with his scorn and illustrates his points with the dirtiest of the stories, and there are no dirtier anywhere, that can be picked up drifting around the fleet. And all the time on the other side of the town, there's the marines under the Arkadian, picking out the stones from a hurriedly walled-up postern gate discovered by our scouts.

He's still talking, as I hears the story, when all at once Athenian helmets starts bobbing up all round the Agora, and the whole place begins to squawk and scurry like a poultry yard under the shadow of a hawk, all the good folk thinking that the town must be in our hands. But Alkibiades, he raises his voice—and lisp or no lisp, he's one of the few men I know who can make their voices carry the length of a war galley from the stern to the ram fighting-gallery against a full gale—and he holds the whole crowded market-place with it. "My friends," says he, "I have talked long enough." (And that was true!) "Any of you here that are of the Syracusian party,

I suggest that you retire to your own homes or your places of business, or to Tartarus if that suits you better, and take no further interest in these proceedings. Those of you who's hearts are with us, those of you who value freedom, remain here, and know yourselves free to vote as your hearts and your ancient loyalties bid you."

So—by evening the Syracusian party have somehow melted away, and the remaining citizens of Catana have voted solidly for an alliance with Athens. And the beauty of it is that there can't have been more than two score of our marines in the city from first to last!

Leaning on the stern of the *Icarus* that night, Alkibiades says to me, "Well, we've as good a base now as we shall get on this coast until we get Messana. Pilot, we sail for Rhegium at sunrise to pick up the rest of the fleet. It's beginning to work, this middle course."

Within six days the whole fleet, storeships and transports and all, are riding at anchor in Catana harbour, or drawn up onto the slipways; and the troops are quartered all about the city or encamped just outside it; and we've the free use of the arsenals and repair yards.

From Catana the squadrons comes and goes, sometimes about this "middle course" business of making allies, sometimes bent on raids on the coast about Syracuse itself—small stuff; a few settlements pillaged, a few olive gardens fired; a few of our own men killed in clashes with the Syracusian cavalry.

There's some that accuses Alkibiades even now, of pointless and wasteful raiding at that time; they underestimates the value of the small surprise attack, repeated again and again when and where least expected, the constant dagger-prick that keeps a man's nerves jumping. They underestimates also the difficulties and dangers of keeping a war fleet too long and constantly to the ways of peace. Either it turns ugly, like a yard dog too long chained, or it goes to pieces and is useless when the time comes for using it.

We makes good friends from the first, among the little dark-haired red-brown men who claims to be the old stock of the island. And knowing the land as they do, and not loving the Syracusians overmuch, they makes good scouts. Only once I knows them fail us, and that's when they brings us word that Camarina, far to the south, is ripe for plucking.

But even then, they're only a bit ahead of time. There's trouble for Syracuse ripening in Camarina sure enough, but not yet ripe; so we does what we can to help on the harvest, and back we heads

48

for Catana yet again. I'm beginning to know those Straits as a man knows the way from his own door to the nearest wine shop.

Alkibiades doesn't seem in the least put out. As I remember, he's whistling half under his breath, standing beside me on the after-deck smiling to himself with eyes narrowed into the bright oar thresh. The wind being against us, the sail's down, but we're making a good pace under oars, and the rowers are singing in time to the stroke as they only do when they're feeling good. There's a feeling of luck about the whole ship.

"And what are you so pleased about?" says I. "We've not had much joy of Camarina."

"Not yet," says Alkibiades, "but it's coming."

"So are the autumn gales! And what do we do then? Rot while we wait for spring?"

"Don't be so impatient, Pilot. It begins to come to hand. Catana has joined us, so has Naxos; Camarina—no not yet, but all the signs are there. Before Pyanopaion's out we shall have Messana, and with any luck that will bring Camarina's fruit to harvest. And after Camarina . . . Syracuse must be beginning to feel a little uncomfortable—a little queasy in the pit of the belly."

"There's still the autumn gales," I says.

"Surely. And the kingfisher weather between. With the first storms, Syracuse will feel more secure; soon she will relax her vigilance a little and begin to take things easily. Oh I know the ways of the Corinthian blood; their horses have more fire and more sense than their men . . . But you know the ways of ships and the sea, my dear, you're no mere summer sailor." And he grips his hand on my shoulder and gives it a little shake; and then licks his lips against the salt and the drying wind, and begins to whistle again, softly but very merrily, the tune that the rowers were singing.

We rounds the last headland and comes in sight of Catana; and there in the harbour, lying alongside the outer mole, there's a trireme that's none of the fleet.

I feels as though I'd taken a small sharp jab in the belly, and I looks round quickly at Alkibiades, and sees his eyes widen all of a sudden; and he stops whistling. I looks back toward the outer mole; and catches the blue flutter of Athene's owl on the new-comer's stern pennant. But I don't need that to tell me. Fifteen years and more I've served with the war fleets, I knows the *Salamina*, the Athenian state galley when I sees her.

# The Trirarch

I never counted myself among the circle of Alkibiades' friends; indeed I think not many of the senior Trirarchs would claim that honour. The young ones, such as Konon, the hot-heads flocked round him like bees round a pot of finest Hymetos honey, and in those days the fleet were his to a man; but that's another matter. Still, I've spent more of my life with the fleet than most of my kind; the Commander of the *Salamina* has to be at least something of a seaman, with less time for politics accordingly. Maybe it was that . . . At any rate I didn't much like my orders when the Council gave them to me. They were the kind of orders that leave a foul taste in the mouth after one has carried them out.

I liked them even less when I stood facing Alkibiades on the after-deck of his flagship in Catana harbour. I gave him the salute his rank demanded, and I remember my face felt stiff, as though I were wearing an actor's wooden mask.

He stood watching me through the eyes of his own mask. He said pleasantly, "My dear Trirarch, what brings you so far from home waters?" But his mask was not quite perfect, and I saw a muscle flicker once in the angle of his jaw.

That insufferable red-headed master of his was close beside him, and the young men of his staff. Even the stern rowing benches were so close that one could as good as feel the rowers' breath on one's ankles. There is seldom much privacy to be had in a warship. And I knew I could not risk telling him there, because I could not see, behind his mask, how he would take it. I said, "A matter best kept between ourselves, I think. You have quarters in the city where we may speak in private?"

He made a small courteous gesture. "One of Catana's leading citizens, finding his health demands a long stay in the country, has most kindly put his house at my disposal. May I offer you its hospitality?"

We went ashore in the *Salamina*'s boat, that being already alongside; and walked through the city. I think we even talked—a casual, well-bred talk of surface matters—only he never once asked for news from Athens.

In the long andron of the house, he sent for wine and saw it mixed to his satisfaction, then dismissed the slave, a pretty boy of the island breed, with eyes like a deer, saying that we would pour for ourselves. When the boy was gone, he poured the Libation still standing, with as much punctilious grace as though he were host at some rather decorous party.

He dipped the wine from the krater into two beautifully painted cups, and not until, cup in hand, we had taken couches facing each other across the low table, did he say at last, "Now, tell me of this matter best kept between ourselves."

I said, "I am sent by the Council of Archons to invite you to return with me to Athens." And my voice sounded wooden in my own ears. The voice of a man who is no actor, speaking lines learned by heart.

"For what purpose?" Alkibiades asked politely.

"To answer to the old charge of blasphemy," I said.

The air in the room seemed to grow thick and hard to breathe, as though there was a storm coming. The room was filled with an intense, high-pitched silence. He had known, in the moment when our eyes met on board the *Icarus*, I was sure of that; but there is knowing and knowing. Then he raised those thick golden brows. "Do you know, for one moment I thought you said 'to answer to the old charge of blasphemy'!"

"I did."

"But that's an old charge indeed. It blew up before the expedition sailed; and I was confirmed in my orders to sail, none the less."

"With the charge against you still to be tried on your return."

He set down the beautiful wine cup in his hand, "Am I under arrest?"

"No, no. My orders are to request—" I stumbled over the word as though I were a callow boy—"to persuade you, with all respect and courtesy, to return. No more."

"And if, with equal respect and courtesy, I refuse?"

"I think you would be wiser not to refuse."

"In fact, your orders are to bring me back to Athens with as little disturbance as may be; but to bring me, none the less."

"Something like that," I said.

He spoke again after a short silence. "Nikomedes, we have not been close friends nor drinking cronies—which is maybe as well for you—but I think you have not counted yourself among my enemies?"

"You do not lack for enemies," I said. "But not many of them are to be found in the fleet or the Army."

"That I believe." He glanced across at my wine cup, which I had not yet touched. "Then drink with me, man, and tell me, in

Typhon's name, what has been going on in Athens since the fleet sailed."

The irony of the situation struck me. "Is it fitting, do you think, to sit drinking with a man one has come to—"

"Carry back to drink the hemlock? You're over-particular for these days, Nikomedes." He picked up his own cup again, and drank off a good half at a gulp. "Tell me what I asked."

So I drank likewise, and told him, examining the black-painted wrestlers on my cup while I did so, for there are times when to watch a man's face is an unwarrantable intrusion.

"At first—this you know—there were only vague rumours and suspicions; even after the slave came forward to bear witness. If they had put you on trial when you demanded it, they knew that they could scarcely have made the charges stick; and so, I think, did you." I glanced up then, and found him waiting for my look with perfect understanding and something very like amusement.

"Go on," he said.

"But as soon as you were out of the way, your enemies in the Council—Kritias and his faction, Androcles the Orator, I believe most eagerly of all—went to work more thoroughly. The destruction of the Herms became joined to those mock Eleusinian Mysteries—nobody seems quite clear how that came about—and both have grown in men's fears to be part of a great conspiracy, to overthrow the Democratic state and bring back the rule of the Oligarchs."

"They were saying that before the fleet sailed."

"Not so widely, not as a certainty."

"So it has become that, now, has it? And yet, you know, it seems an unlikely charge to lay at my door. All men know my Democratic leanings. Why, man, it's one of the chief things that you and your kind hold against me."

He was right in that; a good many of us feel that rule by a few men with understanding of their task and the fitness for it that comes of good birth and the administering of large estates, is better than rule by the common herd, wise man, fool, honest and rogue alike. But it was not the moment to be drawn into political argument. "All men know, or at least they guess, that when Alkibiades says Democracy, he does not mean quite what the modern Democrat means by it," I said. "But be that as it may, the mood and mind of a city is a somewhat unpredictable thing, and prone to faithlessness."

"Faithlessness?"

"Everyone accused of being in any way linked with you in this has been thrown into gaol without trial. Oh yes, even well-respected citizens, on the unsupported word of any known rogue who chooses to accuse them. So have any friends of yours who have dared to raise a voice in your defence. Athens hasn't been a very pleasant place, these past few months."

Alkibiades said, "The gutter curs!" very softly, but with extreme vehemence; and then, "Between these walls, I will admit the mock Mysteries. We were drunk, and the fools' play went further than we intended. But we never mimicked the Forbidden Thing. That I swear."

"The slave who gave evidence had the whole thing to the last detail," I reminded him. But still I knew that he had spoken the truth.

"The slave who gave the evidence could have been primed by someone else. There are always those, not many, I grant you, who will declare even the Forbidden Thing for enough gold. It is my word against his; and I scarcely think they'll dare to give more weight to the word of a slave than to the word of Alkibiades."

"There's still the mutilation of the Herms, to throw into the scales against you."

"The mutilation of the Herms I utterly deny any part in."

"Deny it to the Council when you get back," I said.

"What need? What possible means have they of bringing it home to me?"

"The evidence of witnesses; and more than one, this time."

"*Witnesses?*"

"Notably two, Diocleides, I believe one of them is called, and the other Teucer. They have been very busy in all this, and suddenly rather rich."

"Fake witnesses."

"Maybe, but they swear to having seen the Herm breakers at their work, and to have recognized you and your friends."

"How, in the dark?"

"By the light of the moon," I said.

I remember there was a long silence. Alkibiades was frowning a little, circling his cup and watching the swirl of the wine in it. Then he looked up, and said slowly, "But there was no moon that night."

"No," I agreed.

He was silent again. Then he got up, and carrying his wine cup with him, crossed to the open doorway. Dusk had come, and beyond the door the sky that was clear crystal green behind the acanthus tiles of the roof ridge across the courtyard was flushed every now and then by a reddish glare. "Etna is restless tonight," he said. Then, "And even that did not smash the case?"

"No."

"By the Gods! The Council do want my head, don't they." He even sounded amused. But there was no amusement in his voice when he spoke again. "They refused me my trial because they could not count on turning the troops against me. So they let me off the leash, to be called back presently, with the Army and the fleet safely out of the way—very neatly done, really; I don't think I could have thought of anything neater, or dirtier, myself. But the people . . ."

He said it quite quietly, nothing in his voice except a faint note of wonder. But I remember that as he spoke, suddenly the whole sky was suffused with a livid copper glare such as hangs above the furnaces in the street of the armourers but a thousand times more intense. It was as though all that lay concealed beneath this wrought and polished quietness of Alkibiades, the fires of Etna—the fires of Tartarus—were showing forth in his stead.

It has seemed to me since, that I should have had misgivings then; should have thought that I'd been a fool not to arrange for some of my own men to be within hearing. He was younger than me and as quick on his feet as a cat, and could probably have got me down before I could so much as cry out. And after that he had only to call up a few of his own troops . . . He could have had the whole Athenian force in revolt on his behalf by midnight. But at the time I had no misgivings at all, not of that particular kind. I had too much faith in Alkibiades' sense of the pattern and the fitness of things.

He turned from the doorway at last. The evil copper glow was drying out of the sky, leaving the deepening night blue dark, unreadable beyond the yellow lamplight.

He said, "I accept your invitation to return to Athens with you—in my own ship and with my own crew."

"That shall be as you wish," I said. "But you will understand that I must put my second master on board."

"And why?"

"Alkibiades, your own master is named with you in the charge."

He nodded. "Poor old Antiochus. He would be, of course. Nevertheless, I sail in my own ship with my own crew—and my own pilot."

He still spoke quietly, rather too quietly for Alkibiades; and I had been ordered to avoid trouble at all costs. I said, "Very well."

"When do we sail?"

"At first light."

"Too soon. I must hand over officially and in public to my fellow Generals. If I slip away on the morning tide, the troops will say that I have been taken by force, no matter how little disturbance there is."

Then it was my turn to be silent. Increasingly I felt that Alkibiades and not I was in charge of the situation.

"You shall be there to see how beautifully I shall behave; what happy sentiments I shall express as to my swift return, with all this foolish misunderstanding quite cleared away. That way, there will be no trouble."

And I knew that he was right.

"I will arrange all things as you wish for tomorrow morning. Meanwhile, I must ask you not to leave this house."

"Of course. You have my assurance," Alkibiades said pleasantly. "In any case, I shall be fully occupied here. I intend, if it does not in any way interfere with your plans, to apply myself exclusively to the task of getting drunk tonight. Oh, quite quietly; more beautifully and imperially and obliviously drunk than even I have ever been in my life before."

But as I went out, I had a curious and unpleasant sensation between my shoulder-blades, and I glanced round at Alkibiades standing beside the table. I think I have never seen such a devil looking out of a man's eyes before or since.

# 5

## The Seaman

They tells me that the *Icarus* is ordered back to Athens, and no
more. But when I says that I takes my orders from the Commander and no one else, the Trirarch of the *Salamina* makes no
objection to my going up to Alkibiades' quarters. Maybe they
thinks we'll be easier to keep an eye on, both together. I don't
know.

So then, officially, I don't know a thing, when I hands over to
my second and goes ashore. But I've a fair idea; and I'm not the
only one. Young Arkadius looks like a sick monkey. Anyways, you
can't keep that kind of thing quiet for long, certainly not in any
company as close knit as a fighting fleet. The city's running over
with it, too; and by the time I gets to the house I knows just about
as much as the *Salamina*'s Trirarch himself.

I'd not have been surprised to find Alkibiades under guard.
But there's no sign of a sentry on the street door, nor anywhere
else that I can see. Seemingly the whole dirty business is being
carried through in the most gentlemanly way. I've never understood the ways of gentlemen. And when I goes into the room, there
he is, sitting at the table, quite alone. He's broken his favourite
drinking cup, the one with the chariot race on it that he always
uses. Crushed it as though it was a duck's egg, and cut his hands
again and again on the jagged shards, so that his blood was mingled
with the spilled wine on the table. He's smiling down at the
mess—and it's the kind of smile you might expect of something
that turns into a wolf when the moon is full.

I checks in the doorway, and maybe I gives back a step; and he
looks up. "Why that face?" says he. "Oh yes, I've cut my hands.
It's no great matter; more wine than blood—see, it has almost
stopped. Did the Trirarch of the *Salamina* send you up here?"

I pulls myself together. Quite a pull it takes, too. "I'm told
we're recalled to Athens. I came up for your orders."

"And my orders, Pilot, are that we sail for Athens at whatever time the *Salamina* decrees," he says, and his smile gets more like his own. "I'm recalled to Athens to stand my trial for blasphemy. You too, Pilot; you remember that second strophe? I've always warned you against keeping low company, and this time you've kept it once too often."

Well, I haven't thought of that side of it. And he looks at my face and his smile broadens. "I don't imagine you have much to fear. It's me they've set the hounds on, not you. All the same, I'll not blame you if you go missing before the *Icarus* sails. Nikomedes I know can furnish us another pilot."

I don't bother to answer that one—don't think he really expects an answer. I've followed Alkibiades too long to go round protesting dog-like devotion. "You're going back, then?" I says. I'm none so sure what I was expecting, but not that, anyway.

He hesitates for just a flicker of time. "Shall we say I'm accepting the invitation. You will remember I demanded a trial before the fleet sailed, and it was refused me."

Says I, "I've told you, and I'd tell you again but that you've no need of telling: you have only to say the word, and the troops will rise for you as one man."

He ups with his eyebrows. "My dear, you're almost as much of a fire-eater as Shoe-Leather Lamachus! If the troops were to rise, here in enemy territory, the full strength of Syracuse, with Corinth and Sparta to back them, would be down on our un-defended backside by suppertime." Then even the pretence of laughter goes out of him. "I could have given Syracuse to Athens, and then—all the rest; all that, by the Gods, I swear they'll never get now. But there are a few things I find are still beyond my powers, though doubtless I shall come to them in time; and that is one of them . . . Tomorrow morning I formally hand over my command to Lamachus and Nikias. Have the *Icarus* ready for sea, Pilot." He looks at his hands, and dabs a still oozing cut on the purple stuff of his mantle. "Antiochus, you know the little one-eyed weasel who keeps the wine shop beyond the temple of Apollo? Will you send for him to bring me some of his best wine. Tell him it will be made worth his while."

"Surely there's enough here in the house, however drunk you want to get," says I. The house doesn't look the kind to go short of the needful things of life.

"But I've a fancy to taste the Golden Lily's wine—brought by the shopkeeper himself. Ah—before you go, will you pass me my tablets—on the chest over there?"

I all but throws them at him. Only one word he'd have to say, just one word. And he'll not say it.

All night we waits for Alkibiades to change his mind and give the order, and it never comes.


## The Wine Shopkeeper

Me, I've nothing specially against Syracuse; but there's no denying the Athenian force that came against them was good for trade in those first months after we opened the city to them, sailors and fighting men being notoriously thirsty; and that tall blue-eyed godling their General, him they called Alkibiades, the thirstiest of the lot. I did him the odd service from time to time; girls and such like, and he'd always pay well. Besides, there was something about him. Don't ask me what it was, but I'll not deny I was sorry when suddenly all Catana was buzzing with the news that he was being hauled back to Athens to face a trial for blasphemy. But all the same, I was in two minds about going when that great red-headed pilot of his came rolling into the Golden Lily and bade me bring him up a jar of my choicest Etruscan wine to his lodging immediately. Bring it up myself, mind, and the shop fuller than it had been for months. But in the end I thought, 'It will take more than a blasphemy charge to keep that one down; and when he comes back, maybe he'll remember them that did him a good turn when things looked black for him.'

So I hands the shop over to Helen, my woman, and I takes a jar of my best Etruscan, and off I goes.

Seemingly somebody had left word with the doorkeeper, so there was no trouble about getting in. And then there I was, standing in the doorway of a big room opening off the summer court, and blinking at a pool of lamplight on the table, with a pair of hands in it; all cut, they were, and there was wine or blood or both all over the table, and the pieces of a broken cup. And they were writing, amid all the mess, just as if it wasn't there at all. I knew them for Alkibiades' hands by the great gold signet ring that he always wore. But for that I'd not have been sure it was him, in the first moment, for when I looked beyond them, his head was bent so low over the tablets that I could hardly see his face at all (and one eye isn't as good as two, whatever they may say, especially after dark).

When he had finished writing, he looked up. "Ah, Demetrios, you have been quick. Come in and set down the wine."

So I came to the table and set down the jar in its stand; and he lays down his stylus, closes the leaves of his tablets and knots the crimson thread, all very deliberate and slow, and sort of gentle. Then he softens the ball of beeswax in the lamp flame and seals the knot with his ring.

Then he sits back and smiles, like a man finished with a job well done. "I am returning to Athens tomorrow, but I had a whim to taste your Etruscan wine again before I go; and I find it—inconvenient, to go into the city tonight."

He put money on the table. "That's for the wine and your trouble. But there's another matter, a message to be delivered." And he jingled more money in a little embroidered leather bag.

I grinned. "A girl is it, My Lord?"

"Not this time, Demetrios," he said. "I believe Alexandros the magistrate is still in the city, though lying low with the rest of the Syracuse party? You told me once that he bought his wine from you."

"Yes, General, still here, though he keeps to the house as close as any virtuous great lady, these days."

Alkibiades dropped the purse on to the table beside the tablets. "The message is for him."

I looked at the purse. It looked reasonably full, and it had made a satisfying jingle as he tossed it down. But still—"It won't mean trouble?" I said.

"Not for you, not for Alexandros." Alkibiades picked up the tablets and sat weighing them in his hand. "Give him this from me; and bid him see that it reaches Messana—the Chief Archon— as quickly as possible."

That rocked me back a bit, and it was a moment before I could find enough tongue to speak.

"What is it, Demetrios?"

"Your pardon, Lord, but—he being all for Syracuse, and you being who you are, won't he be wondering a bit . . ."

"Demetrios of the Golden Lily," says he, "don't tell me you have not heard why I am being summoned back to Athens? Remind Alexandros that Athens has called me back to stand trial on an old trumped-up blasphemy charge; and I think you'll find he will not wonder any more."


## The Soldier

It only needed one word from him. One word, and the whole

59

Athenian force would have gone roaring up in revolt. We waited all that night for it to come. I hope Nikias and Lamachus spent a sleepless night; I know we did, feeling the whole of Catana, city and fleet alike, working under us like yeast. And we grew sullen and uneasy as the time of darkness passed and the one word did not come. Antiochus looked like murder as he set about readying the trireme for sea. Normally, with the *Icarus* sailing shortly after noon, I would have had to have my lads back on board early in the day. But we returned only to report departure and collect our kit. This was no time to be sending home even one ship's complement of marines, and we had been transferred to the land forces. So I got my lads up to the Agora instead, to hear him formally hand over his command; and we pushed our way through the crowd to get as near to him as possible, just in case. We hadn't quite given up hope, even then. Several of his staff had done the same, and we made a kind of unofficial bodyguard about the foot of the rostrum.

He did it beautifully. Dignified yet a little amused, as though the whole thing was some ridiculous mistake that could quite easily and quickly be sorted out. He seemed as confident of being swiftly back with us again as most men are that the sun will rise tomorrow. He paid a most generous tribute to the qualities of his fellow Generals (I didn't dare catch Corylas' eye, having too often heard Alkibiades' real opinion of his fellow Generals), and he wished them all success in the campaign during his absence. Nikias looked yellower than usual.

He was in full armour save for his helmet, which he had under his arm, but as always except on horseback, he wore, not the regulation military chlamys but one of his long mantles gathered in great folds across his shoulder and forearm and trailing a carefully casual corner onto the ground. He trailed it from step to step after him when he descended from the rostrum; he trailed it after him through the dust and garbage all the way down to the harbour, carrying his head as though there was a crown of golden laurel on it, and talking pleasantly to the Trirarch of the *Salamina*, by the way.

We followed him down; his staff, who he had turned over with his command to his fellow Generals, and the *Icarus* marines. We should have been reporting to our new company by that time, but I don't think any captain of hoplites would have been foolish enough to question our movements just then.

We were angry and wretched, feeling ourselves somehow betrayed, that he should leave us like this, to the leadership of

Shoe-Leather Lamachus and the priest-ridden Nikias, when he must have known that if he had said that one word, he need not have left us at all. But still, we followed him.

He went on board without once looking back, laughing at something Nikomedes had said. We might not have been there at all. And the last we saw of him, as the *Icarus* followed the *Salamina* to sea was a figure in a crocus-purple cloak leaning casually against the after-deck rail, and watching the circling gulls about the masthead.

"He'll be back," we said, "he's got some plan." But we did not quite meet each other's eyes, and something of the heart was gone out of us.

I looked at the boy, Astur, who chanced to be standing next to me, and saw that he was indecently near to tears. I had had little real contact with any of the staff lads before, they came of a somewhat different world to mine; though of course, physically, war galleys being what they are, we had spent a good deal of time packed close as spearheads in a barrel. But seeing him swallow, and his chin begin to quiver under the new dark chickendown of his beard, I wanted suddenly to reach out a hand in comfort. But above all I wanted, with an aching intensity, as one wants such things for the beloved, that he should not cry now and have to remember it afterward. So I edged up closer and muttered, "Behave! Or we shall have Phaedo" (he was one of the most notorious womanizers in the camp) "tumbling you in the bushes by mistake!"

He looked round at me; his chin cocked up and his brows whipping together in anger. For a moment he looked as though he would walk away. But I knew that at least he would not cry now. And then he swallowed; and his face lightened into that quick smile of his that left it so grave again the moment it was gone.

It had never happened to me before, and so I had never realized that falling in love could be so quiet and simple a thing.

A few days later, news reached us that a pro-Athenian party in Messana had been discovered and rounded up. It seemed that they had been planning to hand over to us the city and the great harbour that we needed so sorely. Alkibiades had known it all. And Alkibiades had sent word to the Chief Magistrate before the *Icarus* sailed, betraying the whole plot. So we lost Messana. I don't really know what happened to the men who had made the plot and trusted him with it; but I believe they got the hemlock. I hope it was that; it's an easy death. Presumably that side of it didn't matter much in his scheme of things, so long as it cost Athens dear enough. They say there was a girl among them, too.

I think if it hadn't been for Astur, I would most truly have wished myself dead in the brush that we had with some Syracusian cavalry, before ever the word came from Messana . . .


## The Priest

There have been strange things happen to me, in the thirty years that I have served the Sanctuary of Poseidon here at Thurii.

All men who tend the Sanctuaries of the Great Ones alone and at night have known such things. Strange comings of the spirit, strange sights and shadows in the altar flame, certainties that one has but to turn and look behind one, and the Splendour and the Terror will be there. Once, when I turned so, it was a ewe with her lamb at heel, strayed in from someone's flock. But there was the one night—the one night when for a space I thought that the Blue Haired One himself had indeed come to me.

At noon, the two Athenian triremes put into the harbour. That was usual enough, Greek vessels are forever putting in to the harbour to take on water and provisions for the long seaway across to Korkyra. But my serving-boy, returning from an errand into the city, brought back word that the trireme with the lion's head prow (I knew by that, that he had been down to the harbour for a good look, instead of coming straight back to the Sanctuary as I had told him), was the flagship of Alkibiades the Athenian General, and that she was taking Alkibiades himself back to face a blasphemy trial in his own city.

I had heard of this Alkibiades, especially since the fleet came west; the great war-host that was to conquer all Sicily for Athens. And with all else, I had heard of the shadow hanging over him. It is long ago, so long, and I begin to forget the details—or maybe it is not long enough, for as I grow older I find that I remember very clearly the things that happened when I was a boy, and often cannot remember the things that happened yesterday or last year at all—but it was something to do with the Eleusinian Mysteries; and he was supposed to have castrated all the Herms in Athens before the fleet sailed. But what reason could any man have to do such an accursed thing? Deliberately to call down upon himself the hounding of the Gods? Or—what reason for another to falsely accuse him of it? No, no, I grow confused and I forget. But the rest, I remember well.

It was one of those nights with a little fretting wind that brings the sound of the sea right up into the Sanctuary, and makes the big lamp that burns always as a guide mark for shipping jump and flare against the wall. The back wall of the Sanctuary is always black with lamp-smitch, no matter how one tries to keep it clean. One does one's best, one does one's best; but it is never enough. What was I saying?

The wind was making a deep lyre-string hum that came and went among the branches of the sacred pines, as I went across from my own little house to make the midnight sacrifice and see to the lamp. I left the boy sleeping. The time was near when he would have to learn to perform all the rituals, night as well as day; so that he might follow after me when I grew too old, as I followed after my master. But not yet; young things need their sleep.

I trimmed and refilled the lamp, but nothing could steady the flare and flutter of it while that wind blew. I cleaned the black streaks of soot from the bronze reflectors on the wall so that they shone out bright again, and cleared the feathery white ash of the evening's sacrifice from the altar (but the wind had blown most of it away long since), and laid and kindled the fresh bed of pine chips, and scattered into the small new flames the brittle brown tear-drops of Korax. The scented smoke rose and feathered away on the wind; and I raised my arms with the smoke and began the Invocation to Blue Haired Poseidon. I was not yet halfway through, when I felt the first touch on my spirit of something, someone, some presence drawing near to me out of the night at my back. The hair on my neck rose, and a coldness and a stillness came upon me, such as comes upon men when the Gods are near; and my own voice raised in the Midnight Prayer echoed like a stranger's in the empty places of my head.

And then I heard a long light footstep, and a brushing through the tamarisk scrub; and then a silence hollow under the wind. I finished the prayer, and turned round.

For one heartbeat of time, I thought that the God had come to me, even to me, Phyloctetes the priest of His Shrine.

He stood naked on the edge of the lamplight, with all the windy sea-sounding dark behind him. His eyes in the leaping light were like holes in his face with the dark sea showing through. His hair was wet and wild and clung about his neck, and the drops from it trickled and shone on his breast and shoulders. He was beautiful with the potent and terrible beauty of a stallion, and full of power. I was an old man even then, and it was many years that I had served His Sanctuary, and such shocks are not good for an old man . . . And then I saw the other man behind him, a big ugly man with a drunkard's nose, naked as himself save for the barbarian ornaments of coral and silver swinging in his ears, and carrying a dripping bundle under one arm.

He was so completely of the flesh, that second man, that I knew the first, too, was man and not God.

I said, "What is it that you seek, here in Poseidon's Sanctuary?"

The first man came forward into the full light, and I saw that if I were to take him for a God, I should have taken him, not for Poseidon but for Dionysus, the older Dionysus of the corn and the beasts of the wilderness. He moved long and light, like a mountain leopard.

He said, "Bravo, priest! No time wasted on needless words. We seek food and an old cloak—two old cloaks; later, a ship sailing for the Peloponnese. But in the first moment, sanctuary."

And then I knew—the need for sanctuary, the seawater already showing the faint whiteness of its salt where it had begun to dry on his body. I thought of the Athenian flagship in the harbour, and I knew.

I took them back to my house, and woke the boy. He might linger in the city when I had bidden him to come straight back, but I knew that I could trust him in such a matter as this. Round-eyed with astonishment and still half-asleep, he set to blowing up the brushwood and smouldering charcoal in the brazier. And when it burned clear red, spread out to dry the dripping tunics which the second man had brought from the bundle. Food I got for them myself, oatcake and goat's milk cheese; and the rugs from the bed-place to wrap their chilled bodies in. And Alkibiades sat down by the fire and held out his hands to it as though it were the depth of winter. His hair began to feather, coppery gold at the ends as it dried.

A leather money purse and a few gold ornaments had come out of the bundle also; he saw me looking at them, and said, "Now arises a nice point: are you, or are you not, one of those to whom one offers gold for the God in return for sanctuary?"

"If the charge against you is false, then the Lord Poseidon asks no gold for sheltering an innocent man."

"And if it is true?"

"Then His Sanctuary would profit little from the gold of a man lying under the curse of the Gods."

"Then you know what they accuse me of?"

"I have heard somewhat," I said.

64

"And you think that if I am innocent I should go back to Athens and face my judges."

It was true, but I do not know how he read it in my face.

"Hemlock tastes as bitter to the innocent as to the guilty," he said.

"If you are innocent, can you not trust your own city?"

He looked at me a while in silence, and the brushwood flared in the brazier, making strange upward shadows above his jawbone and in the hollows of his eyes. And Great Lord Poseidon! I never saw a man's eyes so bright, nor, behind the brightness, so full of the dark. Then he said, "I would have done so, once, but I have lately learned a little wisdom. Even now I think I might trust them in, say, the matter of the city drains—supposing of course that their moneybags were not too closely involved. But in the matter of my life, I find that I would not trust my own mother, any more."

And he flung up his head and laughed.

If Dionysus laughed, seeing the Maenads closing in, it will have been such laughter as that. It set the dogs howling in the farm below us.

They ate and rested, while the boy found them another cloak to add to my old winter mantle; and before dawn, they were away.

I watched them heading inland into the faint 'fore-dawn light. The search was out for them, and they would lie up in the hills till the *Salamina* gave it up and the two ships sailed without them; and then come down to find a trading vessel bound for the Peloponnese. But they would not return to me. I was glad to see them go, yet my house felt oddly desolate for their going, as though something bright that had blazed up with their coming, had burned out, leaving a little grey ash over everything; even over my own heart.

# 6

## The Seaman

We landed in Cyllene in Elis, and found lodging with an old Olympic friend of Alkibiades, while he sent to Sparta, asking for political asylum. Of course he gets it. The Spartans may be slow thinking, but they know what's good for them, and My Lord Alkibiades, outlawed from his own city and hot for revenge might be very good for them indeed!—only Alkibiades doesn't seem so hot for revenge by then. It's as though that ugly business over Messana has quenched all that in him, quenched everything.

It frightened me, and I don't frighten easy.

Well, we goes to Sparta, walking every mile of the rough mountain tracks that turn into quagmires with the first autumn rains. There's horses to be had in Elis, but they cost money, and the gold that Alkibiades had brought away with him would have to last the Gods alone knew how long. Beside, I think the idea of trudging into Lacedaemon on foot like a soldier at the end of a long march suited the character he was minded to play among the Spartans.

I'll never forget my first sight of Sparta. The track comes over the Taygetus saddle and drops away from our feet through the grey-leaved scrub whose hot peppery sweetness always makes me long for the good salt smell of open water. Lower down, there's kerm oak forest, dense as a ram's fleece; and on the far side of the valley it all begins again, dark forest running up in tongues that mark the river gorges, to threadbare grey scrub and naked rock; and above the treeline, the huge angry masses of the farther mountains with the eagles flying below the snow crests. And between the two, all the plain of Lacedaemon spread out; corn and olives and the river winding down past the city and its litter of settlements, southward towards the sea.

They say Sparta used to be four villages, and from up there on the hill-saddle, it still shows; four districts, the city has, still carrying their old village names, joined together by the market-place and the temple area. Even the temples of Sparta are of timber without even a lick of paint such as a galley needs to keep her seaworthy. And the houses, even the joined houses of the two Kings are of timber and thatch with here and there a wall of rough piled stones, and the hearth smoke finds its own way out through holes in the thatch. Oh yes I know, I couldn't see all that, not from such a distance. I learns it later. But when I thinks now of that first sight of Sparta, it seems as though I can see it all at once, and catch already the prison stink of the place. It's olive harvest, and between us and the city the Helots are hard at it, gathering the olives. (You never sees a Spartan lift a finger on his own land, even at harvest time.) And way off on a piece of level ground north of the city ants are moving about, solemn and purposeful—only that ants don't drill in straight lines and wheel and counter-march.

"Looks like a colony of old rooks' nests, doesn't it," says Alkibiades. "A good place to be out of, one day, Pilot. Meanwhile, it will serve its turn."

And we goes on down the track.

They lodges us in the house of a man called Endius, as dour as he's dark—and he's so dark that it's my guess there's Helot blood in him. You find that darkness sometimes among the Spartans; and when you do, better not ask questions. The Spartans talk a lot about keeping the breed pure, but the men are often away fighting, and like enough to a woman left too long alone, a black-eyed Helot boy from the family farm may seem better than no man in her bed at all.

This Endius is a man of wide cornlands and many olive groves; and his house is one of the finest in the city. So we lodges almost as well as King Agis himself, which is to say almost as well as the pigs in Attica. Me, I'm used to sleeping hard, and I'm as used to fleas as the next man, but I'll swear the fleas they have in Sparta could keep the ship-board kind as hunting dogs. And in all the three years we spends there—Praise be to Poseidon I'm not knowing it's that long at the outset, or I'd be howling to the moon like a mad dog—I never gets so that I can sup that foul black broth of theirs without a crawling in my guts.

Three days we kicks our heels and waits, and then Alkibiades gets his summons to go before the Kings and the Council of Ephors. After he's gone, I can't breathe in that stinking city, and I goes out and walks about the cultivated land. I've an eye for land, as most of my kind have. It's born in us, along with our hunger for the sea, the hunger for a little plot of good earth, a few olive trees and a radish patch when our seafaring is over. And it's beyond me how men who own such land, the richest land in Hellas, can leave the working of it all to their slaves and never know the good feel of looking at their corn whitening towards harvest, and thinking, 'That plot is doing well, because the Gods have been kind, and because I have sweated over it.'

I comes to a pile of stones marking a boundary. Someone has left a garland of withered flowerheads at its foot, and that's all there is to tell that it's a wayside Herm—a pile of stones is the nearest they can come to a Herm, even in the city. I stands and stares at it, I don't know how long, thinking 'Gods! what a place and what a people!' and not knowing I said it aloud till Alkibiades' voice just behind me says, "Do I gather that you do not care for our Spartan fellow-men?"

I swings round, and he is standing within arm's length of me; with that queer emptiness in his eyes, and his teeth just showing between his lips.

"Do you?" I says; but I'm not waiting for an answer, I knows he'll not give me one, anyway. "What news from the Council?"

"If I hadn't had to search half Lacedaemon for you, you might have had it sooner," he says. "There's a full muster of the Assembly called for tomorrow before the Council of Ephors. I am summoned to speak before it."

"To what purpose?" I says bluntly.

He shrugs. "There are more guests in Sparta, lately arrived—envoys from Syracuse, no less; with a couple of partridge-plump Corinthian noblemen thrown in. The Assembly is being called chiefly for them, but they think they may as well hear what Alkibiades has to say at the same time. It's humiliating, Pilot, to be cast for the second attraction, but doubtless very good for the soul."

We turns back together towards the city; and I looks round at him after we've walked a good way in silence.

"What will you have to say to the Assembly, then?"

"Oh, you know what I am, my dear; whatever the Assembly most wants to hear. Not that they matter here, anyway; it's the Ephors that I have to satisfy."

But I knows that he's not quite sure, even now. There's only that emptiness in him, waiting to be filled. And, it's wondering what will fill it that gives me the shivers.

He laughed then, and flung his arm across my shoulders. "Or

else I will tell the lot of them to go to Tartarus; and take to the sea with you in good earnest, and we'll turn pirate and grow rich preying on the Black Sea corn trade."

He'd have made a good pirate, would Alkibiades; I've often thought so.

That night with the newly arrived guests, we eats in the Royal Mess; the long Mess Hall linking the Kings' houses, where the Kings and their bodyguards eat their two meals a day.

The food was no better than in Endius' house; barley cakes and olives and more of that stinking black broth with the taint of bullock's blood coming through the salt and vinegar. They don't keep the grown men hungry, as they do the boys to teach them to be thieves; for the men have learned their lesson, and can live off the land wherever they find themselves in time of war; if anything, I'm thinking they eat more than we do in Athens, but the food's vile, none the less. The talk round the long bare table is good, though—camp talk, such as one gets around the cooking fires and under the sterns of the beached galleys on campaign. A bit more heavy-handed, maybe, for every Athenian camp has its jesters, and usually there's a good deal of laughter. The men don't laugh much in Sparta. But it's good nutty talk, and Alkibiades seems able to talk it with the best, his face straight, and his laughter, when it comes, short and sharp in his throat. But I think the envoys of Syracuse and Corinth feels themselves somewhat at sea.

Never in all my born days have I seen men look more out of their own place than those nicely polished envoys among the shaggy Spartans. In their pretty soft tunics and curled hair—one of the Corinthians even wore bracelets strung with little bells on both wrists—they looks like striped tulips growing in a thistle patch. Very odd I feels, eating with men I'd by rights be viewing at the other end of a galley's ram, and on the whole I'm more comfortable watching the Spartans.

King Agis sits at the head of the long central table; shortish and thick-set, a good few years older than Alkibiades and me; decked out like all the rest in a rather dirty soldier's tunic of goat's hair dyed blood red so as not to show the stains in battle (can't think of anything but battle, these Spartans), with his hair in a greasy bush, and his weapons beside him, and nothing to set him apart from his bodyguard save that he sits in a great chair with a brindled wolfskin slung across the back, while the rest of us sits on benches. Certainly there's nothing special kingly in his face. He looks rather like a boar, come to think of it, with a long snout and his eyes very small and bright, looking as though they'll turn red when he's angry. I thinks to myself, 'He's dangerous, that one, and not because he's a King', and then I finds myself looking at another sitting not far from him, and thinking, 'But maybe not as dangerous as you.'

I knows, having heard him spoken to by name, that he's called Lysander, and I'd a known him for a seaman anywhere, without being told that he's Sparta's senior triarch. He's got one of the most open faces I've ever seen—too open by half, like those perfect autumn mornings among the islands that brew up half a gale by noon; and he looks very straight into anyone's face that he's speaking to, but there again, somehow *too* straight, as though he's doing it deliberately. I thinks, 'I wouldn't trust you the length of a galley's keel, my lad.' You can see that he's got more wit in his little finger than Agis has in his whole boar's carcass, and I've a feeling I'd like to take him to a certain wine shop in Troizen and get him dripping drunk and see what comes out.

Meanwhile the company have begun to talk of the things that tomorrow they'll be arguing before the Assembly.

"Sir," says one of the envoys, "if you will only strike *now*—"

"The Ephors have the matter in hand," says Agis, making pellets with the grey bread. "They are resolved to send envoys back with you, to hearten your people so that there is no thought of surrender in them."

The Syracusian says stiffly, "Syracuse has no thought of surrender."

And another, an oldish fellow who plays with an amber ball while he talks, says, "If the Athenians had attacked at once, while the size of their force still seemed to us a matter for nightmare, who knows, Syracuse might be in Athenian hands today." (I catches a glance at Alkibiades, but he's squinting into his wine cup and seemingly aware of nothing else.) "You see then, there is nothing that we seek to hide from you. They did not attack at once; doubtless they had good and sufficient reason; and since the foremost of their Generals was removed from them—" And then he checks and glances under his wrinkled papery old lids at Alkibiades, kind of apologetic.

And Alkibiades takes a sip of his wine and sets the cup down, and smiles at him cheerfully. "Speak freely, my friends. We have parted company, Athens and I. Let last summer's flowers blow down the wind."

The old man makes him a small courteous bend of the head, and turns back to Agis. "The remaining Generals have divided the force between them and keep it sailing to and fro on raids and slaving expeditions until—especially now that they have attacked Hybla and failed to take it—they no longer seem so vast nor so invincible as they did at first."

I thinks, 'Fool! That's not the way to ask for help! Better to have left the talking to the Corinthians!' And then I changes my mind. He's no fool, that old man; perhaps with the Spartans it is better to ask proudly than to beg; it is seldom good to beg from a bully. But then the Spartans are not mere bullies; I don't know. Does anyone know much, where the Spartans are concerned? I looks at Alkibiades again, to see if he does, but he's wearing his mask, the rather bored one, and I can't see in.

They goes on talking, and I sits listening while they mulls over the whole ugly story of the fleet's mishandling through that early autumn when so much might have been done with what Alkibiades has left behind. Most of it's stale news, of course, but the sourness of it's in my belly yet, and comes up like the after-taste of vomit at every hearing. Gods! What a confusion of muddled tactics and old men's half-measures!

Lysander leans forward on his arms, and says with a kind of bluff directness that only just shows the iron underneath, "Despite which, being men of good sense, you know that you have no reserves to call upon, whereas Athens has many more fighting men still unused, where her present force came from. And so you come here to see what Sparta will do for you."

"We turned first to our Mother State for aid; Corinth deemed it best that we should come to you, the greatest soldiers of all Hellas." The old envoy glances across at the plump Corinthian with the bells on his wrists, who's seemingly half asleep. And I fancies there's a kind of faint wryness about his mouth, as though he's just bitten on a bitter almond. The Corinthians are noted for their skill in passing anyone who comes to them for help on to somebody else.

"We'll make blood-puddings of Athens when the time comes," says one of the King's bodyguard, spitting olive stones on to the floor. "But these things can't be buried, we're not at war with Athens."

"At peace, then?" Alkibiades says sweetly, into his wine cup.

"There's a truce between us."

"Oh yes, I was forgetting the truce."

Agis puts in suddenly and loudly, "All this will be dealt with before the Council tomorrow. It's not a thing that can be settled

71

round the mess table. Let's have the boys in to do a spear-dance for us."

When the gathering broke up for the night—for the Mess was for the most part made up of older men who didn't live in barracks but had homes of their own to go to—Alkibiades and I went back to Endius' house.

Endius hadn't eaten in Mess that night, and met us in the foreporch, saying in his clipped Spartan way, "There's one waiting in the andron; a merchant from the north. He brings news which it concerns you to hear."

Traders do not come often into Lacedaemon, though from time to time one will bring in a consignment of that dark heady resinated wine they make in Thessaly, and exchange it for Spartan hunting dogs to sell in Athens. And it's my belief that Endius, knowing of his coming, had remained at home that evening to be the first to hear what news he brought. Our host was well in with the secret police; indeed, I'm none so sure he wasn't one of them, and high up at that. If so, I wonder how sound he sleeps at nights. Ah well, the Spartans are strong stomached.

The andron of his house was like any other building that I had seen in Sparta so far; beaten earth underfoot and things that rustled in the thatch overhead. But a brazier burning brushwood and charcoal drove out the worst of the autumn chill and made the place seem almost cheerful, compared with the Mess Hall we had just left. There's a man sitting on a stool beside the brazier, mired from his journey, and with a scarlet Phrygian cap pushed far back on his head of greasy curls, in the way that a man pushes his bonnet back when he's mortal tired. He gets up stiffly at our coming; and it doesn't look to me as though he's been given food or drink in that house, though by the looks of him he could make good use of both. (When I was a small boy and dropped food from too large a mouthful, or made water on the doorsill because I'd left it too late to get properly into the yard, my mother used to cuff me and say, "You have no more manners than a Spartan!") But I suppose it's a case of 'Eat when you've earned your supper', and Endius doesn't consider it earned yet.

He says, "This is the man." And then to the merchant, "Speak now—all that you told me."

The man looks troubled, as though he doesn't above half like the story he has to tell. He scuffles a bit, and swallows, and blurts out, "You are Alkibiades, son of Cleinias?"

"Who else, fool?" says Endius; and suddenly I gets the feeling that behind that dour face of his, he's fair hugging himself with amusement at what's going forward.

The General sits down on the stool and stretches his feet to the warmth, and says, "I am Alkibiades, son of Cleinias; and (you know how curious we Athenians are) waiting with pricked ears to hear what you have to tell me."

The man swallows again, and brings out all in one rush, "I'm from Athens, before this; the whole city was full of it. They've tried you in your absence, Lord, it's all over."

"They found me guilty, of course. Did they condemn me to death?" Alkibiades says gently.

"Yes, Lord."

I was watching his face as the man spoke. His mask had slipped, and he looked for an instant like a man who has been hit between the eyes. I think until that very instant, something in him, deep down, hadn't believed that it would happen. He says just as quietly as before, "Give me details."

The man nods, rummaging inside the folds of his waistcloth. "I managed to get a copy of the indictment. I thought maybe there'd be those in Sparta that'd be interested; though I couldn't guess that Alkibiades—"

He stops short, and there's one of those silences that make the back of your neck prickle. Then Alkibiades holds out his hand. "May I see it?"

And when the man hands over the small papyrus scroll, he unrolls it and sits rocking the stool back on its hinder legs, glancing along the lines. Then he starts reading aloud, half to himself and half to us.

"'Thissalis, Son of Kymon, of the Deme Lacidae' (may his soul rot) 'impeaches Alkibiades son of Cleinias of the Deme Scambowdae, for committing crimes against the Goddesses of Eleusis, Demeter and Kore, by mimicking the Mysteries and showing them forth to his companions, wearing a robe such as the High Priest wears when he shows forth the Sacred Secrets to the Initiates; and calling himself High Priest; Polytion Torchbearer and Theodorus of the Deme Phagaea Herald, and hailing the rest of the companions as Mystae, contrary to the laws and institutions of the Heralds and Priests of Eleusis . . .' Were we really as drunk as that, that night, Antiochus?"

My memory—I admit it's a bit cloudy—is that it wasn't anything like as elaborate as that, and certainly didn't go as far. But I knew he didn't want an answer.

"And so they found me guilty and condemned me to death.

73

They have been busy. Well, since I'm not there to drink their hemlock there seems not much they can actually do."

"They did what they could," the merchant says.

"Such as?"

"They have ordered the whole priesthood of Attica, formally and publicly to curse your name; and the curse to be inscribed on iron tablets, that it may endure for all time."

"That seems carrying things almost vulgarly far," Alkibiades says. "Anything else?"

"Yes—as you are now dead in the eyes of Athenian Law, they were selling up your property when I left. As soon as that was done, they were going to start pulling your house down. It was a nice house, too."

"Yes, wasn't it," Alkibiades agrees, and then after a silence. "Do you know what happened to my horses?"

The merchant shook his head. "I am sorry, no."

"Pity, I should have liked to know who they'd gone to."

Just for the moment I wonders whether he's going to ask about his son; but after all, there's no need. When his wife died, her brother took the boy over; and as Callias' ward he'll be well clear of any trouble. Besides, he's not a child that any father in his senses would trouble himself much about. It's odd how a family like that, the kind that breeds lions and princes all along the line, seems now and again to gather up all its bad blood and throw off something that should be drowned at whelping.

We're all waiting for something to crack; some lightning-blast of fury. But Alkibiades only gets up and walks over to the doorway, and stands for a little with his back to us, as though he were looking out. But it's in my mind he's not seeing much of the dark courtyard, nor hearing the sudden pattering of the autumn rain. He gives his shoulders a little shake, and turns back to us. He says, "It is a mistake to try flaying a lion before one has made quite sure that he is dead. I will show Athens that I am still alive."

And that was all.

Except that later, alone in the guest porch where we slept, he says, "So the Herm charge was dropped altogether."

"Perhaps too many people remembered about the moon."

Next morning in the Agora, Alkibiades, chosen for the rough work of speaking first, mounted the hummock of beaten earth that served as the rostrum, and made the speech which, in the end, brought Athens to ruin.

74

The rain had cleared, and there was a cold wind blowing down from the north. I can feel the edge of it now. And when Alkibiades stands up to speak, it's as though his eyes catches up the reflected snowlight from the first winter whiteness on Taygetus, and it makes them burn in the way that cold burns; with a bright, bitter blue.

He begins by justifying himself for his own success against Sparta in the past; reminding the Spartan Assembly of old family ties between himself and them. (I'd forgotten that his grandfather had been the Consul for Sparta in Athens, and that at one time he thought of trying to get the Consulship back.) None of it mounts up to much, but the start of Alkibiades' speeches seldom did, in his politician days. It's different when he speaks to the troops; they don't need warming up; but with others, especially those stolid bleak-faced Spartans, he needs time to tune up both himself and them, and get the feel of them. I'd not have known that of myself, but he once tells me.

And then, when he's ready, he comes to the part that matters. So far as I remember, it goes like this.

"You Spartans are a monarchy, and an aristocracy; and here I stand up to speak before you, a known Democrat. Therefore, before you judge mistakenly of me in this, I must break down all cause for misunderstanding between us. I have been always, as my father and my grandfather before me, one of those who stand opposed to tyranny. In Athens, all who stand against tyranny in political life go by the name of Democrats. That democracy I uphold. But the thing that democracy has become in Athens, its insane policies, its jealousy of any who possess more than others of skill or courage or beauty, so that all must be dragged down to a grey and greedy mediocrity, this I utterly repudiate."

'That's clever,' thinks I. Furthermore, in a way it's true. And I feels the crowd stirring round me and knows they're beginning to answer to the helm. Not that the crowd matters much, this being Sparta. It's the Kings, and even more the Ephors, he has to make his mark with.

"So, that is dealt with, truly and in good faith, that there may be no shadows of hidden things between us. Now I am free to turn to those matters of which I came here to Sparta to speak with you.

"The Athenian fleet sailed for Sicily to conquer Syracuse. That you know. This you do not know, though maybe some have guessed: we sailed for Sicily to conquer Sicily. After that, Italy;

75

after that, Carthage. After that," he shot it out at them, *"you!"* and waited a heartbeat for the word to strike home. "With fighting men from Iberia to reinforce our own, with a fleet enlarged by galleys built from Italian timber, with gold and corn of Carthage to pay and victual our troops, *your turn*, my friends! A fleet greater than has ever been known in these waters to blockade you from the sea; an army stronger than all Hellas has seen since the Persians were driven back, to siege or sack the cities—Oh not of Lacedaemon alone, but of the whole Peloponnese not already our subjects or allies. All Hellas ruled from Athens! And what of Sparta? What of all the pride and power of Sparta then?"

The men round me growls uneasily; a deep sound and ugly. And the Ephors are leaning forward in their seats. Alkibiades has them now all right.

He says, "There is no man better qualified than I to tell you of these far-reaching plans; for it was I who made them!" The mutter of the crowd deepens and for the moment takes on a note of menace. And I thinks 'Be careful! For the sake of all the Gods, be careful!' But he's made his point, and sidesteps neatly on to the next thing; and the crowd's beginning of anger turns to admiration for his cool effrontery. It's harder to tell what the Ephors are thinking. "My plans," says he, "and much as they hate me personally, my fellow Generals will carry them out if they can. As things stand, I see little to stop them. The Syracusians" (he makes a little bow towards the Envoys) "for all their confidence and their undoubted courage, are unused to our kind of fighting, unused to fighting at all for two generations. They cannot long survive alone. And if Syracuse falls, all Sicily falls. The rest I have already foretold to you. In the spring, you must send out ships, not manned by rowers and a dozen marines, but with fighting men at the oars, ready to become infantry the moment they beach the galleys. But more even than this, you must send them a leader; a Spartan General to bring them the certainty of your full support—and who can hammer their new levies into a single disciplined force. At the same time, you must thrust against Attica, thus making sure that the Athenians have nothing to spare from their needs at home for reinforcing their army in Sicily."

Agis, sitting in his high seat, speaks for the first time, then, holding up his rod of office, according to the Spartan custom. "You have a plan for this, too?"

"I have," says Alkibiades; and he stands rocking lightly on his heels and looking at the Council and down at the crowd. We're all silent now, waiting. "It is a very simple one. Do you remember how it was every year before the truce? Every spring your raiding bands came down into Attica by the pass at Dekalia. Every autumn they returned by the same way; and behind you the people swarmed out from the city to reclaim their farms and undo the summer's damage. Next year you must build a fort at Dekalia and keep your quarters there through the winter. From that strongpoint you can cover the road in from Thebes and Boeotia, thus forcing Athens to bring the entire corn supply round by sea. With a Spartan force so near, they will not dare to work the silver mines at Laurium from which comes the chief wealth of the state; and if they try it, the mine slaves will desert to you in droves. For ordinary folk, there will be no going back to the farms to make good the summer's wreck or to gather the olive harvest. I tell you, Athens will be hamstrung lacking the means to live, let alone make war."

It was odd to stand there and feel the dull Spartans stirring and pricking their ears around us, and feel nothing myself except maybe a bit sick. Not very, just a bit.

He says, "Maybe you are saying in your hearts 'He has broken faith with his own state and joined himself to her strongest foe; will he then, not break faith with us as soon as it suits him?' Remember that Athens first broke faith with me! You have harmed only your foes, and that is the right—the duty—of every people and every man; but Athens has declared war on me, who was her own. And therefore, outlawed from my own people, I come to you. I loved and love my state, but I am not a dog to fawn on the lord who kicks me, and crawl back to be kicked again. Indeed, I do not feel myself to be turning on my own country, but seeking to win back the country which was once mine but is mine no longer. That, for me, is the way for a man to love his country! Therefore I beg you to trust me as I will trust you. Use me for the hardest and most hazardous work; I shall not fail you!"

(Oh there's a lot more of it, of course, but not being Thucydides with his little note tablets, I've only my memory to rely on; and that's the gist of it, anyway.)

Gods! The clamour that rose then! The deep harsh shouting of the crowd make it clear the fighting men are his! But when the garboil falls away a bit, King Agis sits forward in his chair, his head thrust out on his thick neck, his little bright eyes thrusting among the crowd, though it's to Alkibiades he speaks. "The plans are good; but there is one point that you have forgotten. The truce of Nikias still holds, as you yourself have said. To send troops to

77

Syracuse would be only to support an allied state in giving aid to one of her own colonies; but in the instant when we set warlike foot in Attica, we violate the truce. And shall we, the Spartans, stand before the world as truce breakers?"

Says Alkibiades, with that silky softness, the fur over the sheathed claws, "You'd not be forgetting the plain of Cynera? Argos has been a touchy point between Athens and Sparta since the old dispute. I believe that a couple of raids into the Argolid will bring a return raid from Athens on the Lacedaemon coast. So the Athenians will be the ones to break the truce."

After that, there's little need for the Syracusian envoys to speak at all.

All Alkibiades' proposals were put to the Assembly and passed within the day. But that night in our quarters, he says to me, "Talk is a fine thing, even in Laconic Sparta."

"Meaning?" says I.

"Didn't you notice that there was no time limit set? There'll be endless delays. For all that they cheered me, I have not fully gained their trust yet."

"You've not made so bad a start without it," says I. "How does it feel to have ruined Athens?"

He leans back against the wall scratching behind the ear of a big red hound bitch that has come padding in after him. "My dear Antiochus, I never knew you for a patriot."

I shrugs. "I leave that kind of thing to other men. I'm thinking of the farms, the burned thatch patched up each autumn, the hacked-down olive trees replanted. And in the six years since the fighting stopped, the farming folk have slaved their hearts out to bring the land back to life. Now, they'll never harvest the olives from the new trees they planted. Everything will be destroyed; and there'll be no more going back to make good the damage. You said that yourself, this morning, standing out there on the Speaker's Rostrum, and proclaiming in the next breath that you love Athens still!"

"Love—hate—the balance is very delicate, you know." He went on playing with the bitch's ears a few moments longer. Then he looked up at me. "Yes, I do love Athens still, Antiochus."

I stands looking at him, trying my damnedest to understand—though why I wastes my time in trying to understand Alkibiades I don't know. Then I thinks I have it. "A jealous lover! If you cannot have Athens you'll break her—and have the jagged shards to tear your own heart to pieces with afterwards."

"Congratulations, my dear, I never knew you could think like that," he says.

"So I'm right."

He smiles at me, long and lazy. "You're wrong; quite beautifully wrong. Will you bid the slave listening at the door to bring me some wine?"

# 7

## The Seaman

We gets news from time to time through that long dreary winter.
We hears of a fight before Syracuse itself, lost by muddled
generalship. We hears that the Athenian force is wintering at
Catana. We hears that they're building a siege wall along the
heights behind Syracuse. Towards winter's end we hears that old
Shoe-Leather Lamachus is killed—sorry about that—and Nikias
and the other Commanders have sent back Tydius (a good choice,
he being Lamachus' son and having got himself honourably
wounded) to get more men and more money out of Athens.

That's about the time the Spartans gets moving enough to send
out the General that both Alkibiades and the Syracusian envoys
have been howling for. Just four months, it's taken them! They
sends out Gylippos, a big rawboned fellow with as many scars on
him as an old boar hound; and under him a picked force of six
hundred Helots. (I've never been able to make out why the Helots
don't desert in a body, when sent overseas to fight for their
Spartan masters. Unless it's because Lacedaemon is their own
earth that they belong to even more than they do to their masters.
Unless it's because the Spartans still hold their women and
families. Unless it's just habit.)

Coming with such a small force, Nikias must have thought
Gylippos not worth troubling about. At all events, he lets him
through. It seems beyond belief, then and now; but it's true.
Nikias lets him through; and by the time he discovers his mistake,
it's too late.

Gylippos isn't one to stand while the bindweed grows up his
legs; and it's not long before we hears that he's contrived to throw
up a cross-wall to stop the Athenian siege wall in its tracks; and
he's raising fresh troops from the Sicilian cities.

And then at last Sparta wakes up and decides the time's over
for holding back. The Ephors presents their plans (Alkibiades'

plans) to the Council, and the Council summons the Assembly; and slow and heavy at first, then gathering way like a wagon when the oxen sets their necks into the collar and takes the strain, Sparta begins to grind into war. In March, half a regiment of hoplites actually sets off on the Argos raid to make Athens break the truce.

Alkibiades goes into a queer silence, seemingly a long way off in some wilderness of his own, and wanting no company but his own shadow on the grass. I leaves him to it, judging that there's nothing else to do unless I wants trouble. And there's trouble coming sooner or later without any help from me. The beer's strong in Sparta, and the Helot girls hot and willing, so I'm not lonely.

My Lord stays in his wilderness the best part of a month, and then one morning he comes out of it and whistles for me to go down for a morning swim with him, exactly as if he's never been away.

Afterwards, we sits among the tall feathery reeds on the river bank, and dries off in the growing warmth of the sun. Oh, the good warmth of the sun, after the fiery cold of the Eurotas coming down in green spate from Taygetus' melting snows! Alkibiades lies on his back, whistling to the river birds. And I looks at him, and an odd thing happens behind my eyes; perhaps because of the time he's been away on his own business, suddenly I sees him—I mean *sees* him—as though he's someone I haven't seen before. I sees the leanness of him and the flat hollow of his belly below his ribs, and the clear brown of his skin, and the little white scar on his left temple that he brought out of the fighting at Potidea. I sees his gold-and-copper streaked hair and rough like a stallion's mane in need of grooming, and the paler brown of the lower part of his face, where he's shaved off his beard to follow the Spartan fashion.

I says, "Until you open your mouth you could pass for a Spartan, now—one of the fair ones. Well, you've been practising hard enough all winter, with all this exercising and cold bathing and hard lying, and keeping a wooden face and speaking in two words at a time."

He says, watching the flight of a bird overhead, "It's something to do."

"You're wasted. You should have been on the stage," says I.

We're halfway back to the city when we hears the women wailing. And we both checks in our tracks. We've both of us forgotten till that moment it's the first day of the Hyakinthia. I have known two more feasts of Hyakinthos since then, and got

81

to know the way of it. All that first day the women wail and the whole land mourns with Apollo and makes sacrifices to their own dead along with the boy they say Apollo loved and slew by accident while teaching him to throw the discus. On the second day they rejoice, for Apollo caught the boy's escaping life between his cupped hands and breathed his own strength into it and changed it into a blue flower springing in the grass. So on the second day they sing and wear garlands for Hyakinthos risen.

Alkibiades turns on his heel and walks off in the opposite direction without a word. And I wonders if he's remembering the women wailing for Adonis through the streets of Athens and down to Piraeus on the day the fleet sailed for Syracuse. So I don't follow him.


## The Queen

I was eleven years old when they betrothed me to Agis; but I had known almost as long as I could remember, that I must be Queen of Sparta one day. I did not mind; but it would have been no matter if I had. It was my proud destiny. My sister Dionyssa and I were the only two of the right degree of kinship in the Royal Houses, and I was the elder by almost two years.

Agis is thick-necked and heavy in the shoulder. His hair grows low on his forehead and always looks dusty. And when he is angry his eyes go little and red like a boar's. He smells like a boar too, at times. But he is boar-brave also, a fine soldier when once he starts to make the ground move under him; and no true Spartan woman should ask more of her man than that. I asked no more. I should be a Queen of Sparta. I was well enough content.

That was until the Hyakinthia; the seventeenth Hyakinthia of my life. I had not thought that that year I should be still among the maidens who take the new robe to Apollo Amyklae; for most women are wives at sixteen, and Agis was already forty; ten years past the age at which most men leave living in barracks to sleep openly with their wives. But he was—he is—one of those who do not change from the ways of their young manhood when young manhood is passed. Everyone knew that while King Pausanius had become so much a family man that he seldom even dined in Mess except during the men's festivals, King Agis still turned to the boys' barracks for his needs, and was in no hurry to take a woman into his bed. I was in no hurry either; I was happy; being not yet awake.

82

I was happy, that second day when mourning was over, to be still with my sister and the other maidens who carried the sacred robe that we had all shared in weaving through the winter. We had been out in the woods since before dawn, searching the lower glens of Taygetus for the blue hyacinth flowers that bear, shadowed at the heart of each petal, the God's cry of grief—Ai, Ai—for his slain darling. It was still cool in the Taygetus woods, the streams running cold as ice under the fern, and my fingers had grown damp and chilled seeking the sappy stems among the grass in the clearings. We came back wearing the garlands that we had woven up there under the trees, and bearing the blue flowers piled high in our rush baskets. And the lightness of heart was in us that comes always with the second morning of the Hyakinthia.

In the market-place, between the Kings' Houses and the Temple of Athena, the crowds were gathering, and men called to each other "Hyakinthos is risen!", and called back "He is risen indeed!" Every shrine and altar in all Sparta was spilling over with blue—blue—blue. And everywhere was the music of flute and cithara. We went to the weaving shed and took the new robe which had been cut from the loom last night, and hung it carefully on its mast and cross-piece, and carried it out to the waiting people.

In the weaving shed the light was dim and diffused, but as the early rays of the sun struck upon it, it kindled into coloured flame, red and black and gold woven upon the deep blue-violet of grapes at vintage; the lyre and the bow and all the emblems of Apollo, and in the midmost part of it, the figure of the God himself, poised with his discus in the instant before the throw.

The procession was already forming; first the priests, with the sacred flute players, and the puzzled beasts garlanded for sacrifice. Then after an empty space, the Queen's chariot being edged into position, and chosen girls from all over Lacedaemon with their flat rush baskets piled and spilling over with the blue that was the colour of the day. We took our places behind the Queen's chariot, and as we did so, out from the forecourts of the Kings' Houses rode first Agis and then Pausanius, with their bodyguards about them, the Ephors walking stiff and stately behind, to take their places in the emptiness left waiting for them. The flutes shrilled, and already the women along the wayside had begun to raise, very softly as it goes at first, the Hymn to Apollo.

So we wound our way out of the city; the dry smell of the dust-cloud mingling with the cool woody sweetness of the hyacinth flowers; and singing as we went, took the way to Amyklae. And I thought, 'Next year, maybe, I shall ride in the Queen's chariot

83

beside Gargo.' And the sudden joy rose in me till it was sharp as pain, that I was not yet Queen of Sparta, that for this one time more it was given to me to walk among the other girls with the knot of my girdle not yet loosed, and dance the Sun Dance of the Youths and Maidens.

We came to Amyklae in the loop of the river; Amyklae in the level cornlands, shut in by dark woods of kerm oak and Apollo's own laurel, where the God slew his boy-love. The meadow was crowded, as always on that day of the year, but a broad lane had been left clear, stretching before us to the dark waiting Apollo standing against the curve of the woods; and a wide space clear about him, as though he cast a bright shadow in which men feared to tread.

The Kings dismounted, and their horses were led aside; Gargo stepped down from her chariot, slowly, for she was heavy with child again. And the procession moved on following the shrilling of the flutes.

One must not look to right or left, but be aware only of the God.

He is very ancient, our Apollo, almost black with age and weather, for no shrine holds its roof over him to keep out sun and rain. From the far side of the meadow, he seems no more than a great baulk of timber, a column growing broader towards the head, and deep-rooted in the grass as the kerm oaks behind him. Then as you draw nearer you begin to see the carven head and shoulders of him, and the proud, erected phallus; and then the smile on the closed lips, the secret, half-moon smile, and the painted eyes that are more than painted eyes, wide and far-gazing, coming to meet you and draw you towards them.

And all the while you must answer with your whole heart to the silent Call of the Lord Apollo, and be aware of nothing else. It was the fourth time I had walked among the maidens at the Hyakinthia, and always, until now, I had been able to put away from me all awareness of the crowds pressing along the way, to let the flute music flow into me, and fill myself with the presence and the calling of the God so that all else passed by me as a dream. But that day I was aware of all things, of the flutes and the rising dust and the scent of the blue flowers in my garland, and of the crowd and something that seemed to be coming out to me from the crowd, disturbing me to my finger-tips. I must not look round, I must keep my gaze straight before me, to meet the summoning gaze of the Lord Apollo; but I saw them as we passed, out of the tail of my eye: faces—and faces—and faces, pressing in . . .

I had made my wreath in a hurry, for we had been long in the

84

woods gathering the hyacinths; and as we came close to that inner open space where the crowd ended, a flower fell from it. I felt it go from me in loss. My flower, as though it had been something of myself; and there was a quick movement on the crowd's edge as we passed, and a swoop of shadow on the grass, and I knew that someone had caught it up from under the feet of those who came after.

The flutes shrilled into silence, and we halted, and up at the head of the procession, where the Kings and priests were, there was a murmur of prayer and invocation, a sudden movement and the bleat of a ram cut short, and then the smell of the burnt offering mingled with the drift of storax and frankincense on the air; and the voices raised to Apollo. And we moved forward until we stood among the priest-kind, and the offering burning on the altar before the waiting God, strong and terrible with his courteous close-lipped smile. And then again the voices and the flutes fell silent, and again we moved forward, the chosen three of us who bore the sacred mantle. The priests had already taken away the remains of last year's garment; and where it had lain in fallen folds about the feet of the God, I saw the new dark stains, wet splashed and fresh-blood smelling, above other and older stains that had sunk year by year into the grass. I had never seen those stains before, but today it seemed that I saw all things, was aware of all things . . . The High Priest took the new robe from its crossbar and began to swathe it about the sacred figure. And I remember now the silence; the little wind stirring the kerm oak tops, and the yellow flowers of the laurel booming with bees. And we were piling the hyacinth flowers already wilting in the noon sun, over the bloodstains on the grass, where the ram had died, until the feet of Apollo were lost in a spreading stain, a whole lake of pulsing blue.

We made the Round Dance, the Sun Dance, maidens together with youths on the edge of becoming warriors, spinning with the sun; and I knew that for me it was the last time; and I longed for the dance never to break its circling over the grass. But it broke when the time came, and the hands of the boy on either side of me were gone from mine.

The procession re-formed to carry last year's mantle, stained by the winter rains, tattered by the wind, back to the city. Soon the rags of it, stiff here and there with the blood of the sacrifice, would be bound about the King-tree of every olive garden, to bring a rich yield at the harvest.

The crowd pressed forward as we passed, crying to us,

"Hyakinthos is risen!" and we gave back the answer, "He is risen indeed!" And the flutes took it up so that it became the chant of the return, flung to and fro between us like a shining golden ball . . .

And among all the faces of the crowd that beat upon me like a wave, I saw one, blue-eyed under a lion-coloured crest of hair.

Alkibiades, the Athenian. One saw him everywhere, in the gymnasium, about the city, among the men setting out on the hunting trail, coming up from bathing with his wet hair bright in the sun. I had even felt a little sorry for him, thinking what it would be to be cast out by Sparta and driven to help her enemies for the sake of revenge. But indeed both his exile and his revenge seemed to sit so lightly on him that after a while I had ceased to feel sorry.

Yet in that moment I saw him as though for the first time; as though a shadow had fallen from my eyes. I saw the blazing blue of his eyes, reaching out to pierce me, and the laughter at the corner of his mouth; and my fallen hyacinth flower caught into the shoulder knot of his cloak.

## The King

It was early summer when the messenger I had been waiting for so long, brought in word that the Athenians had attacked the coast above Parasiae.

We were at supper in Mess at the time. Alkibiades was there, and he sprang up like a man hearing the trumpets for the onset; and shouted that his plan had worked and the truce was broken, pounding his fist on the table-boards until the beer cups jumped. That's the worst of these Athenians; no control, all laughter and tears, and as impatient as women. He seemed to think that now, instantly, all his other plans must be put into operation, whereas, having learned in a hard school that such things must be taken at marching pace and not at the blind run, we knew that the time had not yet come to do more than deal with the raid itself. (And make sure, of course, that all the world understood that the truce had been broken.)

We dealt with it handsomely; but for the rest, we held our hands. And indeed the Higher Command were proved right, for long before we could have got an expeditionary force into Attica, news came that Athens had got together another five thousand men under their last remaining General of any ability—Demosthenes the name was. And after that of course we must hold back to see how Gylippos did in Sicily in the face of this new Athenian thrust. Nobody but a fool would get the flower of our fighting men pent up in Dekalia, and then have Demosthenes prevail—or even bring off the Athenian army safe back to Athens, after all. It seemed possible from the first that his real purpose was to evacuate the Athenian troops, if their situation grew hopeless. All this had to be taken into account, and watched.

Meanwhile we put in a hard winter of preparation, not that our men needed much extra training, they are always at the finest peak of fighting condition; but the Gods know that there are matters enough to be dealt with before so great a step as the invasion of Attica must be.

Alkibiades never began to understand all this. They are all alike, these Athenians; just as I say, always in a hurry and all born above themselves. Look at the way they rushed into the Syracuse business in the first place. And Alkibiades was Athenian, sure enough! He came to me the year before, to join the raid on Argos. He might have understood his true position in Sparta after the answer he got *then*; but his kind never learn.

As soon as the Council decided that the time was indeed ripe, and the orders were issued for Dekalia, the fellow came demanding speech with me. I was busy with the muster rolls. He had become maddening as a hornet through the past year, though we remained outwardly on good terms; and I all but sent back word that I had too much on my hands to see him. But suddenly I was minded to make his position clear to him once and for all. So I bade the guards let him through.

He came swashbuckling in past their parted spears, trailing his pride behind him like one of those golden Persian pheasants trailing its tail. And he came and stood over me in my own quarters, with the whiteness of a late sleet squall melting on the shoulders of his cloak. And my old hound bitch went and thrust her muzzle into his hand.

I whistled her back, and she wagged her tail to show that she heard, but did not come.

He laughed and said, "Women! They're all faithless or too damned faithful for comfort! I'll come straight to the point. I learn that we are marching for Attica at the full of next moon. Many of the captains have already received their orders. I have received none as yet."

I said, "The orders have gone to all who are concerned in the matter."

87

It was pleasant to watch his eyes go blank for a moment.

Then he said in a tone of polite enquiry, "And I am not included in that company?"

I said, "Why should you be included in it? You are not Spartan, skilfully though you have played the part this year and more."

He said, "The whole Dekalia plan was mine in the first instance."

"It was. And we are acting on it. What more would you have?"

He said, "My rights! To go with the force to Dekalia."

Left to myself, I think I'd have taken him. It would have been amusing to see whether he would really fight against his own people when it came to it, eye to eye and hand to hand. But the Council of Ephors had decreed otherwise. So I said, "You mistake your position in Sparta, my friend."

We were both standing by that time, facing each other across the table with the muster rolls. He said, "I have sometimes wondered what it is, myself. Will you make it clear to me, Agis the King?"

I said, "I will make it clear past all mistaking. We have treated you with the courtesy due to a guest among us. You are no more than that; and there are those, particularly among the Council, who feel that you are something less. You came to us for sanctuary, and to bring us certain information and advice for the ruin of your own state. We are acting on the information, we are following the advice, which seems to us good. But your usefulness is over; you have nothing more to offer us that is of any value."

He broke in, leaning forward across the table, so close that I could see the sweat-beads starting among the hair-roots on his forehead: "Nothing more of value? Which among you knows Attica as I do? Who else can tell you what the Athenians are thinking? What move they will make to counter a move of yours? Leave me here in Sparta, and you leave your best weapon behind you!"

I laughed at that; and it takes a good deal to make me laugh. "Listen," I said, "whatever value you had for us is in the past. There is nothing you can teach the Spartans when it comes to actual push of spear. And do you think I'd let my men's lives hang by such a slender thread as your faith-keeping? You have betrayed your own state." I saw that he was going to cut in again, and I thrust on. "And we lay no blame to you for that; revenge is every man's right. Nevertheless, betrayal is a habit that grows in the heart. You will be better here, out of the way of temptation!"

He said, "As a prisoner, in fact."

"Free to come and go *within* the borders of Lacedaemon. But remember that Sparta has a very efficient secret police."

"And needs it," he said softly. And I understand well enough that he meant it for an insult; but any fool can see that a good secret police is necessary for the well being of a state such as ours; and before I could think where the insult lay, he straightened back from the table, and smiled and stretched himself like a sleepy cat. "It seems that I am to have a dull time of it. What shall I do to amuse myself in the coming months?"

"Anything you please," I said.

And he looked at me through a long hard moment's silence, smiling still. Then he said, "I will, Agis my dear friend, I will."

And he turned, and strolled to the door and out between the guards' parted spears.

The bitch came back to me then; I kicked her in the belly to remind her that she was mine; and she yelped and cowered away into a corner. But she came out, whimpering and sniffing, when I called, and came to crouch under the table against my legs.


## The Queen

Afterwards I scarcely thought of him again. Only from that second day of the Hyakinthia I began to be restless, to feel always that I was waiting for something. I did not know what; but my body knew. It was as though the sap was rising in me and did not know how to break free into flower. My old nurse recognized the signs, I suppose, for I heard her saying to one of the other women slaves, "I have seen heifers like that, when they are ready for the bull. It will pass when her man takes her." But I did not think that it was my wedding to Agis that I was waiting for.

I waited almost a year; and then Sparta began making ready to march on Attica, and suddenly my marriage day was a fixed and settled thing. Agis would be leading the war host, and it is the duty of every Spartan going to war, more than all others it is the duty of the King, to leave behind him children to take his place if he should be killed; at the least a wife with child.

So Agis would have to turn from the boys' barracks at last; at any rate until I was safely breeding. Once I heard three young men of the guard talking together. One said, "I wonder if he can?" And the second shrugged. "Well, he's got upward of two months to practise." And the third said, "He'll need them. It's my belief he's never lain with a woman before."

And sometimes I caught the women whispering, who would break off as soon as I drew near. I began to understand what lay ahead of me, and be a little afraid. My nurse said, "He will do his duty by you, for that is his duty to Sparta; and many women would be glad to have a husband who will make so few demands on them."

The time passed, and my new tunics and the veils that I should wear when I was a married woman, were ready in my olive wood bridal chest; and with them the earrings and the pair of heavy gold bracelets that had been my mother's, and the fine wolfskin rug for the bride-bed, which by custom I must bring with me to my husband's house. Agis had already paid to my father the remainder of the bride-price left over from our betrothal. And the thin petalled crimson anemones were in flower.

Three days before my wedding, I took a little pot of wild honey and a handful of corn bound in a napkin, and with Dionyssa for company (one may take a single companion, though no more), I went up into that narrow hidden glen of the Taygetus gorges where no man cares to go, to the Place of the Lady. Nearly all girls go there before their weddings. The Lady is very old, older even then Apollo Amyklae, older than the city of Sparta. She was here long and long before we conquered the land; and the Helot girls come there still. It is the one place in all our land where it matters more to be a woman going to a man, than it does to be a Helot slave or the Queen of Sparta. Some of us go half laughing, but still we go.

I made the sacrifice—it is only a Little Sacrifice; no blood fresh spilled, but only the smearing of the honey on the breasts of the black stone, and the pouring of the grain before her. I made the ritual gestures and spoke the prayer, and tied my ribbon of crimson wool among the others already there, to the branch of the terebinth tree that arches over the place; and then we came away.

It was dark and chill in the woods—the woods of Taygetus do not generally seem to me so, but I have heard others who have been to the Place of the Lady speak of the same chill. And when the ground began to level under our feet and we came out from the trees on to the track leading back towards the city, the hollow land seemed very wide and filled with light, light that was caught like golden dust in the air. There was a faint haze of green over the cornland, and here and there on the edges of the olive gardens the white feathering of an almond tree breaking into flower. Somewhere in the woods a cuckoo called. Soon it would be the

Hyakinthia again, but I should not walk free among the maidens this year.

Only a stade or so from the place where we had joined it, the track rounded a grove of very old wild olive trees and crossed one of the streams that came down to feed the Eurotas, and there we came on a man sitting by the way just short of the log bridge and rubbing his ankle. I knew Alkibiades before he looked up.

I stopped beside him and said, "You have hurt your foot?" It was the first time I had ever spoken to him.

He looked up at me ruefully. "The stupidest thing, I have twisted it on a stone. It is a small matter, I do not think that I have pulled the tendon."

If he had not said that, I would, I might, have gone on and perhaps sent back a slave to see if he needed help. But anyone who has ever trained in the gymnasium or on the running track knows the trouble that a pulled tendon can cause, especially if it is walked on before being properly strapped. So I said, "Let me look at it."

"It would not be fitting," he said stiffly—but I could have sworn that there was laughter somewhere behind the stiffness.

"It would not be the first racetrack injury that I have dealt with," I said. "I am not one of your shut-away Athenian women." And I squatted down and held out my hands for his foot.

"So I should guess," he said, "even if I had not seen you running with your sisters and the young men on the training grounds."

"To every land its own ways," I said. "Give me your foot."

And he let me have my way.

"One day," he said, "far enough from here, I shall tell people that I have had the Queen of Sparta kneeling at my feet."

"Timea," my sister said, "we must go on. It is growing late and there is still so much to do."

I said to my sister, "There is time enough for everything," and to Alkibiades, "I am not yet Queen of Sparta."

"You will be in three days," he said.

My heart had begun to beat in little sharp bangs high under my collarbones, and for a moment there seemed a faint mist before my eyes.

I had the napkin in which I had carried the corn and the honeypot: I held it out to my sister. "Dionyssa, go and wet this in the stream."

She shrugged, and took it and went down the bank. The stream was only a few paces away, but as she stooped to the water her back was towards us, and the branches of a half-fallen oleander

91

came between us and her. Alkibiades leaned toward me and said,
"I still have your flower."

"My flower?"

His hand moved as though unconsciously to the breast of his
tunic. "The flower that fell from your garland at the Hyakinthia."

"How foolish! What use can it be to you?" I said; and he
laughed suddenly, the sun making a blue devil-dance in his
narrowed eyes.

"Maybe it will bring me luck," he said.

And I knew that he was teasing me because he saw that I wanted
him to say that it was precious to him because it was from me.
And yet I do not think I believed for a moment that he still had it,
and was half minded to bid him show it to me. But I knew he
would have some tale ready on the instant if I did; and truth to
tell I did not care whether he had it or not. I loved the audacity
of him; and the laughter rose in me to meet and mingle with his,
for the waking joy in me that chose laughter because it must either
laugh or weep. Yet I do not think that there was any sound to my
laughter; it was part of the world and the shining moment and
the sudden flash of gold on the air as an oriel flew out from the
smoky shadows of the olive trees and darted away downstream.

Then Dionyssa came back rather prim and cross, with the
dripping napkin, and I bound it tight about his foot and ankle,
while he watched me, and I knew that I must not look up and
meet his eyes.

When it was done, he thanked me, and got to his feet, putting
his weight testingly on the bandaged one. "You will be wasted as
Queen of Sparta; I could walk a hundred stades on this, now."

"Can you walk as far as the city?" I said.

And he said gravely, "If I may walk it with you and your little
sister."

So we all three walked back to the city together; and he never
once forgot to limp, all the way.

# 8

## The Queen

The day of my wedding came. A strange brooding day with little flurries of wind that blew from all quarters, raising the dust and making a rainy sound among the olive trees; and long calms in between when the air lay heavy against one's forehead and was too warm for so early in the year.

"Earthquake weather," said our old cook-slave; but to her every day that was not like any other meant earthquake weather; so nobody took any notice of her. The household was much too busy.

At first light the slaves brought the garlands of myrtle and arbutus to wreath the wooden pillars in front of our house. The olive wood chest containing all my bride gear, including now my distaff and spindle, was brought out from the women's quarters together with the wolfskin rug, and carried away to the King's House. I watched it go, feeling that something of myself had gone with it and I was already beginning to be a stranger in my father's house.

My mother and Panthea, my nurse, baked the little sesame cakes which I must eat for my last meal in my father's house and the first in my husband's, so that I should be fruitful and bear many sons for Sparta. They went about it crying a little as most women do at such times, even the women slaves cried too, and they all ran about doing three things at once. But for me there was nothing to do but sit in the women's apartment with my hands in my lap and wait for the time to pass, and watch those little uneasy dust-devils in the inner courtyard.

Twilight came at last, and Panthea brought me a lamp and set a platter of sesame cakes on a low table at my side, saying, "Eat, and bear a hundred sons."

I ate, though they turned to sawdust in my mouth and were hard to swallow. In the King's House now they would be holding the marriage feast. I wondered if they were giving Agis plenty of sesame cakes, too. And then suddenly, almost for the first time since I was a child—except sometimes on the running track at the end of a race—I felt sick, and could eat no more.

My nurse tried to coax me, but when she saw that in truth I could not, she was kind, and shooed away Dionyssa and my girl friends who had come pressing round me. "I have seen it so with many brides in my time. Tomorrow she will be proud and happy, and when next she feels sick, it will be time to start asking Artemis for a boy . . . But now I must be making her ready."

I have heard that in other states of Hellas the marriage customs are quite different from ours; the bride is present at the wedding feast, wearing fine robes and veiled in saffron. But we still keep to the older way, remembering the days when a man must carry his chosen woman away by force; and we make a ritual pretence at disguising the bride and hiding her away before the bridegroom's coming.

So Panthea and my mother bound my hair up close about my head—in my grandmother's day they used still to cut it off—and dressed me in a boy's tunic, and took me up to the loft above the women's quarters, and left me there alone. I might not even have a light; but I bored a hole in the thatch with my finger and let a thread of moonlight through, because I could not breathe the thickness of the dark.

It seemed a long time that I crouched there waiting; so long that it felt as though the night must be three parts worn away, only that the flake of moonlight had not moved a hand's span on the straw. I watched it, the white light and the tiny shadow of a bent cornstalk; the light trickling down it on to another stalk, and the shadow changing. It was very hot under the rafters, and it seemed to grow hotter and more airless instead of cooler as time went by. I wondered if there was a storm brewing; but no dimming came over that trickling white drop of moonlight. Below me the house was by turns silent and filled with soft whispers, and breaths of excited laughter.

And then I heard the voices and the footsteps coming up the street. They checked beneath our garlanded porch; and there was a beating on the door, and Agis' quick harsh voice demanding Timea, and my father's deeper voice denying that there was any daughter of that name in his house, and then the scuffle as the bridegroom and his companions thrust him aside. It was all part of the ritual, no more, but suddenly as I heard them questing like hounds through the house, the terror of the hunted woke in me, and it was all I could do to bide still in the straw. They were calling to each other from room to room; and then a shout told me that they had found the loft ladder.

Red torchlight burst up through the hole in the floor, turning my silver moon-fleck as thin as skimmed milk. There was a rush of feet, and then the feet of one man alone, on the rungs. His shoulders blotted out the torchlight sending a great gout of shadow before him. He came, not hurrying, not hesitating, and as he came I shrank back into the straw. He climbed clear of the ladder head, and stood for a moment with the torchlight and the thick voices beating up about him from below; his head lowered and swinging a little from side to side like a boar's. I could feel his small red eyes looking for me in the dark. Then he gave a grunt, and came striding across to me, his hands coming before him.

His hands came down on me, spread and crook-fingered . . .

It is allowed to a woman to put up a fight at her carrying off, so long as she yields at the last, and I have known some women make their men pay heavy for their capture. But I did not dare, because I was afraid of what would happen if I once began; afraid that I should not be able to stop, and so be carried from the house at last clawing and biting, pitiful like a captured wild-thing. So I let him catch hold of me, and tried not even to tense as he swung me up from the straw. He was rough and clumsy, his hands seeming to shrink from me even as his grip tightened, and he flung me up across his shoulder. The boar stink was on him, and the stink of neat wine. He turned back to the ladder. And all without one spoken word between us. He is not a tall man, My Lord King, but strong; in those days he was very strong, and I felt the strength of him, the hard slow beat of his heart, the heat of his body, and the ease it was for him to carry my weight, even though his feet were made unsure by the wine. He carried me down into the tossing torchlight and the faces crowded in the inner court below.

It was all like a dream, vivid but confused. Faces that were all eyes or gaping mouths, hands that reached out of nowhere. Yet I remember it all so clearly, every detail. I remember how he carried me out between the garlanded pillars of my home, and the scent of myrtle and rosemary mingled with the resin smell of the torches.

The companions closed about us, each with his spear in his right hand and a torch held high in his left, so that there seemed fire all about me, fire and faces and the male glint of spears. And I remember in my hurrying dream, looking up at the moon, as we turned from the narrow street into the Agora that was murmurous

95

with women crowded in doorways to watch the King's wedding party go by; and seeing that it was a strange colour as though all the gold had been drained from it leaving only the cold, glaring white behind.

We came to the King's House, and there too the scent of the bridal garlands hung heavy in the air as scent hangs before a storm. He carried me in through the foreporch and across the outer court where the stables and storesheds are. The horses were restless; I heard them stamping in their stalls, but it might have been only the sounds of coming and going so late in the night that disturbed them. At the entrance to the inner court, Agis checked and turned to his companions, and said, "The King thanks you. The bride is safe. There's still wine in the Mess Hall, go back and quench your torches in it."

Often the closest friends and mess-mates of the bridegroom escort him to the door of the bridal chamber, and there is laughter and men's jesting, and sometimes even, one especial friend must hold the door after the groom has carried his bride within. But no one attempted to follow Agis through the inner gate. He was the King, and in any case he had no close friends.

He carried me across the inner courtyard, his footsteps sounding sharp-edged and alone, the torchlight falling away behind us. There was a scurrying of slaves in the moon-shadows, and I saw lighted doorways ahead. He carried me over a threshold, across a long chamber and up three or four steps that I knew must lead to the women's quarters; and just within another door, he set me down, and snatched his hands away from me the instant my feet touched the ground.

Strange women slaves came forward, and he said, "Get her to bed and then get out." And turned on his heel and tramped off, never once looking at me.

The strange women brought me into a further sleeping chamber. They stripped me of my boy's tunic and unbound my hair and rubbed spikenard between my breasts and on the palms of my hands. And all the while I felt a gathering uneasiness in the room. It was not the women, uneasy of me and the new pattern my coming must bring to the household, as at first I had thought that it might be. It was not personal at all. Suddenly it came to me that the uneasiness was not within this one room alone, but filled the whole night.

They spoke soft words to me, as though they thought that the unease in the room was my own fear of my wedding night. I scarcely heard what they said; only their voices—the Helot women have softer voices than ours. They led me to the broad bed-place, piled with rugs, my own wolfskins over all; and when I lay down, they would have drawn a coverlid of saffron wool over me. But the skins were warm beneath me, and there seemed even less air in this place than in the loft at home. And when they were gone, I flung it off again and lay naked. The room turned on me the blank look of a stranger; in the light of the lamp hanging from its bronze standard at the bed-foot, I could see a couple of spears propped in a corner, a great armour-chest against one wall, with a well-worn soldier's cloak flung across it. Only my own painted olive-wood chest standing ready opened, with my spindle and distaff lying on the beaten earth beside it, was a part of familiar things and the life I knew. It was very quiet, the wind had died utterly away. There were sounds of movement and distant voices in the house. Once I heard Agis' voice raised, and a boy's, angry and near to tears. But always, beyond the sounds, was the silence, and the waiting.

And then I heard Agis' footsteps, stumbling a little; and he was back, standing on the edge of the lamplight, freeing the shoulder knot of his cloak, pulling off his sword. And still he never looked at me. I said, "Did you get rid of the boy?"

He said, "Yes," and then he turned and looked at me for the first time. He had been a little drunk before, and he had been drinking again. He stood rocking on his heels, his eyes were red-rimmed, and the hard lines of his face were slackened and blurred by the drink in him. And I saw for that one moment my boar brought to bay. The moment passed, and he looked me all along as I lay there naked on the bed-place, and his face settled into cold distaste. I said, "Do you want your son so much?"

And he said, "Sparta wants my son."

And I knew he would give Sparta what his duty demanded, like the good Spartan he was.

He pulled off his tunic and came to the bed, and looked down at me; and I saw that he was shaking, through all his strong thick-set body; and I thought, 'Maybe he will kill me with this; with his striving to force his son into me against the will of his flesh.' And even as he bent over me, suddenly a bird gave its alarm call to the night, and there was a great fluttering of wings, the courtyard pigeons and the swallows that nested under the eaves flying out from their roosting places. And then I heard it: a distant mutter of sound that seemed to come from far, far down below the King's House, as though in some cavern of the underworld, something stirred from sleep. In the same instant the lamp-flame began to jump and flutter, sending weird bursts of shadow up the walls and rafters as though a great wind had leapt into the room. The lamp itself had begun to swing on its chains; and the mutter that had died away, came again, deeper and louder and more menacing, and the earth shivered with it, and was still. I had known it before, the wrath of Poseidon the Earth-shaker, but only as a child, and it was a few moments before I understood. Then the beaten earth seemed to rouse and shake itself and slip sideways under me. Part of me noticed, as though it stood apart from the rest of me, looking on, how my spindle rolled a little way in a sharp curve over the floor, then back again to rap against the side of the chest. Dry chaff and old dust and small many-legged things showered out of the thatch. A narrow crack started beside the bed-place and ran like a lizard up the wall. I waited for it to widen into a mouth and the King's House to come crashing down. It seems strange to me now that I did not spring up, but only lay there waiting—and watching Agis' eyes. But it was all over so quickly; a few heartbeats of time, and the earth was still again; nothing left but the crack in the wall and the fallen roof-stuff, the crying and calling of voices, a horse neighing in terror in the stable court. And then those too began to fade. And strangely, like a great sigh of relief, I heard the birds coming back to roost.

The wrath of Poseidon had been mild and swiftly past. I learned later that little damage had been done. One house on the outskirts of the city had been burned down by a lamp setting fire to a fallen rafter, a few Helots' hovels had caved in, a few stones had been shaken out from the big Boundary Herm on the North Road, two or three people had been killed by falling debris.

At the time I could know none of that. I only knew Agis' small bright eyes staring straight into mine and the sudden relief in his drunk face.

He passed his tongue over his lips, and said, slurring the words, "It is the warning of Poseidon! The warning of the Gods!"

I said nothing; and after a moment he gathered himself together and hid the relief with care. He said again, "The warning of the Gods." And then, to himself as much as to me, "They bid me not to lie with you before we march for Attica. They demand this of me as the price of victory." And his eyes dared me to say otherwise.

He flung his cloak round his shoulders and caught up his sword and strode out of the room.

Next day it was known everywhere that in obedience to the

Warning of the Earth-shaker that had struck Sparta as he entered the marriage chamber, Agis had vowed not to lie with his new Queen until he returned from Dekalia.

It was a good enough reason for my own people, who have been bred with a proper reverence for the Gods; but I seemed to hear the laughter of Alkibiades everywhere, even in my solitary bed at night.

I thought at first—when I had had time to think the thing out at all—that since Agis did not want me, I should have at least as much freedom as other Spartan wives, maybe more. I did not yet know Agis the King. He had no desire for me in the way of a man for a woman. But I was his, like his cloak, his sword, his hunting dogs; indeed he was like an old hunting dog with a bone that it does not want itself but is determined no other dog shall have; crouching within reach, eyes half-closed and hackles a little raised.

I found myself keeping to the women's quarters almost as close as I have been told Athenian women do, because of the eyes that followed me whenever I went abroad, no matter how modestly I drew the unaccustomed veil across my face; the eyes of the Palace women, of the guard, of my old jealous hound himself. I was Queen of Sparta, as was my appointed destiny. But I had not known when I ran free with the other girls and the young men at training, that it was appointed also that I should be caged.

So I heard only the distant sounds of Sparta making ready for war. The distant shrilling of flutes from the training grounds; the tramp of marching feet up the narrow street behind the women's quarters; the occasional talk of My Lord and his Generals, when he sent for me as he sometimes did late in the evening, to sit beside him where the lamplight fell on my hair, while he talked over plans of campaign or went through the muster rolls. At first I used to wonder why he sent for me; there was nothing for me to do, there were always boys to mix and pour the wine. But later I came to understand that I was simply to be there, so that other men might see, and know that I was his.

On the morning that the Army were to march, I was working early at my loom when one of my women checked her spinning and glanced quickly at the door and then at me; and a little flurry among the rest made me turn that way myself. And there on the threshold stood Agis in his favourite position, legs apart and hands behind his back, his head down a little, watching me under the rim of his helmet, for he was already fully armed. And under the thorax-straps and the heavy folds of his cloak, the breadth of his shoulders filled the doorway from side to side.

I gestured to my women, and they drew back to the far end of the long room.

"It is always good to see the mistress of the house busy at her loom," he said. "But I wonder how many women are weaving in Sparta this morning while their men make ready to march?"

I said, "It has not seemed to me that you find so much pleasure in my company that I should come to you unsummoned."

"I waited for you to come to arm me for war."

"Your Helot has done it quite as well as I could do."

He said, "That is not the point. It is the duty of a Spartan wife to arm her husband at such times, to show her pride in him."

"You have not treated me as a wife," I said.

His brows drew together. "The Gods forbade it, that you know."

I think by then he had forgotten the truth, had made himself forget, and believed that he was obeying the will of the Gods in this. I was the only person in the world who had seen the sick relief in his eyes when the shuddering of the earth gave him a good reason for keeping out of my bed. But I did not remind him. If I had, I think he would have had me killed while he was away.

So I bowed my head, and said nothing.

He said in a kinder tone, "This has been hard for you, and you have played your part well. I have not failed to notice how properly you have kept to the women's quarters, and held yourself, now that you are married, from the company of other men. If you have not been in truth my wife, you have behaved yourself as a Queen of Sparta." And then, while I was still shaken by the unusual kindness of his tone, the iron crept into it again, and he was looking at me with the hard narrowed eyes that I was used to. "I shall expect you to hold to the same conduct while I am away. Remember that, for if you forget it, if you should think, maybe, to follow the ancient custom of women when their men are long at the wars—which is a good custom for the carrying on of the race, but not for a Queen—there are those watching who have their orders from me."

I went close to him, and put my hands on his breast, and felt him shrink a little. I said, "You do not want me. Why does it mean so much to you, that no other man should have what you do not want?"

He said, "You are *mine*." And I saw that to him that answered everything.

Later, I called my women after me, and went out across the forecourt to the broad timbered porch; my veil drawn decently across my face, to watch the men march away. Every woman in Sparta would be crowding out to see husband or son or father depart; and the Queen must be there with the rest. The broad space of the Agora was full of troops, the early summer sun glinting on bronze helmet-combs, on spear-points pricking the morning, on shields blazoned with the scarlet Lamda. Agis had already taken station at their head, his staff officers about him and his bodyguard close behind. The King-Standard with its painted Lion shivered in the little wind that was driving light clouds across the sky. The smoke of the sacrifice was still curling up from the altar before the temple of Ares. The augurs had read the omens in the entrails of the slain ox and proclaimed that they were fortunate. And the voice of the High Priest speaking the final words of invocation sounded thin in the morning air. It ended, and the flutes shrilled their order, and as one man the long ranks swung forward. The flutes broke into marching time; the steady, swinging rhythm of the tunes that would lead them northward through the mountains and across the Isthmus, and down at last from the north again, through the Dekalia Pass into Attica. The ranks passed—and passed—and passed—and were gone. The music of the flutes and the tramp of many feet, moving as one, faded into the distance. In the training ground beyond the city, the rest of the Army would fall in behind them. But for us, here in the city, it was over, and they were gone.

There was a ragged murmur from the crowd that had gathered to see them away; the women and the old, and the boys as yet too young for war; very little weeping. The women of Sparta are accustomed to watch, without weeping, their men march out to fight. But I, I wished all at once that there was some need in me to weep, something to bind me to the other women already beginning to drift away. But I could feel nothing, not even relief, at Agis' going; I had no brothers, my father was too old, for they had not called up the veterans, and the boys who had trained with me were as yet too young by almost a year.

For me there was nothing save an empty and impersonal pride in the bronze and crimson ranks that had left their emptiness in the sunlit air. Once, even though I had no special stake in them, my heart would have swollen and raced with a warm agony of pride as the marching ranks went by; but it seemed that close on two months of being Agis' unused property had frozen something in me quite dead; and I missed it; I missed it with a longing beyond the need for tears.

I do not know what made me pause as I was turning to go back into the King's House, and look once more across the emptying Agora.

Alkibiades was standing not far from the still faintly smoking altar, leaning one shoulder against a timber column of the temple, as though it was too much trouble to stand up. He was looking away down the street as though still watching the rearmost ranks that were long since out of sight, and the Helots who plodded after them carrying their baggage and spare weapons. I knew that he had applied to go with the Dekalia Force, and been refused, just as he had been refused when he applied to go on the Argolid raid the year before. He was a captive, even as I was, forbidden to leave Sparta till My Lord the King returned, a hostage for the success of his plan to ruin Athens. I wondered if there was anything of relief in him that at least now he would not be called on to draw sword against men of his own people. Or had he nursed his hate so well as the months lengthened into years, that there was only rage in him that he who had made the plan was left contemptuously behind while other men carried it out. There was nothing to be read in his face; it was the face a man wears in the wrestlers' pit. As though he felt my eyes upon him, he turned his head and looked at me. For maybe the time that it takes to run five paces, it was as though we stood alone within touching distance and had reached out. Then he turned and said something to that drunken redheaded lieutenant of his, flung an arm across the man's shoulder, and strolled away.

# 9

## The Queen

The outer gates shut behind me. The pigeons came fanning all about me with the sunlight rimming their wings with fire; pitching at my feet, strutting and crooning, for it was the hour at which I often threw them a little grain.

I had plenty to do all day, the maids to oversee at their spinning, the household to attend to; except at festival times when she must perform her priestly duties, the life of a Queen is little different from that of any other woman, save that she has a larger household to handle.

And all the while I felt, as I had felt for so long, that it was not Timea doing these things, but another in Timea's shape, while Timea herself stood by in some kind of half-country, not living at all, but only waiting—for a beginning or an end; I did not know which.

Evening came, and the slaves lit the lamps; night came, and I went to my sleeping chamber that should have been mine and Agis', but now bore no sign that ever a man had had part or lot in it.

It was a hot night. One of those early summer nights when the wind drops quite away and the belly of the darkness swells with unspilled rain. I longed for the rain, as though its coming could ease and slacken me and let me sleep. (I had not slept well for a long time, I who in the old days had slept when my head touched the pillow.) But failing the rain and failing sleep, I longed to be alone—not presently when the ritual of the Queen being put to bed was over, but now, now! I could not wait! When my women had taken off my tunic, I told them to leave me.

My old nurse, who had followed me into my new life, said protestingly, "But Mistress, your hair!"

"I will comb my own hair," I said. And then I heard my voice rising, growing shrill as a market woman's. "I do not need you, I do not want any of you! Go away from me! Get out! Go!"

I suppose they thought the day's happenings had been too much for me. Indeed Eurynome the youngest of them said gently, "Mistress, he will come back."

I remember looking at her with a kind of surprised pity, and thinking that I had not known before what a fool she was.

When they were gone, I unclasped the two heavy gold bracelets from my wrists and laid them on the table. The lamp by the bed-foot cast my naked shadow on the wall. I stood and looked at it, and it was a good shadow, narrow at the waist and broad at the hip and shoulder, the kind of shadow that many women must bind tight strips about their waists to achieve. I turned sideways, so that it turned sideways too, and I could see the outline of my breasts and belly on the wall; I was still hard and flat-bellied from the running track. Once that had seemed to me good; but there is a time for all things; and suddenly I could have wept for pity of myself, wondering if I must go lean and flat-bellied until I withered into an old woman with empty hanging dugs and flanks that might as well be a man's.

I pulled off the golden ribbon that bound my hair, and it came tumbling down over my shoulders. I took the comb from the table, and my little bronze mirror and began to comb it.

I sat there for a long time, parting it with my fingers and combing it this way and that, and thinking. Thinking of the long solitary months ahead; thinking of what might happen if Agis did not come back, thinking of what might happen if he did. The lamp flame burned blue at the heart as a hyacinth flower; the turn-over of the wick was sparked and seeded with red in the way that foretells rain.

Presently I heard it come; the first heavy drops on the beaten earth outside. It quickened to a spattering, and the scent of rain-wet earth came breathing in at the high window. And then I heard another sound; a faint stirring of movement outside that was not the rain. I looked towards it, and a hand came over the sill.

I sprang up, my mouth was open to cry out—but I knew the hand; the great ring on the signet finger, too, but the hand more than the ring. Artemis pity women! I did not cry out. And Alkibiades drew himself up and dropped into the room.

I remember that for a time, I do not know whether it was short or long, we stood facing each other. Part of me was terrified, listening for a shout and a running of feet and the jar of weapons in the night outside, and hearing only the soft hush and spatter of the rain. Part of me felt as though all the blood in my body had turned to a strange cold fire and rushed back to my heart so that I could not breathe. Part of me said, 'This is what you were waiting for. Now be content.'

He said, "Your hair is the colour of Hymettus honey where the lamp shines on it."

I said, "Why have you come?"

And he answered, with the laughter twitching at his lips, "I asked Agis the King what I should do to amuse myself while the Dekalia Force was away, and he bade me to do whatever I pleased."

"And this is what you please," I said.

"This is what I please. We shall do better, I think, without the lamp." And he crossed to it with that long light stride of his, and pinched out the flame between finger and thumb. For a moment darkness hung like a web before my eyes; then as the slurred moon swam into some rent in the clouds, it paled, and I saw him again, a man-shaped darkness blotted against lesser darkness of the window.

I said, "Get back as you came."

"Presently," he said.

"Now! My women are close by; I have only to call."

His voice was softly amused, "But you are not going to call, are you, Timea?"

It was the first time he had spoken my name, and the first time it had ever seemed to me that my name was beautiful.

"No," I said.

And then I felt more than saw, how he held his arms out to me; and I went into them as though there had never been any other place for me from the day that I was born. He caught me against him, and I felt even then how his hard body was alight with laughter. His tunic was wet with the first spattering of the rain, and there was rain on his lips, and the cool wetness of rain in his hair that fell forward across my face; and the fresh sweet smell of the rain was all about him, mingled with the smell of wine.

I said, when I could speak again, "How did you escape your guards and get past mine?"

And he said, "Love, your brave Spartans are no match for an Athenian in guile. Antiochus is on watch outside; there is nothing to fear."

As though discovery was all I had to fear that night.

And as though it was a thing of long agreement between us, he picked me up and carried me across to the bed-place and laid me down on the wolfskin rug that I had brought with me to furnish my marriage bed.

He hurt me, then, for I was a virgin, having been bred up to give proof of that to My Lord the King. And Oh, the pain was sweet! I took it and drew it up into my body, writhing and gasping beneath his thrust, until his man-spear broke through and I gave him the proof that had been meant for Agis the King.

Afterwards, when he lay quiet with his body all along mine, and his head driven into the hollow between my neck and shoulder, I said, "Was it only to be revenged on Agis?"

"That I came? I had other reasons."

"Tell them to me."

"Small foolish reasons. Because the little hairs on your arms and legs make a silvery bloom over the brown of your skin; because your mouth is wide; because you have the scar of an old spear-thrust below your left knee—thin and white as the sliver of the New Moon. Did you come by it on the practice grounds?"

"Yes," I said, "when I was fifteen. One of the boys playing the fool with his weapons."

He turned his head and kissed me on the throat. "It would be hard to find an Athenian girl with the mark of a spear gash below her knee . . . Because I knew your hair would smell of sweet-grass. Because I knew you would be fierce and sweet in the taking."

And fool that I was, because they *were* small foolish reasons, I believed him at least half the way; and the half was enough for me.

I wish I had died that night, with the first fiery pain of love upon me!

It was full summer when I went to my nurse, the only woman in the world I could trust, and said, "Panthea, I think I am with child."

"That was in my mind also," said she; and then, "Pray to the Gods he does not lisp when he comes to talking."

I said, "You knew?"

She took me in her arms, and held me as she was used to do when I was small, and said, "There's not much that you can keep from me, my lamb. There were still traces on your marriage wolfskins for all your sponging, on the morning after the Army marched for Dekalia—you may thank your fortune it was old Panthea that found them. And well enough I know that you haven't slept lonely every night since then."

"Why did you never say anything? Never seek to stop me?" I asked childishly.

"Because I wanted you to have something from life, no matter what came after. It is better for a woman to have her springtime and pay for it, than never to have known the spring at all."

"Panthea, what shall I do?"

"That depends. Do you want to do away with the child?"

"No! Oh no!" I wanted Alkibiades' child more than I had ever wanted anything in this world. But I clung to her, frightened as a child myself, with the newness of what was happening to me. "Will he kill me, when he knows?"

She was silent a moment, then she said, "You must tell Agis that the child is his."

I almost laughed at that. "I am not one of his bodyguard nor from the Boys' Barracks! He has never lain with me, all Sparta knows it!"

"All Sparta knows he *says* he has never lain with you. He was here in the bride chamber with you on your wedding night."

"But he never lay with me. The earth shook. Panthea, don't you understand?" I shook her, wondering desperately whether age was making her wander in her wits.

"He was drunk, that night," Panthea said. "All Sparta knows that too. Men often do not remember clearly when they are sober again, what things they did when the wine was in them . . . There was confusion in the house—Oh, I was not there, but one learns things—his latest boy made trouble; and I doubt if there's anyone with a clear idea of how long before the earth shook, he went to the bridal chamber. Swear he got you with child that night. Tell how he came for you like a leopard in the coupling season—you can swear you found means to smuggle something into his wine, if you like—and when the earth shook, the thing was already done."

"He will never believe me."

"He will never be able to be quite sure."

But I had thought of another thing. "Unless the child is born early, it will be more than ten months—close on eleven—since that night."

"I've known first children carried as long in the womb before now," Panthea said. She put back my hair from my forehead and looked at me fixedly. "Swear that he lay with you that night before the earth shook, and when you found that he had forgotten, and taken the oath, you kept silent for his sake. Swear it is the King's child and let nothing shake you from that. Part of him will want

107

to believe you, the more so if it is a boy, for then he will have done his duty by Sparta and his house, and need never come to your bed again."

After she had held me for a little while in silence, she said, "Will you tell Alkibiades?"

"Yes," I said. "It is his right to know. But not yet."

I do not know why, not yet. I could not know then, that when he knew his seed had quickened in me and taken root, I should have already begun to lose him.

It was a night of late summer with the moths blundering into the lamp, when I saw my side-cast shadow on my chamber wall, just as I had seen it the night he first came to me, and knew by the faint swelling and softening of my belly, that the time had come to tell him, before all Lacedaemon knew that Agis' Queen was with child.

In the heat of the summer's end when people sleep in the courts and porticos, it was not so easy for him to come to me in my chamber. But we contrived to meet at times, still, with the help of old Panthea. Most often we met in the mouth of the wooded glen that ran up toward the Place of the Lady. It seemed natural enough to my women that I should go there, taking only my old nurse for company; while Alkibiades was free to come and go as he would, so long as he made no attempt to cross the border. I did not think the Lady would be angry, seeing that I was about Her business.

It was there that I told him, lying in the shade of myrtle and kerm oak and arbutus trees, his arm under my head, the cicadas filling the noontide heat with their shrill churring, and beyond the trees the cornlands were cut stubble, drained of colour, shimmering in the heat.     .

He rolled towards me, and cupped his hand over my belly, and said, "A child of mine, so small that I can cover him with the palm of my hand." And then, "What shall you say to Sparta? And Sparta's King?"

And love-blind as I was, I did not see then, only in remembering long afterward, that he was not concerned for me, only curious as to what I would do.

I told him how I was prepared to swear to Agis that the child was his own. "No one else will ever know," I told him.

"They'll guess," he said.

"They'll never be sure. Only you can be sure."

"Only you and I," he said. "Bear a son for me, sweetheart."

I said, playing with him a little, "Would not a daughter serve as well? You'll not have to find her dowry."

"Nor my son his armour," he said, and pulled me to him. "Every man wants a son by the woman he loves."

"You have one son already," I said. "For me this is the first time, and it seems strange to me that you have one son already."

"One lawful son." His voice was muffled in my hair. "I have told you what manner of son he is."

"He was little more than a baby when you saw him last," I said, driven by sudden pity for a son of Alkibiades who had nothing of his love. "You could not be sure what manner of son he will be."

"When I saw him last, he was sitting in the sun with shallow eyes. He had caught a frog and he was pulling it to pieces," Alkibiades said. And then, as though that explained and disposed of everything, "I never loved his mother."

And then just as suddenly, I could not bear, with his child lying curled in my own belly, to think of that other child his words had called up to shadow the summer noon. I turned quickly to the last thing he had said, "Why did you marry her, then?"

For somehow the laws that bind other men did not hold for Alkibiades, and the idea that he had married simply because his guardian had arranged the marriage, never came into my mind.

"I married her for her money—I was somewhat short at the time—but the money ran out. Poor Hipparite, unsatisfactory in all things. And so damnably faithful. That wouldn't have been so bad, but she would have had me faithful too."

"She could not help it that you did not love her," I said.

"There were so many things that she could not help."

"And you love me! I am glad, I am glad!"

"I love you—till the moon darkens in the sky," his arms tightened round me, and I felt a kind of ripple run through him, as though his whole body was shaken with silent laughter.

"What is it?" I asked. "What are you laughing at?"

"A foolish thought, a man's thought. You would find no laughter in it."


## The Citizen

At first the war seemed far off, and I remember my own furious rebellion—Gods! How the young can rebel!—against the short leg that kept me safe in Athens. More, I think, when the news began to be bad, than in the early days when it was all good.

But we were to have our fill of death in Athens too, before all was over.

It began even before our General Demosthenes was sent out with reinforcements. We scraped what seemed at the time to be the bottom of the barrel to gather those reinforcements, and all Attica began to go short, and part with family treasures to pay for them. My father gave the gold earrings shaped like tiny hanging vases, that had been his wedding gift to my mother; and felt it deeply that he could not give me. (I felt it deeply, too; a fact which I think he overlooked.) But even so the fleet sailed short of sixteen hundred Thracian mercenaries who we could ill spare, simply because we could not raise the money for their pay. They raised what they could of it themselves, on their way home, by looting the towns and villages they passed through.

But it was not until early the following summer that the war really broke over us. That was when Agis and his Spartans came over the Pass at Dekalia, as they had used to do in the old days before the truce. Then for the first time in twelve years we saw the smoke of burning farms, and the Meltemi blew the ashes south into the streets of the city as I remembered it doing when I was a child. Now, suddenly, it came howling in upon us that this was no mere summer raiding. The Spartans had taken and fortified Dekalia; they had come to stay! Agis swept across Attica like a plague, leaving black destruction everywhere behind him; and our slaves deserted in hordes to join his raiding parties, and it was no longer possible to work the silver mines of Laurium—old Nikias would have felt the pinch there, if he hadn't been sweating a cold sweat before the walls of Syracuse. Our corn supplies from the north were cut off, and every day Athens became more full of pitiful refugees from all over Attica, to squat in the streets and build themselves shelters against the very walls of the temples, and hold out their hands for help.

No one came to buy at my father's shop any more, there was no money for perfumed rubbing oil in Athens now; but the men came to talk, as they always had done, old men looking more and more like shadows as the days went by. Everyone knew whose brain was behind the seizing and fortifying of Dekalia; no Spartan would have thought of it. "He has betrayed Athens," they said. "He has betrayed his own people."

But I thought of him riding down to the Piraeus Gate, on the morning that our fleet sailed for Syracuse, with the sun in his eyes and the crimson Adonis flowers trampled beneath his horse's hooves. And the young man in the crowd saying, "The Gods help him if ever he betrays us." And the old man saying, "The Gods help him and us, if ever we betray *him*."

And I went down into the darkest corner of the storeroom and cried. But I am still not sure whether I cried for Athens or for Alkibiades, or for something that was dead within myself.


## The Seaman

I've seldom grown more heartily sick of anything than I did that summer of playing watchdog for Alkibiades while he tumbles the Queen of Sparta. I'd got myself a regular Helot girl by that time, too, and could have spent the nights pleasantly on my own account. But Alkibiades never considers anybody's nights but his own . . .

No, that's not it either—I was maddened that he should go running his head into such a hazard simply because he was bored.

I tells him so one evening, when he comes up with me on the track below the Taygetus woods where he meets her now that the heat of late summer's come. I tells him, crawling out of the bush where I'd been watch-dogging for him as usual; and he stands stock still in the path and laughs at me with his hands on my shoulders. "Oh my Antiochus, my soul of circumspection, it's overlate in the day for you to turn mentor!"

And there's a triumphant devilry in his laughter that makes the hair rise on my neck; and I says, "That's as maybe. In Poseidon's name, what madness is it now?"

"No madness," he says, laughing still. "I have lain with a Queen under an arbutus tree and listened to the cicadas and sworn to love her until the moon darkens in the sky."

"It's full now, that's twelve nights," I says, picking twigs out of my hair.

But I was wrong. There was an eclipse of the moon that night.

If I had been about my proper way of life I should have known that it was coming, for a seaman's business includes the sky. But stranded long enough on the beach, a man loses touch with such calculations. I was busy with my Helot girl in the loft over Endius' stables when I heard the sounds of fear in the street, and somebody crying on the Lady Artemis and somebody banging on a cauldron to drive demons away. And I rolls over on the straw and pushes my fist through the thatch to see what's to be seen.

The moon's hanging huge over the roof of Endius' house, bloated and red—the dull ugly red of blood that's beginning to dry at the edges; and even as I lies there watching, a shadow begins to creep across it, deepening as it goes, as if the darkness were eating the moon away.

I doesn't think of it that Syracuse also will be seeing what Sparta sees in the sky that night. I certainly doesn't think of the effect on an army and a fleet near to breaking point, with a priest-ridden old fool like Nikias in command—not until the news came through, best part of a month later.

Demosthenes had enough sense, it seems, to see by that time that the only chance of saving anything from the wreck, was to pull out the whole Athenian force while it was still possible. Athenian morale was about as low as it could get, their losses had been heavy and they were eaten up with fever. But if they could be brought off, Athens would suffer a hearty kick in the soft under-belly of her pride, but she would have a sizeable army again to run Agis out of Attica; and once that was done there'd be fresh hope for salving something out of the general wreckage. Demosthenes had even managed to drag Nikias round to his way of thinking, which can't have been easy for the old man was of the weakly stubborn kind who will go on blindly carrying out his original orders even when the changed shape of things has made them insane as well as suicidal. The order for withdrawal had actually been given and all things made ready in secret for the fleet to sail next day. And then the moon had darkened, and Nikias had listened to his soothsayers and cancelled the orders. The fleet must wait until the moon had purified herself by another circle and come to the full again. Another month in those stinking swamps I remembers below Syracuse, with the men dying like flies of dysentery as much as wounds. I had never much liked the little I had seen of Demosthenes, the man was so worthy; but Great God Poseidon, my belly sickened for him!

And then of course the thing happened that was bound to happen. Word of the intended pulling out reached Gylippos. I've often wondered if one of Nikias' soothsayers had anything to do with that . . . And now, reported our Spartan scouts triumphantly, the Syracusian and Corinthian fleets had formed a barricade of ships across the harbour mouth. The Athenian fleet was trapped.

"They may break out yet," I says.

Alkibiades says nothing. I've never known him so silent as in those few days. And it's Endius our host who says, "They may try."

And then only a day or so later another report comes in.

Demosthenes had tried his break-out and been driven back with hideous losses in men and ships. What were left of the Athenian force had begun a retreat overland, leaving their dead and wounded behind, and making, probably, for Catana. We heard few details at the time, of that ghastly three-day retreat. Everyone knew the details later, when the few survivors began to crawl home. I'm glad I didn't know at the time; I think I'd have broken the habit of a lifetime, and left Alkibiades to his Royal woman and whatever ugly death was brewing up for him in Sparta, and gone off and turned honest pirate.

About the end of Boedromion a fast penteconta came in to Gythion and the word went round that she brought despatches from Gylippos, and that the last fighting of the Syracuse campaign was over. The Council of Ephors met that same day. But Alkibiades, who I could have sworn would demand to join them in the Senate House to hear the reports from Syracuse, whistled a couple of Endius' hounds to heel and went off hunting. The evening meal in Mess was long over when he got back with a pair of bloody hares to show for his sport. I saw him cross Endius' courtyard towards the rooms that had long since become our established quarters, and went to forage in the cookhouse. Partly that was to put off the moment of going after him, for I wasn't looking forward to telling him the news from Sicily, which had been all the talk in Mess that evening.

But when I got back to our billet with a bowl of bread and olives and cold pig-meat, Endius was with him—that was Endius' year as one of the five Ephors—and I saw that he already knew. The air in that room was crackling, so that if I'd been on board ship, I'd have expected to see the masthead blue with cold-fire.

Alkibiades looks round at me and says, "Ah! Food! The hunting was so good I forgot about supper." And then, "Endius has come like a good host eager for his guest's pleasure and entertainment, to bring me the news of the Athenian fleet and Army."

I says, "There isn't an Athenian fleet or Army, any more," and set down the bowl, and a cup of raw wine—I'm thinking he'll not be wanting it watered that night.

"So you have heard it, too."

"Maybe not in such accurate detail," I says.

"So, we can finish hearing the tale together. Endius, my dear fellow, please go on. Demosthenes tried to kill himself, you said."

Endius nods. "He was too weak to do the job properly. A messy business—in the belly; but he was taken alive out of the olive garden where he made his last stand. He had almost got his lot through to safety; they were within sight of the sea again, only a few miles south of Catana."

And I thinks for the moment there's a note of regret in his voice; almost admiration, you might say.

"And Nikias and the other party?" Alkibiades asks.

"Cut to pieces at the river ford. Nikias was taken alive, too. Not quite right in the head, I gather."

"Was that in Gylippos' report, too?"

"No; the account of the penteconta Commander. However, you'll not have the embarrassment of coming face to face with your fellow Generals here in Sparta. Gylippos says he had hoped to bring them back as living captives—it would certainly have added to the triumph of his own return—but the Syracusian Assembly was not in favour of that idea. The executions were duly carried out, and the bodies left bound to stakes outside the state prison. The dogs and the kites won't have left much of them by now. The rest of the Athenian captives have been sentenced to the stone-quarries outside the city. It seems that it is always difficult to keep them fully manned, the life expectation being considerably shorter than in your own silver mines." He smiles at that—leastwise he shows his teeth. It's one of the very few times I ever sees Endius smile. "Your advice was good, my friend."

There was a long silence after he'd finished speaking. Alkibiades sat staring straight before him at the opposite wall as though he was looking through it into a black pit. Then he smiles too—so nearly that old lazy smile of his that anyone not knowing him as well as I do might have thought it was the same. He leans back, rocking on the hinder legs of his stool, and picks up the wine jug. "My advice was good, as to both Syracuse and Dekalia. I shall drink to Agis remembering that my advice was good, when he returns."

"It's more to the point to drink to the Ephors remembering," says Endius, pointedly.

"Yes, I was forgetting. Does the King—Kings, count for any-thing in Sparta?"

"Only in the field," says Endius, "and in the Queen's bed."

And there's a long look passes between them. Then Endius excuses himself as courteously as a Spartan can, and goes his way.

"He knows about you and the Queen," I says, when he's gone.

"Oh yes."

"Was it a threat?"

"Not so long as our interests run in double harness. Endius has little liking for Agis—something to do with a son, I believe.

Moreover, under that dour face of his, he's that rare thing, a Spartan with a sense of humour."

"It would be his sense of humour that made him take such pains to be the one to bring you the news from Syracuse?" I says.

"No, that was his interest in human behaviour. He was curious to see if I would squirm," says Alkibiades sweetly. He picks up the gutted carcasses of the two hares, which he must have brought in with him and dropped on the ground at his feet; and looks at them with a faint distaste as he gets up. "How very bloody—I should have remembered to give them to a slave for the cookhouse." Then he flings them across the room with such force that they smashes against the farther wall, spattering blood and mess across the lime-wash and leaps apart and back from it again to lie in two small huddles of fur and blood and broken bones on the floor.

Then he walks out past me into the night, like a man who is going to vomit.

# 10

## The Spartan

In the days after our victory off Syracuse, Alkibiades puzzled me.
I like to know what pulls the strings inside a man, but with
Alkibiades I never succeeded. He had come to us for the breaking
of his own people, and now that they were as good as broken you'd
have been expecting him to be crowing like a painted Persian
gamecock, instead of which I really wondered for a time if he was
going to fall a prey to Night's Daughters. His moods swung
between black silence and the kind of wild gaiety which is laughter
flung in the face of the Gods. And the Gods do not tolerate impiety.
I saw men step aside to avoid treading in his shadow.

He seemed unable to be still a moment, ranging the countryside
like something in a cage. The amount of his freedom had been left
to my discretion, so long as he did not cross the borders; and
I used my discretion to the full, giving him a couple of my best
hunting dogs and the run of all Lacedaemon. It was that or
chaining him up in the inner courtyard.

I kept my spies on him, of course; that was how I knew how
seldom he spent his nights, now, with the Queen. It had always
amused me to watch Agis being cuckolded; and beside, it gave me
a useful hold on Alkibiades if I should need one at any time. It was
becoming clear to all beholders, whenever she appeared in public,
that under the folds of her chiton, Timea's belly was swelling up
like a water-melon; and there were a few raised brows; but the
story was already seeping out that Agis had been drunker than he
knew, on his wedding night, and that by the time the earth-shock
came, he had already sowed his wheat. Those of us who knew Agis
best found that story something hard to swallow; but so long as
nobody knew for sure, my hold remained good and strong.

It seems a pity that I never needed to use it; I'm a man who
hates waste.

With Sicily safe again, and our troops firmly dug in to Attica, it seemed, that autumn and winter, that suddenly all the world wanted an alliance with Sparta. Pharnobazus the Satrap of Phrygia sent us a couple of Greek exiles by way of envoys, seeking our aid in stirring the Athenian cities of the Hellespont to revolt; and it was from them we first heard that Lesbos had already appealed to Agis for help in throwing off the Athenian yoke.

"It seems that Syracuse has raised a wind of freedom among the Islands," said one of my fellow Ephors. "But it is strange to say the least, that no report of this has reached us from Agis himself."

"Agis your King sent no report, so far as is known," said one of the exiles. "He has sent officers to Lesbos with a promise of ships to follow."

"Agis," I said, "has been too long away from Sparta. He is forgetting the limits of the King's power."

A few days later came envoys from the island of Chios, with representatives of Tissaphernes the Lydian Satrap, on much the same errand with regard to the more southerly Ionian coast and islands. Tissaphernes' trouble was that he had lately received somewhat pointed demands from the Great King, for the yearly tribute which Persia had collected from the Hellenic cities of Ionia until, for many years now, the Athenian Navy had made its collection impossible. So, Tissaphernes wanted Spartan aid to raise rebellion in the Ionian Islands.

I listened to them with the rest of the Ephorate, through a couple of days of long drawn-out discussions. And by the end of the second day it seemed to me that the time had come to call in Alkibiades. What had emerged from those long hours in Council was that neither Persian Satrap had any mandate from the Great King, who was not in the least interested in helping us or the Athenians, but very interested indeed in getting back the islands lost to Athens eighty years before. And also that neither Satrap had any use for the other, but that each was out to buy us for themselves. Tissaphernes offered a drachma a day for every man we would send against Chios; Pharnobazus' renegade Greeks brought twenty-five talents down, to be ours if we would send a Spartan fleet up to the Hellespont.

On the face of it, Pharnobazus offered the most in immediate results. With Agis in complete control in Attica and cutting off all land supplies, a Spartan fleet in the Hellespont, cutting off the Black Sea corn ships, would finish Athens within half a year. But on the other hand any expedition in that direction would be bound to come under the supreme command of Agis himself, and there would be nothing in it for Endius. But a victory, even if somewhat slower in coming, by way of the Ionian Islands, might have a great deal in it for the Ephorate in general and for Endius in particular, if he could make himself the moving spirit behind it.

My fellow Ephors were all tending to the other view, which was inconvenient to say the least of it. Alkibiades, I felt reasonably sure, would see the thing much as I did, for the very simple reason that he must know by now that Sparta was growing unhealthy for him. It was not only the Queen; men were jealous of his advice that had proved so insufferably successful; they were growing afraid, as men do of too much success (which is interesting and amusing when one comes to think that he was little more than a hostage at the time). The sooner he was out of Sparta the better for his health. And while the Hellespont offered him no more than it did me, Ionia was old hunting ground to him; he had, I knew, powerful friends in Ephesus and Miletus, and would be the obvious choice to go as adviser with a Chios fleet.

So I put it to my fellow Ephors that Alkibiades, who knew the Aegean as we, a land power, could never do, and whose advice had proved sound before, should be brought in as an outside adviser. They didn't care for the idea, and it took most of another day to work them over. But I managed it at last, and Alkibiades was duly called in.

He cast his vote for Chios, and did it with a blazing speech in Council that won the day for us. Chios was the foremost of all the Ionian Islands, he argued, so powerful that her fall would set the whole Aegean Empire crumbling, while her sixty ships would form a valuable addition to the Spartan Navy. Those same ships which would make her, if she were left under Athenian domination, a danger in the rear of any fleet operating in or around the Hellespont. He talked a good deal about liberating the islands from Athenian tyranny; that went down well with the Council, for we Spartans have always had a fondness for such liberations.

At the end of that fourth day, the Council voted for forty-five ships, five of our own, the rest to be drawn from our allies, for an expedition against Chios at winter's end; and Alkibiades was appointed to sail with the Spartan squadron, as personal adviser to our Admiral.

So Pharnobazus' Greeks departed in a fury with the twenty-five talents, while Tissaphernes' envoys went home looking like cats that have got at the fish-trap. Alkibiades and I had each got what we wanted.

## The Seaman

"But why did you do it?" I says. "You were out to smash Athens, and you know as well as I do that cutting off the corn ships would finish the war before next summer is out."

"I'm not much interested in a quick Spartan victory that will leave me in worse case than I am now," says Alkibiades. "I am condemned to death in Athens; and I *think*, Pilot, that I am condemned to death in Sparta. If the fleet sails for the Hellespont I remain here, caged and sooner or later the sword will fall. *So* the fleet sails for Chios, and I sail with it. I am safely out of Sparta, and yet I am still in the forefront of Sparta's war thrust against Athens."

"I'm only a seaman," I says, "I can't keep up with all this. Where do you hope that it will get you?"

"Who knows?" he says. "The islands are my old hunting ground as they are yours, Pilot; and they are in the melting pot. A bold man—the right man—might do almost anything with them, if he was not afraid to take his opportunities as they come."

He's all on fire with the new idea, the new venture, like a wind rising after a flat calm; and I sees plain enough that for the moment at least, he's thrown off Syracuse like an old cloak, lest it hampers him in what comes next.

## The Queen

Long before the baby was born, I knew that I had lost my love. At first I told myself that it was the news from Syracuse, and would pass; and waited for him to come back. He did come, sometimes, but it was as though a drawn sword lay down the bed between us—no—even when he lay in my arms it was there; the dead, all the Athenian dead at Syracuse that lay between us . . .

And then all Sparta was about the preparations for an expedition against Chios, and he was to sail with the Admiral as adviser; and then when he came to me, he was bright-eyed and eager and laughing once more, but when I held him it was as though I held his outward shell in my arms, and nothing more, while the man himself was already away on his new venture, mind and heart and hopes set far ahead among the islands and the shores of Ionia where I could never follow.

I prayed for a son, in those days; in the long dreary winter nights when he did not come; prayed for a son as never woman prayed before: "Great Mother! Ancient One, Reed crowned, give me a son!" for I thought that maybe a son would do what I could not, and draw him back to me.

Our son was born in the spring, some weeks early, so that it was a bare ten months that I must admit to carrying him. It was lamplighting when I began to bear him, and the first light of morning was hanging barred with gold beyond the high window when the last pang came upon me, and I felt as if part of my own body were being torn out of me. I had worked hard all night, bearing down whenever Panthea told me to, though all my body cried out in revolt, to withhold itself from the pain. And then came that last wild pang, and something cried weakly, and for a moment I thought it was myself and was too weary even to be ashamed, though it is as shameful for a woman to cry out in childbirth as for a warrior to cry out under the spear. And then I knew that it was not me that cried, but the live thing that had tumbled out between my straddled thighs. His child, and so eager for life that it could not wait for the midwife's hand nor the cutting of the cord, but must suck in the air and begin living while it was still joined to me.

They lifted it away from me, wiping my mouth with thin wine. "It is a boy," they said, "a fine boy."

Later, when I had slept, and when the room had been purified and smelled of salt and hyssop and no more of hot blood, and they had washed him in cold water and wine, they gave the baby to me to hold. So little and so sweet-smelling curled in my arms. I remember I snuffed the back of his neck as a bitch snuffs her newborn pups; but I thought, 'Now he will send me word. When he hears that I have borne his son, surely he will send me word— and then he will come.'

But the days passed and the nights passed and he sent no word, and he did not come.

The Ephors came and looked him over to be sure that he had no defect in him and was worth keeping; and on the third day the families gathered in the andron of the King's House; my father and mother and my sister Dionyssa who was married herself long since, and the kin of Agis' line. And again the foreporch pillars were garlanded, with olive this time, for a son—and the Priestess of Artemis wearing her tall crown of reeds, took the babe from me and carried him seven times about the hearth, and gave him his name. Leotichides, which is a Royal name. And so he came back to me, passed and accepted and marked as the next King of Sparta.

Such ceremonies are for the family only, and Alkibiades, who of all men should have been there, must be lacking. But after, I thought, 'Now he will come. Surely he will come.'

But the days passed and the nights passed and still he neither came nor sent me any word. And in less than a month the Chios squadron would be sailing. Already the Corinthian and Allied Fleets were gathering at Corinth. I grew desperate and my milk failed so that a wet-nurse must be brought in to feed the baby, who seemed never to be satisfied. And at last I let go all that was left to me of pride, and begged Panthea to get word to him that I must see him or I should go mad.

He came that night, just as he had come the first night of all. But there was no smell of rain about him, only the smell of wine, for he had come, I suppose, straight from the Mess table. And he stood rocking on his heels and staring at me as though he had never seen me naked before, with the smile playing like summer lightning in the shadows at the corners of his mouth. I had half sprung up at his coming, but his look kept me sitting on the side of the bed-place.

He said, "Why do you look so startled? You sent for me, Timea."

"If you have no wish to see me," I said, "do you not wish to see our son?"

"Surely. But I knew that he was born and all was well with him; and I have been busy of late. You will have heard that I am sailing with the Chios fleet."

"I have heard," I said. My voice sounded strange in my own ears. "I have been busy too. It is hard work to bear a child."

He said, "The child, where—" glancing about him.

I pointed to the little olive-wood cradle in the shadows beside the bedhead, and as he came towards it I got up and flung a cloak round me, and reached down the lamp from its stand to give him light to see by.

Leotichides lay on his side lapped in soft folds of deerskin, his thumb in his mouth. Alkibiades touched his cheek with one finger, and said, "Greetings, small son. In some ways it's a pity that we shall not have a chance to improve our acquaintance."

It was strange to stand there with him, leaning over the cradle, with the child asleep between us, and know that this was the last time we should be together.

"He's a fine baby," he said, and stepped back.

I made one last attempt to reach him. "Don't go with the Chios fleet."

"Sparta isn't the safest of places for me any more, my sweet."

"Safety? What do you care for safety?" I said. Suddenly I was shaking. I set the lamp down on the chest top lest I should spill the oil. "Go then—but in the Mother's name, be a little sad!"

And he said, "Timea, I'll be as sad as you please, when I've time for it; just now my mind's on other things."

If I'd had a knife in my hand I think I would have stabbed him then. But I had only words to fight with. "This new venture—if it means so much more to you than my love—"

"If! If—ye Gods, the conceit of women!" he said. "This new venture as you call it, it means not only the escaping of death, it means life! Life, Timea!"

"I could give you life—"

"Not the life that is for me! Timea, did your mother never tell you that no woman should try to hold a man once he wants to go free?"

"That's a fine doctrine for men!" I said. I had no pride left. I am sick with shame to remember it now; I would have clung to him, flung myself down and clutched his knees if it had seemed to me that there was hope in that. "You have told me what manner of son your wife bore you; I have borne you a son who will be King of Sparta!"

"Never call on a man to do for gratitude what he will not do for love. That's another thing your mother should have told you."

I had begun to feel very cold, but I had stopped shaking. "Did you never love me at all?"

"Of course I did! I loved you all last summer, and that is as long as I have ever loved any woman."

And then I knew that I had been wrong when I thought that I was losing him to the Syracuse dead and to the Chios venture. I had never had him to lose. That was the bitter thing; not that it was over, but that it had never been. I stood looking at him in the lamplight, seeing the laughter in him; and thought clear and cold behind my forehead, that if I called in the guards and he was taken in my room, the thing would have passed out of my hands, and the Gods alone knew where it would end. And I had the child to think of as well as My Lord Alkibiades. So I said, "Go now! Go quickly, before I call the guard!"

He grinned at me with no more shame than a boy caught stealing eggs, and set his hands on the high sill of the window, and then he was gone.

Next day Dionyssa came to visit me. We sat in the sun in the women's court, under the trained vine where the buds were breaking, and watched Leotichides waving vague arms and legs on a spread rug at our feet.

Dionyssa, who was with child and suffering miserably from sickness every morning, looked at him and said, "Ten months! Oh Timea, how did you endure it? All those extra days!"

And I caught her in my arms and said, "Oh Dionyssa, swear never to tell a soul! He was no more than nine months within me."

She looked at me, startled. "But Agis—"

"He is not the King's," I said. "He should be called not Leotichides but Alkibiades. Oh Dionyssa, swear you will not betray me!"

She swore of course. She always swore not to reveal the secrets that I was fool enough to tell her when we were children. But I had learned many years since that Dionyssa could never keep a secret.

Just to make sure, I told three or four others of my friends and household in the next few days, choosing always the ones that had Dionyssa's failing.

It is strange; it seemed to me at the time that I was thinking very clearly and coldly; but now, looking back, I know that I was only striking out blind, and all my thinking was confusion. I thought, 'They will have no proof; I shall deny everything, but the seed will be cast and blow where the wind carries it.' And I thought, 'The messengers will have reached Agis before this, both the Ephors', and mine; but if just a little doubt keeps open in his mind until I can see him and talk with him, we may yet be safe, the child and I. If not, maybe he will kill me, but that is so in any case; the odds against me have only worsened a little because of what I told Dionyssa; but he will take no chances with Alkibiades. He will die, that one—a regrettable accident, maybe. He will not sail for Chios.'

And I sacrificed a black puppy to Artemis Orthia, and prayed, "Oh Mother, Lady of the Lashes, Lady of the Lions, give me his life! And if need be take mine in quittance!"

## The King

I got word at last of what had been doing in Sparta all winter without any report of it being sent to me—to me, the King! It was the Ephorate of course, showing me their power because for once I had acted as a King and not a mere figurehead, sending ships to Lesbos without waiting for the express leave of the home government. I swore I'd have blood for that insult, but that must wait.

I broke off my own negotiations with Pharnobazus, and leaving Dekalia safely garrisoned behind me, came down to Corinth, where I found the Allied Fleet assembled in the harbour, thirty-nine triremes in all. Sparta had sent up Alkmenes, who I am bound to say would have been my own choice, and two others, to oversee the mustering. And from them I learned details of the Spartan squadron about to sail under the command of Chalcidius, with Alkibiades as his official adviser—that swashbuckling Athenian who I had left virtually a prisoner. How the change had come about, none of them seemed very clear; and there was no point in troubling about that now. There was nothing to be done but get the Allied Fleet under weigh as quickly as possible, in the hope of making Chios before our Spartan squadron. If I could do that I would have won the game. If not, the Ephors were my masters —and the Gods damn them! They are to this day!

I took command at once; and since the weather is still chancy at that time of year, ordered that for the sake of speed the whole fleet should be portaged by the great haul across the Isthmus, rather than sailing round the Peloponnese as had been intended. But when I gave the order I met with blank faces, and a courteous deputation from the City Council. The Isthmean Games had just begun, and while the Truce of the Games lasted, certainly while the actual three-day Games were in progress, they could not allow the use of the portage-way for a war fleet.

To do so would be to risk the anger of Poseidon in whose honour they are held.

"Then give me leave to work the portage with my own men," I said. "I'll take full responsibility along with the command, and if Poseidon is angry, let his anger fall on me, I'll risk it."

They refused, smiling still; and invited me to a dinner in my honour and to watch the Games next day. It was like battering one's head against a well-padded wall!

We sat on our rumps for two days, until the Games were over; and then at last the Council gave orders to the portage authority, and the first of the ship-carriages was manœuvered into position and the first galley floated on to it and trundled up on to the portage way. By evening the first of the fleet was within sight of the Saronic Gulf, and there were seven vessels already on the track. The Corinthians know how to handle their ship traverse, I'll say that for them. I had not seen the portage in action before, and went up with some of the fleet officers to the highest point (but none of it rises much above sea level) to see how all went forward. And I was impressed. There is always something impressive in the sight of many men working as one coherent whole, especially with something which, if it once gets out of control, will spread death and havoc all about it. I had watched three ships go by, and was watching a fourth come up—the long lines of the hauling teams bent double and moving in time to the chanty man who led them, and the whips of the slave-drivers who moved alongside. The galley, chocked up on its sled, came steadily on up the gradual slope, the drag-rope team following behind, the watermen with their great dripping oxhides filled from cisterns along the way, keeping the traverse-grooves running wet and dashing the runners to lessen the charring. Even so the steam and the smitch billowed up, mingling with the smell of the parched pale earth and the camomile flowers along the edge of the cut. And the dust rose and hung over everything.

I saw a young man come quickly up the hillside from the direction of Corinth, and knew by the blood colour of his tunic that he was a Spartan, and from the way he walked, that he was saddle sore. He came up to me and saluted, and the men with me fell back a little to give us speaking space.

"Permission to speak, sir," he said, and when I nodded, "I am sent by the Council of Ephors to bring you the happiest of news, that Timea the Queen has borne you a fine healthy son!"

I felt as though one of the water-skins meant for the sledge runners had been dashed over me. The fourth ship had drawn almost level with us and I had to walk away, for the roar and creak of the carriage and the shouts of the drivers made it all but impossible to hear him; and that gave me a few moments of respite. Then he was offering me the congratulations of the Ephors. And all the while, as he looked me in the eyes, we both knew, as all Sparta must know, that if the Queen had borne a son, he was not mine. I thought he smiled a little. He never knew, that boy, how near he was to death, up there on the shallow hillside above the portage way . . . I bade him return to the city, and then turned back myself to watch the galley lurch past over the highest point of the track; while already, far down the cut, the next was coming into view.

I don't think, despite my threat, I would have touched Timea, even if she had stood before me at that moment. She had done what many women do when their husbands are long away, and the thought of her woman-flesh sickened me anyway. I was not the only man who would return home to father a child born more than nine months after he marched away; but I was the King. Some raider had taken what was the King's. Mine! Mine to me! A little hammer was beating behind my forehead; beating and beating out the question—what man in Sparta would have taken that which was the King's? And wherever I looked, the same face looked back at me. Alkibiades! I knew now the meaning of that look, at our last meeting.

I remembered my old bitch going to him; that time it was the bitch I had kicked, and Alkibiades had gone free. But standing up there beside the portage-way, I swore before Zeus and before Artemis Orthia that he should not go free again. One of the men with me asked me if I was ill. The fool! I cursed him, and stood to watch the next ship go by, and thought of Alkibiades' hard brown body flung across the nearest traverse groove, and the sledge runners spattered and sodden with blood and offal. It was a good thought. But there were plenty of other ways. I did not care how long it took to bring him to his death, so that it was I who brought him to it in the end.

## The Spartan

The scandal about Alkibiades and the Queen finally broke wide open just at the time that Alkmenes' messenger arrived on the last of the relay horses that had been kept ready for him, with word that the Allied Fleet had sailed from the Isthmus, and orders for our own five to put out to meet him, or rather to meet Agis the King, who had arrived and taken over the command. The scandal made a magnificent excuse for my fellow Ephors; and I have never known them work so fast as they did in stripping Alkibiades of his fleet appointment.

Alkibiades came to me raging. "Hell and Night's Daughters! What am I to do? Sit here in my cage again until Agis has leisure to come home and hang me?"

"You should have thought of that before you started picking forbidden fruit," I said. "Incidentally, why do your scandals always blow up just as your fleets are about to sail?"

He glared at me. "I was bored! Ye Gods! How bored I was. And there was a warm ripe Queen for the plucking; and the chance of fathering the next King of Sparta. What would you have me do?"

"The question is rather," I said, "what shall you do now? Timea, whatever she lets drop to her friends, will undoubtedly deny the whole thing to Agis, and he'll never be able to be quite sure. He was drunk on his wedding night, and first children have been carried ten months before now, if the talk of the women's quarters is true."

"My dear Endius, do you really expect me to remember and play up to a story like that? I might just as well tell the truth. Agis will find means to kill me if he once gets his paws on me—on the offchance, as it were. No, if I don't fancy dying in Sparta—and to be quite frank with you, I don't, it's an unpleasant place to live in and it would be an equally unpleasant place to die in—I've got to get out."

"There's one point you're overlooking," I said. "The King has taken command; supposing that you do continue to turn Fortune round in her tracks and still sail with the Spartan squadron, you'll be joining a fleet under Agis' command. That doesn't sound to me like safety."

"Better take my chance that way than caged here waiting for the end."

"You're mad!" I said.

"Fortune sometimes favours the mad. She generally favours me at sea."

"The question remains—how do you propose to *get* to sea?"

But suddenly Alkibiades' fury had left him; and he flung up his head and laughed. "I have, at the moment, not the least idea. And when a man reaches that stage, it is time to rely on the Gods—or luck! I shall rely on my famous luck to cast something up for me before the squadron sails."

"Then she'd better work fast," I said, "with the squadron sailing in the morning."

And she did—somewhat expensively for Sparta.

Before the night was out, another messenger came in at foundering point—no relays waiting for him—with tidings of disaster. The Athenians at the Isthmean Games must have kept their eyes open and their wits about them, and sent home word of what they saw. So the Allied Fleet had been met by a hurriedly scraped-up Athenian one, under a mere trirarch, Konon by name, and driven aground in one of the bays below Epidauros, where they were now blockaded. Agis, quite sensibly, had left them there and was returning to Sparta to take over the war plans from this end. But it was hard to see what he could do.

Sailing orders were immediately cancelled and a meeting of the Council called. In the grey dawn light the situation looked damnable, and the gathering of unshaven men in hastily flung on cloaks decided that whatever the King's orders when he returned, to send the Spartan squadron now would only be to lose five more ships. For the present at least, the Chios expedition was off. The orders went to the fleet.

I got home to find Alkibiades waiting for me in my own quarters, unshaved and hurriedly dressed as the Ephorate, but blazing with eagerness. I never knew a man who could catch fire and kindle the fools around him as that one could! He was pacing up and down when I came in; but he swung round and caught me by the shoulders. "What decision?"

I told him; and he made an impatient gesture dismissing it. He must have known all along what it would be. "That's madness, of course. If you delay now, the news of the Allied Fleet aground and blockaded will get out, and your chance will be gone for ever. Chalcidius must sail this evening, and with me beside him."

"You?" I said, and laughed in his face.

"Listen!" he said. "We talked of this before. Your credit, your whole position in relation to our friend Agis depends now on this Ionian revolt; and an Ionian revolt can't succeed without the Satrap's support. You know well enough that I'm the only man in Sparta who can get it for you." He flung away from me, then back again, his eyes blazing in his head. "Get the Council together again and make them reappoint me, and when that's done, get a vote out of them and send orders down to Chalcidius. The fleet must sail by tomorrow."

"A fleet of five triremes to capture Chios?" I said.

"It will not need capturing. Half the Council and many of the people are on our side already—only we must get to them before they hear the state of the Allied Fleet. Then we can tell them we are only the forerunners; that a fleet of forty ships have sailed from the Isthmus to their aid, that Sparta is backing them to the hilt—that Athens is bleeding to death."

"Great Lord Apollo!" I said. "Five ships to start an Empire's revolution!"

"It can be done! It's a gamble—a glorious gamble, but I can pull it off for you, and there's not another man who can! Beside—" Suddenly his whole manner changed. It made me think of a sword blade thrust into some fine-wrought dark coloured scabbard. "Don't you see, this is your perfect chance. You will be the prime mover in the affair, and if you can get all settled ahead of Agis, think of the kudos you'll gain, Endius, my friend."

"And you?" I said.

He smiled deprecatingly, but his eyes never wavered out of line with my own. "I am only your lieutenant in this."

. . . . .

128

Somehow I got the Council summoned again, before noon, and somehow the thing was done. I put Alkibiades' own arguments to my fellows and after much discussion got the vote for the squadron to sail. Getting Alkibiades back into his appointment was still more difficult; I got to the stage of pointing out that a man's private morals had nothing to do with his gifts as an admiral or a diplomat—which had little effect. I also suggested that Sparta might be a healthier and more peaceful place for quite a lot of us, if our Athenian friend was out of it—which had rather more.

I got both votes eventually, and sent the order off to Chalcidius (I had previously sent him private word to stand by), and next morning the little fleet slipped out to sea; Alkibiades aboard the flagship and that red-polled pilot of his with him. I made the rather surprising discovery that I should find life less amusing if I were never to see Alkibiades again.

I never have.

# 11

## The Citizen

Everyone knows how we first heard of the total destruction of our forces outside Syracuse, from a Sicilian merchant who talked about it in a barber's shop, thinking we already knew. It's a tale that doesn't bear telling again. It seems to me now, looking back, that it was all that long hopeless winter and late into the next spring before we heard anyone laugh again. And then suddenly all Athens was rocking with laughter at the news that Alkibiades, left behind as a semi-hostage for the success of his own plans, while the Spartans were wrecking Attica, had amused himself by cuckolding the King of Sparta. How we could laugh like that, with even something of our old shocked delight in him, with the sorrow of Syracuse still upon us, I don't know. But we did. Men would stop each other in the street, grinning with hunger-pinched faces, and clap each other on the shoulder and say, "Have you heard?" Laughter is a strange thing, almost as strange as love.

It was soon after, that our athletes (we had managed to keep a few of our best in training, mostly youngsters serving their first year as Ephebes, who are never taken for fighting overseas) sent back word from the Isthmean Games, of the whole Peloponnesian fleet waiting at Corinth to be portaged across the Isthmus. That could mean only one thing, fighting on our own threshold or in the Aegean. We scraped together every quickly available fighting ship, including the *Thetis* and the *Halkyone*, which, since they had been acting as dispatch-vessels for Demosthenes, and in home waters at the time, had escaped the Syracuse disaster; and we continued to intercept the enemy fleet and drive them ashore below Epidauros.

It was our first success for so long that it went a little to our heads, as wine goes to the head of a hungry man.

Then came more news, unbelievable—no, it would have been unbelievable of any other man—that Alkibiades was away from

Sparta with a squadron of five ships, to raise the Ionian islands in revolt. Chios had welcomed them with open arms, declaring for Sparta almost before his ships were past the mole; and other islands and mainland cities of Ionia were following their lead.

I think a good many of the ordinary folk of Athens began to wonder, as that summer wore on, just how wise we had been in turning against Alkibiades three years ago. It had been generally accepted by now that the mutilating of the Herms had been the work of Corinthian agents, hoping to cause such consternation in the city that the expedition against Syracuse would not sail at all. And as for the charge on which he had been tried in his absence, found guilty and condemned to death—the priests had publicly cursed him, and the curse by the order of the Council of Archons, had been inscribed on tablets of iron, that it might last for all time. And he had turned, not unnaturally, to our enemies, and had prospered. Apollo Far-Shooter! How he had prospered! It was we who had suffered. That could only mean that the curse had been an unjust one. I had always been one of those who believed the case against him to be a false one, rigged by his enemies; now, more and more citizens were coming to the same belief; and even my father, not much given to doubting his own judgement, was beginning to have a doubt or two.

A good many of us in Athens, then, would have been glad to call him home from his Spartan allegiance, but of course it could not be done. The proud city of Athens to go crawling on her knees to one angry man, and then as like as not be refused . . . I could imagine how his eyes would look.

I cast my vote with the rest of the hurriedly called Assembly. Twelve ships were detached from those blockading the Peloponnesian fleet, and the dwindling store of gold in the treasury was put to good use, getting together and fitting out another thirty—new galleys near to completion, old ones that had been judged not worth another refit, a few bought from neighbouring states.

It had to be done quickly. From Chios the revolt was spreading like a stubble fire, and if it was not stopped short, we must go down beneath the ruins of our Aegean Empire. We gathered up our hearts and did what must be done as though we made plans for a great victory, and not to stave off defeat. Suddenly the mood of the city was both grim and gay. We were thrusting out once more from the position we had held too long with our backs to the wall. But in these later years I have wondered whether it would indeed have been so impossible to make some approach to Alkibiades while the fleet was fitting. It would have been humiliating, but it might have saved Athens. And then again, in these later years, I have wondered whether Athens was already not worth saving . . .

The Oligarchs had quite other ideas; headed by such men as Kritias, who would gladly let Sparta in, if only they might rule Athens for the new overlords. But at the time we knew nothing of this. We knew only that we were making our last desperate throw, loosing our little polyglot fleet to the relief of Chios.

But it seems that the human heart is very narrow, except among the few great ones like Socrates, and we must remember always the events that shake the world by small personal joys and sorrows of our own. So I remember of that time, chiefly, that my friend Theron returned with the *Halkyone*, and that with the *Halkyone* he went away again, leaving me still to help my father in the perfume shop.


## The Seaman

Aye! it was good to feel the lifting deck of a galley under foot again, and taste the salt spray and see the dazzle of the oar-thresh after two long years and more on the beach. If I live to see a hundred summers, it's that one—not the autumn that came after, mind, but that summer, that I'll remember of them all.

Chios was only the beginning; from our base there, Alkibiades and Chalcidius swept down on port after port. The *Lion* was our galley; Chalcidius hoisted his pennant on the *Agamemnon*, but I think most people forgot that we weren't the flagship, and wherever the lion figurehead and the sail with its sun-coloured beast appeared, men burst into cheering, seeing freedom within their grasp for the first time since their grandfather's day, and not recognizing it, poor bastards, for a mere change of masters.

Athens lets loose on us twelve galleys under Strombichides from the blockade of the Allied Fleet, to strengthen Samos the foremost of their remaining islands, and from somewhere they scrapes up thirty more to re-take Chios.

But we runs them out of Chian waters and down to join their friends in Samos. And then towards high summer, we takes twenty or so of the Chian fleet to swell our own squadrons, and leaving the rest to hold Chios, we're off and away to spread the revolt to Miletus. We puts out in squally weather, and has quite a trip of it, with one thing and another. The Athenian squadrons puts out after us as we heads down the western side of Samos, and gives chase all the way to Miletus; hare and hounds. Normally in weather like that and with the possibility of action, the mast and mainsail would have been struck and we'd have relied on the foresail and top bank of oars; but Alkibiades says to me, "Are ye seaman enough to give her full sail without capsizing her, Pilot?" And him grinning like a schoolboy with his hair flying all on end.

"I am," I says, "but I don't know about the rest."

"We'll risk it," says he, and we crowds on full sail, and the *Lion* leaps forward, taking the wind, and we scuds down on Miletus like a skein of wild duck—and makes harbour five good mile ahead of the Athenian fleet. I suppose its best seamen had gone at Syracuse.

Miletus was ready for us, and the first thing we sees as we sails in between the stone lions at the harbour entrance, is the Spartan Lion flying from the Arsenal.

That evening, having come up, and found Miletus closed to them, the Athenians makes camp along the shore of Lade across the straits. We saw their camp fires strung between the water line and the smoky darkness of the hillside scrub, between the beached galleys. But *we* lies soft in Miletus, our galleys, save for those standing off, on patrol duty, drawn up safe on to the strands and slipways, our men billeted in the city. Alkibiades and the Admiral had one of the largest houses in Miletus for their own use. The floor in the andron was tessellated with an elaborate design showing Leda and the Swan. Chalcidius' face when he saw it was the funniest thing I'd seen in years. He was a good fellow, Chalcidius, Spartan or no, and not at all a bad seaman, but when he was shocked he looked as some tarts do when they don't consider you're treating them like a proper lady. And he was shocked by that pavement—not by the clear intentions of the swan, I don't mean, tho' a randier swan than that one I never saw, but at the sheer immorality of all that expensive luxury just for walking on!

Well, he didn't have to walk on it long; only till a messenger to Tissaphernes had time to go and return; then the two of them are away to Sardis—Alkibiades exchanging the fleet officer for the diplomat as easily as a man might change his mantle—in search of the alliance with the Satrap that we must have if the Ionian revolt is to get anywhere.

I spends most of my time down at the harbour while they're away, seeing to re-fitting and careening and drying out. After half the summer at sea, the galleys are timber-sodden, and green as spring grass below the water line, and sluggish as so many cows in calf. And a good few of them have taken damage of one sort of another in the fighting. So I've plenty on my hands.

Well, so I was down at the harbour overseeing the lashing of the *Lion*'s new hull-cable, when Alkibiades comes strolling down to see how the work goes, as though he's never been away. I gives the needful orders to my leading topman, and we strolls on together along the foreshore and out on to the mole, well beyond earshot of the docks and slipways. Below us, the water laps green at the foot of the wall, changing blue and then deep as cuttlefish stain far out. Across the straits, the Athenian fleet's still strung along the shore.

"Well?" I says.

"Well?" says My Lord, leaning against the plinth of the great stone lion and watching the gulls.

"How did you fare?"

"Well enough."

"What manner of man did you find him?"

"Tissaphernes? Stoutish, in the way that a man who lived hard in his youth runs to flesh when he starts to take life easy. Eyes sticky and soft in his face like fresh dates; mouth like a woman's. Too fond of wearing rose colour and it doesn't suit him."

"What manner of man to *treat* with?" He knows well enough what I'm after; but he's in one of his blasted fantastical moods.

"A trifle slow to bring to the point; he was beginning to make a new garden below the palace—paradises they call them—a delightful place; shade and water everywhere; and the most charming little pavilion with pillars of gilded cedarwood, and at first he seemed too interested in my opinion as to the best placing of his young frankincense trees and oleanders, to show much interest in the making of treaties."

"To Hades with the oleanders!" I says. "Did you get round to the treaty in the end?"

He looks at me, pained. "Really, Pilot! You have been too long in Sparta and picked up Spartan manners! In Sardis we do these things with an exquisite leisureliness quite beautiful to behold. It is like a game of draughts played with rose-quartz and crystal pieces. Oh yes, we got round to the treaty at last."

"So?"

He begins quoting, softly, and by the sound of it, word for word. "Whatever country or cities the Great King has, or the King's ancestors had, shall be the King's. And the King and the Spartans together shall prevent those revenues from them which formerly the Athenians enjoyed, falling henceforward into Athenian hands. The war with the Athenians shall be carried on jointly by the King and by the Spartans, and it shall not be lawful for one to make peace with the Athenians except both agree. If any revolt from the King, they shall be enemies of the Spartans and their allies; and if any revolt from the Spartans and their allies, they shall be enemies of the King in like manner."

"That sounds pretty binding," I says.

He smiles at the wheeling gulls. "There are ways and ways. One could drive a four-horse chariot through it if need be."

"If you say so—just as long as Tissaphernes doesn't understand that too."

"He probably does. But it needs to hold for only a short while to do its work."

"What was that first bit again?" I says after a moment.

"Whatever country or cities the Great King has, or the King's ancestors had, shall be the King's."

I gives it time to sink in, but when it's sunk it still means what I think it means. "But that's the whole of Ionia, islands and all! It's the Athenian Empire!"

"Yes," says Alkibiades.

"Name of the Dog! How did you get Chalcidius to sign away Sparta's prospects of pouching the Athenian Empire?"

Alkibiades brings his gaze down from the wheeling gulls. "The Spartans are none too well versed in any history but their own. I don't think Chalcidius was very clear in his own mind as to how much of the Aegean Darius' forebears did in fact hold." He smiles, reflective like. "I like Chalcidius, despite the fact that he's worthy and straightforward and simple, which should make him a quite distressingly dull companion. But there's no denying that he *is* worthy and straightforward and simple: I don't think he was too clear about anything by the time Tissaphernes and myself had finished our talks."

I can imagine it. But back in Sparta there's keener brains than Chalcidius—Endius, for instance.

As though he sees that showing in my face, Alkibiades says, "There's no need for Sparta to receive too exact a copy of the terms of the Treaty. They'll be just as happy without. As I said, a four-horse chariot can be driven through it if need be, but probably Endius is the only man in Sparta with the wit to see it."

·     ·     ·     ·     ·

135

It wasn't more than a few days after that that Samos revolted and overthrew the Oligarchs. The island and the city had been governed by Oligarchs from time out of mind, but I suppose the strange winds that were blowing through the Aegean that summer whipped them up. At all events the people rose against their government, helped by the crews of the three Athenian triremes that happened to be in port at the time. I *have* heard it said they wiped out some two hundred nobles and banished twice as many more. At all events Samos became a democracy overnight, and closer bound to Athens than ever before.

In a queer sort of way, that change-about of Samos is like a sort of turning of the tide.

Through the rest of that summer and on into the autumn, the fighting is mostly a tangle of skirmishing that swings first this way and then that. But as time goes on, a thing I'd not have believed possible begins to happen; Athens begins to regain something of her power at sea! If I hadn't been on the wrong side, I'd have cheered! It's not all their own doing, of course; the islands have had time to think, and seemingly some of them's got around to the idea that there isn't much freedom lying about loose, after all, and if it comes down to a choice of overlords, Athens might still be better than Sparta. So when Athens starts to send out whole new squadrons for their recapture (the Piraeus shipyards must have worked harder that summer than I reckon they've worked in the memory of man!), they don't put up much resistance—not as much as they'd have put up three months before, anyway. Next thing we know, the Spartans have sent out a second fleet to join the Allied squadrons that had broken out from Epidauros by that time, and the Athenians have hunted them half across the Aegean and got them penned at Chios. So there's Chios blockaded again, by the other side. Lesbos and Clazomenes goes next; and all of a sudden, between drink and drink as it were, Samos has become the base and rallying point for a whole new Athenian Navy.

Soon after that, Chalcidius gets himself killed in a land brush with the Athenians before the Walls of Miletus. I liked him better than any other Spartan I ever had dealings with; but with him out of the way, Alkibiades has the undivided command of a small Spartan and Chian fleet—the only Allied Fleet still at sea in the Aegean—and we has a lively time of it the rest of that autumn. But we were too small to do much more than play gadfly on the flanks of Athens, until storm-weather put an end to serious sea warfare for that year, and we were forced to lie up in Miletus till spring.

One day in late autumn, going up from looking to the *Lion* in dry dock, I daunders along the harbour wall, having nothing else to do in a hurry, and stops to watch a couple of fisher lads mending their nets. There's an Argolid trader made fast to one of the jetties (the deep draught trading tubs can always keep to the seaways later in the year than a war galley), and while I'm watching, a strange seaman who looks as though he might belong to her comes up to speak to them. They talks a few moments, and then one of the fishermen looks up and sees me and points, as though he would say, 'See, there he is now.' And the man from the trader comes quickly towards me.

"You are Antiochus, pilot of the *Lion*?" says he.

"I am that," says I.

"Where can I find Alkibiades?"

"And what would you be wanting with Alkibiades?"

"I have a letter for him."

I knows well enough that my bonnie boy'll be where I left him, a couple of hours since, up on the house-top where he can get a good view of the straits, with a wine jar and no wish for unexpected company. It's always like that with him when he sees a stretch ahead without enough to fill it. So I says, "I'll take it to him."

"Your pardon, sir, but my orders are to give it to the Lord Alkibiades and to no one else."

I shrugs. "He won't be best pleased to see you, but that's your affair. I'm going up to his house now; you'd best come with me."

Alkibiades is exactly where I expected, sprawling on a pile of rugs in the lea of the windbreak of myrtle and oleander bushes in tubs, with the all but empty wine jar beside him. His eyes are bloodshot, and he curses soft and foul at sight of the messenger, then sits up and reaches out a hand. "Give it over."

I keeps a tight eye on the man as he does so. 'Twouldn't be the first time a murderer has used the guise of a messenger, since the world began. But it's only a little roll of papyrus, sweat darkened as though he's carried it a good while next his skin.

Alkibiades looks at it as though it's a dead mouse. "Who gave you this?"

"A man, who had it from another man."

"Where?"

"In Epidauros, just before the ship sailed."

Alkibiades nods and tosses him some money. "Go below, and

tell the kitchen slaves I sent you to be fed. Then wait; there may be an answer."

"There is no answer," the man said.

"So? Well go and tell them to feed you, all the same."

When the fellow had gone, he still sits turning the letter over in his hands, till I asks, "Am I to go and tell them to feed me, too?"

"No," he says, "I've a feeling this is from Sparta, in which case it probably concerns you too. And it certainly won't be a love letter."

He slips his thumb under the sealed thread and snaps it, and unrolls the small strip of papyrus and starts reading. And as he reads, all the lines of his face that are heavy and blurred with drink and boredom comes up keen again, like a rusted spear-blade under the scouring-sand. When he comes to the end, he looks up with an odd expression on his face, and holds it out to me. "Read it."

I takes it and looks at the thick lines of writing. The Spartans always write as though even their Alfa Beta Gamma was standing on parade, a stiff outlandish script. "A few words I can manage," I says, "but not this lot. Read it to me."

So he reads it again, out loud. "Apollo alone knows why I should trouble myself to send you this warning. You're no further use to me, living or dead; and I'm like to run into trouble enough on my own account. It will be no news to you that you have left enemies behind you in Sparta, it's a habit of yours. You have the offensive habit of being too successful and therefore dangerous. Also others have not failed to notice that the child which the Queen carried so unusually long has a strong look of you. Agis has especial cause to wish for your head—or other parts than your head. He has disowned the Queen's son, though he has not put the Queen herself away. I suppose he can never be quite sure enough for that. She sent him word of the child's birth—it was an extremely clever letter, I read it—which, if her messenger had not been delayed so that he did not receive it until some while after the Ephor's somewhat blunter announcement, I really believe might have convinced him that the boy was his. As it is, how annoying for King Agis to find that it is all to do again. His annoyance has taken the form of drawing him closer to the Ephorate in this one thing (I of course have served my year and am no longer one of that august body; but I have my useful contacts still), and between them they have decided upon your death. The order has gone out to Admiral Astiochus at Chios; it may well have reached him by

138

the time you get this. If I were you I would take my leave of the Spartan Navy as quickly and quietly as maybe."

He let the scroll snap back on itself. "That's all."

I felt rather as though I had taken a blow amidships, and yet I wasn't altogether surprised. "Who from?" I asks, after a moment.

"It's unsigned and all Spartan writing looks alike. But can you think of any of the Ephorate, any man in Sparta except one, who would write to warn a man of his impending demise in quite that chatty style?"

"Endius," I says. "But he was never your friend. He'd have been in on this murder plot himself if it had suited him."

"Of course. But as I told you before, he has small love for Agis. And in an odd way we understood each other." He was still sitting on the pile of rugs, his hands hanging from lax wrists across his knees, the letter dangling from his fingers. "How very depressing, not to have sired a line of Spartan Kings, after all."

"Did you really think you would? What are you going to do now?"

He ignores my second question as though I hadn't asked it. "I didn't know, but with nothing more amusing to do, it was worth the try."

And then without warning, he springs up; and for all that he had to keep it quiet, I have seldom seen him in a worse rage. He's grey-white with it, shaking. He crosses to the roof parapet, and I saw how his hands gripped and worked on the stonework till the knuckles shone white and waxy as bare bones, as he stood there staring out with wicked slit eyes towards Samos. He says in a voice as though he can't quite get his breath, "May Night's Daughters have them for their own! They have had three years of me, and in those three years they have brought Athens almost to her knees. And now, like Athens, they plot my death by crooked ways behind my back. They shall learn, as Athens did, the unwisdom of that! They shall weep blood in the learning, those brave Spartans!"

"So what now?" I says again.

He swings round from the distant view of Samos tawny in the evening light. "I take my leave of the Spartan Navy as quickly and quietly as may be." He's still shaking like a white poplar, his nostrils flaring, but suddenly there's a kind of marshlight laughter flickering round his mouth. It fair gives me the creeps! "Coming, Pilot?"

"I told you before, the last time you asks that," I says. "I've followed you too long to break the habit now. Besides, I reckon the Spartan fleet might not be too healthy for me after this, either."

We rode out of Miletus that night, crossed the river at the head of the estuary, and turned the horses' heads towards Sardis.

# 12

## The Seaman

Sardis is a big sprawling town, perched on one of those crumbling outcrops of the hills that border the Lydian Plain. The markets and the Temple Area are bad Greek—at least Alkibiades said it was bad Greek, I'm no judge—the fortress-palace, behind its bronze-sheathed doors and its Nubian guards, part Persian and part peculiar. We were given rooms in the Court of Strangers, the guest place, between the inner curve of the palace wall and the chariot court where the Satrap's hunting leopards also had their cages. And we ate there alone on that first night.

The slaves had already unpacked our saddlebags, and the few things that Alkibiades had been able to bring away with him were scattered about the bare rest-house chamber, making it at once personal, his own quarters and nobody else's. Any room that houses Alkibiades, however short a time, takes on his colour like that. There's his sword in one corner and his high Phrygian riding-boots in another, his spare cloak flung over the big cedar-wood armour chest, and beside it a small rose-quartz hermaphrodite which I had last seen in the house in Miletus. I picks it up and looks at it to be sure. It's beautiful in its way, and quite foul. I don't know how the maker did it; it was only a slender little figurine not much more than the length of my hand, combining breasts and cod in the usual way of things; but there it was, in every line, in the eyes and the curve of the lips, beauty and the stink of corruption. I put it down again. "How did that get here?"

"In my saddlebags," Alkibiades says.

"In Aphrodite's name, why?"

"It happened to be the choicest thing lying to hand at the time we left. With the breed of Tissaphernes, friendship generally begins with a gift."

"It makes my gorge rise to think of courting the Persians!" I says.

"You have been bred, like the rest of us, on too many stories of Marathon and Salamis. The great days, the clean days are past, Pilot. I need Tissaphernes' friendship if I am to do Sparta justice, and—carry out certain other plans of mine."

"You'll not find it so easy to use the Satrap against Sparta," I says. "Have you forgotten he's still bound to them by the treaty you and he and Chalcidius signed, back in the summer?"

"Oh, I think we may contrive to—modify the treaty. But first I must gain our plump Persian's confidence and make him the friend of my bosom." And he picks up the figurine and wraps it in a bit of that fine coloured stuff they weaves in Cos from wild silkworm thread, as tenderly as though his whole revenge for the past and hopes for the future's bound up in it.

## The Whore

Tissaphernes made a garden—a paradise, the Persians call it.

He began it in the spring after I came to the palace, on the cool northern slopes of the hill. He laid out terraces, and had cisterns and channels made for falls of water; and in the autumn he had trees planted. Quite big trees, planes from the north and frankincense and rose bushes from the south, and almond trees from my own Black Sea coast, all brought with their roots in baskets of earth, in ox-carts or slung on the backs of camels. But at the same time the masons began to build a wall round it, so that the delights of the paradise might be private from the eyes of the world. And the wall grew until the garden was hidden, except for the tops of the tallest saplings.

I could see them from a certain window in the quarters of the palace slaves. I watched the few twigs above the wall, bare through the winter and then growing woolly with leaf buds, and here and there a pale spark of blossom at the winter's end. Some of them put out no buds—I suppose the tree-spirits sickened and died at being torn from their homes even to make beauty for a Satrap of the Great King. And they were torn up by the gardeners and forgotten, and others put in their places. The ones that lived grew taller through the year; and through their bare twigs that winter I saw workmen setting tiles the green of the flash on a mallard's wing on the topmost part of a roof that I supposed must shelter a garden house of some sort.

When spring drew near again, before anything else broke from bud, suddenly above the mud-brick wall the almond trees were in flower. And every pale star pierced my heart like a sword; I who had seen them flower so many springs from the rich black earth of the north. Suddenly I was wild for freedom as in the first days after I was sold, one with the talking painted bird that fluttered on clipped wings in the Satrap's private court, and the hunting leopards with collars on their necks, and the falcons in the mews, and the yearling colts that the young men broke to the chariots. For it is not with me as it is with most of the dancing girls and fan bearers and the Satrap's soft-fleshed concubines, who were born and suckled in slavery. I was born free, and my father was a chieftain's younger son, of the Thracian people who crossed the Narrows where the Black Sea stretches its hands to the Propontis, and conquered the people who were there before, and are called Bythinians now. I was bred free and rode my horse with the other girls and the young men on the hunting trail—until war came between our tribe and another. They were stronger than us, and when the fighting ended my grandfather's great timber hall was a blackened shell and most of the horses were dead. And without the horses, the people also die. Then the Strangers came, the slave dealers who come always on a people in the wake of war or famine, as the buzzards and the wolves gather to a carcass. I did not think that I had anything to fear, for I have never had anything of beauty except my hair. Small breasts and narrow flanks and crooked teeth are not what the slave dealers hunger after. But my father bade me fetch my reed flute and play for the strangers after supper. And no flute in the world of men has the soft note of our Phrygian kind. I played my best—I did not know how else to play—and they smiled to hear; and when I played, they gave my father good money for me, and took me away.

I was sold in Sardis slave market, to a man who kept a house where merchants and caravan captains go for their pleasures, and sometimes some lesser one from the Satrap's Court. And after I had been there a while, one of Tissaphernes' agents heard me playing my flute for the pleasure of the guests; and so I came to be a flute girl in the Satrap's palace. Sometimes the women told me that I was lucky.

One evening when the almond trees were in full flower, I was summoned to the new garden-house to play for the Satrap and his guest, who were supping there. I had seen this guest of the Satrap's in the distance, more than once, that winter; the tall Athenian with hair the colour of the Black Sea cornlands; riding out with the Persian nobles, with furs over his gay silks and a falcon on his fist; walking in the outer court with Tissaphernes, deep in conversation.

Once, when I had been called on to play my flute for a festival, I had seen him spring out into the midst of a circle of laughing courtiers, together with that flame-headed comrade of his, who they said was always master of any ship that he commanded; and each with a hand on the other's shoulder, spin off into some quick-footed seaman's dance to their own mouth-music since no one there knew the tune.

We all knew (slaves know most things) that he carried two death sentences on that bright head of his, one set there by his own people, and one by Sparta; and I never saw a man carry a death sentence so lightly. He had become something of a favourite with Tissaphernes; indeed the new garden had been named after him, the Paradise of Alkibiades. The Persians love their gardens so much that I suppose there was no greater compliment that the Satrap could pay him.

I remember that at the thought of playing for Alkibiades in the little garden-house beyond the almond trees, of seeing him close for the first time, a breath of pleasure and interest woke in me. It was so long since I had felt it, that I scarce knew what it was; but because of it I took more pains than usual in putting on the loose trousers striped like a wild tulip and the tunic of peacock gauze that were provided for me to wear at such times, and in painting my eyelids with green malachite and lengthening them with kohl. It was done for my own pleasure, not for any foolishness of thinking that the Athenian would look my way. I took my flute; and then with the three dancing girls who were summoned with me, went and stood before one of the harem eunuchs to be inspected and approved. In the usual way of things it was Arbaces the chief eunuch, but he was ill that day from overeating, and so we were spared his fat hands and womanish pokings and tweakings. Phaeso, who looked us over in his stead was not quite as most of his kind, and never touched us. Then we were turned over to two of the palace guard, to be taken to the garden-house.

It was still very cold after the sun had set, and braziers burned at each corner of the garden-house, giving off the scent of burning amber mingled with the sharpness of wood-smoke, and the fretted walls had been hung with embroidered cloths on two sides, to keep out the thin evening wind that had been scattering the first petals from the almond trees outside. I had expected that there would be several of the court there, but at the low table in the centre of the room, with a pair of slaves to wait on them, only Tissaphernes and the Athenian reclined on piled cushions and played with the dried fruits and little sweetmeats of camel's milk curds and honey that ended the meal. I had seen the slaves before; Tissaphernes always had them to serve him at table when he did not want the talk to be spread around, for they were deaf mutes. But I suppose they thought that we four, slipping quietly in through the hangings, to take our places in a little knot on the cushions set for us at a little distance, were out of hearing, or that none of us would understand, for they spoke in the Attic Greek which is the common tongue of diplomats everywhere. But if so, they forgot that it is also the common tongue of traders. And I, who have a quick ear for such things, had been more than a year in that house in the lower town where the merchants came.

Although we had been sent for, it seemed that they did not want our music or dancing, yet, at all events, for they talked on as though we were not there. At first I did not listen. I was content only to watch Alkibiades under my lids, while pretending to gaze into my lap. He wore Median court dress, like Tissaphernes. Loose trousers striped violet and white, his tunic deeply green as the heart of an emerald, two gilded daggers stuck crosswise in his fringed silken sash; a diadem of braided silk and silver wire on his head, silver bracelets showing on his arms where the wide sleeves fell back, kohl rimming his eyes. He might almost have passed for a Persian, save that his bones showed too clearly. The Persians live hard when they are young, but turn too much to luxury as they grow older; and by the time they are thirty, their bones are fleshed over. His hands were bigger than a Persian's too, horseman's hands, as theirs are, but I knew that they would never be able to fit easily round the slender grip of a Persian sword . . .

Gradually I began to hear what they were talking about, and I understood and remembered most of it. It seemed to me that they had been talking of the same thing for a long while, and maybe had talked of it before. Alkibiades was saying, "In my view a drachma a day is over-generous—unwisely so."

And Tissaphernes put a sweetmeat into his mouth—he had a red passionate mouth like a woman's—and said, "That did not seem to be your opinion before we signed the treaty. A drachma a day, even for the rowers, was your own demand."

Alkibiades spread his hands. "I admit it. It was in my mind that by paying high, you would outbid Athens for troops and rowers. But now—I have had leisure to think, and I believe that I was mistaken." He smiled. "It is not every day that Alkibiades admits to being mistaken . . . I should have thought that you would have looked with favour on the lower price."

145

"That depends . . . When I am offered something at a reduced price, I smell it carefully before I buy. Do have some of these sugared figs, they really are delicious."

Alkibiades said, "Am I to take it that you do not trust me, for all your protestations of affection? I am cut to the heart, and the birds no longer sing for me," and took a handful of the figs. I felt as though I were watching two men play a game of skill.

Tissaphernes said, "My dear, I love you like a brother, as I know you do me. Have I not called this paradise by your name, that you and all men may know the delight that I have in your company when we walk in it together? But a man does not necessarily trust his brother with his neck."

I thought that there would be a quarrel flaring between them at that; among my own people it would have been a matter for knives. But they were both laughing like two men who perfectly understand each other. But I think now that they only thought they understood each other . . .

Then Alkibiades said, "Listen, the matter is simple enough. Half a drachma a day is all that Athens pays, and Athens, you will admit, have a long naval experience. The Athenian War Council— of course they may be wrong—consider that high pay has a demoralizing effect on troops on active service."

Tissaphernes nodded, and with his wine cup refilled, began to eat sugared rose-leaves, very delicately, one at a time. "This is also your opinion?"

"On the whole, I think, yes . . . I would suggest also that even this should be paid irregularly, and kept somewhat in arrears, as a guard against desertion."

Tissaphernes nodded. "Very sound reasons, my dearest friend, and now—what is the true one?"

Alkibiades crooked his finger for one of the slaves to refill his wine cup, and did not answer until it had been done and he had taken a mouthful of the wine. "I think the results might well be—disappointing, for Persia, if Sparta was to finish Athens too quickly and too completely."

"How so?"

"Oh I know it would be easily done." Alkibiades seemed to be talking into thin air, much as a man talks when he is alone and talking to himself. "You have but to bring up this Phoenician fleet that you are building, and a regiment or two of Persian troops, and you could crush Athens once and for all." He held up his hand and clenched it slowly into a quivering fist as though all Athens were inside it. And it seemed to me for an evil moment that I saw the blood dripping between his fingers.

"So?" said Tissaphernes softly.

"So you are left with Sparta the supreme master of Hellas; and all the Greek states and islands would flock back to the Lion Standard. You, who wish to be the Lords of Hellas, would be confronted by a Hellas united under Spartan command. That, my friend, would be a tough nut to crack; and with no Athens to help you, because Athens will be dead. Hard fighting, there'd be then." I thought there was a shimmer of laughter in his voice. "You might even have to put on again that beautiful inlaid fishscale corselet you were showing me the other day."

I did not think, from the look on the Satrap's face, that he cared much for the thought, after the silken years. He cleared his throat. "And what has all this to do with half a drachma a day, paid in arrears?"

"It will cause disaffection and a fine variety of other troubles in the Spartan Navy; and if there is no increase of pay to be expected, their ranks of rowers will not be swelled by deserters from the Athenian benches. Hold out hope to Spartans, of the arrival of the Phoenician fleet—not too much hope, just enough to keep them tame to the fist. But on the whole I would suggest that there is no point in spending men or money in intervening on one side or the other, when it is only a matter of waiting while they wear themselves out against each other. When both sides are exhausted—what simpler than to step in and annex the whole of Greece?" He looked as though a sudden thought had come to him in mid-speech. "Indeed it might be best to give just that featherweight, that merest breath, of extra help to Athens."

Tissaphernes raised his brows over those full dark eyes of his. "Explain."

"As a sea power," Alkibiades said, "Athens will be content with naval supremacy; if you handle them in the right way, they will help to subjugate the Hellenes of the Ionian islands and mainland to the Great King. But Sparta—" I remember how he paused, and again the flicker of amusement came. "Sparta is a land force with a certain—missionary zeal. They intend to save the islands from you as well as from Athens."

They looked at each other a long moment, and then it was as though by common consent, Tissaphernes had shut the games'-board. "So. Of all companions you are the most enthralling and delightful in your conversation."

"The pleasures of good conversation depend as much upon the

listener as upon the speaker." Alkibiades smiled. "May we now turn ourselves to pleasure of another kind, from your dancing girls?" He glanced round as he spoke. And he saw me looking at him before I could look away; before I could guard my face. And his eyes widened on me; they were full of cold blue light between the darkened lids; they held me so that I could not break free but must give him back look for look. And he knew that I had heard and understood the main part of what had passed.

At the same instant Tissaphernes snapped his fingers for us to begin.

My fingers and my lips felt numb, my head empty of all save the cruel probing blueness of the Athenian's eyes. But somehow they must have remembered their own skill though I forgot; for I found that I was playing, and the other girls had risen from their cushions and begun to dance. Their skirts swung out, pretty and spangled, the little bells round their ankles chimed foolishly above the throaty softness of the flute; and I played on and on, alone with fear.

When the dancing was done, Alkibiades applauded lazily and threw nuts and sweetmeats among the girls—he had learned all the Persian ways—and I felt his glance flicker over me and leave me cold, though this time I would not meet it. It seemed that they had returned to the old talk even while they watched the dance, for Tissaphernes was saying, ". . . Tomorrow, then, I will get in my confidential scribes, and we will have these slight—amendments made to the treaty; purely as a matter of interest between ourselves."

Alkibiades took something from the folds of his sash. "But meanwhile,—seeing the beauty of this pavilion as it grew through the winter to open like a flower on the edge of spring, I sent back to Miletus for this. Among my own poor treasures it was the only one I felt to be worthy of such a setting. I had meant to ask you to accept it from me this evening, that it may stand here to grace other pleasant evenings when I have gone my way. Now let it also be a gift to seal the bargain between us, if you will have it so."

Tissaphernes received it ceremoniously, speaking of its beauty and the delicacy of its workmanship; and leaned forward to kiss Alkibiades on the mouth, as men greet their equals among the Persians; and after, Alkibiades kissed him on the cheek as men greet those above them. He said, "It is a poor gift, but I am a poor man in these days. If it finds beauty in your eyes I am content."

There was a tiny click, as the Satrap set his gift on the tiled floor, and cold with fear as I was, curiosity made me glance that way. The thing stood among the fruit bowls and tall wine jug between them; a figurine of some moon-pale pinkish stuff such as rose-quartz, that seemed to gather up into itself all the light of the palm oil lamps. It was too far off to make out the detail of a thing so small. But whatever it was, part of me knew suddenly in the little silence, that to Tissaphernes it was a gift to win his favour, and to Alkibiades it was more like the dice thrown down in a game played for high stakes. But all the rest of me was taken up with cold scurrying fear of what would happen to me now. Would Alkibiades consider a slave too small a matter to trouble about, even one who knew what had passed between him and the Satrap? Or was he one of those who attend to even the smallest detail? If he were, then how would the end come for me? A thong round the neck in a dark passage? A fall from a window?

I heard Tissaphernes say that he could only accept the gift, if his guest would honour him by accepting one in return. That is the Persian way; among them it is unthinkably bad manners for any man save the Great King to accept a gift without giving one in return. A bribe is different. And suddenly I saw how carefully this gift had been chosen, beautiful to flatter Tissaphernes' taste, but far too slight to be counted as a bribe by a Satrap. Under my lids I saw Tissaphernes' hand in its loose silken sleeve, gesturing as though to include anything in the garden-house, even the garden-house itself. "All that I have is yours, my beloved friend. Choose, then, what you would have in memory of this evening, and if it is not here, then speak, and my slaves shall fetch it for you."

"The Satrap is the prince of givers," Alkibiades said. "But for a man such as myself, a wanderer on the face of the earth, it is best to travel light. Give me your gift in another kind."

"You have but to ask, and it is yours," said Tissaphernes. But I thought he sounded a little uneasy. When men ask for unnamed gifts, it is time to go warily.

And then Alkibiades said, "Give me the services of your flute girl to play me into sleep tonight, for sleep is slower in coming to me, these latter years, than it was when the world was young."

I looked up then, and met his blue gaze full upon me; lazy now, and mocking; and I have never been so afraid—not for myself. There was a stirring among the dancing girls. I felt envy running through them like a little wind through a field of flax. They did not believe that it was for my flute playing that Alkibiades had asked for me. And nor did I.

The Satrap cast a careless glance in my direction, and said, "My dear, if you are lonely at nights, why did you not say so before? I had assumed that you made your own arrangements; but now that I know, you must allow me to find you a more worthy play-mate than this. She is really quite ugly—why, man, she has scarcely any breasts! You would not rather have a boy? Well then, allow me to choose something more worthy of you from among the harem slaves. I have one in mind now—a honeycomb girl, and almost a virgin."

"But can she play the Phrygian flute?" Alkibiades asked, his gaze still holding mine.

In the end the other girls departed, and I was handed over to two eunuchs, and led out of the Paradise of Alkibiades and taken to the guest court and handed over to the slaves there with many nods and winks. The slaves brought me to an inner chamber, where there was a couch resting on gilded griffons, and left me there to wait for Alkibiades' coming. Palm oil lamps burned in fretted niches in the walls, casting soft shadows and blurred webs of light about the room. There was a chair with rose and purple cushions on it, a great painted chest with some clothes flung across it—I suppose he had left them there when he changed to sup with the Satrap. A long straight-bladed sword lay there too. A little shiver ran through me at the sight of it. But that was foolishness; if he was going to kill me it would not be with a sword, when he had already the little Persian daggers in his sash. For a while I sat on the griffon couch. And then I saw—I had been looking at it long enough without seeing—that the archway into the outer chamber had nothing but curtains to close it, and through the gap where they had been carelessly drawn, showed the blue spring night beyond the courtyard doorway. The slaves, in departing to their own quarters, had not even shut the door. At the far side, I knew, was a postern which opened on to a narrow way behind the chariot court. The slaves could not have been so careless; there must be guards about, or it was a trap of some sort. But sometimes a trap could be sprung. I got up and prowled into the outer chamber and across to the door.

And yet I do not think that I would have tried to escape, even if the way had been clear. The sense was upon me that whatever was coming to me that night, for good or ill, it was written on my forehead . . . In any case I had no choice. That red-headed henchman of his, was sitting very comfortably outside the door, with his back propped against the wall. He sat there and grinned up at me, and the light from the open doorway caught the white flash of his teeth, and his quirked devil's eyebrows and the swinging lumps of silver and coral in his ears.

I went back to the bed and sat down again. After a long time I heard a step in the court, and Alkibiades' voice. "No trouble, Pilot?"

And my gaoler answered, "No trouble that a drink will not cure; my throat's as dry as a lime-pit, where in Typhon's name have you been?"

"I could scarcely rush away like a green lad with his first girl waiting for him," Alkibiades said. "Well enough; go and get drunk with my blessing, Pilot dear."

I heard the other make a sound between grumbling and laughter, and his footsteps tramping away. There was an aching quietness after they had gone, and in the quietness, I heard a long light step in the outer room, and Alkibiades was standing in the archway.

I do not remember getting up and moving back from him; but I must have done, because suddenly the coldness of the wall was pressing against my shoulders and rump, biting through the thin stuff of my garments.

He came on, until he could set his hands flat on the wall at either side of me, and I could smell the wine on his breath and the perfume of saffron crocus that he wore.

He said, "Where did you learn the Attic Greek?"

"Chiefly in the pleasure house beside the temple of Hermes, where many traders come," I said. I wondered how long we must talk like this before he killed me.

"Those who overhear what is not meant for them, should not show it so clearly in their faces."

I said, "Sparta is nothing to me; and if it were, how could I betray you? I who am a captive and a slave?"

"There are ways of sending messages," he said. "Slaves have been known to escape. I can't take the risk, darling."

His hands left the wall, and he set them lightly, almost caressingly, round my neck.

I said, "If you are going to kill me, do it with your dagger, and quickly."

He smiled a little, and shook his head. "You have pulled your front teeth out of shape with all that flute playing—I have always said no man should disfigure himself with the flute, let alone a woman. But your hair is too bright to be quenched in the ground and your eyes are too beautiful to be filled with dust before their time." And as he spoke, his fingers went to work on the silver clasps that held my bodice, and stripped it off; then to my girdle— he knew very well, with much experience, I suppose, his way about the fastenings of a woman's garments—and everything fell from me in a drift of striped silks and golden gauze. And I stood before him naked except for my bracelets and forehead ornament. And he stood and looked me over, with suddenly lifted brows.

Always since I was taken from my own land, I had shrunk from being naked, even among the other women; for in Bithynia as in Thrace, tattooing is a mark of rank, and not only for the men, as it is in some lands. I had been proud of the lilies and star-flowers on my thighs and shoulders, the running stag below each breast. I had hated them to be looked at by curious alien eyes who saw in them only a matter for sidelong glances and laughter and foolish questions; but time makes one used to all things, and I had almost ceased to care. But with the lazy blue gaze of the Athenian moving over my body, I was proud of them again, proud that they would show him, if I was a barbarian, at least I had not been bred a slave. I forced my head up and back, feeling the hardness of the wall behind it, drawing up my belly under my ribs and pressing my shoulders flat to the wall, making myself proud and taut like a strung bow.

He said softly, "Now who would have thought it, under the Persian gauzes?" He put out a finger and touched the centre of a star-flower, then traced the curves of its stem where it forms a pattern, interlacing with the stems of others of its kind. And his finger seemed to leave a thin white trail of fire behind it. "Curious, twined and twisted beauty. Here's a lily, crimson-lipped, and here's a running stag . . . are you always patterned so? Or does it come to you with the leaves to the trees, only in the spring and the rutting season?"

"These patterns are the marks of rank, in my country," I said. "I am from Bithynia before the slavers came."

"And you were born and bred a free woman. You do not need to tell me so." He put his arms round me, laughing a little, his hands loose-linked in the small of my back between me and the wall, and kissed me, tonguing my lips apart. "No, and you do not need to tell me that you are no soft harem woman for a man to take his pleasure on, among soft smothering cushions in the dark. You should be hunted down and stallioned on the bare ground under the stars!"

Abruptly, he let me go, and crossing to the couch, swept together all the rugs and soft coverlids spread upon it, into one great dragging bundle and thrust them into my arms. "But the bare ground will be cold tonight. Go and spread our bed-place in the court, and make it warm for me until I come."

There was a narrow colonnade all round the little guest court, and the small open space in the centre floored with fine turf that would be bare brown earth when the summer came, and roofed with the twisted dragon-branches of an old almond tree that grew in the midst of it. I spread the quilted coverings beneath it, the great bearskin bed-rug with its lining of embroidered crimson over all. Then I lay down and drew the rug over me.

Under the warm weight of it, I ceased in a little while to shiver. The sky above the almond tree was green, like the heart of a beryl; and as my eyes grew used to the dark, I could see the faint pale flecks of the almond blossom; and above them were the stars. A great waiting came upon me, but I was not afraid any more. And deep within myself I said, "This was written on my forehead on the day that I was born."

Then there was movement in the lamp-lit doorway, and I turned my head and saw Alkibiades. He had stripped off his court dress, and stood there in the instant before he quenched the lamp, naked save for a narrow crimson sash bound tightly about his waist, with one of the gold hilted daggers thrust into it. Then he reached up and pinched out the lamp flame; and the soft amber shape of the doorway turned black, and out of the blackness of it, he came.

He stood over me, and I saw how his hand went to his dagger, and for an instant my breath checked in my throat. And then I knew that he had felt for it only as a man feels for his spear before he lies down to sleep in wolf country, and it came to me that in this palace where he was an honoured guest, he never lay down to sleep without making sure that his dagger was to hand.

He lay down beside me, and pulled the great bearskin rug over us both. And then his darkness came between me and the stars, and I felt the hard urgent weight of his body on mine. Yet he did not seek to come in to me at once, as I have known some men do; instead, he began to make a fierce sweet love-play with me, such as the stallions on my father's runs would make sometimes with the mares at mating time. I had not known that kind of play since before the slavers came, I had never known it like this; and all my body woke and answered to it in joy.

I lay with my first lad when my breasts had scarce begun to swell, for in my country we let our girls run free, though when once the bride-price is paid, it is a different story. We had coupled freely as young animals, though less sure at first of how it should be done. And after the slavers came there had been others; in the house near the Temple of Hermes, and in the Satrap's palace. There had been a few who made me want to laugh, because they were too fat or not up to what they wished to do, a few I would have liked to kill. There had been a few who had made me sorry—those every pleasure-house girl knows, who came because they were ugly or crippled and could never have except for payment, what other men can get free and for love. There were a few who had even given me pleasure. They came and went, and I had learned long since to take them as they came.

But when I opened my thighs for Alkibiades, it was as though it was for the first time. And when he came up into me, the great waves of his coming were made of flame, beating, beating through all the dark woman-parts of my body, filling all of me, shimmering through me like the high notes of a flute, until the shrill white sweetness was almost past my bearing; and I clung to him, while all my body seemed to melt and I no longer knew which was flesh of his flesh and which was flesh of mine, or where his spirit ended and mine began.

And that too, was for the first time.

The tide ebbed, and we parted into our separate bodies; and he slept. He slept deeply and quietly, as a man sleeps who has eaten his fill after a hard day's hunting; arms and legs wide-flung and almost all the bed-rugs tangled round him. But there was no sleep for me, through what was left of that night. For I knew that I had found a more bitter bondage than ever the slave market had forged upon me. Something, some part of my life, he had taken from me, and I belonged to him now, whoever had paid the slave price for me. And he would go away and forget—I thought suddenly that he had never asked my name, so I would not even be a name in his memory—and laugh, and lie with other women on other nights that would mean as much and as little to him as this one night of all my life had done. And I should be left with nothing, yet still bound to him past all breaking free.

He was a boy in some things, and cruel as a boy. He was a great lover of women, and proud of his skill with them, but he never understood what it meant to a woman to be loved by Alkibiades.

It was the one thing in which he ever thought too little of himself. But that knowledge came to me at a later time. That night I knew only that I loved him and hated him. I heard his voice again in the darkness, saying, "I can't take the risk, darling." He had made sure of me by a way as certain as death and more cruel. He had taken all that remained to me of freedom; bound me to him so that I could not betray him to Sparta. And for no other reason.

I remember propping myself on one arm, and looking down at him as he slept. The first water-grey light of dawn was creeping into the little courtyard. A bird was singing in the Satrap's new paradise; and from the young men's quarters of the palace I heard a gamecock crow, answered by another, farther off. Soon the slaves would be astir, and all night there must be guards within call. But he lay defenceless, sleeping, his face turned a little toward me. I did not know that I had reached down to feel for the dagger at his waist, until my hand closed on the grip. Afterwards the guards would come running. Afterwards it would be death for me too, but I did not care. Hair's breadth by hair's breadth I eased the curved blade from its sheath. It came free into my hand, and I sat back, looking at his exposed throat. But I could not do it that way, as one slaughters a sheep; not to Alkibiades. I had only to draw back the rug a little, to come at the place where I had felt his heart beat slow-pounding against my breast and belly.

I drew back the heavy folds of fur. He stirred, but did not wake. The marks of my teeth were on his shoulder. I sat there for a time—it could not have been as long as it seemed—with the knife in my hand, before I knew that I could not kill him.

I let the rug settle again, and got up—I was crying I think—I think—it is so long ago; and went quietly into the sleeping chamber and huddled on my clothes. On my way to the postern I had to pass again the place where he lay. I checked and looked down at him. He had stirred a little, flinging out his arm, but not toward the empty place beside him where I had lain. He would be waking soon, and I must hurry. But when he woke, he should know what had been in my heart. The naked dagger lay where I had left it lying on the grass. I picked it up and reached for a low-hanging spray of the almond tree and cut it through; three newly-opened flowers shone on it, fragile and grey as the ghosts of flowers in the morning twilight. I laid it with the dagger among the dark harsh folds of fur on his breast.

Then I ran for the side entrance. The door opened easily, and

I was out in the narrow way behind the chariot court. Two guards loomed out of the shadows and barred my way. But when I showed them my face, and the flute that I carried, they laughed and let me through. They must have been well used to the night-time comings and goings of Alkibiades' women.

# 13

## The Seaman

Alkibiades and our fat Satrap walks everywhere with their arms on each other's shoulders and seems uncommon pleased with each other all that spring. On the edge of summer a Spartan commission arrives in Karia, and Tissaphernes goes down with a splendid retinue to meet them. There's not much need to wonder what they come for, what with Tissaphernes cutting the promised daily drachma to a half, and no sign of the long-promised Phoenician fleet; and the state of things in Ionia can't have suited the Ephors too well.

Alkibiades, left behind in Sardis, wanders up and down that fine new garden like a caged leopard, or sits with his hands across his knees whistling half under his breath and staring at nothing, or joins me by fits and starts in the pleasure houses of the lower town. Well, I won't deny it's good to have his company again; but when he was left behind in Sparta, it wasn't *that* way he passed his time, and it seemed to me that Sardis was taking its toll of him. I says to him one day, "We're going to pieces in this place, you and I—let's cut adrift and get a few ships together—"

He was lounging on cushions in a jasmine arbour, feeding a little tame green bird with millet seeds from his hand, and lazy as a eunuch. Soon, I thought, he would grow fat. "The old sweet dream of piracy," he says, and laughs. "Ah now, Pilot, it does a man no harm to rest for a while in the shade before he turns to the next stage of his journey."

"And that is?"

"Tissaphernes' return, in the first place."

"And after that?"

"That depends on what happens in Karia; on what kind of mood he returns in; on a great many things." He looked up from the little green bird. There was kohl on his eyelids and he reeked of the saffron crocus perfume that the men wear in those parts. He says, "I'm playing a lone tune, Antiochus dear, I have to play it by ear."

A few days later Tissaphernes gets back, and word goes round the palace that he's in a foul temper and his wives and his slaves will suffer for it. But Alkibiades isn't his wife nor yet his slave. And he comes back from talking with the Satrap on the morning after his return, with a new spring in his step and a new brightness in his eye, like a man who has been ill and suddenly begins to feel better. He calls out the horses and bids me ride with him to try out a new falcon that he had just been given.

We rode out over the Magnesian plain, the grass already beginning to dry with the onset of summer. But we did not try the falcon. Instead, when we were well clear of habitation we talked. There is nowhere one can talk safely in Sardis.

I says, "Well?"

"Well enough. Tissaphernes has quarrelled with the Commission. They were sharper witted than poor old Chalcidius where the treaty was concerned, for one thing."

"Of course you never did send a full copy of that treaty back to Sparta," I says. "It must have come as something of a shock to them."

"It did." Alkibiades smiles between his horse's ears. "They told Tissaphernes what he could do with it, and I gather he swept out in a passion. The Spartan Commission will not have reassuring news to take home with them."

"Is that a good idea, so far as we are concerned?" I asks. "Forgive me, I'm only an ignorant seaman; my brain can't keep pace with all these doubles and twists."

"If our aim was to bide friends with Sparta, no," Alkibiades says, and then, "There was a time—I think you know it—when I considered allowing Sparta the honour of returning me to Athens. But I can scarcely be expected to remain on kissing terms with a state that plans my—liquidation."

"You certainly didn't, before, when the state was Athens," I says.

We rides a little way in silence, and a deer breaks from cover of a thicket and runs across our path; and Alkibiades turns and watches it out of sight. "It was not the people," he says at last. "Not the people in their hearts; it was the party."

"The people suffered for it," I says; and again he doesn't answer, but his horse jumps and flinches as though from a sudden jab on the bit.

But when at last his looks round again, he's half smiling, though not with his eyes.

"Our fat Satrap has cut the Spartan's pay *and* it's in arrears, and the morale of the Spartan fleet is doing exactly what the morale of a fleet always does when pay is long in arrears. He has kept the Phoenician fleet out of action—though they could sweep the Athenians out of the sea. All this will be known in Athens as well as it is in Sparta. And as well as it is known that Alkibiades is in Sardis and has the ear of the Satrap. Add that Tissaphernes is out of humour, to put it mildly, with all Sparta, for their stiff-necked commission; and I think we have enough in the pot for the moment. We will leave matters to simmer for a little."

"And when you reckon they've simmered long enough?" But in my bones and belly I know already, and the whole pace of life seems to quicken round me.

"Then, my dear, I shall send you with a message to the senior fleet officers at Samos."

And so a bit more than a month later, there I am, standing in the colonnaded terrace of one of the tall houses of Samos, looking out over the town, while behind me three Admirals of the Samos fleet sits round a table and discusses a letter from Alkibiades.

I seen that letter before it was sealed, and it was beautifully to the point; not a word wasted. Alkibiades offered to return to Athens bringing with him the friendship and support of Tissaphernes and through him, of the Great King; and he made only one condition; that the democracy which had outlawed him must be overthrown.

Behind me, I hears their voices murmuring on. There'd been a spot of disagreement as to whether, though I know what was in the letter I brought, I should be present at the meeting. Strombichides, the senior Naval Commander, had been dead against it, but Paesander had persuaded him and Charminius that it might be useful to have me there in case there was some question I could answer or point that I could clear up. We knew each other, vague like, having met at one or two of Alkibiades' parties; but I don't think 'twas friendship for me that made him take that line. I think he wanted to be sure that if there was trouble, I was up to my ears in it; and his sense of humour made him enjoy the thought that every word of their discussion, however uncomplimentary, would go straight back to Alkibiades, and him not able to do a thing about it. Anything he was not to know would be said at some other meeting that I shouldn't be told of at all. Incidentally, I was interested to see that Phrynichus—the fourth of the Samos Admirals, and a Democrat of the more rabid kind—hadn't been told of this one.

"How do we know that we can trust him?" Strombichides asks, point blank, behind me. "He has betrayed us once already, and now he betrays Sparta."

"As to that," says Paesander, the politician, "one can hardly blame him. Athens condemned him to death on a false charge of blasphemy."

"If it was false," puts in Charminius in his dry smooth voice.

I looks round at them over my shoulder; Strombichides, who couldn't have looked anything but a sailor if he tried for a thousand years, and Paesander with his clever, big-jowled face, and little grey Charminius with his dry cough; and Alkibiades' future lying on the table between them. "It was false," I says.

Paesander looks round at me. "Ah yes, I believe you were present at that unfortunate supper party."

Charminius gives his damned little cough. "But—forgive me—I believe you were drunk. Your recollection may be somewhat hazy."

"We were all drunk," I says, "but not as drunk as that. If you're going to condemn to death every young man who joins his friends in a mock invocation or a bawdy version of a hymn after supper, you'll be hard-pressed to find enough survivors in Athens to fight your wars."

Strombichides nods. He's a good enough fellow in his way, and a great one for justice.

And Paesander said soothingly, "Shall we say, at least, that the charge was greatly exaggerated." And I felt myself dismissed from the discussion, and turned my back on them again, propping myself comfortably against one of the painted columns.

Below me, the town curved out on its horned headland, glowing honey-coloured in the evening light, and across the straits that were dark as lapis, stood the hills of Ionia. Alkibiades and I had come down to the coast together, and somewhere among those hills he waited for the word that I was to bring him. I did not wonder he had chosen to send his messenger to Samos instead of to Athens direct. Athens herself, by all accounts, with barely enough ships and men to defend Piraeus and the Long Walls, counted for very little now. All the power and strength of Athens was here, with the whole Athenian fleet that lay at anchor in the harbour, or drawn up on to the strands and slipways, save for the guard-squadron patrolling beyond the harbour mouth. Even from

160

here I could see the swarming activity of the docks and harbour-side; the galleys stripped down for refitting, the forest of masts, the brilliance of new paint reflected in the water. I hadn't known until then, how homesick I was for the sight of ships and the men of the sea.

Behind me, the three had got back to an earlier stage in their debate. "There's still his betrayal of Sparta," Strombichides says. How the man harps on faith-keeping.

Again it's Paesander who answers him. I begins to realize that of the three, it's Paesander, for his own good reasons, who's on Alkibiades' side. "Sparta also has condemned him to death—chiefly, one gathers, for the crime of being too successful. Beside which, he is when one pauses to think, not a Spartan, however good a showing he made as one."

There's a silence; and then Strombichides says, "Supposing that we admit his excuse for treachery, supposing that we believe him to be acting in good faith now, in this promise of support from Persia, how can we be sure that the Great King will carry out his promise?"

"It is, of course, quite impossible to be in the faintest degree sure of any such thing," says Charminius. "Alkibiades has always had an overwhelming notion of the power of his own charm and—ahem, personal beauty."

I wants to turn round and push his yellow teeth down his throat, but I remembers it isn't a good moment; so I just cherishes hopes for the future, and goes on watching a Samian pentaconta heading across the harbour.

"A couple of months ago I would have agreed with you," says Paesander's plump and soothing voice, "but since then, Tissaphernes has quarrelled with the Spartan Commissioners. Now, I think we may give considerable weight to his promises."

"It's a hideous gamble," says Strombichides.

And Charminius' dry voice slides in again, "It is. But there is more to it than that. Even supposing that the gamble comes off, there is still to be considered the price that he demands—and he drives, you will not deny, an extremely hard bargain."

"A full scale revolt to overthrow the government is certainly not a thing to be entered into lightly," Strombichides agrees.

"No one imagines that it is," says Paesander. "I suggest, in the first place, merely that testing approaches should be made to certain of the officers and men."

"Which is to say that you are yourself already committed, at least in mind; and the moment these approaches are made, we are committed with you."

"That is so," Paesander says, after a moment.

Strombichides says flatly, "The fleet are Democrats almost to a man."

And Charminius in his dry polished voice, "That in itself might not be an insuperable difficulty. I imagine the power of Persian gold might have a certain effect on the fleet's political opinions."

"I don't know the fleet as intimately as you two," Paesander says, "but it has seemed to me from time to time, that the promise of Alkibiades' return might have its effect, too."

"Aye." I knows from the rasping sound that Strombichides is rubbing his short harsh beard up the wrong way, a trick of his when he's uncertain. "It's a strange thing about that golden boyo. Even after all he's done against us, after Syracuse itself, he still lies at the bottom of men's hearts like lees at the bottom of a wine cup. Any mention of his name—you can see it in their faces."

"And even Strombichides waxes poetical."

"Oh for Zeus' sake, Charminius!" Strombichides' voice goes rough at the edges. "I'm simply speaking the truth. And it goes against the grain quite enough, to admit it, without your sneer! If the thing were put to the vote among them, I honestly don't know which would win, their democratic loyalties, or the combination of Persian gold and something that Alkibiades trails behind him as he does those ridiculous great cloaks of his."

"The overthrow of the government is still not a step to be taken lightly," says Charminius. "Can we really afford so high a price for the luxury of Alkibiades back among us?"

There's a long pause, and I turns round from looking over Samos. The shadows is gathering under the portico, and the three men round the table has their faces thrust in on each other. Then Paesander says, "Whatever he has done or not done, it is because he has the ear of the Satrap that the Spartan fleet is short both in pay and morale and the Phoenician fleet has so far been held in leash. My friends, given the least chance of getting him, can we afford *not* to have Alkibiades back among us?"

## The Citizen

It was early autumn—the fourth since the young men marched for Syracuse; and the city, a city of old men and young boys and cripples, was still free; and that was about all that could be said—

when a customer at my father's shop told us that the *Paralos* was in from Samos with General Paesander on board. And soon after, we heard that he had been with the Council, and would speak before the Assembly, summoned for three days' time.

My father and I went up to listen and cast our votes. There was no difficulty about leaving the shop with only a slave in charge, the man who brought us news of Paesander's arrival had been the first customer in days, and there hadn't been another since. All Athens had a fairly shrewd idea what Paesander had come to say; and I remember there was a kind of uneasy quiet, a great sense of waiting, about the crowd gathered on the Pnyx. It was one of those days when the Meltemi falls asleep, and there seems no air to breathe. Parnes, far off beyond the wooded slopes of Colonus shook in the heat haze, and southward the sea was like burnished silver, hot in the sun, that will burn the fingers at a touch. On such a day the stink of a great crowd is almost suffocating; but that day there was another smell, of fear and expectancy and anger held ready for use; and running through and under it all—how can I describe it?—a kind of unwilling hope. The smell of the crowd's mood, that was almost as tangible as the stink of its sweat . . .

I am not Thucydides, with his copies of speeches after they are made; I remember only the gist of what Paesander said, but it is enough.

After the usual preamble which is seldom more than the beating of the gong in the theatre before the play begins, he led up to a very direct statement of facts. Alkibiades had sent word that he was willing to return to Athens and lead her war effort.

I have said before, that all Athens had some idea what was coming; but speaking for myself, the sheer valiant impudence of it took my breath away. Rightly or wrongly the Athenian Assembly had condemned him to death, and he was still under that sentence. He had gone over to the enemy and handled *their* war effort (Oh, we all knew whose brain was behind Dekalia and the loss of Syracuse), for more than two years, with a notable success. And now, with Sparta too hot to hold him, he did not ask us to forgive him, but as good as told us that *he* would forgive *us*.

But not without conditions.

Paesander was saying now that Alkibiades and only Alkibiades could detach Persia from her Spartan alliance, and bring in the weight of her gold and her ships on the Athenian side; and Alkibiades would not lift a finger in the matter unless he was recalled to Athens, and the government which had outlawed him and then so criminally mishandled the war effort, were in its turn thrown out.

At that, the crowd raised a furious outcry—two separate outcries that met and mingled with each other. The one was led by the priestly families of Eleusis, furious at the idea of recalling the man who had profaned the Mysteries and so brought the anger of the Gods upon Athens; the other, and much larger, a general protest at the bare suggestion of overthrowing with our own hands, our own hard-won democracy. My father joined in that. I remember him, his face dark red and the veins on his neck standing out like whipcord, shouting, "Maybe the Oligarchs aren't enough! Let's have the Tyrants back, while we're about it!" I did my own share of shouting, partly I think because it was the easiest way to get rid of the clamour of conflicting emotions pent up within me. Athens *was* the democracy, often as we grumbled at it; and to overthrow it, and set up an aristocratic rule of the few instead of the free voice of the many, seemed to me in that moment a kind of snuffing out of the spirit. It was too high a price.

I have known men try to shout down an angry crowd, and a few, a very few, who succeeded. Paesander didn't attempt it. He just stood there until we had shouted ourselves out, and then went on.

"My friends, it goes hard with all of us, none more so than myself, to consider this change in our way of government, but we must consider also that it need not be for ever. When the war is over, there will come a time for changing the government again—" (The dirty dog! said something within myself, but at the time I scarcely noticed it.) "It is no bad thing, in wartime, when quick decisions are needed, that they should be made by the few. And Alkibiades, coming of our greatest democratic family, will be the first to see when the time is ripe to return to the way of government that is natural to us."

There were doubtful mutterings among the crowd, and a few shouts of dissent began to rise again. Paesander held up his hand for silence, and when he got it, went on. "As to the blasphemy charge—remember that most of the men who brought it have since fallen into disrepute; several are in gaol for one cause or another. I tell you frankly, that it is not Alkibiades who has brought the wrath of the Gods upon the city, it is Athens who has brought the disasters of these past years upon herself, by driving her greatest and most brilliant General into the arms of the enemy!"

He paused then, to see the effect of his words, and from the crowd came an uneasy murmuring. "You all know how it is with Athens. The Spartans from Dekalia are loose in our land; we have less than twenty warships at Piraeus, barely enough to beat off an attack from the sea; the rest of our fleet, and the citizens to man it are at Samos and cannot be recalled unless we are to lose Ionia. Our treasury is empty. The Spartans on the other hand have risen in the scale of seapower until their fleet about equals ours, and they have the whole sea strength of the Peloponnesian league behind them, backed by Persian gold. The gold has been cut and is in arrears, you say; yes, and we all know whose doing that is. We must all know too, that if Alkibiades can sway the Persian Satrap in one direction, he can sway him in the other." He leaned forward, his heavy face seeming to kindle with the urgency of what he said; his eyes moved to and fro over the crowd. Then he flung out his hands as though in a last appeal. "Tell me, if there is one man here who can do so, what hope have we, apart from Alkibiades?"

Men looked into each other's faces and away again up to the big shape on the rostrum. The uneasy muttering and the stray shouts of dissent died away. No one had any answer. We had no hope apart from Alkibiades.

Before the Assembly broke up, we had voted that Paesander and ten of our leading citizens should go to Sardis to negotiate with Alkibiades and the Satrap, with full authority to accept their terms. And since it was clear that there would be trouble with certain of the Samos senior officers, including that redoubtable democrat, Phrynichus, we had passed another, relieving them of their command. Having once accepted the idea that Alkibiades was coming back to us, nothing must stand in the way.

Years later, Aristophanes put a line into his play *The Frogs*, "Athens loves and hates him too—but wants him back." We wanted him back; and he was coming . . .

We did not know, then, the full price that we should have to pay.


## The Seaman

It was late autumn when the embassy came from Athens, and the weather turning cold. They had given Alkibiades a brazier burning charcoal and scented logs in his quarters, and he checked a moment to hold his hands to it every time he passed in his caged pacing. Once he checked at the window end of his track, and twitched back the crimson hangings that were supposed to keep out the whining draughts, and peered out through the star-shaped window-fret into the darkening courtyard. "The almond tree is almost bare," he says, disgusted. "We've been a year in this well-cushioned abode of the damned; while the fleets of Athens and the League scuttle about the Aegean taking and re-taking islands, and fighting six-a-side battles that get nobody anywhere. Isn't there *one* commander worth the name on either side?"

He'd been like that for weeks, months; impossible to be with, and somehow impossible to abandon. I'd been near changing my name and taking out my earrings and slipping off to Miletus to enlist as a rower more than once; but always I'd known in the end that I couldn't leave him up there in Sardis to go to the dogs by himself.

But now that the embassy from Athens had come, now that he had supped with them . . . "Soon will be," says I. "At least, that's the word going round Sardis."

"May Sardis rot," says he, letting the hangings fall across the window and turning back to his pacing. "Meaning me, I take it?"

"Meaning you." I takes a good look at him as he comes back to the brazier, the first real look I've taken in a long time. And I don't like what I sees; his face is puffed and blotchy, the old scar dark on his temple, his eyes heavy and hot, set in bruised circles like the eyes of a man as hasn't slept for so long that he's almost forgotten what sleep is like. "What's amiss? Athens hasn't been fool enough to refuse you?"

He gives a shout of laughter. "Refused me? No! Listen, my dear anxious old drunken pirate—Gods! Antiochus, have you any notion how appalling you look? Paesander has been bringing me good news between mouthfuls all evening. The magic of my name—or the hope of what I can do for them—has raised me a strong party in Athens; the Assembly has voted for my recall, and in order to oil the skids, they have removed Phrynichus from his command at Samos."

"Well then, what in the name of the Dog—" I begins.

"All this depends—it *must* depend—on my ability to bring in Persia's support on our side."

I nods. "That's the message I took to Samos."

"And it was a message in good faith. That's the howlingly funny part! I've used trickery before now, what politician hasn't; but I sent that letter in good faith. I had Tissaphernes' promise, and

I trusted to it. I even believe that he meant it at the time. But that was in the summer; now the almond tree is almost bare, and *Tissaphernes has had second thoughts!*"

I gets up from my stool beside the brazier, and stares at him through the fronding smoke, feeling a bit sick. "Why? He can't have!" I said stupidly.

"He has bethought him of earlier council I gave him when I was—warming him up—that keeping both sides equally balanced and letting them waste each other is better policy—for Persia and for Tissaphernes, that is. He's right, of course; it's cheaper for one thing, and less trouble, and offers better chances for a clean-up by Persia with proportionately rich pickings for the Satrap of Lydia, in the end. Only I thought I'd got him safely past that point. I had, but he's doubled back on me." We stands facing each other through the smoke, Alkibiades breathing through flared nostrils; then he adds—oh, quite pleasantly—but the pleasantness makes the hairs crawl on the back of my neck, "May he die slowly and screaming, in the hands of the Merciful Ones!"

The sour taste of the wine I had drunk earlier came back into my mouth. I gagged, and spat into the hot charcoal.

"So what do we do now?"

"There's only one thing to be done, and that I've done already," he says. "Persuade Tissaphernes to demand impossible terms."

"And how will that help us?"

"It will force Athens to be the one to break off negotiations. With any luck it will mean that the people will spit on Paesander's name rather than on mine—if they don't look too closely at the terms, but see only that they had the chance of getting me back, and Paesander lost it for them."

"Alas for Paesander," I says. "You're very sure of your charm for the Athenians."

He says, looking into the red heart of the charcoal, "I know Athens. I don't think anyone ever knew her as I know her, or as she knows me."

And by Blue Haired Poseidon, he said it as lover speaks of lover!

The negotiations ran on for three days; and Alkibiades spent the days in the conference chamber and the nights in the brothels of the town. (I had asked him once why he never had his little flute girl back; it was reputed that she was good in bed; but he only laughed and said that he liked variety.) And then on the third night, when I was drinking in a wine-shop not far from the Temple of Cybele, I looks up and sees him standing in the doorway. He sees me at the same moment and comes lurching across the crowded court and crashes down on the bench beside me and yells for wine. "They told me I might find you here," he says, and leans sideways to smack the plump pink-draped backside of the girl who brings the wine jar. I remember I was as shocked as Plato might have been. It was the kind of thing other men do, as a matter of fact I'd done it myself a short while before; but it was all wrong for Alkibiades; a kind of deliberate grossness. The girl darted off giggling to attend to another customer, and he turned to me. I thought he'd been drinking already, for his face was darkly flushed and his eyes bloodshot, and when he put out his hand to the wine cup it wasn't as steady as it might have been; but I meets his gaze straining in his head; and he's stone cold horribly sober.

"It's all over," he says. "The embassy have broken off negotiations."

I says under my breath, "Hadn't we best get out of here? Somewhere we can talk without being overheard?"

"It's not much matter whether we're overheard or not," he says. "It'll be public property soon enough, anyway." But he keeps his voice down, all the same. "The Satrap made his demands—firstly that the whole of Ionia, coast and islands alike, should be ceded to the Great King. There was a good deal of argument of course, but Paesander agreed to that at last. He actually agreed, Pilot! Oh I suppose he thought that with Sparta crushed by the aid of the Persian fleet, we—Athens—would still have her Thracian colonies and the cities of the Hellespont—corn trade safe, and no Sparta to stand between us and the sun. But that was only the beginning—do I not know it, I who framed the demands! He made more demands, and more, and Paesander and his troop accepted or half accepted or asked for time to think; and at last he demanded that the Great King should build what ships he pleased and send them *where* he pleased, even along our coasts and throughout Greek home-waters."

I set down my wine cup so sharply that a few drops flew out, and spattered the table top with crimson. "But that means only one thing—"

"One damnable thing," Alkibiades says. "With Sparta crushed, Persia would turn her new Navy on to us. To agree to that would be as good as selling out to the Persians here and now. Incidentally, I'd almost certainly become Satrap of Athens, which is a pleasant thought, if I could make up my mind whether to laugh myself sick or howl like a dog. Well, at that even Paesander dug his toes in, as I'd banked on his doing. And proceedings came to an end, with Tissaphernes gathering his furred robe round him and stalking out of one door, while Paesander and his envoys stalked out of the other."

I says nothing. There doesn't seem much point even in cursing; and when things gets beyond cursing, it's better to keep quiet. Alkibiades is watching his own hand on the table, playing with the light in that great signet ring. In a little, he says carefully, "Tissaphernes pretended he wasn't fluent enough in Attic Greek and made me act as his interpreter, so that the demands came from my mouth. I think he found that very amusing."

And then suddenly he looks up at me. "Do you know what nearly broke my heart, Pilot? That Paesander so nearly accepted. I—you can imagine what conditions at home must be."

"You don't know your own strength," I says.

# 14

## The Soldier

Seven thousand men went into the stone quarries at Syracuse; and half a year later, rather less than seven hundred came out, to slavery of one kind or another.

I was sold to a farmer, and worked most of my time among his pigs. Pigs are surprisingly good company, when you get to know them as well as I did; and their smell is sweet and wholesome compared with the smell of the quarries. I wake up with *that* smell in the back of my throat sometimes, even now; the smell of despair and filth and old grey stone dust, and the sickly-sweet stench that came from the dead bodies of our friends. The guards would not take the dead away, and we had nowhere to bury them—you cannot dig graves in solid rock; so we piled them on top of each other in the worked-out galleries of the quarry. We had a great many flies. They swarmed on the dead, and blew in the wounds of the living. Anyone with an open wound almost always died, you couldn't keep the dust out of it; and the fly maggots hatched out, and that was that. We began to know after a time.

Astur died in the early days. Quite quietly, with his head on my knee. We were together all through the long hideous campaign, and the desperate retreat that ended at the Assinaros ford. We never knew one quiet hour together, save for some odd spell on watch. We never swam together, or lay in the shade and laughed holding hands; or played kotobos, trying to make the initials of each other's names in the wine lees after supper; or hunted with a shared pack in the oak woods of Colonus. Because of Astur, I have never known these things—oh in the way of friendship or with casual companions, yes; some of these things at least; but not as lovers know them. His grave bright-eyed shade with the sudden laughter would never have held me back; I have simply never wanted it with any other. He was the one and the only one. And after him, I became a man for women, and even that, not for a long while.

Yet at the time I scarcely felt anything. I stacked his body with all those others, and crawled out of the gallery, and vomited up the bean bread that had been my evening meal, and settled down to get what rest I could in the little time remaining before another day.

And as the days passed, and passed, and passed, and the towns-folk who had used to come to stare at us ceased to come because the smell from the quarry mouth had grown too foul, the chief thing I felt about him was envy. It would be easier to be dead than living; at least one could stay lying down.

Only when at last they let the survivors of us out to slavery above ground, and we crept out like tattered ghosts from the half land of Hades, into a world where colours were too bright and voices too loud, and spaces too wide, and I saw the Adonis flowers, the little blood-red anemones of the spring fluttering among the rocks at the quarry entrance, I knew that I was leaving Astur behind me, deserted; never to see the spring time again, or fondle the warm soft hollows behind a hound's ears; never to go home. Then I felt all that I had not felt before, and paid for the months of feeling nothing . . .

Oh well, I had the pigs. Only I missed my friends. The society had been better in the stone quarries.

There were men in Sicily—some from the garrison at Catana, some Sicilian, who helped quite a number of us away. One heard whispers; but I didn't pay much heed. And then, more than a year after I came up from the quarries, one day it was my turn. I got a message—no matter how—concerning a faulty bolt on the door of the shed where I was caged at night, and a fishing-boat that would be at a certain place at a certain time; and with the message, gold enough for passage money and a cloak to hide my lash-scarred back.

And so, three years after the army had left for Syracuse, I came ashore from a trading vessel at Piraeus; and stood on the jetty and looked up and saw the blink of light, four miles away, that was the sun striking on the blade of Athene's upraised spear.

That was about the only thing in Athens that was as I remem-bered it. For the rest, I walked up between the Long Walls into a city of old men and boys and the odd cripple, and silent close-veiled women doing their own shopping—and very poor shopping at that, for the stalls in the market seemed to have scarcely anything to sell—because they had neither menfolk nor slaves to do it for them. Every face I saw was gaunt and pinched; clearly the city was on the edge of famine. It seemed to me a strange city, even before I reached our house and found that my mother was dead and the place sold up.

I remember standing in the street and wondering what I should do now. My friends had mostly died in Sicily, and I could not bear the thought of going to their houses and coming face to face with families who would be looking, not for me, but for sons who would not be coming back. Finally I decided to go up to Kymon's perfume shop. It had always been a favourite meeting-place, and it would be a likely spot, always supposing that it was still there, to find out how things were in the city, and maybe get news of any friends I still had. All Athens seemed so strange and lacking that I half expected it to have crumbled away like so much else. But it was still there, and looking much as it had always looked, from the outside, save that the blue pillars had chipped and faded and were badly in need of a coat of paint. But inside, it was empty. The first time that ever I had seen Kymon's shop empty of customers.

The old man must have been out, and it was the son Timotheus who got up when I came through the door. He was about my own age, but with a game leg that had kept him clear of the call-up. Except for some guards down at Piraeus, his was almost the first face of my own generation that I had seen since I landed that morning. He stood with one hand on the selling-table, and looked at me—and suddenly I realized what I must look like, and waited for him to order me out into the street, that being the right place for beggars. But instead, after a moment, he said, "From Syracuse?"

"How did you know?" I said.

"There have been quite a few of you, these past few months," he said, "and more than one has found his way here. I've begun to know the look."

"But you don't know which one I am," I said; and then, as he hesitated, "I'm Arkadius, lieutenant of marines. I used to buy iris perfume here when I could afford it."

"I'm sorry," he said, "it is unpardonable of me to forget an old customer," and limped round to take my hand, and then drew me in to a cushioned bench. I sat down on it wearily, my legs feeling suddenly weak.

"I've changed," I muttered. "Nobody would know me in Athens now."

"Some of the change will wash off," he said. "Vasso will bring you hot water." And he smiled, "Oh we're very grand, we still have a household slave, like the very rich folk. She's too old to run away to the Spartans, and too old to sell—even if we could find a purchaser who could feed her better than we can."

He fed me, though, after I had washed, and apologized that he could not give me fresh garments, for he had given his spare tunic to one of my kind a few days before. He said the name, but it was no one I knew.

And then I realized that I was probably eating his supper. The stone quarries and the pigs had made me forget my manners. I did not beg his pardon, because I knew that would only make him uncomfortable, but I remembered to thank him; which I had not done before, and said that I must be going.

"Where?" he said.

"I don't quite know. I went home when I arrived this morning, but my mother is dead and our house sold up. I did not like to go to the homes of any of my friends."

There was a rather painful silence. And then Timotheus said that I must stay there for the night, anyway. The shop could see to itself for the evening, there would be no customers anyway, nobody could afford to buy perfumes these days. So I stayed—and asked if anything had been heard of one or two of my friends who had left the stone quarries alive, or escaped capture; but he only shook his head.

"Well, it seems the sooner I get back to the ships the better," I said. "I only saw about a squadron as we came in, is that all we have now?"

"Just enough ships and just enough men to defend the harbour and the Long Walls," he said. "Every ship and man that can be spared is at Samos, keeping the seaways clear."

"Then I'd better make for Samos." It all seemed oddly dream-like; but my heart snatched at the hope that in Samos I should see a few faces that I knew.

And then I remembered something that had alerted me at the time and then passed out of my head. "Timotheus, on my way here, I thought I heard Alkibiades' name spoken two or three times in the streets as though there was some special news of him, or . . ." I did not know how to finish the sentence.

He was silent for a moment, then he said, "I did not quite know how to tell you that part. It cannot be a name that sounds very happily in your ears. Alkibiades is coming back. He sent word to the senior officers at Samos, offering to come back and bring the help of Persia with him, on the one condition that the Democratic

173

government is overthrown. The Admiral Paesander and some other officers are over here now; they spoke to the Assembly yesterday and we have voted for his return, at the price he demands." And then he added pleadingly, "You can't altogether blame him. The Democrats—the leaders anyway—condemned him to death on a trumped-up charge—they drove him into the arms of Sparta."

"That's the talk of a man who stayed at home. Oh, I know it must have been bad in Athens all this while. But I was in the stone quarries; I saw my friends die there. I can blame him a good deal."

I saw him wince, and realized that that was an ugly taunt to throw at a lame man who had probably eaten his heart out to march with the rest of us. But just then I didn't care.

"To overthrow the government! Great Gods, man! Athens has been a democracy for a hundred years!"

"The Government *has* mishandled the war," he said. "Most of the men's clubs are Oligarch in secret already. They are sick of the muddled rule of the many. They think that at least in wartime the government is better in the hands of a few skilled men who know their jobs. I don't think it'll be skilled men we'll get, only rich and powerful ones."

"And you still cast your votes for his return."

"We need him, Arkadius, he's our only hope."

He had been looking at his hands on the table before him while he spoke. But suddenly he looked up, full at me. And I saw his eyes.

I said, "Need him, yes, it seems so; but want him is another word for it! Great Gods! Timotheus—you too! What's the matter with us all?"

"I don't know," he said. "I once heard an old man say that men had created Gods in their own image. Maybe we of Athens created Alkibiades in ours. He's part of us, woven into our soul, we may hate him, but without him we are barren and lost."

So I went down to Piraeus again next day to look for means of getting to Samos; and there I had a stroke of luck. The *Paralos*, which had brought Paesander to Athens was due to sail, taking him and the other envoys to Miletus for Sardis, and one of the marines had gone sick. It was not Samos, but at least it was out of Athens, and there would probably be a chance of leaving her and getting across to Samos before she sailed on the return trip with Alkibiades aboard.

We made Miletus, and lay there for fifteen days, I, biding my time, while the envoys went up to Sardis. At the end of that time they returned, in foul tempers, with Paesander the foulest of them all. Tissaphernes, it seemed, had demanded impossible terms. It was quite clear that Alkibiades had tried to trick them. The *Paralos* was ordered to Samos instead of returning to Athens at all. At the time, not knowing that Samos was riddled with Oligarchic plots, I wondered why.

My first sight of Samos I shall never forget. Even in late autumn, the city seemed to be basking like a great pale-coloured cat between wind-ruffled blue sea and tawny hills. And as we rounded the headland with its high rock-perched citadel, and came in under shelter of the mole, the harbour and waterside was all that Piraeus had used to be; and I thought—Oh Gods, how I thought—of the day the fleet sailed for Syracuse . . . We had passed one squadron on patrol outside the harbour mouth, exchanging signals with the leading Trirarch; but inside, the harbour was rich and running over with shipping, the Samian fleet and the whole new Navy of Athens, in peak condition like chariot horses ready for their race. And all along the foreshore, from the great Temple of Hera away to the westward, out to the citadel on its spur, was the bustle of a great seaport. Troops and seamen and citizens coming and going among docks and rope-walks and warehouses; ships drawn up on the strand for careening or refit.

Paesander and his fellow envoys landed first, and disappeared, presumably to their own quarters in the town, or to some council or other to make report of Alkibiades' perfidy. And we landed next, and were marched off to the Athenian camp, under the plane trees between the city walls and the Temple of Hera.

At Rhegium we had camped in much the same way between city walls and temple; but then we had been there on sufferance, shut out from the city. Here it seemed that the city was not only open to us, but that we were its masters.

Samos in those months was a place to go to the head like wine. And here, more even than in Athens, one heard the name of Alkibiades at every turn. The embassy's news was out within the hour, so of course that wasn't surprising. What was surprising was that there was a feeling abroad that despite what had happened, still somehow, at some time, he was coming. It was tangible, something that breathed out from the men who felt it. It was all too heady for me, fresh from my Sicilian pigs.

But in Samos I found, here and there, a man I knew from the old days before the world fell to pieces. Notably some days after Paesander had gone on by another ship to Athens, I came upon Ariston, a fellow lieutenant of marines some years older than

myself, who I had served under before I gained my own lieutenancy. We came face to face halfway up a street as pretty and
indigestible with gilding and coloured marble as the sweets
children buy at festival time. And like Timotheus, he did not know
me. When I told him who I was, he said, "But the Arkadian was
three years younger than me."

"We aged rather quickly in the stone quarries," I said.

After that, he swept me into one of the wine-shops that are
everywhere in Samos city, and would have poured enough wine
into me to put a mule driver under the bench, as though he hoped
in that way to wash the quarry-dust and the stink of dead men out
of my throat. But I had little taste for wine at that time. Afterwards
we wandered out into the barley terraces and olive gardens beyond
the citadel headland, and sat in the sun, where the next terrace
kept the wind from our backs; both glad to have found each other,
for we had been good enough friends in the old days; and both
wanting to be quiet.

For a while, we talked of small unimportant things, not much of
the Sicilian campaign. Ariston was never one to trespass in
another's private places; and I was grateful to him for that. But
presently he asked my ship, and when I told him the *Paralos*, he
spoke of Alkibiades and the failure of Paesander's mission.

I said, "Everyone speaks of Alkibiades; his name blows on the
wind, here in Samos."

"It's a very potent name," Ariston said.

"The Gods know it. But they—the people, the troops,
are speaking as though he was still coming. I've heard them,
Ariston.'

He was silent a short while, staring out towards Ionia, which in
the evening light seemed very near across the straits. Then he said,
"Arkadius, when I first realized that it was you, back there in the
street of the Golden Grasshopper, the obvious thing seemed to be
to celebrate and—well, celebrate, with Samian wine. But then
I began to think. I want to talk to you, and that's why I brought
you out here where there are no ears to listen. You're right, the
people do speak of Alkibiades as though he might still be coming.
That's the Oligarchs' doing. They are putting it about that if the
Democrats here in Samos are swept away, and Alkibiades presented
with the accomplished fact, he may yet come back. And even
without Persian help, Alkibiades could win the war for us, as he
has been winning it for Sparta these three to four years past."

"I should think that might even be true," I said.

"Very likely. But the Oligarchs aren't interested in whether it's true or not. They're interested in overthrowing the democracy and putting themselves in power."

"I'm no Oligarch," I said, "but I suppose that's natural enough in a way. Samos has always been an oligarchy until a few years ago, and you can't blame men for wanting to get back what they've lost."

"Only these are not the same men who lost it," Ariston said.

I stared at him. "Not the same men?"

"Oh no, the men behind the present Oligarch clubs are not the old landowners. They're the men who were in the forefront of the democratic revolt, three years ago, and then abandoned it as lightly as they'll abandon Alkibiades once he has served his purpose. They're simply out for what they can get; and the Gods help Samos, and Athens, if they get it."

I felt stupid. I had grown unused to using my brain. "Paesander?" I said, after a moment.

"Paesander is the perfect political opportunist. He'll take what offers, and use it in whatever way seems to promise the best advantages to himself. It's almost a game of skill with him."

"What will happen?" I asked, after a little.

"It's a situation in which anything might happen."

"But surely nothing much can, while the Athenian fleet's here. They're still Democrats, aren't they? All those rowers out of the slums of Athens, never forgetting or letting anyone else forget that they're free citizens with the vote."

"About three-quarters of the fleet are Democrats, as always," Ariston nodded. And then he said abruptly, "Where have you been all day?"

"Asleep, most of it. I was out on night manoeuvres with the scout squadrons."

"So you won't have heard that except for the *Paralos*, the *Vixen* and my own *Hesperus*, the fleet is ordered out on another pointless sortie against Chios tomorrow at dawn?"

In the silence that followed, I remember the sea sound of the wind in the olive trees, and the gulls calling.

Then Ariston said, "Keep your wits about you, and don't go too far from the town when you're off duty."

On the way back, he said, looking at my plain hoplite's uniform that had been issued to me out of the war chest at Piraeus, "My second has just got promotion. If I have a word with your Triarch and with my own, would you like to take his place? You'll get a lieutenancy of your own again soon, but meanwhile?"

"I'd like that," I said, and we gripped hands on it.

Two days later, when my transfer was through, Ariston sent me down to the arsenal to deal with a hitch in the supply of three barrels of javelin heads. Getting javelin heads out of a master of armament is always like drawing teeth; as a breed they seem unable to grasp the fact that a throw-spear used at sea is in the nature of things generally a throw-spear lost.

In the arsenal the air was warm and heavy after the gusting-up of the thin north-easter outside; thick with the smell of sailcloth and pitched rope. And down the shadowy sides of the long building loomed the unshipped figureheads and stacked oars, the arms' racks and the great bronze rams with their fangs wrapped in old sailcloth for safety. From the waterfront below, I could hear men at work on the slipways, and the calling of the gulls and the lapping and slapping water. And then from somewhere behind in the town, a distant murmur that swelled into a crackle of angry shouting.

The master of armament (I had managed to get past the clerks and arrive at the great man himself) broke off in what he was saying about javelin heads not growing on bushes and the barrels having to be signed for in triplicate anyway, and we listened, meeting each other's startled and questioning gaze.

And then there was the sound of running feet and somebody outside shouted, "Get up to the Agora! They've murdered Hyperbolus!"

(Hyperbolus, originally exiled from Athens, had become one of the most vocal of the Samos Democrats, a veritable gadfly of a man. At normal times one could not really blame anybody for murdering Hyperbolus; but these were not normal times . . .)

I ran out; men were coming up from the galleys. I saw several of the *Paralos* marines and joined up with them as we ran, seamen joined us, some few shipyard workers, but not many of those. Thrasybulus, Trirarch of the *Vixen*, appeared from somewhere. He shouted to us, "Up to the Agora! The Oligarchs are out for blood, and Hyperbolus won't be the only one!" And we ran headlong for the great open market-place in the midst of the town.

Angry crowds began to press in on us, with more of the galley crews and the troops pushing through to swell our ranks. There were shouts of "Kill! Kill!" and shouts of "Get the arsenal!" and shouts of "Alkibiades!"

Everyone knows how that day went. It was fairly hot work for a few hours, but fortunately some of the citizens realized the plot, and most of the troops stood firm by their officers, and little tough Thrasybulus was there to take the lead. Even so, if the Oligarchs had got the arsenal things might have gone differently; but they lacked a leader to match the *Vixen*'s Commander, and Ariston and some of our lot got there first and with the master of armament and his own guard and its clerks and storemen, contrived to hold it in the face of a sharp attack. By the end of the day it was over, with a couple of our own men lost to about thirty of the Oligarchs'. And when the rest of the fleet returned in due course, we were maybe a trifle loud-mouthed, and prone to admire the length of our own shadows in the sun.

We called an Assembly, all together though, townsfolk and fleet; we banished certain of the ringleaders including Charminius, and pardoned the rest. They were poor stuff, for the most part, not worth troubling about. Then we elected new Commanders in place of those we had exiled. Thrasybulus was an obvious choice; the other, Thrassylus, was less obvious, for it isn't often that the troops elected an ordinary captain of hoplites to the high command. But he was a natural leader, if a bit of a rogue, and popular with the troops. Both of them were the men for the moment. And we had no cause to regret the choice.

The *Paralos* sailed for Athens at once, to carry the news of the attempted uprising and its crushing, to the city, in the hope that this, reaching the Athenian Oligarchs in time, might prevent a similar attempt there.

The trireme returned after some weeks' delay, lacking several of the crew, left behind imprisoned; and the Trirarch, who had barely escaped himself, had a desperately ugly tale to tell.

The *Paralos* had been too late with her news; too late by many days. Paesander and his crew had gone straight ahead with their plans, and in Athens the Oligarchs had prospered better than on Samos. The orator, Androcles—he who had originally indicted Alkibiades—had been murdered like Hyperbolus. That had been done in the name of clearing the way for Alkibiades' return; but Alkibiades or no, it had removed one of the most potent of the Democratic leaders. And other deaths had followed already, of men opposed to the Oligarchs; the Gods alone knew how many more were to come. Athens, a democracy for four generations, was being ruled by four hundred men, and the four hundred controlled by a mere five, of whom our good Democrat Phrynichus was one. I suppose, having spoken out so hot against Alkibiades' return, his skin felt safer that way. Fines and banishment were becoming the small change of life, murder walked the streets, and the whole city was in the grip of terror. I was rather glad, then, that my mother was dead and I had no family any more. I was in better case than the men who kept watch or lay down to sleep that night in fear for wives and kinsfolk at home. The men from the *Paralos* were spreading through the streets and wine-shops of Samos, the rumour that the Oligarchs, caring only to save their own estates, were preparing to treat with Sparta. They had sent an embassy to King Agis back at Dekalia, ran the report; and there was a fort already going up at the mouth of Piraeus Great Harbour, which all men knew was to cover the Spartan fleet against attack from *us*.

All this in a few weeks.

The story had gained a good deal in the telling (though the bare truth was evil enough), but at the time we could not know that; and in the wake of the news the whole Athenian force went up in flames. Red rage swept through the port of Samos, and for that first night after the news came, the danger pressed more sharply than it had done on the day of Hyperbolus' murder, for now the chief peril was within ourselves, in the fact that a quarter of the fleet at least had Oligarch sympathies; and with men frightened for families at home, and red-angry, roving at large through such a town as Samos, that was a danger to be reckoned with. A split in our forces now would bring the Spartan fleet down on us from across the straits.

Thrasybulus reckoned with this, and gave orders that all shore leave was to be stopped and the men got back to their ships. Ariston and I spent a busy night rounding up the *Hesperus'* marines, and it was close on dawn before we found the last three, good Democrats very drunk and hurling grubbed-up cobble-stones against the street door of one of the pardoned Oligarchs, and got them back on board.

Next morning, with everyone still ordered to remain on board their ships, or in the case of those whose ships were beached and dismantled, to take parade order beside them, our new Commanders came among us and went personally from ship to ship, binding every topman, every rower and marine by solemn oaths, to maintain the democracy, to hold together in undivided loyalty despite any personal differences in politics, to carry on to the full the war with the Spartan League, to have no dealings by herald or in any other way with the Four Hundred in Athens.

It is wonderful, the steadying effect of an oath taken all together. It is akin to the habit of holding formation acquired on the drill-ground, that helps a man not to give back before an enemy thrust on the battlefield. The night before, the troops had been ready to fire Samos or fly at each other's throats. That morning they had been only sobered up and sullen. But by the time Thrasybulus and Thrassylus had been their round, we felt ourselves comrades again; and had taken a long clear look at the fact that Athens must now be counted out, and we were alone; we, the Samos fleet, against the whole strength of the Spartan League.

We took that first long look, and in an odd way, we found it good. At least we knew exactly where we stood now. We had no one to depend on but ourselves. It was for us to prove that ourselves were enough.

After the Generals had made their round—it was evening by then, the black-plumed clouds of early winter breaking in the north-west as they did most evenings, and the sea beginning to shine—we sacrificed, the whole fleet together, the scented smoke of the storax drifting down from the after-deck, and we sang the Paean. We were a brotherhood.

Now that we stood alone, it was for us in Samos to take upon ourselves the powers that had belonged to Athens. Citizens and fleet together, we held another Assembly a few days later, and voted Alkibiades a full pardon on the old sacrilege charge. Next day Thrasybulus sailed for Sardis to bring him back.

Sitting over a jug of wine in the Golden Grapes with Ariston that night, I said, "Will he come, do you think?"

Ariston had no need to ask who I meant; when men said "He" in Samos at that time, they only meant one man. "It's what he's worked for, all this while."

"I know. But just look at it, Ariston, it's a situation from some crazy comedy. We're calling him back because he and no one else can get us the help of Persia—and it's become pretty plain that he can't get it. He made the overthrow of the democracy a condition of his return, and now it's the Democrats of Samos who are demanding it. In his place, wouldn't you suspect a trap?"

"Yes, I expect I would. But then I'm not Alkibiades."

I turned to him, not sure of his meaning, and he explained himself in his quiet careful way, as though I had asked the question aloud. "If he was merely intelligent, he might very well smell a trap—that would be cold reason. But he doesn't function on reason, our Alkibiades. He'll come."

And I remembered Timotheus at the perfume shop, saying, "We of Athens created him in our own image. We are part of him and he of us, woven into the fibre of our soul, and without him we are barren and lost." No, cold reason had no bearing on the case.

It was a good while before the *Vixen* returned; but we did not find time hang heavy on our hands for lack of occupation. We had been hearing for a good while past that the Spartans at Miletus were growing restive, waiting for Tissaphernes to bring in the Phoenician fleet that never came; and after the crushing of the Oligarchs' plot on Samos, I suppose they grew somewhat desperate. At all events they came against us soon after with their full strength, something over a hundred triremes. With the ships that we had in port at the time we were well and truly outnumbered, and so we refused them fight until Strombichides who was up at Abydos, came sweeping down with three squadrons to strengthen us. Then the Spartans pulled back to Miletus and it was our turn to sail against them, and theirs to refuse battle. It was all a bit like cockerels squaring up to each other, all crow and stretched necks and ruffling feathers, with nothing to follow. But it kept our hands in and helped to pass the time.

And no sooner was that over than a scouting vessel brought in word that ten ships of the Spartan League, had got through to the north, to Pharnobazus the Satrap of Phrygia (presumably he offered more regular pay than Tissaphernes had been providing of late), and that at their coming, Byzantium had revolted and gone over to them. That looked ugly for our Black Sea corn trade, but there was nothing we could do for the present but send up a squadron to keep watch in the Hellespont; a mere stop-gap move to hold the situation until Alkibiades came. We all knew that he was coming and over the whole fleet, as winter turned to spring, there was a sense of marking time, of lying to the wind until he came and the world and life itself moved forward again.

And then at last, when the olive trees were in flower and the cuckoos calling, one dusk there was a fire on the beacon headland, signalling that the *Vixen* had been sighted. And next morning all Samos, citizens and fleet, crowded the waterfront of the harbour to see her come in.

The day was hot for the time of year, one of those spring days that hark forward toward summer, and I remember the heat of my helmet scorching my forehead; and the sun-dazzle off the water as we strained our eyes toward the nearing trireme, trying to see the figures on the after-deck, the flash of the sun on the oar-blades, the white arrowhead of foam and oar thresh spreading from her prow.

Then we saw him, standing alone save for the steersman in the stern. Bareheaded, with his helmet in the crook of his arm, and the sun beating on his bright head. The *Vixen* passed quite close to the *Hesperus*, so close that we lifted and rocked in her bow-wave; and I could see the look on his face as he stood with his head tipped back just as I remembered. It was the look of a man who has come back from the realm of Hades into the sunlight again; too grave for gladness; a look that greeted all things with a long, questioning, remembering touch.

At first, as the *Vixen* came in past the mole, silence had held the fleet. But as she swept across our bows the cheering began; and ship after ship caught it up until it reached the harbour walls, and swept all along the water-front, and crowded wharf and boatshed and rope-walk went up in a roar of joy to greet him. We knew that we had longed for him as he had longed for us; and we cheered Alkibiades home, back to his own again, as never man was cheered before. Some of us wept, too, I think. I am not even sure that I was not one of them.

# 15

## The Soldier

The next day, Alkibiades spoke to the Assembly. It was a magnificent speech, touching more in sorrow than in anger on his exile, and going on to assure us that Tissaphernes had promised that if he could only trust us he would sell his own silver bedstead before the Athenian Navy should want for anything.

When he had done, we shouted ourselves hoarse for him, voted him to the chief place among our Generals; and then the rank and file came pressing about him, demanding to be led at once against the Oligarchs at home.

We are a people very fond of pulling down the memory of our great men; and I suppose one day they will say in the streets of Athens that Alkibiades cared for nothing but himself and the popularity that was meat and wine to him. But such a man, finding himself our darling again, would have done as we wished; and he did not. He had gained what he had been working for so long—he was back with his own again, shouted for, kindled by our love; and he risked it all, rather than lead us on a course that would have left our rear unguarded to the Spartan fleet.

He refused, telling us, when he could make himself heard above the clamour, that now we had given him the official status of a General, his first task must be to return to Tissaphernes and see that the Persian's promise was made good.

I have wondered since, if he still thought he could steer the Satrap into giving us the help we needed; but truly, I think he did. He was no fool, and it would have been foolish to make that speech about the silver bedstead, except in good faith.

He sailed for Sardis next day.

I was sent aboard with a message for the Trirarch, just before the *Vixen* sailed; and my message delivered, I had just turned to go over the side again into the waiting boat, when I found myself face to face with Alkibiades. He looked at me for a moment, and then he did what no one else had done (but perhaps I was becoming a little more civilized to the eye by that time), he recognized me.

He said, "Arkadius! You here!" And despite myself, it was as though the sun came out.

I said, "Sir," as woodenly as I knew how.

"Who are you serving with? What ship?"

"Second of marines with Ariston of the *Hesperus*."

His golden brows jerked up under his helmet rim. "That's a step down from lieutenant of marines with the *Icarus*."

"It's a step up from the stone quarries," I said.

His face went stiff for an instant. "Are you the only one of the *Icarus* marines left?"

"So far as I know. Some were killed in the earlier fighting, or the retreat of course."

And then he asked for young Astur.

It was likely that he would, of course; but I had forgotten that they were some kind of kin, and I was silent a moment; and I suppose my silence told him most of the story, for he said, after that moment, "Leave it. The boy's dead and it makes no difference how he died."

"He was wounded before we went into the quarries. Scarcely any of the wounded lived; the flies and the stone-dust saw to that."

A kind of darkness came over his face. He said, "Men die in every war. It is not a thing to hold against the Gods." But I think he meant "against Alkibiades".

"We all came too near death to hold it against anybody," I said. "We were just very tired."

All about us on board was the last moment bustle of departure. A few moments more and they would be hauling in the anchor cable; already the bos'n had gone to his place, his pipes in his hand, and the Trirarch was glancing our way impatiently. I said, "May I go, sir?"

"Yes," he said; and then, "No, wait."

I turned back, enquiringly, and he said, "Arkadius, when I return I shall be taking the old *Icarus* as my flagship again. There'll be a place for a lieutenant of marines."

I remember we were silent for maybe a heart-beat of time, looking at each other; and then I shook my head. "There are plenty of other men to fill it. I am well enough as Ariston's second." He looked surprised. I don't suppose he was used to men turning down the chance to serve close to him.

185

I still don't know why I refused. I told myself I couldn't just abandon Ariston the moment something better came along. I suppose it was Astur, after all. Never let a dead friend spoil your chances.

I went over the side and dropped into the boat, feeling him looking after me, and wondered if I had damned my chances in the Samos fleet.

But soon after he returned—still unsuccessful in the matter of Tissaphernes—I was promoted to lieutenant of marines again, and ordered to join the *Trident*. And I found later that it was on the recommendation of Alkibiades.

Soon after that, envoys arrived from the Four Hundred, among them our unlamented Democrat Admiral, Phrynichus, who had gone over to the Oligarchs to save his unpleasant skin. What possessed the Four Hundred to send him, I cannot imagine. Their reception would have been chancy enough without that . . .

When they mounted the rostrum to speak to the Assembly that had been called to hear them, the air was as thick with shouts of "Death to the traitors!" as it was with rotten vegetables and bad eggs. One of my lads had got a very dead cat from somewhere. I should have stopped him throwing it, but I took care not to see until it was too late. There began to be an ugly surge forward among the troops, and I really believe the thing would have ended in murder, if Alkibiades himself had not sprung on to the rostrum and got them a hearing simply by being there.

When he could make himself heard, their spokesman took over boldly enough, telling us that the Oligarchs had taken power in Athens, not to subdue the city or betray her, but to save her from the bungling of the Democrats who were so hopelessly mishandling the Athenian war effort. As for the accounts that we had heard of murders and floggings, they were gross fabrications. To hear him talk, you would have thought there never had been such merciful and high-minded men in Athens since the days of the Kings. We heard him out, with Alkibiades' bright amused blue eye on us; and we did not believe a word of it.

And when he had done speaking, the clamour broke out again; a new clamour, this time, or rather an old one revived; for the shout began among some of the crews, that Alkibiades must lead them against Piraeus, to be done with these liars and traitors and restore Athens to her old state.

Alkibiades stood there; the envoys looking small beside him and nothing but his presence saving them from a very unpleasant death.

Some of us began to shoulder through to make a guard about the rostrum; several of my lads came with me, even the hero of the dead cat incident, for this was a different and an uglier thing. And gradually Alkibiades got them quietened again. When they were in a mood to listen once more, he looked round at us, gathering us all in. He still had the power of making the least and furthest man in a crowd feel that he was speaking to him direct. Then he began. "Lads, are your memories so fogged with Samian wine that you can't recall raising this self-same garboil less than a month ago? Or the answer that I made you then? It is the same answer now, and for the same reasons. If we go back now as you wish, to deal with the Oligarchs, it means civil war. Do any of you want civil war running through the streets of Athens? Also, if we go, leaving the squadrons of the Spartan League at Miletus with the Phoenician fleet maybe joined to them, the Island Empire, with none to guard it, is going to fall like ripe fruit when someone shakes the bough. If that's what you want, you can choose out a new Commander and sail for Piraeus tomorrow, *but I'm not leading you!*"

And they were quiet. I don't believe anyone but Alkibiades could have done it. It was like watching a superb driver bring a bolting chariot team back under control again. The men quietened, and out of the quiet someone shouted, "What are we to do, then?"

"This," Alkibiades said. "We will send these men back safely as they came, to carry our orders to the Athenian government." Then turning to the envoys, he spoke to them, smiling courteously, but in the same tone pitched to carry to every man in the Assembly.

They were to carry back to Athens his orders that the Assembly of five thousand, which, though not the full Assembly of the old democracy, was reasonable enough, might remain at least for the present. But the Four Hundred must go. Above all, the five who ruled the Four Hundred must go. Phrynichus turned a dirty yellow when he said this. And having said it, he became all at once honeyed. "When that is done, and Athens is fit for decent men to consort with again, we will look for some means of healing the sad rift between her and Samos." And then last of all, when he was already half turned to leave the rostrum, he added as by an afterthought, "If anything—unfortunate—should happen to either Athens or Samos, it would be a sad thing for the survivor, left with no one to be reconciled *with*, and the full strength of the Spartan League to face alone."

Next day the Athenian envoys went home. It must have been annoying for them to realize that their being alive to sail at all they owed to Alkibiades; and that he had quite clearly found the situation amusing.

## The Citizen

Athens had become a strange city, in which men dared not speak their thoughts aloud lest the friend they spoke to should be an agent of the Four Hundred. Indeed it seemed to me at that time that Athens, the Athens I had known, was dead and stinking. But before the Four Hundred had been much over a month in power, there began to be signs of a rift among them, between the extremists led by Paesander and Phrynichus, and the more moderate men such as Theramenes; and when the envoys returned from Samos with Alkibiades' order that the Four Hundred were to be abolished, or rather, since nobody else could do it, that they were to abolish themselves, the rift not unnaturally widened. Not that that helped Athens. The extremists had still the upper hand, and used it with the ruthlessness of desperate men, while it was still theirs.

The embassy they had sent up to Agis at Dekalia had come back with no success behind them. Now they sent another to Sparta itself; and meanwhile they pressed on with building the sullen great fort down at Piraeus, and at home in Athens itself they took steps to see that any spirit of revolt was kept well trampled down, among ordinary people.

It was at that time that they called at our house one night, and took my father away. He had always been too apt to speak his mind in politics. I got between them and the door (I don't know what I thought I could do, there were four of them), and I remember my father looked at me, his hair rumpled and his face a reddish grey, and a dignity about him quite different from his dignity in the shop, and said, "Don't be a fool, Timotheus, you can't help me, and who's to look after your sister if she is left with no man at all?"

Next day we heard that he had drunk hemlock in prison, rather than face trial for his heinous crimes. That was the usual story. If he had lived a few more days he would have escaped the hemlock altogether, for the time of the Four Hundred was almost all run out.

They gave us back his body. I had never got on well with him, but I suppose he had something of my heart. I know that I felt closer to him in the moment they took him away than ever I had

188

done before; and I gave him a decent funeral as funerals went in those lean times; a better one than I could afford, with Tekla dependent on me. I had scarcely buried him when news came that Euboa, which had revolted from us some while before, had called for Spartan aid, and a fleet was making ready to sail from Gythion in answer to their call. But in a few days more, the rumour was running through Athens that the fleet was not intended for Euboa at all, but had been invited by the Four Hundred to enter Piraeus, to take possession of the city. Theramenes had said as much, standing up in Council. Instantly the trouble between the moderates and the extremists flared into the open. The moderates claimed that the extremists had meant treachery all along, and that the new fort being built on the mole was intended for covering the ships of the Spartan League and holding the harbour against the Samos fleet if they came to interfere.

Next day it was known that the Spartan fleet, after raiding Aegina, was waiting off Epidauros for a wind to attack Piraeus. That morning Phrynichus was murdered in the Agora; and the man who did it got clean away. I don't think the crowd were too eager to catch him.

By noon, word came flying up to the city that the Spartan fleet were standing off Piraeus. The soldiers employed on building the mole fort had struck work. The whole port had gone up in revolt. The Four Hundred had issued orders for its instant suppression, but since the soldiers were in it too, there was nobody to carry the orders out. We heard that Theramenes himself had gone rushing down to cope with the situation; but it was beyond him, or any other man, except possibly one. By evening we heard that the Spartan fleet had made for Salamis for the night, and troops and townspeople were combining to pull down the fort.

"It's the end of the Four Hundred," said old Episthenes, our next-door neighbour. And it was. They met once more, early next morning, but by then the troops had actually marched into Athens and encamped with their arms in the old cavalry base by the Temple of the Dioscurii. I shut Tekla, my sister, in the women's chamber and forbade her to come out. It looked unpleasantly like civil war.

But before anything else could happen a horseman came drumming up from Piraeus—all the men of Athens were out in the streets, and I saw him come—shouting that the Spartans were out from Salamis and heading straight for the Great Harbour.

To judge by last night's accounts, there would be little of the mole fort left standing by now; and the port was largely undefended. I remember turning and going back to the shop and through it into our house, to the chest where my father's old equipment was kept, and getting out his spears, as though it was a thing I did every day. My sister heard me and came running despite my orders, to see what was happening and to demand the meaning of the uproar in the streets.

I told her, and bade her get some food together if there was anything in the house. She said, "This isn't for you, Timotheus."

I said, "It is for anybody who can hold a spear."

And she began to cry again; she had cried so much since the funeral that my own head ached with it, and said, "Not you as well as Father. Timotheus, you can't go, you're a cripple."

I heard the trumpet sounding from the Temple of the Dioscurii.

But in the end she got me the food and a cloak, then went back to the women's chamber as I bade her, and barred the door; and I was out in the street in time to join the stream of boys and old men heading for the port. The troops had of course gone ahead by then. I could not keep up even with the old men, but I've always been able to walk a good distance if I could take my time, and I arrived at last, though somewhat late. Our few ships, partly manned, were strung across the harbour mouth, and the quays and the long mole right out to the remains of the fort were lined with what troops we had, and every last man and boy, even slaves and foreigners, who could carry a spear. I took my place among them, and in that unlikely moment I was happy, with a young man's happiness in the feel of a spear shaft in my hand and another man's shoulder against mine. Happy also in finding that my city could still stand like this, united in the face of an enemy. These might be her last moments of life, but at least she was not dead yet as I had thought, and when she died it would be a cleaner death.

We could see the Spartan galleys out beyond the harbour mouth, so close that we could make out the devices at their prows and catch the sun-flash on dripping oar blades.

There was a long murmurous silence all along the quays. My leg ached from the long walk, and my mouth was dry, and my hand suddenly slippery with sweat on the unaccustomed spear shaft. The waiting time drew out long and thin . . .

And then, small and clear across the water, we heard a trumpet call from the foremost Spartan trireme. It was echoed from another, and another, and before our eyes the whole fleet went about. It seemed like a dream, and we dared not believe what our eyes told us; but it was true; the galleys were broadside on now, heading past the harbour mouth. They passed almost within bowshot of the mole, and stood away for the open sea.

Rag tag and bobtail that we were, we must have made a better and more warlike showing than we knew.

"What now?" said a trader beside me, shouldering an old spear. "To look at all of us you'd think the war was over! Don't forget the Spartans are still at Dekalia and with Euboa in revolt half our remaining corn supply is gone."

The same thought must have occurred to Theramenes and his party; and the extremists, their plans miscarried, dared make no counter-move; for within a couple of days all the ships in the harbour that had been so hastily manned that morning, had been as hastily victualled and equipped for a longer service, and with hurriedly gathered crews, were off on the trail of the Spartan fleet.

We heard no more of them for several days, and then a single battle-scarred trireme limped back into Piraeus. I was in the shop, checking over the little stock that remained, when I heard the wailing in the street. I went out, with a sudden cold fear on me; and a man was standing by the fountain at the end of the street, shouting his news in a hoarse cracked voice. "Twenty-two ships," he was shouting. "It wasn't a battle, it was a bloody rout! What could you expect with ships half-equipped and half-manned? We're done for—finished; it's all over with Athens I tell you!" And then he sat down on the steps of the fountain and began to cry.

Looking back, I still cannot think what saved us then, unless the Gods made the Spartans mad. We were wide open, and must fall at a touch, no possibility of holding off a single enemy squadron; and they remained at Euboa, and never came.

In the breathing space Theramenes and the new Democratic leaders (not merely moderates now, but Democrats!) made one last desperate effort and got together twenty ships, to guard Piraeus—half-rotten hulks, converted merchantmen, craft half-finished off the slipways like premature children—and while that was doing they formally dispossessed the Four Hundred, who in fact had already ceased to exist, and called an Assembly of the Five Thousand.

I was not one of them; it was not the old days when every citizen was free and expected to attend the Assembly. But the news of their first vote was in the streets almost before they had cast it on the Pnyx. It was a vote to recall Alkibiades.

That night the first autumn rain fell in Athens, pattering on the hot, parched ground, drawing out the scent of the dark scrub from Lykabettus and Colonus to breathe cool across the city. And the whole thirsty earth seemed to sigh and stretch itself and drink. I remember that a lovely lightness of heart seemed to come upon the city. Our prospects were as black as ever, but the magic of Alkibiades' name was in every mouth, and the little myrtle tree in our courtyard lifted up its head and drank in the rain.

## The Seaman

Phrynichus and his bunch of beauties had only departed a few days when Alkibiades sent for me one evening. I dropped whatever I was doing and went up, for the summons had an urgent sound to it; and found him on the terrace of the fine white house above the town where he had taken up his quarters. He was leaning on a saffron painted column and looking down toward this merchant-man that had put into harbour earlier in the day.

He swings round as I comes out on to the terrace, and says, "Tissaphernes has bestirred himself it seems. He's off to Aspendus, and the Spartan Commander with him."

I whistles. The idea of Tissaphernes doing anything more active than taking a morning's ride on a well-schooled horse with a belled falcon on his fist seems unlikely. "Who brought you that news?"

He jerks his head in the direction of the merchantman.

"And you're sure it's true?"

"No. But my scouts don't generally make mistakes."

He was wearing the dress of an Athenian General again; but the difference in him was deeper than that. He had done another of those changes of his that seem to reach down to wherever it is a man keeps his soul. He had laid aside the Persian noble with the eye-paint and the silk diadem; and he looked now as though his whole life had been spent on the deck of a galley; like a man doing the thing that he knows and loves best in the world, and burning with a restless inner fire.

"The Phoenician fleet is at Aspendus," I says.

"I hadn't forgotten. Close on a hundred and fifty strong, and if they link up with the Spartan League that's the last hope gone for Athens."

"Do you think that's what it means?"

"I can't think of anything else likely to take Tissaphernes and the Spartan Commander to Aspendus. They must have decided that the time has come to close in for the kill."

"And has it?" I says, feeling my mouth suddenly a bit dry.

He stands leaning against his saffron column with his thumbs stuck into his belt, looking at me, and I sees the old lazy sunshiny look back in his eyes that most times means foul weather brewing for somebody else. "What do you think, Pilot?"

"I think you've another of your neat bits of devilry in mind."

"It's a time for devilry," he says. "You know as well as I do, that the last hope of getting Persia in on our side is gone. But that's not to say we have to sit back and watch them go in with Sparta. I've done my humble best to foster distrust and ill-feeling between them; and I must admit I thought I was doing none so badly—till now."

"And now it's pretty clear that they're planning to join forces after all, and attack either Piraeus or Samos."

"So we must try sowing a little extra distrust and dissension—a catch-crop, as it were—and without undue loss of time. Have the *Icarus* ready to sail by noon tomorrow. I have already sent orders to the Trirarchs of the First Squadron."

I suppose I goggles at him, for he grins, and says, "I know; a Commander of any intelligence would see at once that the only chance was to keep the fleet together, and head for Athens to try to prevent a blockade, or bide here at Samos and try to save the Island Empire. But which, Pilot, which? No, my way is better."

Next morning he takes a fine lighthearted farewell of the troops on Samos, telling them fairy-tales about bringing them back the Phoenician fleet for allies if they're good, and don't burn down the island while he's away; and at noon we sails for Aspendus with a squadron of thirteen triremes. But I'm the one standing close enough to him to see his face, and I knows him better than most; and it's the face of a gambler making a desperate throw.


## The Soldier

In the Bunch of Grapes that evening, Callias of the *Hypolita* said, "Well, that's the last we shall see of him."

I put down the shared wine cup on the bench between us. "Meaning?"

He shrugged. "My dear Arkadian—he's going over to Sparta again. With things looking as ugly as they do for us at the moment, it's the obvious answer."

"Not to me, it isn't," I said.

"Oh come! Have the stone quarries robbed you of your wits?

Or your memory?" And then he laughed. "Oh, you needn't pretend to be so much his man; all Samos knows you could have had the *Icarus* marines and you turned the offer down."

I wanted to say a great many things to Callias at that point, but could not think of words sufficiently foul for any of them. I picked up the wine cup—I remember doing it very carefully, as though it was something that needed to be done with great accuracy—and poured what was left of the wine over his head.

He came for me like a bull, then; poor Callias, his size, next to his stupidity, was always his undoing. I tripped his feet from under him and threw him on my hip. He went down with his mouth open, all arms and legs, and we fought it out under the benches among the feet of the other customers, until the shout went up that Thrasybulus was coming up the street; and then several of them pulled us apart.

Thrasybulus was a great one for discipline, especially among his officers, and we'd probably both have lost our lieutenancies if he'd found us at it. But we grew good at standing by each other in the Samos fleet. Samos City was a plague spot in many ways, but I never knew men so close knit as we were. Perhaps it was because of that that our hates, as well as our loves, grew so strong.

## The Seaman

We joined the Spartan fleet at Aspendus, a little apart from the great Phoenician squadrons that I didn't like the look of at all. Alkibiades sent word across to the Persian Satrap's state galley, beginning with all the formal courtesies, and suggesting a meeting between himself and Tissaphernes, for he had something of great importance to discuss.

"And what would that be?" says I.

And he laughs, and says, "I'll think of something. The main thing is that it should sow a little fresh distrust where it will do most good—and that the Spartans and the Phoenicians should see what a dear friend is Alkibiades to the Persian Satrap."

And in due time, off he goes in the ship's boat, with his best cloak on and oil of rosemary in his hair and the beginnings of his re-grown beard.

I sees him on the deck of the Persian galley, with his arm lying across Tissaphernes' plump shoulders, and I reckon the Spartan Admiral sees it, too; and then they goes ashore together. I've no idea what story Alkibiades tells the Satrap, or what excuse he makes for joining him. All I know is that for four days they sends each other wine, and sups together in the little blue and crimson pavilion Tissaphernes has had set up for him ashore under some shade trees beyond the town, and walks the decks of both ships leaning on each other's shoulders. And the Spartan Admiral, the couple of times I sees him, looks like squally weather.

On the last evening they sups on board the *Icarus*, and plays kotabos after, laughing like boys as Alkibiades teaches Tissaphernes the Greek game; and tries to throw each other's initials on the deck in the lees of the wine.

And when Tissaphernes has gone back to his own ship, My Lord says, "Get watered and victualled at first light, Pilot, we're for Samos again."

"With the Phoenician fleet for allies?" I says, jerking my head at the long lines of them drawn up and blackening the moonlight all along the shore. "And talking of water, will you look at my deck? I've been half a day in battle and come out with a cleaner deck than that."

"At least with the Phoenician fleet not as enemies," he says, "and talking of water, your damned deck will scrub."

So we pulled out for Samos at noon next day; and when we beached the squadron at their old berths, found that while we were away two things had happened: over half the remaining Spartan fleet had sailed from Miletus, heading north and Thrasybulus had sent off three fast scouting vessels to keep them in view, but there was no further news of them yet. And a fast penteconta had come in from Athens, with word that the city had thrown out the Four Hundred, and bringing Alkibiades' recall.

He read it when the envoys brought it to him, standing beside the beached galley. And when he had finished he let the parchment roll up on itself and looked up and said, "This is the second time Athens has called me home in mid-campaign, gentlemen."

The envoys did their best to look pleasant and as though they did not know what in the world he meant. But he only smiled at them affably and shook his head. "Not this time. Not yet. I'll come when the time is ready. But now for a while, I've other things to do."

Three days later he took the first squadron and a few more, and headed for Cos. Cos itself is nothing, but it is easily held and makes a good base; and just across the straits from it is Hali-carnassus, where the East comes and goes and the markets drip with gold and Tyrean purple and essence of roses as a honeycomb

195

drips with honey. The merchants were no more keen on lightening their purses than most of their kind; but the fleet sorely needed paying, and so we strung the squadron across the harbour mouth with their rams smiling at the merchant vessels along the mole, and all our marines on deck, and that made a powerful argument.

We'd have got still more if we could have waited a day or two longer; but we got news of the Spartan fleet that had sailed from Miletus; they had gone to throw in their lot with the Persians of the Hellespont, and the Samos fleet was out after them. "It's pleasant to think we didn't waste our time at Aspendus," Alkibiades says thoughtfully when the dispatch came. "Our visit must have decided Admiral Mindarus against waiting for Tissaphernes' help any longer; so he'll try Pharnobazus in his stead . . . Make ready for sea again, Pilot; it's a pity we can't stay to milk the cow dry, but I've a feeling we may be needed elsewhere."


## The Soldier

We got twenty-one of the Spartan League ships off Cynoscura, for fifteen of ours, and the Commanders called it a victory, and sent word back to Athens—chiefly I think because they knew that Athens needed a victory as a sick man needs hope to hold on to. But it did not seem like a victory to us who fought it; there is too little difference between fifteen and twenty-one, and the Spartan fleet was not driven off the seas. Indeed, the fighting that began at Cynoscura never really ceased, but trailed on into a series of skirmishes and small scattered dog-fights about the mouth and southern reaches of the Hellespont; and they in turn intensified and became more general until on a squally autumn morning, we found ourselves drawn up in battle formation, facing the whole Spartan fleet in the narrows opposite Abydos, where the mountains of Phrygia come down almost to the water's edge. The lower land of Chersonese Thrace to the west was growing green with the autumn rains; and the rain squalls came sweeping over it, spattering on the decks as we waited, hissing in the water about the oar blades that scarcely moved, just holding us against the current. And then the trumpets sounded and we raised the Paean, and the rowers bent to the oar looms and sent the galleys springing forward. We lined the fighting deck; and I remember how the *Trident* lifted and nose-dipped to the swell; and ahead of us, shadowed below the foamed and rain-pocked surface, the Spartan rams . . .

We fought them all day; but in the eddies and racing currents of the narrows it is not possible to hold to any intelligible fighting pattern; and by evening, the battle had become a scattered dog-fight, and seemed likely to end as inconclusively as Cynoscura had done. Marsyas, my second, was gone, shot below the breast and toppling over the side with the air of surprise men so often wear in their dying. And I remember the chill greyness closing on my heart, dragging it down within me, because once again we had lost men and galleys to no purpose; and I knew how a wave feels when it breaks with all its power and forward rush spent, and begins to fall back upon itself. That is dangerous knowledge for a fighting man—and I would not be the only man in the fleet to have reached it.

And then, as we hung on the turn, suddenly from the galley astern of us a shout went up. I was busy just then, but I snatched a glance that way; and there, ruffling up the straits came a new squadron. The evening light struck on the gilded leopard-head prow of the *Icarus* in the van; they came on at racing speed, the white water curling back over their rams; and if a squadron could be said to swagger . . .

For a moment the breath caught in my throat, and I wondered if Callias could have been right after all. Alkibiades to our aid? Or Alkibiades acting spearhead for the Phoenicians?

For that one long moment, both fleets seemed to hang in uncertainty. I suppose the Spartans were wondering exactly what we were wondering ourselves. And then from the *Icarus* there broke out the blue and white ensign of Athens. The oars changed their rhythm, and we saw the steersman swing his whole weight over with the steering oar; and the *Icarus* came about in a curve like a sea swallow, her whole squadron behind her, and bore down from windward into the densest massing of the Spartan fleet!

Gods! How we cheered him! The *Alcestis* and the *Marathon*, the *Trident* and the *Vixen* and the *Hesperus*! Every ship in position to do so swung in behind or beside him, thrusting through the water like hounds slipped from the leash. I remember leaning out from the fighting deck, sword in hand, as we swept on, and the crash and shudder as our ram took toll of a Spartan trireme below the water-line, and the heave as the rowers backed water to shake off the kill.

The ships of the Spartan League broke and ran before us, and we drove them toward the land.

Again and again the rams made their killing; and others we engaged quarter-bow to quarter-bow, and swept from end to end.

Some of the galleys grounded in shoal water close in to Abydos, and their men splashed ashore, and still we went after them, till we were within a finger's breadth of grounding ourselves; and we went over the side and after them still. Pharnobazus' cavalry that had been waiting on the shore, pushed forward to cover them, thrusting their horses even down into the shallows. But the light was growing uncertain by that time, the light of a stormy sunset that shone in their eyes and not in ours, and showed us the tall blue crest of Alkibiades way up ahead of us; and among shallows and sand-dunes and rocks and tamarisk scrub, there's not much to choose between horse and foot.

By nightfall, when the fires of the burning galleys began to bite, we had regained every ship that had been captured from us earlier in the day, and had taken thirty of the Spartans', beside those wrecked and sunk or burned out.

Athens had her victory.

# 16

## The Seaman

Tissaphernes must have found himself an uncommon worried man, because next thing we knew, he was up from the south to confer with Pharnobazus, and they're not what you might call drinking cronies, those two.

And the very day that we hears of his coming, Alkibiades starts making ready to go visiting yet again.

I says, "You've made enough trials at getting Persian help for Athens; what in Typhon's name makes you think you'll stand a better chance this time?"

"Abydos," he says. "A naval victory might just tip the balance and decide our dear friend to come in on the victor's side. There's a chance—a damnably slim one I grant you; but it's worth the taking."

So he gathers his Admirals together and bids them keep a tight eye on Abydos. "For I've an idea the Spartan fleet may be getting reinforcements soon, and our own position at Sestos is none too secure." (We'd made fleet headquarters at Sestos by then.) "If the need arises before my return, take the fleet round Cape Helles and make winter camp on the west coast out of their way." They didn't above half like the suggestion that they couldn't handle the Spartans without him. Then he orders out the choicest of the Halicarnassus pickings—if any other Commander had done it there'd have been a mutiny—and sails stuffed below deck with bales of silk and jars of oil of roses, with amber and storax and gold. There's a magnificent black-maned lion's skin, too. I says, "You wouldn't like purple sails worked in silver while you're about it?"

And he says, "Very much, Pilot, but I'm in too much of a hurry to wait for the dyers and embroiderers."

So we sails for the Propontis with three others of the squadron; leaves the galleys at the port for Daskylon with their crews to guard them, and gets horses for ourselves and pack-ponies for the gifts, and pushes on up to the Satrap's capital; Alkibiades and me and a couple of Trirarchs, with the *Icarus* marines by way of escort.

Daskylon clings like a colony of swallows' nests under the eaves of its mountain; but Tissaphernes had his camp on the level ground below the town. He had come to talk with Pharnobazus, but I'm thinking they weren't sure enough of each other to share the same city walls. From the outside the great dark tents had something the look of crouching animals on the mealy paleness of the first snow; but inside they were coloured and rich enough to make a man think of the pavilion in the Paradise of Alkibiades at Sardis. The tent that was made over to us had rugs patterned like a flower garden, with lilies and fishponds and pomegranate trees and flying birds spread on the cold ground, and the dark skin walls lined with hangings of blue and violet cloth; and cushions of fine skins were piled high for our ease; and they brought us good food and better wine; but none the less, the place had the smell of a trap. I tells Alkibiades so, but he only laughs and says it's the camels.

The pack-ponies were unloaded, and slaves carried Alkibiades' gifts away, with his message to Tissaphernes; and the pack saddles were stacked about the tent-poles; and we made ourselves comfortable and waited. It was well on into the next day when messengers came from Tissaphernes, bringing Alkibiades a present of a talking bird with a gold chain on its leg, and bidding him into the Satrap's presence.

He had been ready for the summons since first light, his best cloak on and his beard scented; and walking up and down the tent, looking dangerous, while the rest of us played draughts and pretended not to notice. But the summons, when it came, was courteous enough. Only, when I and the lieutenant of his marine guard got up and would have followed him, we were met by crossed spears in the tent opening; and the official who had brought the message, said, "The summons of the Satrap is for his dear friend Alkibiades alone."

I knew the man of old; and many's the time I'd have liked to flatten his smirking face for him. But Alkibiades turned and looked at us, one long look, and we fell back and let him go on alone. I watched from the tent opening, how he went up through the camp, past the picket lines and the dark humped tents toward the great tent of the Satrap with its fluttering pennons, in the midst of all.

And then we sat down again and waited. I don't think any of us was too happy. The day dragged on, and Alkibiades did not return. And presently slaves brought lamps, and the fading daylight beyond the looped back tent-flap turned deep blue. By that time we had given up trying to play draughts, and half of us were standing and walking about. Great bowls of steaming kid's flesh were brought to us at the time of the evening meal; and we heard the ponies stamping in the picket lines, and a thin wind came siffling over the steppe-lands, thrumming faintly through the taut tent-ropes; and beyond, were the evening sounds of the camp.

And then suddenly, I had had enough of it. I remember getting up from the food bowls with my mouth full of kid, and hitching at my sword in its sheath—we had none of us unarmed—and saying to the faces that turned towards me, "I'm away to see what's happened."

The Trirarch of the *Marathon*, the senior officer there, gets up also, and looks at me with narrowed eyes. "Our orders were to stay here, and I'll not have you running this whole company into trouble."

"I'm away to see what's keeping Alkibiades."

"I forbid it," says he, with his jaw jutting.

"Forbid and be damned!" says I, and out I goes.

I'd half-expected to find my way barred by crossed spears again, but there was no guard on the tent opening.

I goes towards the great tent; the acid smoke of the camel-dung fires drifts low in the cold air, and the ragged flares burns between the tents and the picket lines. A group of tents makes a kind of forecourt to the Satrap's huge pavilion, and as I comes up to the first of them, the same court official steps suddenly into my way. I'd have thrust past him, but I sees that the open space before the pavilion is full of the Satrap's Nubian guard, with the flare-light shining on their spears; and I've enough sense to know that if Alkibiades is in any kind of trouble, tangling with the Satrap's guard isn't going to be the best way to get him out of it.

The official says, "Ah now, here's a fortunate meeting, for I was about to send for you."

He's eating sugared rose-petals out of the palm of his hand.

I says, "Were you so? And why would that be?"

"Because your Lord Alkibiades wishes to see you, and the Satrap has graciously given orders that his wish is to be granted," he says.

I don't much like the sound of that; and I likes it still less when he makes a gesture with the hand that isn't full of sweet stuff, and two of the Nubian guard steps up on either side of me. But before I can ask what it's all about, he nods, and turns back into the tent behind him, still eating sugared rose-petals.

One of the Nubians points the way we should go, and we goes. Across the open space and between two tents on the far side to another space beyond, walled in as far as I could make out, with uprooted camel thorn, which looked to be the Satrap's baggage park. The dark humped shape of yet another tent rose in the midst of it, with more guards posted about it; my own two falls back, and I goes in alone—and finds Alkibiades sitting very comfortably on an embroidered camel pad beside a brushwood brazier. I thinks for the moment that he's alone, but then another man stirs in the shadows and gives a dry cough. I suppose I glances that way, for Alkibiades says pleasantly, "Only one of Tissaphernes' friends, one of that illustrious body, the Eyes and Ears of the King, set here to keep a check on our conversation."

"In Poseidon's name, what's happened?" I demands.

"Have they not told you? My dear, you behold in me the Satrap's most wretched prisoner. You said it was a mistake to come, didn't you?"

And all I can think to say is, "Why? Why?"

He says, "Our friend the noble Tissaphernes is uneasy. Really uneasy this time. It seems that evil-minded men have made complaints against him to the Great King, accusing him of dilatoriness in aiding the Spartans." (This he says, flicking up an eyebrow at the faint movement from the man in the shadows.) "Therefore he seeks to prove his good faith—as though it needed any such proof—by the capture of the Athenian Admiral."

My first real thought is to tear the place apart, and he must have seen that in my face, for he says quickly, "No, Pilot, not a good idea."

I'm not clever with words, and I don't know how to put it, not with the King's Eyes and Ears listening in the shadows. So I drops the Attic Greek for the clicking patois of the seafaring kind from Sidon to the Pillars of Heracles. "Not now, with no more than a dozen of us, but when the fleet hears—"

He says carefully, still sticking to the Attic, "My poor friend, you speak wildly, and forget that I do not understand that tongue. Now listen, Antiochus, for it was to tell you this, that I have been howling the place down to get word with you—apart from the fact that I knew you would run amok and end up with a spear in your belly, my old hothead, if you were left long without word of me. Listen as you never listened before; any attempt to break me out, either from here or from Sardis, or during the journey between the two, would be disastrous. It might very well bring the Persians in after all, and on the Spartan side. And if the attempt failed, the Athenian Navy would then be called on to face the Phoenician fleet as enemies, lacking the only Commander it has who could handle the situation."

"So we leave the Commander in the Persian Satrap's hands for so long as he likes to hold him—likely until he meets with a fatal accident," I says. "That's fine counsel, that is!"

And I sees the warning flicker in his eyes. It's not the easiest thing to hold that kind of talk, with every word of it going back to the Satrap—and the Son of the Sun himself for all I knows.

"Oh not so long. I am convinced that I shall rejoin you before the winter is out."

"How?"

"My dear Antiochus, you mistake the situation. There is no question of my being held indefinitely nor of the—fatal accident that you suggest. Tissaphernes is at heart still my good friend, I am convinced of it; and when this unfortunate coil of false accusations against him is disentangled, I shall be immediately set at liberty." That's for the King's Eyes and Ears in the shadows. For me, he adds grinning, "My famous luck is with me yet. When it deserts me again, I shall know. And then I'll turn cautious and sit at home by the fire."

And I knows what he's really telling me is that he'll break himself out before winter's end, and we're to leave him to it. And I believes him. He has the look of a man with his luck still on his forehead. And ye Gods! I'm angry! So angry I can barely speak to ask if there's anything more.

"Tell the fleet Commanders all that I've told you," he says, "and make very sure that they understand. Remind them of the orders I left with them, and do what you can to see that they're carried out. Go now; I've been promised safe passage out of this camp and back to the coast, for you and the rest of our party—but that of course goes without saying, since *Persia and Athens are not at war*."


## The Whore

In the women's quarters there are screened windows and galleries that look down into the palace forecourt; and when we heard the trumpets, the Satrap's wives ran to see the cavalcade ride in.

When one spends much of life shut behind the walls of the women's chambers, the sight of a few men and a handful of steaming horses makes a change. Something to look at for a few moments and talk about afterwards for days.

The rest of us, slaves and concubines, ran to look, too. The scene below us was cut up into four-petalled shapes by the fret of the window screens. Snowy forecourt and running figures and the flare of torchlight, all held within the dark blurred outline of the rose-fret as I pressed my face against it. I saw the horsemen come through, the hooves of the horses skidding a little on the half-frozen ground; the dark faces of the Nubian guard under their pointed helmets; and then the Satrap himself, riding with his officers around him, all drab-coloured in furs and sheepskin with here and there the glint of a jewelled hilt, and the bird-wing gleam of coloured silks beneath; and the little bells chiming on the horses' bridles. The Satrap looked like a bear, hunched in his furs on his horse's back—swag-bellied as a bear looks when it sits up like a man.

Behind him followed more of the guard, and riding in the midst of them hedged with their spears, a tall man swathed in sheepskins. He was bareheaded, and when the torchlight struck on his hair it shone the colour of newly burnished bronze; and the heart in my body knew him even before he looked up in passing close beneath the gallery, and the torchlight showed me his face.

All along the gallery there was a murmuring and exclaiming and twittering; a little flurry of excitement.

Then someone thrust between me and the girl peering over my shoulder, crying, "Let me look! Let me look, it's not fair!" And I lost my place and could see only the blue dusk and the shifting gleam of torches gilding the undersides of the window-fret; and hear the voices and the horses' hooves.

When there was nothing more to see, the women began gathering into little knots. "It is the Athenian!" "It is Alkibiades, and a prisoner!" "What can it mean? Have we had a great victory?" "But I do not think we are at war with the Athenians." "He has hair as bright as a Persian's!" "He has hair like a lion's mane!"

And some were mobbing Arbaces the chief eunuch, with soft coaxings and promises of presents, to find out what had happened and bring them word.

I went away and found a quiet place under the stairway to the fountain court, and crouched there with a fold of my wide skirt pulled over my head. It was very cold there, but it is not easy to find a place in the women's courts of the Satrap's palace where one can be alone and think.

I thought, with my head on my knees and my forearm pressed across my eyes until bursting flowers and coloured sun-wheels spun before me against the blackness. I had not tried to forget the night under the almond tree. I had not tried to remember it. It was, it is, part of me, it breathes with my breathing and beats with the heart in my breast. I had not waited for him to send for me again, in the after-time, before he was gone from Sardis; I had not looked for him to come back. I had accepted the bondage he had put on me, in the dawn when I left the dagger and the white almond flowers on his breast instead of killing him. It was complete and for all time, and needed no renewing.

Crouching in the chill darkness of the fountain court, I did not even know or question whether I most loved or hated him. I knew only that he had returned to Sardis a captive, and that though my own life paid for it, I must find means for his escape. In that brief moment when he looked up into the torches before I was thrust aside from the window, I had seen the look on his face. It was almost gay, his eyes wide and bright, his mouth touched with an east wind smile; and behind it, something I have seen in the eyes of a wild stallion captured in the nets. I knew that given time, a very little time, he would plunge into some reckless attempt at freedom, and end on the spears of the guards.

Somehow, I must get word to him; and quickly, or he was marked for death. And to do that I must have a man to help me; some man that I could trust. My thoughts were scurrying now, like mice; and suddenly they came to rest, not on a man, not a full man, but on Phaeso. He that had looked us over, the dancing girls and I, on the night we went to amuse the Satrap and his dear friend at supper. In the ordinary way there is no one less to be trusted than the eunuchs of the women's court. No use to a woman, cut off from the fellowship of men, they have nothing to gain in life but wealth and power; and nothing else to lose. But Phaeso was a captive like me, taken by a dealer in castrated boys and sold through the market of Cos; and in his case the gelding had been done too late. When that happens, it may take years for the manhood to die. Sometimes it never quite dies at all, and that must be hard to bear. Phaeso had still something of a man's heart and a man's needs in him; and a great bitterness under the gentle rounded outer-seaming. I knew the bitterness because my own cried out to it and found an answer, and I thought I might rely on that bitterness now, as well as on a certain friendship that we had for each other.

I went in search of Phaeso, and when I found him hurrying down a corridor with two more of his kind, I made him a certain signal that we had between us. He went on with the others, but I waited where I was, and in a while he came back. I asked him to find out for me where the Athenian was lodged and how he was guarded.

"You will hear all that soon enough," he said in his light cool voice. "The women's courts know everything almost before it happens."

I said, "But I want to hear even more quickly and in more detail; and I want to be sure that what I hear is the truth."

He said, "Why do you want these things, Timandra?"

"For good reasons that I have. Do this for me, Phaeso, there is no one else in the whole palace that I can trust."

He took my hand, and I let him, though despite my liking for him, my flesh crawled a little at the touch of his. He said (it was the only time I ever heard him speak so), "In a few more years, I shall have ceased to care. You will be able to buy my favour for a gift, and I shall betray you to any who offer a larger gift than yours; and the Head Wife will fawn upon me as she does on Arbaces. But for this while, you can trust me, Timandra."

He was so young; far younger than I, though not in years, and his manhood had been taken from him just as he began to feel it stirring; and one day he might be as he had said, but not yet. And grief rose in me because I was prepared to pay his life as well as my own, for Alkibiades'; and in that, as in the loss of his manhood, he was having no choice in the sacrifice. I kissed him then, not as a flute girl fondling a eunuch whose favour she needs, but as a woman kisses a boy.

The next day he sought me out, and told me that Alkibiades had been lodged with all honour in the Guest Court, with two of the Satrap's personal bodyguard constantly before his door; and that the word was that presently he was to be sent to Susa.

So then I bade him do another thing for me. Two or three times in the past—the first time when I was still in the pleasure-house below in the city, I had lain with a certain one of the Nubian guard when he wanted a woman; a man with not much in his head, but the body of a black panther. Some women say black men make the most enjoyable lovers, for their man-part is larger and more potent than a white man's; but I would not myself count him among the few who ever gave me pleasure. It was some time since we had been together, but I thought that I had enough skill in the ways of a woman beneath a man, to draw his interest back again if need be. So I said to Phaeso, "Now get a message to Hanna of the guard, for me. Bid him meet me tomorrow night in the pavilion of the lower paradise. Say that I have a secret to tell him that may make us rich, and that I keep it for him alone, because of certain joys that we have known together."

He said, "Timandra, I have gone blindfold into this for your asking. But now I must know—what wild business have you in hand?"

And then I took the biggest risk of all. I told him the whole truth. If I had been right in believing that I could rely on his friendship and on his bitterness, I should know now.

He said, "It is a small revenge, but even a small revenge is sweet." And then, "But with you, I think that it is a greater matter."

"No," I said. "For me it is a thing that must be done, as a flower must open and die, and the swallows fly north in the spring time."

"And what will happen to you? They will find out."

"I think that they will kill me; but that is no very great matter. But take great care that they can bring nothing against *you*. If they do, I will swear upon the horns of the Lady Ashtaroth that you were nothing in all this but my unknowing tool."

The next night I rubbed spikenard between my breasts, and took a flask of wine with certain herbs added to it. The women of my people have been skilled in the use of herbs since the time of the witch Medea, and they were all quite easy to obtain. Then I slunk out by one of the small postern doors of the Lion Court and down to the lower paradise. It is not hard for a mere flute girl to get out from the women's courts, even at night. If I had been one of the Satrap's wives, it would have been a different matter.

The lower paradise had sunk into disuse since the new Paradise of Alkibiades had come into being; the bushes had not been pruned that autumn, and desolation lay upon the place that was not merely the desolation of winter. At first I thought that it was empty, and I cried out within myself, "What shall I do? Mother of All, tell me what I shall do if he does not come!" But as I drew near to the deserted pavilion he stepped out from the overgrown myrtle bushes and stood in my path, straddling, with his thumbs in his belt.

My breath went out of me in a sigh. "You are come!"

"The little gelding said that you had a secret for me." His smile was a white blur in the darkness of his face, and he cocked his head on one side. "Come now, and tell me what it is, my girl."

"Later," I said. "Let us go into the pavilion." For the door was unfastened and creaking a little in the wind. "See, I have brought you some wine to keep out the cold."

He shrugged and laughed, the soft guttural laugh far back in his throat, of all his kind. And we went into the pavilion. It was almost as cold within as without, but at least we were sheltered from the wind. And I gave him the wine, and when he had drunk, crept close to him, murmuring that his cloak was big enough for us both. I pressed my body against his and as we wormed under the cloak the smell of the spikenard came into his nostrils; and soon the herbs of Ashtaroth were in his blood and his loins, and he thought no more of asking what secret I had to tell.

When he had finished, I felt bruised and sick; for the herbs of Ashtaroth are not gentle. But I knew that he would want me again and again.

We met twice more after that, but those times I mixed no herbs in the wine I brought him, and so, his needs being less urgent, we had time for love-play and even for talking, as well as for the other thing. And so I learned that Hanno was among those who kept guard on the Athenian. And the days and times of his guard duty, which held him from coming to me every night. He told me this to show me how important he was, and how greatly the Satrap trusted him. And then I knew that the Lady of the Moon, the Mother of All things, was indeed holding me by the hand.

Just as we were parting the third time, I asked him with my arm round his neck, "Hanno, will you do something for me tonight? For you and me?"

"What is it?" he asked, cautious as an animal snuffing the wind.

"Give the Athenian a message for me. You can do that?"

"I might be able to, if it's Budas or Narko with me," he said grudgingly. "What is the message, then?"

I took a deep breath, knowing that this was one of the danger moments, like the one when I told Phaeso my plan. I said, "Tell him to wait seven days, and then send word to the Satrap that he sleeps badly in captivity, and would have a night's loan of the palace flute girl he had before." The request was just the kind that Alkibiades would make, as much for devilry as anything else, so that it would not seem strange in the Satrap's eyes. And since he was being kept less like a captive than a guest under guard, it seemed to me most likely that Tissaphernes would grant it. Also, I thought that Alkibiades, if he remembered me, if he remembered that night at all, would guess at some other meaning behind the message, and so it might hold him, for those seven days, from running upon disaster in some mad attempt at escape, on his own. But could I persuade Hanno to take such a message? Already I could feel the anger in him as he caught me by the arms and dragged me against his body. "You ask *me* to tell him that—you bitch!"

I let myself go, yielding under his sweaty hands. "Listen, he means nothing to me; no more than any other of the men I have lain with, excepting you. You are a *man*, strong and black and potent; beside you they are children." I laughed softly. "Black darling, I have lain with many men before you came; have I had less to give you because of that? I shall be with many after you have turned to someone else, and you will care no more than for the swaying of a seeding grass-head in the wind. Listen now, last time I went to him he made it well worth my while; and this time—they have not stripped him of his jewels?—this time he shall make it doubly worth my while; and what he gives me, you and I will share between us. And we will laugh! Think how we will laugh!"

I gentled him round at last, and made him repeat the message over and over again, to be sure that he had it right. And then he had another thought, and asked why seven days.

I said, "Look up there into the sky and tell me what you see."

And he said, "The horns of the Old Moon."

"And in seven days, when you look into the western sky at sunset, you will see the white horns of the New Moon; and that night there will be a great feast of Cybele. But in the dark nights between, among my people the women keep themselves apart from all men."

"I never heard of that custom before," he said, grumbling. I had not, either, but it made as good a tale as any other. And in the long run, no man comes between a woman and the Fierce Mother. So despite his grumbling and cursing, he would leave me in peace for those dark nights; and Alkibiades would get my message, and wait. And I should have time for working out the rest of my plan, and for the gathering and brewing of certain herbs not so easy to come by as the others had been.

A horse I must have too, but there were several posting stables in the town. I gave Phaeso my silver bracelets with the turquoise and enamel mounts—one of the Satrap's wives had given them to me for my help in a certain matter—and bade him see to the hire of a post horse and the providing of food and a thick cloak for the winter journey; and be careful to let no one see his face too clearly. And he came to me two days later, and told me that all was arranged. He would have the horse waiting at a certain place on the night of the feast of Cybele, with a cloak—old he said, but thick and warm—and a wallet of food, and what money was left from the sale of my bracelets.

I did not see Hanno again, and could only trust that he had given the Athenian my message; and I walked in the moonless nights in the wild tangle of the lower paradise, and about the place where the Persians expose their dead to be torn by dogs and kites, and sought out and gathered the herbs I needed.

On the day of the New Moon, I was practising with the dancing girls in the fountain court—we had to practise every day—when Arbaces himself came waddling down the stair and called to me. I laid down my flute and went to him; while the girls huddled together, looking on. He said, "It seems you must have pleased the Athenian, when he sent for you last time he was in Sardis."

My heart leapt sickeningly in my breast, but I managed to give no sign, only wait submissively for what he would say next. He said, "He has asked for you to be sent to him again, since he cannot sleep; and the Satrap has given his leave. Though what the man can find of pleasure in that scrawny body of yours, to warrant a second visit . . . Phaedime, now, *there*'s a plump pigeon for the taking!"

I said softly, "It is maybe that he likes my flute playing."

And he snorted and leered, and said that I should put on my new gold and purple bodice.

For the rest of that day I had to endure the jealousy of the other women, their side-long glances and small barbed words. But living in the women's courts, one grows used to such foolishness.

When the evening meal was over, I put on the bodice of purple and gold striped silk, and the full, rose-coloured Median trousers, and painted my eyes with stybium and green malachite and reddened my lips and cheeks. In my own land we keep such painting for the faces of the dead, so that whenever I looked in the polished silver mirror and saw mine painted so, I thought, 'This is my dead face.' Only there would be no one to paint my face for burial when the time came, here in the alien south.

And when I had been looked over and approved by the chief eunuch, I covered it all with a thick cloak, and went out from the women's courts with my flute. And on the way I took from the secret place where I had laid it by, the last flask of wine that I should take to Hanno.

The guards on the double doors of the Guest Court knew of my coming, and parted spears and let me through with a jest. The latch lifted easily to my hand, and I went in and closed the door-leaf behind me.

I looked up and saw the bare branches of the almond tree. It had snowed a little, earlier, but now the sky had cleared. The new moon was set, but from the city below I could hear the soft bronze throbbing of the Moon-gongs, and the bright flash of cymbals, where the procession of Cybele still wound through the streets. Across the tiny court, a torch flared under the colonnade, and before the door of the same chambers where Alkibiades had been lodged before, two more of the Nubian guard stood with crossed spears. The one on the left was Hanno. I had been wondering all the way, what I should do if his watch had been changed that night. I walked towards them. Hanno challenged; and I said, "It is I, Timandra. The Athenian asked for me, and I am come by the Satrap's order." I stepped into the torchlight, and hovered a moment, smiling up at him, to show that I was grateful and would not forget to show my gratitude; and brought out the wine-flask from under my cloak. His teeth smiled white in the dark ripe-fruit red of his lips. "It is a cold night. I have brought you something to warm you. Both of you—there is plenty for your comrade."

"There's my girl," he said; and to the other, "That's the kind of girl to have, eh, Buba? Even if her bones do show through her skin." And he put out his hand for the flask.

I would have mixed a harmless drug with wine if it could have been done that way. I bore him no ill will, and his comrade I had never even spoken to. But if he lived, he would tell things that were death to Phaeso, and to me. For myself I did not greatly care, but I did not want to be the death of Phaeso, and it was their deaths or his. I had used a kindly poison; no more than a coldness and heaviness that creeps about the heart, and a sleep from which there is no waking. I gave him the flask, and Buba unfastened the door for me, and I went in, and they made it fast again behind me.

There were heavy hangings drawn across the window frets to keep out the winter chill; and it was warm inside, and hazy with the scented smoke of the glowing brazier. A lamp burned in its niche high in the wall, and Alkibiades stood beneath it. He looked across the room to me, and he said, "So you have really come."

"Did you not ask for the flute girl who eased your sleeplessness before?"

He said, "There was always the chance that that was only to keep me quiet for a few days. Or even a very pretty piece of woman's revenge."

"If you expect revenge from every woman you lie with in passing, it is small wonder that you do not sleep well of nights," I said, and walked towards him.

He set his hands round my shoulders. "Little she-wolf, not every woman leaves my own dagger and a spray of flowering almond on my breast . . . What do we do now?"

"We wait. I have given the guards before the door drugged wine to drink. Soon they will sleep." I do not know why I did not tell him then that it was the Long Sleep.

"They refastened the door behind you," he said.

"I know. That is why we must wait. At midnight the Officer of the Guard will make his rounds. When he finds them, before he can cry out or summon others of their kind, you must get him in here—groan, and cry that you are poisoned, and when he comes—"

"He may well summon help first, even so."

"That is a risk that we must take; I do not think that he will do so. If you are poisoned during his guard, it will mean death to him also; that he will know. When he comes, he must find you in the inner room and lying on the bed-place. I will be behind the doorway as he enters, so that he does not see me, and when he bends over you, I will knife him in the back—I have the dagger here—and we can get out."

"Have you drugged the guards at the outer doors also?"

I shook my head. "They would be noticed. With the help of the almond tree we will go another way, over the roof-tops."

"Ah, the almond tree again," he said. "And then?"

"There is a postern door in the outer wall close to the women's courts, that is left unguarded during the feast of Cybele, for certain purposes of the Satrap's women—I doubt if the Satrap knows it. And a horse will be waiting for you."

"Perfect," he said, "except for one thing. It is I that will have the dagger."

"I know where to strike," I said.

But his hands had already found the weapon stowed beside my flute in the silk bindings at my waist. "I do not doubt it, she-wolf, wildcat; but I'll do my own killing." I had caught at the dagger, and we struggled an instant, in silence for the guards before the door, before he twisted it from my grasp. And while I stood panting, he slipped his free arm round me, and pulled me close and kissed me on the mouth.

Outside the door, one of the guards—I think it was Hanno—said something in a puzzled tone; and the other answered, but slow and slurred. I pulled away from Alkibiades and signalled to him to shield the lamp; then went to the window and drew aside a fold of the embroidered hangings and peered out through the fret. They seemed to be still on their feet. But it could not be long now; the cold would hasten the working of the poison.

I drew back from the window and shook my head. We stood looking at each other. In the silence I could still hear the throbbing of the Moon-gongs from the lower city. Somewhere a dog howled; a piece of charcoal collapsed with a tinselly rustle into the red heart of the brazier. And then there was a sharp clatter beyond the door as one of the guard dropped his spear.

Alkibiades flicked up his head like a stallion that scents wolf; and it seemed to me that the noise was enough to alert every living thing in the Satrap's palace. I waited, listening until my ears ached inside my head, for the men on the outer doors to come rushing in; but it must be that the sounds of gongs and cymbals from the city had dulled the clatter of the falling spear before it reached them. The slow heartbeats of time went by, and no one came; and at last I let my breath go in a long sigh, and turned again to the window. Hanno was lying face down on the white-speckled ground. His comrade stooped over him, and even as I watched, swayed forward, and gave at the knees, and with a small surprised grunt, crumpled across him.

"Yes," I said, and turned back to the room. "Now we must make all ready, for when the officer comes we may not have much warning."

Alkibiades pinched out the lamp; in the glow of the brazier, he was all red and black like a warrior on a vase. Then he picked up a thick goat-skin coat that lay across a painted chest, and shrugged himself into it. "It will be cold riding, tonight," he said, as though he were setting out on a quite ordinary journey. We went into the inner room, and when he had pulled on a pair of soft rawhide boots, I helped him make a small bundle of such things as he had that might be useful—especially a purse with a little money. "It's a pity we don't wear as much jewellery as we used to do in my grandfather's day," he said; and I thought for an instant of Hanno and the tale that I had told him; but not for long.

When all was ready, it still seemed a great while that we had to wait. But at last, on the very edge of my stretched hearing, I caught the distant sound of feet. I said, "He's coming!"

And Alkibiades bowed to me like an actor, and went and lay

down on the griffon couch, pulling the coverlid over him. And as the footsteps drew nearer, he began to writhe and moan; he began to retch like a man who has vomited up all but the heart out of his body, and cry out that he was poisoned; but feebly, so as not to rouse up the guards on the outer doorway or any others who might be within hearing.

The steps ceased before the door of the outer chamber, and I heard a startled curse, and knew that the Officer of the Guard was bending over the two out there in the puddled sleet. I held my breath for the next thing. But it was only a heartbeat of time before he was freeing the door and flinging it open. He checked an instant on the threshold, then came striding across the outer room. He flung aside the curtains of the inner doorway. He cried out sharply, "Light of the Sun! What has happened here?" and plunged across to the couch where Alkibiades lay moaning and writhing among the bed-rugs. He bent close over him, for the one small lamp high in its niche gave little light; and Alkibiades' hand came out from the tangle of coverings in a flash of movement; I saw the knife blade blink under the lamp; and the Officer of the Guard gave a little wet cough and crumpled forward across the couch. I never saw it done more skilfully.

Alkibiades pulled himself out from under the body, and wiped the dagger on the man's own cloak. He picked up from the darkest corner, the bundle that we had made ready. He said, "So far, very good." Then he went back across the outer chamber, and through the open courtyard door. I followed, and made it fast behind us, lest it should slam in the rising wind.

He glanced at the two lying in the thin speckled snow, but said nothing; I slipped past him to lead the way. I rolled my own cloak into a bundle, and flung it up to the roof; I should need it, both for the cold, and to cover my flute-girl's finery from anyone we might meet, but I could not climb with its folds to hamper me. It caught on a branch of the almond tree and unfurled, hanging there billowing in the wind, but I could gather it up again easily enough in passing.

I went first, for my lighter weight to test the way. It was easy, scarcely a climb at all, for the almond was old and strong, its crooked branches widespread, and in one place actually over-lying the roof of the little colonnade. I seemed scarcely to have left the ground before I was lying full length along the sloping roof, stayed from rolling off again by the Greek acanthus tiles that edged it, and reaching down for the bundle which Alkibiades held up to me. My fingers just grazed the knot; he shifted stance on to the ball of one foot, to gain another finger's breadth of height; I could see the pale blur of his upturned face through the wind-swayed boughs. I eased myself farther over the edge. At any moment a tile would go crashing; the roof was slippery with its scattering of half-frozen snow. But I had the bundle now; I felt its weight carefully released into my hand, and I pulled back from the edge. There was a movement down below, a swaying among the old knotted branches that was not much more than the wind; and Alkibiades was beside me with my cloak flung round his arm.

"And now where?" he whispered.

"This way—along to the end—"

He came close behind me, his soft rawhide boots as silent on the roof tiles as my own slippers—slipper; I realized that I had lost one in the climb. But it made no matter, they knew that I was with him that night, they would know that it was I who had helped him away. Hanno's death might save Phaeso, but it could not save me.

We came to the end of the colonnade and gained a flat roof beyond; and after that it was simple going, with no more than a scramble from one level to another. And twice a narrow chasm between roofs to be leapt, till we came to another sloping roof, and dropped from it, by way of a wall and a clump of cistus bushes, into an alleyway. And Alkibiades gave me my cloak. The sky was darkening above the roof-tops, fresh snow-clouds coming up before the wind; and no one could have seen whether I was man or woman; let alone that I was a palace flute-girl, now; but oh! the knife-edged cold of that wind on my body through the gay silks that were damp with sweat! I dragged the heavy folds of the cloak round me, and went on, longing to run but not daring to, by the winding alleyways and courts, the flights of steps between walls, the tunnels running between and under houses, that riddle the Satrap's palace like mouse-runs. And so I brought him at last to the unguarded postern in the outer wall.

We crept through, and closed it behind us. To one side a track led off close under the walls and down toward the city, ahead, the cliff path dropped steeply to lose itself in the thickets of the river valley below. The sky had broken again for a little while, and the snow, lying thicker there, gave its own light to the hillside, so that it was clear.

"Come," I said, "there is no cover till we reach the bushes. We must put our trust in the Great Mother, and run." And down the path we went at breakneck speed, keeping to the snowy grass on the very edge of the drop, where the softer ground muffled our footsteps. And every step of the way I thought to hear the shout of a guard on the wall-turrets; but we gained the shelter of the riverside scrub at last, and checked for a moment among the willows and oleanders to draw breath after the nightmare of the winding palace ways and the open track.

It was more sheltered from the wind, down there, and it all seemed very quiet, very empty of life. I began to wonder desperately if Phaeso had kept his promise. And then I heard the restless stamp of a horse and the faint chink of a bridle bit, and knew that he had.

Alkibiades said, "They were dead, those two before the door."

"Yes," I said after a moment.

"You are very thorough."

We were moving forward again, keeping now to the shadows of the bushes. "If they had lived, one would have talked," I said. "That would have been death to me and to—the friend who helped me in all this."

He said nothing more until we came out on the river-bank. The water was running high and yeasty, and against the pale swirl of it was the dark shape of a horse, its bridle looped over a low-hanging alder branch. It swung its head towards us, stamping uneasily. There was no sign of Phaeso himself, and I thought, 'He was afraid to wait here till we came. Well, he has been brave already, for a eunuch.'

And then I almost tripped over something dark lying half across the path. He must have meant me to find him. It was as though he had left me a message, and I knew what it was, even before I stooped, and felt the stickiness of blood on my fingers, and his hand fell away from the hilt of the dagger driven in under his breast.

"What is it?" Alkibiades said.

"It is the friend I spoke of. The friend who helped me in this."

He stooped beside me an instant; then I felt his hand whip to the dagger in his belt—my dagger—and his head go up, searching the shadows of bush and rock.

"It was his own hand on the hilt," I said. "There's nothing to be done here, and no time for you to waste."

I felt his gaze on me an instant in the dark. Then he went to slip the horse's bridle from the alder branch. He sprang on to its back, and brought it fidgeting and plunging round.

"Take his shoes," he said.

For a moment I did not know what he meant, and he said it again, impatiently. "His shoes, woman. We shall have to walk a good part of the road we're taking. He's a small man, they should not be so much too big for you."

A few moments before, everything within me had been crying out to him to take me too. That I was his, and I did not want to die; but most of all, that I was his. But I hung back, none the less; for one long moment I hung back; I think it was for Phaeso, lying there in the puddled snow, who was nothing to Alkibiades but a pair of shoes. He had thought that I was better than I was, and would not desert him to face alone whatever might be coming in payment for that night's work; and so he had made sure that there was nothing to hold me back. And all the while, I would have gone; at a word, a whistle, from Alkibiades, I would have left him without a backward glance. So for that one moment, I nearly stayed.

"You will ride the faster alone."

"I shall ride the faster, the sooner we get away from here. *Take those shoes and put them on*; you're a wildcat, but I'll not have you a dead wildcat because of me."

I took the shoes from Phaeso's feet. They were icy, but so were my own, so that I could scarcely feel the shoes when I put them on—it was not until much later that I found that my right foot was torn and bleeding from going bare on the frozen ground. I left my own embroidered slipper beside him, and turned back to Alkibiades.

He leaned down and caught my wrist, his fingers closing round it in a quick bruising grip. "Your foot on mine. Now—up with you."

So I set my foot on his, and sprang, and next instant was sitting before him in the hard crook of his bridle arm. He heeled the horse from a stand into a canter.

# 17

## The Whore

The hen-speckle of snow on the ground made light enough to ride
by, even though there was no moon; and we rode hard that night,
and before morning took to the hills and lay up in the woods
through the daylight hours. They must have been scouring the
countryside for us, but the Gods were kind, and covered our trail
with a fresh flurry of snow, and neither sight nor sound of hunt
came near our hiding place.

We ate some of the food in Phaeso's wallet and lay down on my
cloak with the other wrapped about us both. We mated then, as
much for warmth, I think, as anything else. He was hasty and
harsh with the urgency of life in him. And afterwards we slept a
little, crushed together with our arms round each other; and it
did not seem to me at all strange or wonderful, but as though it had
always been so.

And at dusk we got up and ate a little more of the food, and
rode on.

By the Great Road it takes three days from Sardis down to
Ephesus, but we headed westward, through the broken country
between the mountains and the broad river valley towards
Magnesia, then took to the high hill tracks where we must travel
by day because it was too hazardous to move at night. Tracks
flanking the shoulders of the mountain with only the emptiness
dropping away below; and deep snow over rock for a treacherous
foothold, and much of the time we must walk leading the horse.
Once I said to Alkibiades that we should leave him behind—and
I am of a horse-people so that I would not lightly think of such a
thing; but Alkibiades said that once through the mountains we
should need him on the other side, and that if the worst came to
the worst he was meat on the hoof.

We were two nights in the mountains, with little food and no
warmth but what we could give each other in the lee of a rock or a

tangle of mountain juniper, while the horse shifted restlessly in his knee hobbles nearby. And Horned Lord of the Wilderness! The huge cold emptiness and the thin harping of the wind!

After the high, frozen winter-death of the mountains, there was a softness in the air like spring along the coast, when we came down towards it on the evening of that third day. We had eaten the last of our food, but we came upon a goatherd who sold me a lump of hard strong cheese for three times its value; and there was grazing for the horse. That night we slept warm among pine needles, and the next day we followed the coast.

On the eighth evening after Sardis, we came down to Clazomenea, and saw Athenian ships in the harbour.

Alkibiades took me to a house in a back street and left me there, saying that I should rest and presently he would come again. The woman of the house was kind. I do not know what Alkibiades had been to her in the past, but whatever it was, it was a long time ago. She gave me hot bean soup, and a rug to sleep under; and I ate and slept. And when I woke, the rags of my flute-girl's clothing, and Phaeso's shoes that I had bound to my feet with strips torn from the hem of my cloak, had been taken away, and fresh clothes lay beside the bed-place. And when I reached out for them, I saw that they were a boy's—good, though shabby and weather-stained —and much the same as I had worn long ago when I rode with the other girls and the young men among my father's horse-herds.

I got up, surprised to find myself so stiff and sore—the years in the women's courts of Sardis had made me soft—and began to pull the clothes on; the close-fitting trousers of dark berry-red cloth, the supple boots, the goatskin jacket with the hair inside and the gold threads worked about the neck. My heart was glad to wear such clothes again, and glad because My Lord had troubled to find them for me in Clazomenea. I had scarcely tied the neck thongs of the jacket, and gathered my hair up under the stocking cap, when I heard voices below; the woman's, and a man's; and the man said, "We've come for Alkibiades' new fancy girl. Orders to take her down to the ship."

I opened the door on to the outer stairway and met the woman coming up.

She laughed when she saw me, and said, "You make a fine boy! I hope you do not mind wearing a dead man's clothes."

"A dead man's clothes?" I said, and I thought of Phaeso, whose shoes had carried me across the mountains.

And she shook her head. "There, and I did not mean to tell you. I had a merchant and his boy here a year or two back—from

219

somewhere away north, they were—and the boy was sick, and worsened and died here; and his clothes were left behind. Maybe the man didn't want to be reminded . . . I meant to sell them, but I never got round to it; and when My Lord bade me find you something for ship-board, I thought they'd be just the thing."

A shout came up from below, and she added hurriedly, "I meant to feed you before you went, but the men from the *Iris* are here already."

"I heard them, calling for Alkibiades' latest fancy girl," I said.

Later, squatting under the bull's-hide awnings when the seamen had left me, I felt the lift of the deck under me, and heard the pad of the sailors' feet and the creaking of the timbers, that were part of a strange world to me then; and Fear sat beside me in the almost-dark, and I thought that it would have been better for me to have left Alkibiades to break his own way out of prison. I had grown used to life in the women's courts of the Satrap's palace. I had even a few friends there, or at least a few fellows who were not unfriendly; I had had Phaeso, who was dead because of me . . . Now I had abandoned all familiar things, to follow at the heels of a man with cold blue fire in his eyes, and without mercy, and who I did not know at all. But I knew that if it had been all to do again, I would have done all as before. For making or for breaking, he was written on my forehead.

It was evening, and they had brought me a little lamp and more food before he came, and the anchor-cressets were flaring on the ships, ragged as golden mares' manes in the windy dusk, and I knew that it would be too late to sail tonight. I heard the boat come alongside, and his voice, and a crackle of orders; and I got up and stood waiting. He came, and pulled back the loose leather curtain and stood there, bowed at the shoulder, for he was too tall to stand upright under the awnings, and looked me up and down; and I had the feeling that for the moment he had forgotten he would find me there.

Then he lounged down upon the piled rugs, still looking at me; and said, "You make a valiant boy, Timandra. What a sad pity that I was always a man for women." And I saw that he was mocking me.

I said, "I am still woman, under the clothes that the woman of the house gave me." And despised myself for saying it.

He reached out and caught my wrist and pulled me down beside him. "Has the day been long?"

"The day has been long."

"I have been busy," he said, and I saw the devilry playing at the corners of his mouth and in his eyes. "Would you like to know what I have been doing?"

"If it pleases you to tell me."

"It does. I have been selling the horse, and making certain arrangements for this sea-going. And I have been letting it fall here and there—among such as are good at spreading secrets—that Tissaphernes is none so bad a fellow after all; for having taken me captive to please the Great King, did he not himself arrange for my escape? That should put paid to any better understanding between our plump friend and the Spartans."

He lay back, laughing, and pulled me down on top of him. "It isn't wise to do the dirty on Alkibiades."

"It might have been quite wise, if one of the palace flute girls had chosen to leave well alone."

"Do you think I would not have escaped without you?"

"Would you?" I said.

"Of course. My luck was with me. I always know when my luck is with me."

I said, "Would your luck have killed three men for you, that night?"

And he said, "The Captain of the Guard was mine. Little she-wolf, do not be claiming all the kill."

And I knew that he had forgotten Phaeso already. I wished that I could. Sometimes I wish it when I wake in the night, even now.

He pulled me closer, and kissed me between the brows. "Do not be too eager for gratitude, she-wolf; it's a waste of time that could be better spent . . . Isn't it sweeter this way, than if I had brought you with me out of gratitude?" He began to pull at the thongs of my jacket. "Undo this thing—I want to see if there are still running stags under your breasts and lily flowers on your belly."

But while I was doing as he bade me, he reached sideways and pinched out the lamp.


## The Rower

We are the lowest of the Sea God's creatures we who row the long war galleys. And that winter was not one to raise the heart of any man above his station. The whole war had moved north, and so instead of making back for Samos we rounded the Chersonese and harboured on the western side—I suppose that was because we would be less open to attack from Abydos there, than in the old base at Sestos. The officers, and sometimes the troops and even the seamen got off for a day's hunting now and then—wolf and wild boar among the hills. There were women in the villages, some native and some who had come in the usual way following the fleet; cheap and easy, so I'm told. But even the Captains grew short-tempered, and there was neither hunting nor whoring for the rowers that winter.

Most days, those of the fleet that were not up on the beach for careening were ordered out on exercise; but otherwise, save when one's own squadron was on cruising guard or off tribute-gathering from the coastwise villages of Thrace, there was nothing to do but sit on our backsides and get drunk when we could, and play unending games of knucklebones among ourselves, while the galls on our hands and the salt chaps on our lips and knuckles and knees stiffened without ever really getting a chance to heal—And wait for spring or Alkibiades, whichever came first.

None of us doubted that he would keep his promise to get back to us; the promise that Antiochus his sailing-master had passed on to us when he got back to report Tissaphernes' foul trick. If we had not believed it to the marrow of our half-frozen bones, I think we would have revolted before midwinter; not only the rowing benches, but the whole fleet.

Just before the turn of the year a passing merchantman brought word that Mindarus and his Spartans had left Abydos and were blockading Cyzicus. The news, as usual, was round the whole fleet within half a day of reaching our Admirals. "Where's Cyzicus?" someone asked, three benches from mine. "Somewhere up on the Asian side of the Propontis—at the end of the tunny-fish run." "We shall see some action now."

But there was no order to move; and after the best part of a month, Cyzicus fell. I suppose our Admirals were too busy waiting for Alkibiades.

And in a few days more, Alkibiades came.

He burst on us like a storm at sea, wind and hail and sun together; and drove the drink and the staleness of boredom out of us. He recalled all scattered squadrons, and when the whole fleet lay together once more, he went through us ship by ship, cursing us, laughing with us, setting us straining at the leash. He came aboard the *Halkyone* on the third day, and talked to us, standing in the stern with our Trirarch beside him; his legs a little straddled and his helmet off—always knows when to let his bared

222

face work for him, does Alkibiades. He spoke to us short and to the point; spoke to us all, the rowing benches as well as fighting deck, which was a thing we were not used to. He said that if we were going to smash the Spartan League—and by the grey eyes of Athene, we *were* going to smash them—we must do it quickly, for money and supplies were short with us, whereas Mindarus and his pack were in the pay of the Persian King. (He had a few pleasant things to say about Tissaphernes in that connection; but he didn't spend much time on that, only enough to make us laugh, and see an enemy as the smaller for it.) He said that from now on, he would have every man, marines and seamen and rowers to work as one, and all ready to fight on land or at sea. "I will have the marines of this ship to man the rigging and the seamen to row their guts out, and the rowers to storm Byzantium if I give the word! And I will have them do it gladly, holding nothing back!" He must have said the self-same thing to every ship in the fleet before he was done, but we aboard the *Halkyone* felt, as I suppose did every ship in the fleet, that he spoke to us alone. We had spent the winter grumbling, but we would have cut off our right hands for him after that.

Spring was scarcely thickening the willow-buds when the last trireme was run down the slipways and we cast off for Cyzicus; and the nights were still long, giving us good sailing time; for the order was that we were to move only under cover of the dark. Two nights it took us, to the rounding of Cape Helles; solid rowing, for coming down the coast the winds were for the most part contrary and we could not have the sails to help the oars; so it was a hard pull every oarstroke of the way. We lay up under the lee of Cape Helles that day, while a party went ashore for water; and got what sleep we could in the pitching of the warring currents that meet there. And at dusk we put out to sea again, heading north-east into the straits. The mouth of the Hellespont is like the estuary of a great river; and from our nearer shore there was a nightlong crying and calling of shore birds.

The fleet had been divided into three squadrons, each led by a skilled pilot. We were in Alkibiades' own squadron, led by the flagship, and Antiochus himself. (And drunk or sober, all men knew that he was the best pilot in the Athenian Navy.) And all the rest struggling behind us like ducklings after the dilly.

We were the best part of two more nights nosing up the straits, past Sestos and deserted Abydos and those loathsome muddy river-flats they call Goat's Creek. And if ever a man earned his pay

that red-nosed boozer piloting the flagship earned it. It seemed as
though he knew the straits as a lover knows the body of his love. He
knew from moment to moment where the currents ran our way,
from moment to moment which shore to hug and where to tack
across to the opposite side; and we nosed after him, each galley
following the faint glow of the shielded stern cresset from the galley
ahead; feeling ourselves along as it seemed by the currents and the
inshore eddies and the changes of the wind as it came down through
the hills. Once we were caught by a black easterly squall and had
to row our guts out to keep from being driven on to the lee shore.
I can remember now, thinking that my heart must burst at the
next pull, and looking up through the wind and the hissing rain
and seeing that our pilot had joined the steersman at the steering
oar and they were fighting it as men fight a kicking stallion; and
knowing that I could go on, because I must.

We made captive all the trading vessels that we overhauled, and
ran them aground behind us, that none of them might carry news
of our coming to the Spartan fleet; and we made the passage of
the straits undiscovered, and came out into the inland sea called
the Propontis, and headed eastward. The weather had changed
and the wind fallen away, but a heavy swell was running, and a
thick rain-mist hid the coastline, so that the steersmen held their
course by the sound of the sea beating on the distant shore, and
the leadsman's constant call.

"It will hold overnight, maybe, but it will lift in the morning,"
said my oar mate. He knew those waters better than I did, having
been at the tunny fishing in his youth.

In the dark before dawn, the flagship altered course and headed
in for shore; the signals blinked in her stern, and we followed,
nosing in through the darkness and the murk; then the signals
blinked again, and we backed water and lay with our noses to the
current, while the heavy troop carriers slipped past us like ghosts
with even their stern braziers quenched. We waited, using the oars
just enough to hold position against the current, till presently they
re-passed us, heading out again, and riding higher in the water
than they had done before.

Then we headed back for open sea.

"If it wasn't for this murk, we'd see the lights of Cyzicus over
that way," someone said on the deck above us.

By dawn the mizzle rain was beginning to lift; in the night we
had peeled off a hundred triremes—I learned later that they were
commanded, fifty each, by Theramenes and Thrassylus, but at the
time we knew only that when the sea fret turned grey with dawn,

we were one of the remaining forty, the Admiral's own squadron, and that we were standing in line abreast toward Cyzicus.

The mizzle had almost ceased, and the sky was breaking away into clear lakes of blue among the drifting cloud; and away on our port side, opposite the mainland, rose the high wooded hills of the great Cyzicus peninsular, looking like an island, a little like Salamis, to us on the rowing benches with our backs to the Isthmus. A shout from the flagship's lookout, passed back along the line, told us that the Spartan ships were in sight. All around, there began to be the ordered bustle of a galley making ready for action. The sails were run down and the mast unstepped and stowed along the side of the deck. The leather screens were rigged to protect us rowers, the marines were up in the bows, the Trirarch standing beside the pilot in the stern. The bos'n's flute shrilled, and we swung into a quicker stroke. The feet of the fighting men were close to my head; I heard the lieutenant say, "This is a good trick of the Admiral's, if it only works." And someone answered, "Why shouldn't it work? The rest are hull down over the skyline. To the Spartans it must look as though we forty are all there are." And then there was silence save for the shift and shuffle of braced feet and the bark of an order, the chink of a weapon and the creak of the oars in the oar-ports. And then the voice that had spoken before said, "Look! They're coming out to engage."

Far over the water I heard the bray of the Spartan trumpets. The Trirarch's hand flashed up, and the bos'n's flute fell silent. We had been well drilled in what to do, and we hung on over oars a few moments, as though the Admiral was undecided and the whole fleet hung waiting for his word; then as our own trumpets sounded for retreat, the steersman put the steering oar hard over, the rowers on the starboard side feathered their oars, while we on the port benches strained every muscle, and the *Halkyone*, following the flagship, came about in a wide sea-swallow curve, and the whole squadron was heading out to sea again. But the bos'n's flute set an easy rowing time, we did not want to outrow the lean dark galleys putting out from harbour after us.

We quickened the tempo after a while, when we were well out from land and they were close enough to feel themselves hot on the scent. It was fine to see the low black squadrons straining after us like hounds that think the quarry far spent and smell already the kill. So we drew them after us, and laughed in our bursting hearts to see them come. And then out from the headland westward where they had been lying, and down from the hills to the north out of the departing rain squall, appeared the other two squadrons —and it was as though one heard the trap clash shut.

The Spartans must have woken suddenly to their position, and we heard their trumpets sounding for action stations. They had been deploying into battle-line as they came; but we on the rowing benches never saw the line complete; for once again the Trirarch's hand flashed up, and the steersman bent his whole weight to the oar, and we brought the squadron about, each trireme almost in its own length, in a smother of yeasty foam that flew back from the oar-blades and drenched us in the cold saltness of it that stung like fire. Far off, and close at hand, the squadron's trumpets were talking to each other across the water. Later, I knew that half the squadron had engaged the Spartan centre, while the other, our half, led by Alkibiades himself, swept down on the left wing in wild-goose formation, to smash through and throw it into confusion before the other squadrons came in to finish the work. But that was afterwards. One does not see the pattern of a battle from the rowing benches. I knew only that the bos'n's flute was setting Full Pace and we were driving the *Halkyone* through the water with the short quick, heart-bursting stroke never used except in the last moments of going into battle. I saw nothing but the straining shoulders of the man in front of me; heard nothing but the bos'n's flute and the thunder of my own heart within me.

A rower's life is not a bad one, when he gets his pay and enough shore leave to spend it, in dolphin weather when the sails do most of the work. I saw the world as a rower. I've been luckier than poor old Timotheus tied at home by his game leg to run his father's shop. But there was always that one moment going into battle when I held it against my father that he died in debt and I could not furnish my weapons as a marine. I never learned to like going into battle backwards.

But it was soon over. We had made the Sacrifice, before dawn, knowing that there would be no time when the fighting was upon us; but we drove down upon the enemy, the Trirarch, standing above us in the stern, raised the Paean, catching it up from the flagship, and it swept away down the line of the squadron; even we rowers, who seldom bothered, sang it that day, as well as our bursting hearts would let us. And we were still singing when the first shock of the impact came, all but hurling us forward, each upon the next bank of rowers.

I remember the crash, the grinding and shouting that drowned the Paean, and the shudder of the *Halkyone* as we backed water to shake the Spartan off our ram, knowing that we had made a kill.

I remember the sudden loom of a trireme bearing down on us, and the Trirarch's shouted order, "Starboard oars in!" The steersman bringing her round, and the light grinding as the other ship swept past us after her missed stroke, her oars also hauled in-board.

Two ships we rammed in the first break through, but the order was to capture not sink; and so for us rowers—but indeed that is true of most of our fights—the battle was two things: the sheer physical stress of handling the oars in quick manœuvre, and feet. Feet that came and went trampling the deck, as the fighting men strove to board or repel boarders. The occasional dead or wounded man pitched down all arms and legs among the rowing benches. Sometimes one of ours, sometimes a Spartan. We flung them all off alike, to be rid of their weight clogging the oar looms. There were glimpses of galleys all about us, a great churning and threshing of water; and then I knew vaguely that we were through, and the Spartan line was breached and flung back on itself and the thing had become a dog-fight with Theramenes and Thrassylus' squadrons joining in. One ship we close-hauled, and coming about and shipping over our oars in the last instant, before she could do the same, swept down her starboard side, slicing them off like radishes. That's generally accounted the most skilled and daring of all sea-fight manœuvres, only to be attempted by the Trirarch who has complete confidence in his pilot and in the perfect discipline of his rowers. But few rowers like it; it cuts too near to our own quick. If it succeeds, it leaves a red mush on the enemy's benches, that heaves and struggles somewhat, and moans a little, and cries out like a woman; and one has to get very drunk at the next possible opportunity before one can quite forget it.

So I remember it, now and then, as I remember also, my own oar mate taking a stray javelin in the belly and retching up his life blood mixed with black vomit over my feet, while one of our reliefs clambered into his place beside me.

We suffered a fair amount of damage before all was over; so did most of Alkibiades' squadron, which had taken the forefront of the fighting.

But at the end of the day we had captured the whole enemy fleet, save for those that were rammed and sunk. And Cyzicus had surrendered to the troops we had landed the night before. The Spartan Admiral was killed in the sea fighting, and all the coastwise towns of the Hellespont and Propontis lay at Athens' mercy.

All this I heard later, in a wine-shop near the harbour, through a red triumphal haze of drink; but at the time, as I say, it was only feet, and noise, and fighting the oar-loom, and the occasional dead man.

The wine-shop girl had full brown breasts that showed when she stooped to pour the wine, and stank of musk and jasmine and warm dirt, like a she-cat flying the signal that she is in rut. But I was too tired even to regret that I could not afford her.

I believe the bos'n had her instead.


## Mindarus' Staff Trirarch, to the Government of Sparta

"Our ships are lost; Mindarus is killed; our men are starving; we know not what to do."


## The Soldier

There was a rumour that spring that Sparta had sent an embassy to Athens, offering peace. I remember discussing the likelihood of its being true with Ariston, one evening sitting in his quarters at Sestos, with the lights of Abydos shining across the water and in at the open door. He said, "It's no great matter whether they have or not; there's not a thing Athens can do about it, either way."

I looked at him, not at once catching his meaning, and he added, "They have no power to make peace or war. The will of the Athenian people is no longer in the city, it's here with the fleet."

I must have known it all along, but I had not realized it until that moment. "Of course! If the Spartans want peace, it's here to our blue-eyed boy they'll have to come for it!" Delight woke in us, at the irony of the situation, and something that was like awe, and because of the almost-awe we turned to laughter as young men will, and laughed until we were weak.

If it were given to me to choose for the young men of sad grey future generations, some good, some splendour from the great days, I suppose that I should choose, if there were any wisdom in me, that they should have been friends of Socrates. But we are what we are, and not wiser than our own hearts. I would wish for them the three years that followed Cyzicus.

Those three years in the Northern Aegean, in the Propontis and the Hellespont; in which Alkibiades won back for Athens her empire in the north. I do not think any man ever ran up greater debts than Alkibiades, and certainly no man ever paid them more magnificently. At the beginning of those three years, Athens was at her lowest ebb; at the end she was at full tide again. And make no mistake, oh you of lesser generations, it was Alkibiades and Alkibiades alone who did it. So far as we knew (and a fleet knows most things) no order ever came to him from home. Theramenes and Thrassylus, and later Thrasybulus, who were officially his equals, were in fact no more than his staff officers, and at least in Theramenes' case, a damned inefficient staff officer at that.

Those were years for young men. Alkibiades was always a young man's Commander, as I have said before. He had the fire and the wicked daring that calls to young men following. And in some odd way, despite the hideous discomfort of the campaign, the bitter winters when the fleet never went into winter quarters, the unrelenting sheer hard work, there was something in those years that the older men among us feel the sap rise again. I have heard more than one of them say so, when the years were over. And at the time you could see it in their eyes.

After Cyzicus, we waited only to raise the usual trophy of captured arms, and then we were off about the next job that came to hand.

With Dekalia still in Spartan hands and Euboa in revolt, Athens depended entirely upon the Black Sea corn ships, and so above and before all else, the Propontis and the Hellespont must be made safe for their passage. Alkibiades divided us into three fleets, and sent one of them, under Theramenes, to deal with Chalcedon a few miles inland at the southern entrance to the Black Sea Straits, which had revolted the year before. The Spartan Governor called on Pharnobazus for help, and it seemed that Theramenes was likely to be kept busy there a good while. Meantime, we of the first fleet—the Admiral's fleet, we called it, which can hardly have pleased the other two—were off with Alkibiades to blockade Perinthos, far up on the Thracian side of Propontis, then swept on to show our teeth to Selymbria. But it was drawing toward autumn by then, time for the grain ships to be coming through; and when Selymbria had paid up the year's tribute, we left them alone for that year, and became escort ships, save for one squadron detached to see how Theramenes was getting on with his siege. Broadly speaking, he wasn't. I think there must have been some plain speaking between him and Alkibiades, and after it he was relieved of that particular command. But it was too late in the year to start afresh in that direction, and at any rate with our troops on the spot and the fleet guarding the approaches, Chalcedon was powerless—a boar with his thicket ringed by the hounds—and we took over the little seaport town of Chrysopolis, fortified the place in something of a hurry, with a stockade of green timber, strengthened by piled rocks in the harbour area, the local men standing by and spitting at us while we worked; dumb-sullen but not desperate enough to do anything about it; and left Theramenes there with a squadron of thirty ships to keep the straits open, and exact the one-tenth toll from each of the corn fleet passing through (it came in useful for feeding our own troops) while the rest of us sailed south to pick up the second squadron, already patrolling the Hellespont. That autumn, for the first time in a long while, the Black Sea corn fleet went through complete and unmolested to Piraeus.

We had all of us learned by then to be sailor and soldier in one, and that winter and the next, we turned our hands to the building trade. While a few squadrons were kept at sea for cruising and scout work (they managed to collect quite a bit of most useful tribute, too, from cities that had revolted in the past few years but were suddenly only too glad to return to the Empire), we built forts along the Propontis shore. We strengthened Chrysopolis into a proper stone fort, and raised two more, one at Bisanthe some thirty miles south of Perinthos, and one at Pactye at the northern end of the Hellespont. Good strong places to secure the coast and link up the Athenian settlements of the Hellespont with those of Propontis.

Later, men said that he had built them for purposes of piracy if the luck went against him in the end; but not the men who spent those winters with him in the snow-scurried North of Helles Straits.

At some time in the past, he had made contacts among the Thracian tribes, and a few of those big, rough-riding men in their fox-skin caps came down from the inland hills to work with us. They showed us the best places to quarry the stone we needed—it was odd, the quarrying scarcely brought any memories back, even of Astur, and yet I was not faithless—and helped us fell the iron-hard winter timber. But for the most part we did the work with our own hands, and had the blisters to show for it; spear-butt and rope stay do not harden the hands in quite the same places; I think the rowers had the best of it, when it came to manhandling the rough-cut stone.

Alkibiades himself was like a marsh light, always on the move and never where you last heard of him. He would be with one of the sea-going squadrons, and then we would hear that he was taking life easy in his own house in Sestos with the Bithynian girl he kept there—a fox-haired, fierce little piece with crooked front teeth, and beautiful eyes, who went about as freely as a boy, instead of biding decently in the women's quarters, as often as not in tight breeks and a goatskin jacket, which I know now is not disgraceful among her people, whose girls dress like the young men for riding and in their spring and autumn migrations. And then, while so far as we knew he was still at Sestos, we would be standing to warm ourselves by a brushwood fire in the lee of a half-built wall, and somebody would feel a hand on his shoulder, and the voice with the lisp that was known by every man in the fleet, would ask, "Room for one more?" And there he would be in our midst again. Maybe followed by a slave carrying a wine jar, maybe just himself, muffled as most of us were in a goatskin jacket, under his great cloak, getting more ragged every time we saw it, where he always dragged that corner along the ground.

Just at the time that our first building-winter turned toward spring, two things happened. The first was that Athens took fresh heart and scraped together a new fleet of fifty ships with a thousand troops on board, and sent them out under Thrasybulus to operate with the Samos fleet. They turned aside on their own account to attack Ephesus. They were driven back to their ships, and came limping north to join us. They got a very cool reception; for the Samos fleet (we still thought of ourselves as that) was drunk with victory. We felt that we did not tread the earth like mortal men, certainly not like men who had known defeat. We would not mess with them nor train with them. I have sometimes wondered whether in his heart of hearts Alkibiades was pleased. But as our Admiral, he could not tolerate such a state of things. He dealt with it beautifully. He ordered out Thrasybulus and his marines to raid the country round Abydos, and when, inevitably, Pharnobazus brought out his troops against them, sent a huge contingent of the Samos men to Thrasybulus' aid. Together we hunted them till dusk, and then returned to camp in perfect good fellowship.

The second thing, happening about the same time, was that a squadron of the Spartan League, only fifteen ships, small but admittedly valiant, came up from Megara (King Agis, back in Dekalia can't have liked the sight of the grain ships coming through). They gave our patrols the slip in one of the four-day sea fogs that brew up in spring, and were in Byzantium before we knew it, with troops to strengthen the Spartan garrison. So, once again, for the first time since Cyzicus a year before, there was an enemy squadron in our waters, and the strengthening of Byzantium to make it still more urgent that we should re-take Chalcedon.

There hadn't been much happening in that direction. So to help matters along, the Admiral ordered a stockade to be built from the straits to the Propontis, cutting off the corner of land on which the city stood, and set us to guarding it, so that nothing could pass in or out. It was the same device as Nikias had started at Syracuse. Only this time we had the Commander who had been taken from us then; no dawdling, no gaps left; and when Pharnobazus came up to the relief of the city, he could not get through our lines. It was hot work all the same, for by that time summer had dried out the water course; the one place where the shifting gravel-bed made a secure stockade impossible; and the Spartan Commander made a sally up the dry river-bed at the same time as the Persians came on us from the hills inland. However, we took up back-to-back formation at that point, to face the double attack, and drove the Persians off into Bithynia, while the Spartans retreated—it was a good fighting retreat—back into the town.

After that it was only a matter of time before Chalcedon must fall; and we left Thrassylus to sit there like a terrier at a rathole, and made westward along the Thracian coast to finish with Selymbria.

There's something about the capture of Selymbria, I've never known quite what it is, that makes it stand more clearly shaped and coloured in my memory even than the splendour of Byzantium. And yet it was quite a small affair. Alkibiades had been in touch with the pro-Athenian party in the town; and it had been fixed that on a certain night, if all had gone well with their side of the plan, they were to show a light above the seaward wall as a signal that they were ready to open one of the lesser gates to us. There were some among us, a few who remembered Messana, but we were careful not to speak the memory or to read it in each other's faces. It was past and best forgotten. The whole fleet of course knew that there would be a signal, but only the senior officers and Trirarchs knew the full details. I had become Trirarch of the *Pegasus* by that time. Promotion comes quickly in war, and the old qualification of having to be able to fit out one's ship cannot apply when men die and others must be found to take their places at a moment's notice.

On the appointed night we drew up the ships, and made camp, as we had done often enough before in our comings and goings along the Propontis shores, in the curve of a shallow bay some miles eastward of the town. It was an obvious choice, with a good firm stranding-beach and clean water available, and for that reason we always kept a strong guard when we were there. That night I saw the feathery tops of the tamarisk scrub, and the soft hollows of the dunes in the light of the cooking fires all more clearly and intensely, almost painfully, than usual, as though my body had one less skin than usual and my eyes had shed some shadow cast by habit and familiarity. I do not know how to say it, I am not good at finding words for such things. I think most men have it, in one way or another, this heightened awareness of sight and sound and smell on the eve of battle; I suppose it is partly because we know that it may be for the last time; but also I think it is because the Gods know what battle demands of a man, and if he is lucky, string him in advance to a higher pitch, that he may meet the demands when they come. I remember the lap of the water round the dark stems of the galleys drawn up on the beach, the scattered glow of the spent cooking fires between the tamarisk bushes; the ordered coming and going, the quietly spoken order, where men who had eaten and rested were beginning to arm. I was armed already, as most of the Trirarchs and marine officers were, so that we were free of our own preparations to see to the men. But there was more than an hour to go to midnight, and a knot of us lingered for a few moments round the remains of the fire where we had eaten earlier. It was a still hot night, but the brushwood smoke helped to keep the mosquitoes away. There was a good deal of noise coming from one quarter of the camp; it sounded like a war-dance going on, and someone said, "Listen to those cursed Thracians—I hope to the Gods that hellish noise can't be heard from Selymbria; it will give the whole game away."

"It can't," said Alkibiades' voice behind me. "I've just been up that way. What wind there is is carrying it in the wrong direction. It's pretty, isn't it?"

"If you can call the howling of a wolf pack pretty," said Dion, who was literal minded.

And Cleomenes, Trirarch of the *Clytemnestra*, said, "I've heard them sing that song before. One of the tame tribesmen told me what it meant. It's all about the gold they're going to gather and the wine they're going to drink, and what they're going to do to the boys and women when they get into the city."

"And that," said Alkibiades lazily, "is why I have made careful arrangements that they shall not get inside the gates."

I said—Apollo Far Shooter knows why, for whether I would or no, I loved the man—"My mother's brother was at Melos. You

233

weren't troubled by such considerations then, My Lord Alkibiades."

And he looked round and up at me from where he had let himself down to sprawl in the soft sand beside the fire. "Melos needed a lesson. Other purposes, other methods, Arkadius; at the moment we are rebuilding a lost empire." He was so completely at ease and unashamed as to who had lost it, that none of us were embarrassed. And then he said, "Is there any wine left?" We all apologized, and Cleomenes picked up the amphora and poured what was left into Ariston's cup, which happened to be the first to hand, and gave it to him.

He was just throwing back his head to drink, when he checked, his eyes widening in the direction of the city. Then he lowered the cup again, and said, "There's no star due to rise over Selymbria at this hour, is there?"

I whipped round to look in the same direction, the others with me; and there, above the whispering tamarisk tops, on the dark edge of things, where we knew the city must be, a thing like a star but redder and more fitful, had pricked out in the night.

We were all on our feet by then, staring the same way. Ariston said, "They're an hour too soon." Cleomenes, who was famed throughout the fleet for his gifts in that direction, was cursing in a soft sustained flow.

Alkibiades was already loosening his sword in its sheath. I heard the rasp of it. "Time enough for that later," he said. "Now, we have other things to attend to."

"The men aren't ready yet, sir," somebody said; and somebody else, "The fools must be drunk."

"Drunk, or misjudging the time, or simply scared—or up against trouble, with something gone wrong," said Alkibiades. "In any case we can't sit back and leave them to it. Besides, if we delay and they are discovered, we shall find a poor welcome when we get there, and the gate shut in our faces."

I wondered for an instant, as one does wonder things when it really isn't the time, whether he had any thought of Messana.

He swung round to shout for his trumpeter, then back to us about the fire. "Ariston, you're ready. Cleomenes, Arkadius, rout out any of your men who are yet fully armed; the rest to follow as quickly as possible. Name of the Dog! Don't gape, man! Here, you and you—"

In the end he had about thirty of us. Thirty, so far as I could see to take Selymbria with whatever help (if any) was waiting for us inside, and hold it till the rest came up. But no man ever questioned where Alkibiades led—and he always led in person. I suppose that was part of his power with us. We were running low, through the tamarisk and the shorewise scrub that gave off its hot scents of rosemary and fennel as we brushed by, our swords ready drawn in our hands.

The flare had disappeared from the ramparts when we came shadow-stealing up through the encircling graves to the postern gate. It stood darkly open and unguarded, and two abreast—there was no room for more—we passed through after Alkibiades.

Inside there should have been a whispered password out of the dark, men waiting to receive and join us. Instead, as the last of us stepped clear of the gateway, there was a flare of torches, and in the hissing light we saw the spear points and helmet-crests of men drawn up, to receive us indeed, but not as friends. I realized with a sickness in my stomach that the enemy must have got hold of the plan and showed a decoy light. I suppose they hoped to gain a few useful hostages—and we had walked straight into the trap. For we were enormously outnumbered, and beyond the torchlight was a gathering movement and murmur—full of menace.

They were moving in on us. I was just behind Alkibiades, and I was suddenly aware of the cock of his head. He had not walked blindly into a trap, he had taken a calculated risk with his eyes open. It seemed a long time that we stood in the torchlight, hands rigid on our weapons, confronting the Selymbrian spears, but it can have been no more than a few heartbeats of time. Then Alkibiades spoke quietly to his trumpeter beside him, bidding the man sound for silence.

The trumpeter raised his trumpet to his lips and sounded the call with cool effrontery that matched the Admiral's own; and I suppose because it was so unexpected, the men moving in on us hesitated, then checked in their tracks; and the movement of the crowd beyond the torchlight stopped dead. Silence held us all for a long moment; the whole city seemed to be listening and waiting for what would come next. Then Alkibiades raised his hand and made a proclamation, not very loud, but in a clear tone of authority that must have reached to the furthest fringes of the unseen crowd. "You are to lay down your arms, my friends. If you do this in good order and without delay, no harm shall come to you; Athens has entrusted me with her most solemn promise."

"And what if we do not?" a Selymbrian officer demanded.

Alkibiades said, "Athens does not love those of her own who take up arms against her. I am empowered, in that case, to take such action as I think fit." There was a moment of thick silence;

and when he spoke again his voice had lost nothing of authority but taken on a hint of that familiar charm that could call a bird out of an arbutus tree. "But the action which seems to me most fitting to both of us is that you should lay down your arms and we should talk together as civilized men."

It was the most colossal piece of bluff I have ever known. I thought, 'They'll never fall for this, they can't!' But I don't know—I suppose they thought that no man in his senses would speak like that unless he had troops enough at hand to back his demand, and the rest must have got in by some other way, and be waiting somewhere in the darkness close at hand. I suppose too, they thought his speech had a friendly ring; and so the unbelievable happened, and man after man let his spear clatter to the ground at his feet.

And standing there in the midst of the torches, Alkibiades and the Selymbrian Commander began to parley; and the gate remained open. And while they parleyed the rest of the troops came up, and the Athenian party in the city who had been lying low, ready to come to our aid, but seeing no sense in throwing away their lives by attacking against hopeless odds if there was no need, came from cover to add their numbers to ours.

There was no disorder, no looting. The Thracians were never allowed inside the gates, but given a special issue of wine which Alkibiades ordered the Selymbrians to bring out from their cellars, and sent back to camp on the pretext of guarding the ships.

Next day there was a great discussion of terms with the chief men of the city; and Selymbria paid a good fat fine, and undertook to receive and support an Athenian garrison; and Alkibiades and the Selymbrian Commander embraced each other in the middle of the market-place.

# 18

## The Soldier

When we got back to Chalcedon, we found that the siege was over at last, and Thrasybulus and Theramenes had come to terms with Pharnobazus for the town's surrender. Chalcedon was to suffer no punishment for its revolt, but pay the usual yearly tribute of an Athenian city again as before; and the Satrap had agreed to pay twenty talents of gold on the city's behalf, if Alkibiades would swear to leave his territory in peace.

The treaty was all drawn up ready and waiting to be signed. I was among the officers that Alkibiades took with him to the ceremonial signing—all that the Persians do, is done with great ceremony—it was the first time that I had seen Pharnobazus at close quarters, and I was impressed. I had grown used to the idea of Satraps being plump and luxury loving like Tissaphernes; but this one was a small tough man with a hawk's wide golden eye, and when he rode up to the appointed place, he brought his big tiger-spot horse to a rearing halt that would have had most men off its back on the instant; I saw the grip of his knees. I was interested that this little fierce fighting man judged our danger-value high enough to be willing to pay twenty talents of gold for our promise to leave his Satrapy alone.

After the signing, both companies ate together under the Satrap's great awning; and Alkibiades and Pharnobazus sat together on the same pile of fine rugs and drank from the same wine cup. Clearly in their own way, they were making another treaty, personal to themselves; though maybe in Alkibiades' case Athens had also some part in it.

I happened to be sitting close to Antiochus—we all sat in little groups, each with a bowl of kid meat broiled in milk with raisins and green peppers in our midst—and clearly he did not like what he saw going on in the High Place. He was somewhat drunk by that time, and drink always made him reckless and quarrelsome.

I saw him lean towards an elderly Persian official; jutting his chin aggressively to match the forward swing of those great coral and silver earrings. "The troops aren't going to like it," he said. "When the fighting's been hard they expect a little hunting in the enemy's runs."

The old Persian smiled, and a thousand fine wrinkles gathered round his eyes. "But then, we could scarcely be called enemies," he said, and made a small courteous gesture indicating the Admiral and Pharnobazus. "It is not customary to hunt without leave in the hunting runs of a friend."

"Friend be cursed," said Antiochus. "It'll do him damage with the troops." His voice had begun to rise a little, one or two people were looking round; and I began to wonder if there was going to be trouble.

But the old Persian still smiled, shaking his head. "I think you underestimate the strength of your Commander's hold on their loyalties. Listen, my friend, the Propontis is far from Athens; by the friendship of the Satrap he makes sure of safe passage for the corn ships, and his goodwill towards these little Athenian colonies so far from home, so far maybe from help. That is worth more than the pleasure of a little raiding, a few horses and women carried off, a village sacked . . ."

You could almost see the red hairs of Antiochus' beard beginning to rise like a dog's hackles. "A few horses and women, my arse!" he shouted. "It wasn't to save himself from that kind of raiding that your Satrap hands out twenty talents—"

It seemed to me that it was time somebody did something. I rose waveringly to my feet, turned half round and fell over Antiochus, pouring about half a cupful of wine down the back of his neck. I did just wonder as I landed in his lap, whether the next thing I should know would be a dagger point under my ribs. One normally goes unarmed to a gathering of that sort, but with the likes of Antiochus one can never be quite sure. However, all that followed was a startled flow of curses as he tried to fling me off; while I, tearfully apologetic, clung like a limpet, making futile efforts to mop him up with the tail of my chlamys. There was a roar of laughter, and then Ariston was bending over me saying, "Come on, up with you. You need a spot of fresh air, my lad."

Still apologizing, I allowed him to haul me to my feet, all asprawl like a shock of rain-wet barley, and urge me out through the crowd under the awning. The last thing I saw as I turned away from the group was the faded blue eyes of the old Persian narrowed in amused understanding.

Outside in the thick white sunlight, I pulled away from Ariston, and when he would not let go my arm, tried to strike his hand away, suddenly in a vile temper.

He said, "Softly now, best get out of sight of the guards before you sober up."

And I realized that he knew perfectly well what had happened. When we were out of sight of the encampment, he let me go, and said with twitching lips, "That was very neatly done."

"Why in Typhon's name does Alkibiades keep that lout always with him?"

"Don't you really know?" Ariston said. We were walking back through the dunes towards our own horse lines.

"I know he's the best pilot in the fleet, but that doesn't—"

"He's also about the only one of his senior staff that Alkibiades can trust."

"He didn't show himself particularly worthy of trust, just now."

"He drinks too much, and he drinks quarrelsome," said Ariston. "That's the one thing that makes him a danger. For the rest, he's as brave as a boar and as loyal as a hound. Could you say as much for the rest of our Admirals?"

I thought of Theramenes, the political opportunist; of Thrasybulus the fanatical Democrat; of Thrassylus, who would do him dirt at the flip of a coin; and I cursed.

A few days later we were across the straits and blockading Byzantium, which was ripening nicely for rebellion against its Spartan garrison. We had built a stockade round it earlier in the year, just as we had done for Chalcedon; and news came to us by night out of the town that supplies were running short, and Clearchus had commandeered all the food for his troops, leaving the citizens to starve. You can see his point; Byzantium was essential to the security of the straits, and his orders must have been to hold it at all costs. But anyone except a Spartan might have foreseen what tree would grow from that seed. Probably, too, the citizens had got some word of the good treatment handed out to Chalcedon and Selymbria; at all events we found ourselves with a strong body of allies within the city, and once again, the promise of a gate left open.

But even so, Byzantium with its strong garrison of Spartans and Spartan allies, would be a tougher nut to crack by far than Selymbria. And Alkibiades, calling a Council of War, laid before us a plan by which heavy fighting might be avoided.

On the morning of the day before the gate was to be opened to us, we raised the blockade and sailed off. The Admiral had contrived to let it leak out that matters had gone suddenly and badly wrong in Ionia. But out of sight of the city we dropped anchor and lay waiting for dark, then headed shoreward again, and a little way down the coast, landed the troops in the now familiar pattern; but this time led by Alkibiades himself. It was the first time I had regretted my promotion to Trirarch, which had taken me from one service to the other. But there was plenty of work for the sea-service, too, in that night's plan. As soon as the troops were landed we put out again and headed for Byzantium. If the fools had worked hard they might have got some kind of boom across the harbour mouth, but they had not thought of it, so we came in about an hour before dawn.

We entered the great harbour of Byzantium with cressets blazing and trumpets sounding, the bos'ns shrilling the time for the rowers on their flutes, and every man throughout the fleet raising the Paean as we came. I think some of us even hammered spear butts on the decks or clashed cooking-pots together; anything to add to the uproar, anything that would convince the Spartan Commander of an attack in force from the sea and make him hurry his men down to the harbour to resist it, while at the same time signalling our arrival across the city to Alkibiades and the troops waiting beyond the unguarded gate.

I suppose the first seamen must have sprung ashore just as Alkibiades made his entry on the other side of Byzantium. For a while it was hot work along the water side, and we could make little progress against the defenders. But our orders were not to fight for an advance, but to hold the enemy in play, losing as few of our own men as might be, until the land force could get through to take them in the rear. It seemed a long time, and the struggle to and fro along the dusty quays and jetties with the water lapping at our feet ate itself into my brain. I and a knot of men from the *Pegasus* had swept the narrow alley up from the water beside the arsenal, and were holding it. Truth to tell, I had taken a spear jab below the knee and was not much use for a moving fight just then. The sun was well up into the sky, and the water behind us a harsh white dazzle. I did not think we were going to be able to hold that bit much longer, so I shouted to my lads to raise the Paean, which can generally be counted on to bring out the last ounce of men's fighting strength—and from somewhere ahead of us, it was answered!

Somehow we were charging forward; I hardly felt my knee at that moment; all along the harbour line, on a wave of cheering, and the Paean flung to and fro, the seamen were forcing their way up against the Spartan spears. And then suddenly through the dust of the fighting I saw Alkibiades, his sword red to the hilt and his helmet ripped away, looking like something out of an ancient story—looking as they say Theseus looked at Marathon. We seemed roaring towards each other, and then the roaring was in my own head, like a great sea, and darkness came up between me and Alkibiades' face, and I pitched forward into the darkness and a high singing quiet.

The next time I knew anything I was lying in the colonnade of some building, and someone was half drowning me with water out of my own helmet. I tried to sit up, and the world went spinning sideways and my leg hurt so damnably that I very nearly keeled over into the blackness again.

And Byzantium was ours.

I suppose it was the crown of the campaign, but still it's Selymbria that stands in my mind for those three years in the North.


## The Whore

He brought me up from the house at Sestos to the new fort at Pactye as soon as it was built. When the run of the fighting was along the Propontis shores he made his headquarters there; and he said, driving his head into the hollow of my shoulder, that it was cold without me in the winter nights.

It was lonely up at Pactye when he was not there; but I did not mind the loneliness because of the times when he came. Sometimes he would be away only a few days, sometimes many weeks; and when he came it might be for no more than a hurried meal, or a night in passing; but in the dark storm times of winter it might be for a full course of the moon. I loved and longed for the winter storms when he was there, to hear them beating like black harpies' wings about the walls, and know him doubly sheltered within them and within the circle of my arms.

When he was not there, I listened for news of him. Sometimes I tried to see for myself, in the way of our people, in a polished cup or a pool of black dye held in the hollow of my hand; but though sometimes the bright surface would cloud, and things begin to move in the clouding, I could never see clear. But indeed news of his victories spread swift enough, the length and breadth of the northern waters. And I would hear sounds of celebration from the little guard-post garrison, and send one of the slaves to ask of Philipus the Commander, what news was come. Once in late summer, when I sent he came himself—he had learned the unwisdom of treating me as no more than Alkibiades' bitch-slave —and said, "We have recaptured Byzantium." And I knew that was a great thing, for My Lord had talked to me of it, telling me how the Black Sea Straits could never be secure so long as Byzantium was in Spartan hands. But I thought only, 'Soon, he will come again!'

But the autumn passed, and it was only news that came, news of My Lord and his squadrons, now here, now there, restless as the wild geese.

And then on the very edge of winter, he came. When he came from the sea we had a little warning, a little time to make ready for him; for from the watch-tower on the high rock of Pactye, the look-out would sight the squadron while it was yet far out at sea. But when he came as he sometimes did by land, riding in with a handful of Thracian horsemen, we had no warning at all.

There was sleet spitting down the thin north-easterly wind, spitting in the mare's-tail flames of the torches, as I looked down from the window-hole of the keep chamber and watched them ride in. There was no telling Athenian from Thracian in their long boots and embroidered goatskin jackets and thick felt cloaks, and the fox-skin bonnets of the Tribes. But Alkibiades I knew with the knowing of the heart in my breast. And I thought of the night almost three years ago, when I had watched from the screened windows of the Satrap's palace, and seen him ride in captive. It had been sleeting then, too.

When they had clattered past toward the stable court behind the keep, I ran to the head of the outside stair, and called down to the slaves to bring food and torches, then went myself to mix a krater from our small store of dark Chian wine.

And then he came, and it seemed to me the fire on the blackened hearth-stone leapt up at his coming. The sleet was melting into dark patches of wet on his shoulders, and the shaggy fox-skin of his cap was beaded with it. He pulled it off and flung it on to the chest beside the door, and came to hold his hands to the fire, moving slowly as though he were very tired; not merely saddle sore, but with a deep quiet weariness of the very soul within him. He said, "Is it well with you, Timandra?" as though he had been gone since morning.

And I said, "It is well with me, because you are come," and knelt to free him of his sword. I put my arms round him, round his thighs, and laid my face against him for an instant. Then I got up and laid his sword beside the Thracian bonnet; leaving him still standing with his hands to the fire.

He said, "You have heard that we re-took Byzantium?"

"I heard," I said. "I have looked for your coming, since then; every hour of every day, for your coming."

"There were things to be done," he said. "Clearing up. It is all finished now."

The food came, and I made him sit on the cushioned bench, and fed him and poured wine for him; seeing the blood creep back into his face that had seemed all grey bones when he came in.

We spoke little until the meal was done, and I remember—Oh I remember—how he lay down on the great wolfskin rug that I dragged beside the hearth, with his head against my knee. A couple of hounds had come thrusting into the chamber after him, and his favourite bitch lay suckling her whelps in a corner. He said, "It is good to be with you, Timandra . . . Always remember, whatever happens, that for me, it is good to be with you, Timandra."

Fear brushed against my heart like a cold feather; and I thought it is over. This is the last time that I shall hold him in my arms. But I said only, "For me too, it is good," because every moment that I could hold the thing off from being spoken was one moment more that I should have him, one moment less in the great emptiness that must come after.

And then he reached up and pulled me down into the long harsh fur beside him, saying, "Here, my girl." And he kissed me on the eyes so that I had to shut them, and on the throat and mouth. And I saw the red firelight through my closed lids, and felt the live harshness of the wolfskins under me, and his hands on the fastenings of my clothes; and I put my arms round him.

We made love in the warmth by the fire, with sleet spattering against the wooden shutters, and the little Thracian horses stamping in the stables behind the keep.

Yet even in his love-making there was something changed; something that I had not known before, a desperate urgency and a desperate need that took him by the throat and did what it would with him; he who was always so much the captain of his love-making.

After it was over we lay in each other's arms, quiet for a long while. He lay half over me still; one arm under my head, and rubbed the roughness of his beard against my cheek. But still

I knew that something was changed, something ended—or waiting to begin. I did not know what it was; I did not even know whether it was to do with me at all. I could only fear.

I took his head between my hands, and held it away, to look into his face; and I saw for the first time that he had grown older in the years since Sardis; that the lion's line had deepened between his brows, and there were grey streaks in his tawny mane of hair. I have never thought that age could touch My Lord, and my heart whimpered over him because he was as other men after all.

I said, making it a thing for laughter between us, "How many women have you lain with since last you lay with me?"

He said, "Three." And then, "No, four, there was a girl in Byzantium I almost forgot."

"Poor girl in Byzantium."

"Oh, I gave her a pair of eardrops and she was pleased enough."

I waited for something more, but he only smiled at me, between my hands, a little puzzled. "Do you mind, Timandra? You never minded before."

"Not the girl in Byzantium, nor any of her kind, no," I said. "But there might be one among the other three?"

He said, "Listen, my girl, I'm tired, and I'm a little drunk, and my head is not working very clearly. I do not think I know what you are talking about."

I said, "Something is changed. Something is over, and I do not know what it is." I heard my own voice speaking, lightly, as people speak of small things that do not have to do with life and death. "If it is the thing between you and me that is over—if there is some other woman, that you would have now in my place—"

He gave his head a little impatient jerk between my hands, but his mouth half laughed at me. "Would you have anything to complain of if there were? I have held to you for three full years, Timandra; that's two years and a summer longer than I ever held to any woman before."

"Tell me who she is and where she is," I said.

"Why?"

I let go his head and had him round the neck, straining up against him. "So that I can go to her and *kill* her!"

He was quite silent for a space, and in his silence was a fresh flurry of sleet against the shutters, and far below the sounding of the sea, for the tide was on the turn. And then he flung his head back against my hold, and laughed.

"She-wolf! I believe you would!"

"Tell me!" I said. "Tell me!" and dug my nails into the back of his neck. He broke my hold and caught my wrists and held me in his turn.

"You women! Can none of you ever think of anything that can be over than the one thing? The lying in bed beneath some wretched man you have set your heart on?"

In a few moments I gave up trying to free my hands, and waited for him to say more.

He said, "Timandra, it is not the thing between you and me that is over, it is the campaign here in the North. I have won Athens back the Northern Empire that I cost her. I have lived three years of my life, and I do not think that any years will be so good again. I think, for one thing, that I shall leave the last of my youth behind me, here with you at Pactye."

"You are leaving me here, at Pactye?"

He said, "There is no more need of us along these coasts. I have already ordered Thrasybulus and the bulk of the fleet home. With the first sailing weather in the spring I shall go back to Athens."

"Take me too!" I said. "I will be a slave again—your slave, your flute-girl."

He shook his head. "Eight years ago, I bade goodbye to Athens, under sentence of death. Nearly five years ago they called me back—but the sentence was not lifted; and there was work to be done here in the North. Now the work is done, and I have repaid, the High Gods know it, every wrong I ever did to Athens in payment for the wrong that Athens did to me—which leaves the State heavily in my debt. So now I go home to take my triumph, and it is in my mind that the old sentence will go whistling down the wind. But there are always those who do not forgive a debt when it is they who owe it. I know that when I go back to Athens I shall be walking into the greatest hazard of my life; and the man who walks that road does best to travel light."

"Don't go," I said. "You have saved Athens; she can do without you now."

He answered with his mouth buried in my hair. "I don't believe she can. I know I cannot do without her."

And I knew that it was as though I were losing him to another woman after all.


## The Citizen


We knew that he was coming, for a winter and a spring and the beginning of a summer, before he came. At early winter

245

Thrasybulus came into Piraeus with most of our fleet—a great fleet again, we had scarcely realized how great until suddenly Athens seemed flooded with seamen—bringing word that Alkibiades was returning with the remaining squadron in the spring. And in the spring word came by various traders that he was on his way; and then that he had turned south for Karia to collect that year's tribute; and then that he was back at Samos. A fast penteconta brought his official word from Paros that his bows were even now set toward Athens; but the next we heard was that the squadron had been seen off Gythion on the Lacedaemon coast; that was just a few days after the Assembly had confirmed him in his command, and elected him to serve as a General for the following year.

I couldn't get away from the shop that day; there was quite a lot of custom again by that time, though most of it wasn't the class it had been in the old days. So I wasn't there to drop my pebble in the pot, but the news was all over Athens almost before the vote was cast; and that evening, when I was able to shut up shop at last, I went round to Theron's house in the Ceramicus. Things were not quite as they used to be between Theron and me, since he returned with the main fleet. We had been boys when we were at our closest, and now we were men, and not even very young men any more; and the years between had carried us away from each other. There was always a certain constraint between us now. I knew that he was sorry for me, and looked down on me a little. I was poor old Timotheus tethered to his father's shop by a lame leg; and Theron might be only a fleet rower, but he had rowed through the great three-year campaign in the North, of which he once said to me that even the rowers who had a part in it felt like kings. But the old friendship held between us after a fashion; and he made me welcome, and his sister brought us out a jug of much watered wine, and we sat under the trained vine in the little walled-in dirt-patch that served them as a courtyard, and drank, and watched the tethered dunghill cock, woken by the lamp, strutting among his sleepy hens. Glory is glory, but a rower's wage of three obols a day, mostly in arrears, does not pay for luxury.

I said, "Why is he doing it?"

"He's playing for time," Theron said.

"I suppose so. He can't know all Athens is ringing with his coming, and they have built a fine new house for him in place of the one they pulled down."

"He probably does," Theron said. "But he also knows that the old blasphemy sentence hasn't yet been revoked; and what he

246

can't know yet is that the Assembly have elected him General for the year." He smiled into his wine cup, and in the small silence a roosting hen ruffled its wings in the vine branches overhead. "It seems funny, that, when in fact he has been the General for four years."

"Only by the mandate of Samos," I said.

"Samos has been all that there was of Athens with power to make a General. With power enough to count for anything," Theron said. "Gods! You don't know—you all seem like dozing old men here; waiting for Alkibiades to come and wake you up again!"

"When he *does* come," I said, nettled; no one likes to be told that he is a dozing old man, at twenty-nine.

"When he has had time to know of this afternoon's vote, I think he'll come. But how long he'll stay is another matter."

I got a lift in a cart going down to Piraeus, to see him come in. I did not want to see him first, riding up from the Piraeus Gate, as I had seen him ride out eight years ago. It was foolish, but I had a superstitious feeling about it, remembering the streets of Athens crimson-stained with the flowers of Adonis; especially since the Fates, who had sent him out on one ill-omened day were bringing him home on another. For it was the Festival of Plyntria; the day when our most ancient and sacred statue of Athene is stripped of her garments, and while they go to be washed, is veiled from the sight of her people. It was as if, said an old man in the cart with me, shaking his head, she refused to look upon Alkibiades' homecoming.

But if Athene would not look, her people had crowded down to Piraeus for the first sight of him, until I wondered if there was anybody left in Athens at all. Wharves and jetties were clotted with them like bees at swarming time; they hung out of doorways and windows, clung to every column-base and thronged every ledge and roof-top. Citizens and sailors from the main fleet, everyone staring out toward the harbour mouth; for it was half a day now since the squadron had been sighted out beyond Aegina. The triremes of the main fleet were for the most part drawn up on to the slipways of the covered docks; transports and merchantmen had been warped to one side, leaving the centre of the harbour clear; and the vast crowds had begun to quieten as the scout-boat was sighted scurrying back. I had got a good place right on the edge of the main jetty; for like most small men I am good with my elbows and quick to seize a chance; and the only disadvantage was the likelihood that I might get pushed off the jetty altogether, and into the harbour.

Then the people on the mole began to stir. We could hear their voices across the water; no cheering, just a confused splurge of voices; and round the high snout of the mole, where the Oligarch's fort had once stood, appeared the first of the squadron, coming in under sail and oars.

All round the great harbour the stir and ruffle and murmur of the crowd ceased. As she came nearer we could see that she was flashing with captured Spartan shields along her bulwarks; and fantastic shapes that glowed bronze and darkly coloured in the sun were stacked about the mast—someone said that they were figure-heads hacked from the prows of captured galleys; and the great blue pennant of the flagship flew from the stern. As she drew nearer, we began to see other things: that her paint was chipped and faded, that the blue pennant was battle- and sea-stained and ragged at the ends, and the deck planks gaped with cracks made by sun and salt. But though I remembered these things afterwards, at the time, like every other soul in that huge, waiting, murmurous multitude, I saw nothing but one solitary figure standing alone on the forward deck.

And my throat ached on the edge of tears like a woman's, because Alkibiades who had brought us to the very lip of destruction, was home to us again after eight years.

I heard an order barked across the water; men were aloft in the rigging, the weather-worn sail came rattling down, the oars ceased their rapid beat, rose and feathered, then fell again and held water—somewhere in the crowd, Theron would be watching that with professional interest. The long dark flagship slid up alongside the jetty not a spear's throw from where I stood, bumped lightly against the wooden sheathing of the stone-work, and settled.

Still the cheering did not break; even the murmuring had died away. Save for a small eddy of movement where a handful of nobility and high officialdom were thrusting through towards the trireme, nobody moved or spoke; and surely there was no eye in all that throng that was not fixed on that solitary figure standing unmoving and alone on the forward deck.

He was bareheaded now, having pulled off his great crested helmet and tossed it to one of his staff officers standing below him at the break of the deck; and his hair seemed less bright than when I had seen it last, as though he had rubbed ashy fingers through it. The sunlight cast harsh shadows under his cheekbones and into the hollows of his eyes. I thought, 'Lord Apollo! he is not young any more!' He was like his ship, storm-battered and battle-scarred, worn down to the bones of what he had been, so that suddenly I knew what his skull would look like, clean of the flesh—scoured like a piece of driftwood by sun and salt sea.

He was looking among the crowd; looking, I knew as surely as though he were part of myself, for the face of friends, or enemies, testing their mood as a hound tests the wind for scent. Then he saw the men thrusting through to greet him, friends and kinsmen, the faces of his own seamen and soldiers, among the throng; and it was as though his own face caught fire and he held out his hands to his waiting friends, to all Athens. And the years, and the old wrong, and the old revenge fell away from between us; and then the cheering broke; a great crash of cheering like the crash of a breaking wave, that spread from jetty to jetty and out along the arms of the mole and up the narrow ways from the water-side into the town. And Alkibiades had sprung ashore and had his arms round some kinsman or old friend, and I lost sight of him in the crowd. His officers were coming ashore after him; the other ships of the squadron were coming in to their waiting berths, but no one spared a glance for them; we were all craning and jostling for one more sight of Alkibiades. The next time I saw him, he was being carried shoulder high among his own men. Somebody had crowned him with golden laurel, and the marines were forcing a passage for him up towards the Temple of Poseidon, where the horses waited, forming a ring about him to keep back—not very successfully—the crowds who tried to burst through to touch his feet or his hand or the trailing end of his cloak, as though he were lucky, or a God.

He spoke to the full gathering of the Assembly later that same day, and I was there on the Pnyx to see and hear him. I don't know how I managed it. I got a lift part of the way but I had to walk the rest, and at what was to me a gruelling pace, to get there in time. And when I arrived my lame leg was shaking under me, and aching worse than it had done since I was a boy and the old injury was new. Even so, I was late, and so far back on the edge of the crowd that I'd have seen and heard scarcely anything but for Theron, for I was too spent to push my own way through as I had done earlier, at Piraeus. He had kept an eye open for me—his height made it easier for him; and he shouted when he saw me, and flourished an arm, and came thrusting back from his own place, grinning, and said, "Come on, stick behind me." And somehow, breathless and buffeted, I found myself among a knot of desperadoes with bleached hair and salt-burned faces, who I realized must be some of his rowing mates. They stank to high heaven, but in that moment I would have asked for no better company in all the world.

"I looked for you at Piraeus, this morning," Theron shouted above the tumult of the crowd.

"I was there," I shouted back.

"I guessed you would be, even if you had to crawl," he said, and flung a heavy arm across my shoulders. "You're as daft as the rest of us."

The next time we met, the restraint had come back, but for that time all was well and simple between us, as it had been when we were boys.

Figures were mounting the rostrum, and the uproar began to die away even before the trumpets sounded and the Priest came forward to make the Sacrifice.

When it was done, and the smoke of the incense hanging in the air, Alkibiades stood forward to speak, still wearing his crown of golden laurel. He stood there for what seemed a long time, with the blue sky and the far-off Temple of the Maiden behind him, holding out his hands to us, but not speaking. The crowd rustled and murmured, and waited; and still he stood there. He seemed somehow pinned against that empty blueness of sky; I saw his throat work, and the shadows contract into a kind of grimace about his mouth, and realized that he was fighting for speech, against the barrier of the emotions choking him. I should not think that Alkibiades suffered that trouble more than once in all his life; but seeing him that time, I thought, 'It is a man who feels this way, not a God; and a man can fail; and if he fails, the Gods help him!' The thought, or something like it, seemed familiar, and I remember the old man in the crowd, on the day of the Adonia. But if Alkibiades failed again, it would be a different kind of failing.

And then he broke through the barrier. For the first few words his voice was not altogether under his control, and then it steadied and became the old easy voice with the familiar lisp that our hearts had remembered across eight years. He spoke very simply, saying that he held Demeta the Corn Mother herself to witness that he had never profaned her Mysteries. But he blamed no one by name, for the unjust trial and condemnation; in which I think he was wise. His sorrows, he said, had come upon him from "some envious genius of his own" and there he left the matter, and passed on to other things. He spoke of the broken hopes of the Spartans—making no mention of the years when it had been our hopes that were broken through him; but all that was forgiven and forgotten and out of mind. He promised us that now we might lift our heads with courage and gaze into the future; and we caught his fire, and kindled and leapt up like smouldering touchwood when it feels the wind.

In the end, the Assembly took command, in a kind of frenzy of rejoicing. Something in me knew that it was too bright to last; unless that is only the hind-sight, after all. The keys of his new house were publicly presented to him. We ordered the Heralds of the Mysteries to revoke the curse of eight years before, and throw the iron tablets on which it was engraved into the sea. We had already elected him one of the Generals of the year, but now suddenly we raised the cry that he must be General-in-Chief; that he must have sole power, absolute command of our forces by land and sea. The proposal was put to the vote and carried there and then. It was, I think, the first time that Athens had given such absolute power to one man since the days of the Kings.

Alkibiades tried to refuse; I remember him standing there looking on over the great sea of faces that we must have been to him, his hands going out, almost as though to thrust something away. He said, "My friends, you offer too much, too great a weight of honour, you would set upon my shoulders. Such absolute power is for the Gods, not for men."

We cheered and shouted him down, and though he tried to speak again, for once he could not get himself a hearing, so that at last there was nothing for him to do but bow his head under its crown of golden laurel, and spread his hands in acceptance.

We thought that it had been modesty (as though he had ever known the meaning of the word!) which had made him protest against the honour we would do him. But I think, now, that he saw the deadly danger in this new and unheard-of power that we were shackling upon him too soon.

When the crowd was dismissed and began to drift away, I chanced to come face to face with a man I knew slightly; and it was a hating face, dry-mouthed and narrow-eyed. He looked at me, and said, "Despite appearances, not everyone in Athens has forgotten that the Spartans are still in Dekalia."

# 19

## The Seaman

"Another month," says Alkibiades. "Three months Athens has given me house room, she and I might just about manage one more."

I hadn't seen much of him in that time, for my own days were mostly spent down at Piraeus with the fleet; and so I sees the change in him more clearly than if I'd been with him all the while. His lines had gone leaden and there were dark stains under his eyes. It was the change that always came over him, of late years, whenever the living grew soft.

"I don't know what you mean," I says.

And he grins, "Oh yes you do, pilot, you've heard what they're saying in the streets—or hasn't it reached Piraeus yet?"

I had come up to report on some repair work, and stayed on to supper in the handsome new house. When the meal was over, he had sent the slaves away, and it was just the two of us under the vine arbour of the old house that had stood there before. It was a very hot evening, and the vine leaves overhead, rimmed with light from the lamps, scarcely stirred. I stared up at them until they blurred and ran together at the edges.

"I'll tell you what *has* reached Piraeus," I says, "the feeling that after all these years of muddled government and frittering away of our resources, Athens would do better with one hand to hold the reins, if the hand was strong enough. You're already Master of Athens, it wouldn't be much of a change. I reckon you could be Tyrant of Athens tomorrow, if you reached out your hand."

"But I'm not reaching out my hand," says Alkibiades.

"Why in Typhon's name not? What do you want?"

"Maybe even that, one day," says he, staring into his cup as though he sees things there beyond the reflection of the vine leaves. "But not yet. Not till the time is ripe; and the time is yet only ripening on the bough." He flings back his head and laughs, sudden and soft in his throat. "Besides, I'm ambitious. If I get to the utmost point of ambition too soon, what is left for a later day?"

"So you'll have us back to sea before that happens?" I says, and reaches for the wine krater. If the fleshpots aren't lasting long, make the most of them!

Alkibiades says, looking at me across the wine, "Do you suppose the people are alone in thinking it a short step from General-in-Chief to Tyrant? Do you suppose my enemies haven't thought of that one, too? And the Gods know I've enough enemies in Athens, headed by Kritias and that republican snake Cleontius . . . When I leave Athens it will be for many reasons—not the least among them, that I've no wish for a knife in my back."

"That's not like you," I says.

"No it's not, is it? Perhaps I'm growing old, pilot, or maybe it's just that I'm beginning to know the people of Athens." He takes a drink, and sets the cup down very careful. "It *has* reached Piraeus, hasn't it?"

"Yes," I says, unwillingly. "People are beginning—only a few people—to say why don't you get off back to sea and win us more victories."

He nods. "More victories. I've done it once, so why don't I do it again. They're hungry already for another triumph; and if they don't get it . . . I tell you, Athens is like some women, who can grind a man in their woman-parts until they've sucked the manhood and the very life out of him, and when they've destroyed him, throw him off and take a new lover."

"Athens won't take a new lover," I says.

And he says, "Not so long as I'm her blue-eyed darling and can give her what she wants."

He put his bowed head in his hands and sat there slumped with his elbows on the table, and I thinks, 'It's a good thing there's none but me to see him now.' And then he does one of his sudden changes that I've never got used to in all the years I've known him. He gives his shoulders a little shake, and looks up—and he's Alkibiades again.

"But before I go, I'll give them something to remember me by until I come again. How many days is it to the Eleusinian Festival? Twelve? Eleven?"

"Eleven, the ships are being made ready now."

Ever since the Spartans had been at Dekalia, the Eleusinian Mysteries had been shorn of half their glory; for the procession along the Sacred Way, with its hymns and ritual dances, and sacrifices at shrines by the way, had been too dangerous, and for seven years the whole boiling lot had had to be ferried round by sea.

"We'll cancel the ships," says Alkibiades. "This year the procession will travel along the Sacred Way again."

"There are still Spartans at Dekalia," I says.

"But there's Alkibiades in Athens . . . I and my troops will guard the pilgrims from any attack. The old glory shall return to the Mysteries."

"I'm not a public meeting you're addressing," I says.

But he brushes that aside, and springs up from the table and begins to pace up and down, talking all the while. "Can't you see what it will do for the morale of the troops who have been shut up in Athens all this time? Ever since Agis has been perched up at Dekalia they've scarcely been outside the city, save to patrol the Long Walls. This will be like a trumpet blast to them."

"I can see all that," I says. "Splendour for Athens and Athenian arms, and for the Mysteries, and splendour for Alkibiades—"

"Of course—among other matters."

"There's only one thing—will the Priests of Eleusis accept your escort?"

He stops pacing and looks at me. "They had orders to cast the curse tablets into the sea. If they don't accept my escort, they're publicly admitting that they only did so because they were afraid to disobey the Assembly, and not because they believed in my innocence. That doesn't look well in a priesthood."

"Were we innocent?" I says. "I've always been a bit hazy as to that night."

"Yes," he says, looking at me square, "we got drunk and we played the fool, but we stopped short of the Forbidden Things. I've mocked the Gods from time to time, who hasn't? Even good old Euripides. But if we had played with the Great Secret, do you think even I would do as I shall do—go with the initiates into the Holy of Holies?"

"I'd not put it past you," I says. But I sees that he's in earnest; it really matters to him, this going again into the Holy Place. I shall never understand Alkibiades. I'd have said he was more godless than myself.

"I have certain limitations; even I," he says. "Are you coming with me?"

"Not I. Once was enough for me."

# The Soldier

On the day before the procession was due to start out, Alkibiades posted sentries on the high ground at Daphne with orders to keep watch for any sign of movement from the direction of Dekalia. And those of us who were detailed to guard the pilgrims were turned out at first light next morning, the small amount of cavalry we still possessed, from the Temple of the Dioscurii, the foot companies from our makeshift camp below the High City. We ate quickly hearing the horses clattering by; and marched down to take up our positions outside the Dipylon Gate. It was one of those quiet mornings when the fading night turns green and watery while the owls are still crying. I remember the white flowers of the oleander over a nearby grave beginning to shine faintly as white flowers do in the dusk at either end of the day. The horses stamped and fidgeted, we of the foot companies stood at ease, leaning on our spears, talking a little from time to time, but already drawn up in marching order.

The sentries from Daphne had sent in to report all quiet.

Just before sunrise we heard horses coming down towards the gate, and Alkibiades came out, riding one of the fine new Thessalian stallions that the city had given him, his staff clattering at his heels. He rode up and down the lines, reining in his fidgeting horse here and there to speak to the Pylarchs and company commanders; or to some scarred common hoplite who had served under him. When he came to me, he reined in and gave me my orders in case of a Spartan attack (we already had them, of course, but Alkibiades was always thorough, and I think he liked the excuse to make personal contact, to see men's faces quicken when he spoke to them). He said, "Not quite the usual kind of work for the old Samos brotherhood, eh, Arkadius?" Then he rode on.

My Number Two said, "I wonder if the Spartans *will* attack?"

"It's in the lap of the Gods," I said. "Alkibiades hopes they will."

The boy looked at me, questioning and surprised. He was one of the Athens garrison, and had not followed Alkibiades to the Black Sea and back again.

"If they do, he'll lead the defence in person," I explained. "And everyone will see him, fighting like a God in defence of the Sacred Things, and tell their grandchildren about it afterwards."

He made a small bitten-off sound, and when I looked round, he was staring straight ahead of him as though on parade, his face flushed like a nicely brought up girl's, if you had pulled her veil off in the street.

"I thought you of the Samos brotherhood would cut your sword hands off for him."

"Oh, we would," I said, "but that's quite a different matter."

The rim of the sun was hanging like a golden bead on the shoulder of Parnes and suddenly the world began to cast shadows again as the light spilled over and came trickling down the hills; and far off through the city we heard the singing, winding nearer as the light grew more strong. There was movement within the gate, and the head of the procession came slowly through, out of the gatehouse shadows into the early sun between the graves and the oleander trees. First came the Image of Iacchus, the God himself, garlanded with the golden last ears of the corn, and carried by two tall Priests of the Mysteries. Then the High Priest and others bearing the emblems of the God. Then the first of the musicians, and then the long line of Mystae, white-robed and wreathed with myrtle, and carrying each their unlit torch; young boys and maidens for initiation, grown men and women going to review the wonder of the Mystery that they had known before. All singing as they came, the slow first hymn to Iacchus that begins the day.

The first company, led by Alkibiades, moved off; then it was our turn. I gave the order, and we were on the march, our faces toward Daphne and our shadows reaching out long before us in the morning sun. Presently, looking back, I could see the whole white-robed line of the procession, the myrtle garlands and dark waving branches already hazed by the rising dust-cloud. And all along the line, between them and the menace of Dekalia, the companies of marching troops; and northward again, strung high along the sky's edge, the thin strung-out line of the scouting cavalry.

Everyone knows what it is like, the procession along the Sacred Way to Eleusis; the long hymns to Iacchus and to Demeter of the Corn, and to Kore, the Maiden; the sacred dances to the shrilling of flutes and cymbals, the long pauses to sacrifice at the shrines along the way. The day grew hot, and the soft dust-cloud rose and whitened us from head to foot. The mountains had their pale end-of-summer look, save where the drifting cloud shadows made stains as black as grapes on the high slopes, and on our left even the blue water of the gulf was faded, as though weary in the heat; our helmets burned our foreheads, and the parched ground and sparse tawny grass of the wayside scorched our feet. The very slowness with which we had to travel seemed to make the heat more intense, for it is not easy for men trained to normal marching pace to drift along at the speed of a sacred procession. And all day as we slogged onwards, Alkibiades with his knot of staff officers behind him, passed and repassed us, riding the length of the line like a good sheepdog keeping his flock together and himself between them and any danger of wolf.

It was dusk when at last we reached the gentle lift of country that formed the boundary of Eleusis. The scent was coming out of the scrub, rosemary and thyme and lentisk; and looking back, the lights of Athens, kindled for the festival, speckled the dusk ten miles behind us; and ahead, on the low ground at the edge of the sea, the lights of the Sacred Precinct of Eleusis. After the day, coolness seemed to lie like a blessing over the land and the temple and the dark scented tide of pines that washed it round. We went on down the hill, to the Meeting Place, where the Heralds and Eumolpe waited with their torches, to kindle the unlit torches of the Mystae and bind about the left wrist and ankle of each one the ribbon without which they would not be allowed into the Holy Place.

There, on the border of the sacred ground, with the lights of the dim-seen halls and colonnades below us against the pale sheen of the sea, our task was over, until the time came to escort the procession back to Athens.

There, too, we parted from Alkibiades. He dismounted and gave his horse to his groom, laid by his sword and helmet, and with the help of the staff lads, stripped off armour and linen tunic, until he stood naked and burnished in the light of the torches. He could afford to stand so, before troops and worshippers. His body had thickened a little with the years, but it was as hard as a hound's, and there was no more fat on him than on a boy at his first Games, and he stood light and proud on the balls of his feet. He took from the Priests who brought it to him, the white robe of an initiate, and put on the myrtle wreath. They brought him a torch, and kindled it, and tied the yellow ribbon on his wrist and ankle; and he stepped in among the rest, and moved off with them, laying aside the General-in-Chief, to become just one of the white-robed figures singing under their torches, as they moved forward into the Sacred Precinct. In a few moments I could not even be sure which figure was his, any more.

We made camp among the stone pines outside the enclosure, posted scouts in case, even now, the Spartans tried anything, and got the cooking fires going while the cavalrymen watered the horses.

And there we kicked our heels through that night and the next day, and another night, while below in the Precinct of Demeter and Kore, Alkibiades and his fellows would be fasting and making the purifactory sacrifices. Many of us were initiates ourselves, and knew when they would be eating the sacred bread and drinking the hallowed wine; we knew, even if we had not heard the Herald's trumpet, when it was time to enter the Hall of the Mysteries. But beyond the doorway, and once the torches are quenched, there seems no time; and so we did not know when the singing would begin; nor when the supreme moment, the Showing, would come; for to some of us it had seemed that we were in the dark for many nights and days, and journeying all the time; while for others, it had seemed no more than a breath of asphodel and the time it takes to move from one room into another. But it is forbidden to speak of these things.

We talked a little round the watch fires; once somebody struck up a song, and a few voices joined in, but it fell silent after the first verse. A few of us lay down to sleep, but not many; there was something in all that great hollow of the hills on that night of the year that seemed to hold off sleep.

In the dark of the night, far on towards dawn we heard the temple trumpets again, and far off and thin as the song of grasshoppers, the shrilling of the flutes. And below us suddenly the shore-line was alive with flecks and feathers of light, as the initiates took their torches down to the water and plunged in for the swim that ended the ritual. I remembered how, to me on my own night, the first touch of the torchlit water had been a cold white fire on my body not yet quite returned from the strange places of death and rebirth; and then had changed into the cool strong slap and swing of the sea, into bathing at night with torches, nothing more. And a great lightness and relief had come over me to find that the familiar world which I seemed to have lost for a while was still there, and I had splashed water that shone like flakes of fire over the girl dog-paddling beside me, and realized suddenly as we turned for land (keeping my torch alight had become only a game of pride and skill), that I had never been so hungry in all my life before. I wondered how many of the boys swimming back to land were feeling like that now. I wondered what Alkibiades was feeling, now that it was all over. But save perhaps for Socrates, I doubt if anybody has ever quite known what Alkibiades is feeling.

I had heard that they had come face to face, those two, in the Street of the Tripods, only a few days after our return, and looked at each other once, and passed by without speaking; and had wondered at the time, what the cost was to both of them.

"Well, that's over," said a voice, like an echo of my own thoughts, and Agathos, one of the Cavalry Pylarchs, loomed out of the darkness into the glow of the watch fire. "I wonder what the General-in-Chief is feeling."

"I know one thing I'd be feeling, in his place," I said, "and that's triumph. He must know that this is his full acquittal by the Lords of the Mysteries. Also he'll have enjoyed showing Gods and men, not only that the Lords of the Mysteries have acquitted *him*, but that *he* has forgiven *them*."

"And of course he'll have given a superb performance, the Lord of Athens laying down his olive crown for a pilgrim's wreath. Our greatest stage tragedian couldn't touch it."

We sat silent for a few moments, and then Agathos said at half breath, "If it came to making Alkibiades Tyrant of Athens—"

I looked round at him quickly. "Tyrant!"

"It's being talked of almost openly in the streets. People are sick of the hot air talked in the Assembly, the plots and counter-plots; Oligarch and Democrat pulling Athens to pieces between them. After this, the first time the Mysteries have known their old glory in eight years, they'll be in love with the idea."

I had heard something, but had taken care not to listen. "Then we can only hope that Alkibiades won't be."

"You don't fancy our new General-in-Chief as supreme Master of the State?"

"Democracy may not always be much of a way of government," I said, "but it's the only way for Athens no matter what she thinks she wants."

"Arkadius knows what is good for Athens, better than she does herself," he said, idly mocking.

"Oh, go to Hades!" I said, and rolled myself in my cloak and turned my back on him and tried again to sleep. There was only a short while left before daylight. But sleep was further than ever from me now. I have loved Athens, and the thought of her putting herself once more under the rule of a Tyrant made my belly twist with anger; but the thought of Alkibiades, who we had followed through the winter storms and the blue dolphin days from Samos to the Black Sea and back, with whom we had shared our wine by a hundred watch fires, behind whom we had swept into sea fight after sea fight, and stormed and taken towns, becoming no more

259

than Tyrant of Athens made me want to lay my head in my arms and weep as a boy weeps—or a man for lost youth and lost love.

In the morning the worshippers came out from the Precinct, and we guarded them back to Athens along the Sacred Way, Alkibiades once more in his armour, riding the big Thessalian stallion at the head of his troops.

When we got back, the city was full of news. The Spartans had launched a new fleet of thirty triremes from Gythion, and the new Spartan Admiral, sent to replace Mindarus, had taken them over to Ephesus, which could only mean the beginning of new troubles in Ionia and the Islands. Tissaphernes had been removed from his Satrapy, and the new Satrap of Lydia was Prince Cyrus, a boy not yet out of his teens, a tremendous fire-eater and a great admirer of the Spartans. I began to smell open water again and feel the shock of the galley's ram driving home.

I don't suppose I was the only one in the fleet to do that or to feel in an odd way, glad. Athens looked as it had always done, but it was beginning to have a different smell; a sick smell. Too many crooked undercurrents, too many things happening in the dark. I was beginning to want to go back to war and the ways of fighting men, which I understand.

## The Seaman

I was sitting in my usual corner of the Amber Dolphin with a couple of mates, drinking Chian wine and sweating it out again as fast as I put it in, in the sweltering heat that was beating up for the first of the autumn thunderstorms, and I looks up and sees Alkibiades standing in the street entrance. He jerks his head at me to come outside, and I downs what's left in my cup and goes—most of the wine-shop turning round to gape at him standing there.

"What is it, then?" I says.

And he says, pleasant and conversational, "Come and get a bit of air, pilot."

"I'd sooner have another drink; come in and have one, too, and then we'll find a couple of girls."

"I don't want a drink and I don't want a girl; and no more do you. Come and stretch your legs, pilot."

I says, "There's going to be the father and mother of storms, before dark."

And he grins. "Afraid of getting wet, pilot?"

And his face reminds me of the way it used to look during those last days in Sparta. So out I goes.

We walked straight through the city, in the still yellowish storm light, where everyone had come out to doors and windows and flat roofs to get what little air there was, until we came to the skirts of Lykabettus and began to climb. Cloud stooped low over our heads, and halfway up the thunder began to growl as though the storm were waking and stretching itself among the steep wooded gorges. There was a whip-crack of white lightning, and the rain began.

Like a lot of seamen, I don't care for getting wet on dry land, not when there isn't any need. It would be pleasant now in the court-yard of the Amber Dolphin, cooling down, while the rain hissed and pattered among the vine leaves. But Alkibiades climbed steadily on, and after one hopeful glance at his face in the next flare of the lightning, so did I—grumbling a good deal under my breath, I'll admit. Alkibiades climbed in silence, with his head back and his eyes wide to the lightning; it was enough to give a man the creeps!

We climbs right into the storm, up into the high saddle of Lykabettos, with the clouds all about us, blue-black and copper, and the lightning leaping from one to another and the thunder crashing about our shoulders, and Athens far below us hidden in the drifting storm-murk. We're both long since drenched to the skin, and speaking personal, I'm chilled to the bone, which is another thing I don't hold with on land. I shouts between crack and crack of the thunder, "Well, now that we've got here, can we go down again?"

For answer he sits himself down on a rock on the very edge of the level patch, where the hill drops away into nothingness. I goes to the edge and makes water into the rolling storm cloud below us. It was the cold on top of all that wine, and we'd come up at too fierce a pace to allow of such things by the way.

"I'm not certain that's not blasphemy," Alkibiades says.

"I'll sacrifice to Zeus when I get down again, to be on the safe side."

There's another crash of thunder, and when it's rumbled away, Alkibiades says, "It's time we put to sea again, pilot."

I stands over him, wrapping myself up in my arms and shivering. "Anything would be better than standing around on a hill-top in this deluge. Any new reason? Or just the same ones you had last time we talked of it?"

"Several new reasons. Lysander is in Ephesus, for one—Did

you know he was the new Spartan Admiral?—building ships as fast as the shipwrights can lay down the keels."

"I've heard of that one. You'd wonder what he was using for money."

"Persian darics, I should imagine. The word is that he—Lysander—has been up in Sardis, making friends with the new Satrap. All the world knows that young Cyrus is pro-Spartan to his finger-tips."

Again the thunder crashed about us, and boomed and echoed itself away down the gorges. But the crown of the storm was past, and the rain was slackening.

When we could hear ourselves speak again, Alkibiades says, "I don't like having the friendship between Athens and Persia that I've sweated to build up wrecked by a love affair between Lysander and the Persian Prince; and the sooner we go and do something about it the better."

"Agreed," I says. "Right then—give the orders, and the fleet's ready for sea."

He don't answer at once, then he says through the softening rain, "I've had visitors after dark, more than once lately. They came to sound me out as to what I would do if the chance was handed to me to become Tyrant of Athens. The last one was as good as an offer—and that I think was genuine."

"Not the others?"

"Not sure. I've a feeling Cleontius or Kritias—maybe both of them; dirt breeds strange bedfellows—were behind at least one of the visits."

"The bastards!" I says.

Alkibiades unfurls himself slowly and stands up and stretches. "It would be almost worth staying on and making a bid for it, just to see them squirm."

"But not quite?" I says.

He shakes his head. "Not quite, pilot."

"And so you've dragged us both up here, and probably got us our deaths of cold, just to say that it's time we got out of Athens. You couldn't have done that somewhere out of the rain? In your own house, say?"

He said, looking out to where the storm-clouds were rolling away southward and bright rags of the sunset showing through, "I wanted the storm, pilot. A good storm clears the dark things out. It's as good as hoarhound in the spring—very cathartic." He looked round at me; the storm light had gone, and just enough light came out of the west for me to see his face. He says, "And

I wanted company. It had to be you or a dog, Antiochus, and I haven't known the hunting dogs in my new kennels so long as I have known you . . . I find myself increasingly alone in Athens." And then he grins and says, "We'll go back to my new house now, and get drunk."

We went down the looping goat track, with the air cool after the rain, and full of the scent of thyme and wet grass, and the faint mist steaming up from the hot city, and the lamps pricking out. We were halfway down when he says, "How many sons have you, pilot?"

I was taken aback. "I don't know; a few, I suppose, scattered round the seaport towns. None that I know of for sure."

"Sons are a mistake anyway," he says lightly. "I went to see mine today—thinking I'd better do my fatherly duty before leaving Athens. He's almost ten. It's odd, I had forgotten that he would be so old. His Uncle Callias has told him how I misused his mother, of course."

"So I reckon he hates you. I wouldn't worry. It'll pass when he learns to think for himself."

"He didn't seem to hate me. He was more curious. He had heard that there are pleasurable ways of hurting a woman beyond nature, and not unnaturally assumed that I had practised them on his mother. He wanted to know about them, and thought therefore that I'd be a good one to tell him. It was only when I did not oblige that he started screaming and tried to knife me. He's extremely skilled, I gather, at crushing mice with a brick. His eyes were painted like something out of a boy's pleasure house."

And then I knew why Alkibiades had wanted the storm. I didn't say anything. There didn't seem anything to say. We walked on, down into the mist and the outlying houses.


## The Citizen

I wouldn't have gone especially to watch Alkibiades sail with a fleet of a hundred ships. The mood of Athens had changed, though it looked on the surface much as it had when we welcomed him home; I couldn't put my finger on the change, but it was there; and whatever it was, I didn't like it. But I had to be in Piraeus that day on business; a new consignment of rosemary oil and saffron perfume from Sardis, and I emerged from the warehouse just as a knot of rowers went past, on their way down to the jetty. Theron was in their midst, and called out to me to come and see them off. So I saw the fleet sail, after all.

It was a grey squally day, and the water out beyond the mole was white capped, running high enough almost to hide Aegina from where I stood. There was the usual crowd of friends and kinsfolk; but the city had not poured itself out to the dregs to see him away, as it had to see his return.

I said goodbye to Theron on the jetty before he went aboard the *Halkyone*, which was made fast alongside. He turned and flung up a hand to me in farewell, then disappeared below. The deck and outrigger hid the rowing benches from view, so I could not see him any more; but I waited on, all the same.

The water slapped against the jetty, and the air tasted wet and salt on my lips. I saw Alkibiades go past with his staff, muffled in his cloak and walking purposefully with his head down as a man walks in foul weather. He went down the jetty steps to the boat waiting to take him out to the flagship. And I remember he turned once, as the boat pulled away, and looked back. And for an instant I caught, as I had done that other time, the brilliant blue gaze, unquenched by the day and the chill at the heart of it. But his glance flicked across mine to someone standing at my shoulder.

I looked round quickly, and saw a short squat man of great physical strength, with the face of a satyr, the spread nose and thick-lipped mouth and bulging eyes. I had seen Socrates often enough to know him instantly, though never before, I think, at such close quarters. I saw the long look that passed between them as the gap of water widened; no smile, no signal of the hand, only that look. And then I felt an intruder and hurriedly glanced away, as from something that was not meant for other men to see.

I remembered the talk I had heard of those two, in my father's shop eight years ago.

The boat was growing smaller, the distance narrowing between it and the flagship. I heard the trumpet sounding across the water as it came alongside. I saw the purple pennant run up at the stern—but it looked black in the distance and the sombre morning light.

Trumpets were sounding from ship to ship through the fleet, and the smoke of the offering went up from a hundred altars and the scent of frankincense and storax drifted ashore on the salt wind. On the stern deck of the *Halkyone*, I could see the Trirarch pouring the libation. They did not raise the Paean.

The *Icarus* was already under way; the row-boats were standing by as the ships along the jetties cast off, to warp them out into the channel. A flurry of spray from an oar flew into my face, and involuntarily I turned my head aside from it, and my eyes met the bulging eyes of Socrates. Never having been so close to him before, I had not known how kind they were, or how alight and alive and deeply concerned in all creation. There was a faint smile somewhere at the back of them, and I found myself answering it.

"One should never come to see one's friends off on their journeys," he said. "One can never do anything with the rest of the day. But we all do it, just as we all pick at our mosquito bites, which is equally foolish." He glanced at the *Halkyone* as she swung out from the jetty. "Yours, I think, was the big rower with the red beard."

"Yes," I said, "but like all the rest of Athens, it was Alkibiades too." And then I felt that I had been clumsy and could have bitten my tongue off.

His smile made all well again. "Not quite all the rest of Athens. Indeed I was thinking that the harbour was somewhat less crowded than I had expected."

I said quickly, "Never any man went from Athens leaving more love behind him."

"Or more passionate defenders," he said, smiling with his voice and eyes. "But also jealousy and distrust. Men generally distrust what they do not understand. Enemies enough—and his worst danger of all, in his own colossal prestige."

I was startled. "Why do you say that?"

He was looking out beyond the Mole, and something in his face made me wonder if his Daemon was speaking to him.

"Athens expects nothing but victory from him. He *is* victory. More God than man, nothing he cannot do. If he fails, we shall break him, you and I and the rest of Athens. We shall say, 'He pretended to be a God, and he was only a man', and we shall break him."

# 20

## The Seaman

We raided Andros on the way out. They had been interfering with the corn ships and needed a lesson. At first all went well; we defeated the islanders, and drove the Spartan garrison that sallied against us back into the fort. But we carried no siege equipment, and unless we were prepared to spend time that we could not afford, on a blockade, there was nothing much more that we could do. We made one attempt to take the tower by storm, but suffered heavy casualties among the marines, and in the end Alkibiades whistled them off; and there was nothing for it but to fortify the second town of Gaurium and leave a squadron of twenty triremes there under the command of young Konon, and take the rest of the fleet on to Samos.

I wish we hadn't to detach Konon; he's a good man, and we're going to need good men. But Alkibiades picked him as the best man for the job, so I suppose there's no help for it.

We made Samos on a choppy blue autumn day; the ships of the squadrons left behind there lining the docks and slipways.

But the news that met us there was black as the throat of Cerberus.

Myron, one of the senior Trirarchs, brought it on board with him as soon as we dropped anchor. "What money have you brought with you?" he asked Alkibiades, standing on the quarter-deck, almost before the trumpets had sounded him aboard.

Alkibiades says, "Enough to pay the fleet their three obols a day for something under a month. Athens is a poor city, these days, and Cleontius and his cronies have ways of making sure she puts what she's got to other uses than paying her fleet."

The Trirarch cursed, quietly, but long.

"We shall collect tribute," Alkibiades says. "We've done it before."

"And meanwhile, Lysander has got round young Cyrus to

bring the Spartan's pay up to four obols. And more than half our rowers are bought men from other states."

"Who will naturally go to the highest bidder." There's a silence full of the lap of water and the gulls crying and the voices along the waterfront. Then Alkibiades says, "We must bring Lysander and the Spartan fleet to action before the desertions start."

"The desertions have already started," Myron says. "We're losing men every day."

A few days later—so soon as we'd had time to get shipshape again after the voyage, and before there was time for many more of the rowers to slip away—we has the fleet out and stands across the straits for Ephesus. We cruises across and across just outside the harbour like a whore, with "Follow me" on the soles of our sandals, and our rumps wagging behind us. But Lysander refused to take the bait, and we could not go into the harbour after him.

We tried it for days, till it was clearly no use trying any longer.

"I was a fool to think there was the least chance of getting him out; but it had to be tried," Alkibiades says to me in his own quarters. "Time's on his side and he can afford to wait. He has the support of Cyrus, his men are well-paid and contented, and he has more galleys coming off the slipway every day. It's dead against us, with everything I've worked for cancelled out by this latest flowering of Lysander's love life . . ." He gets up quickly, and walks to the edge of the terrace and stands looking down between the saffron painted columns, at the lights of Samos pricking out in the dusk. "I wonder how many of our rowers are slipping off to Ephesus tonight. Time's running out on us, pilot. It's running out at exactly the speed that the money's running out. The morale of the fleet is dropping like a stone. We have got to get more money. It's not pretty, and that's the first priority now."

"How?" I says.

"Karia and the Islands."

"They've already paid this year's tribute."

He smashed his hand down on the low wall, and I mind how the heavy gold signet ring he always wears rang on the stone. "Then by Night's Daughters, they can pay next year's in advance. They're rich enough, with all trade routes from the East passing at their back door. I'll take ten ships—it's time I had a look at Thrasybulus, see how things are going with him, maybe get his views on the situation." (Thrasybulus has finished the work that he was left to clear up along the Thracian coast, when we left for Athens, and come south. Now he's blockading Phocaea, which revolted in the summer. You can't take your eyes off them an instant.) "Then make for Karia, and gather what I can in the way of a further levy."

"With ten ships?" I says.

"It should be enough. The sight of a few warships works wonders in a merchant port, especially a rich one."

He comes back to the table and pours out more wine, and drinks standing, rocking a little on his heels. I watches him a bit anxious. Men say I drink like a fish, and I'm not denying it; but it don't matter with my sort, so long as we can still handle a ship, and drunk or sober, there's not a pilot in the fleet my equal. Alkibiades drinks different, mostly when he's bored or banging his head against something, and in the long run it dulls him—makes him like a galley clogged with weed below the water-line, slow to answer to the steering oar, a danger to herself and the rest of the fleet. He'd been drinking heavily in the past few days, and I knew it wouldn't be long before it began to take effect.

"When do we sail?" I says.

"I sail as soon as the ships can be victualled and ready."

"Three days," I says, not noticing till after, that he says "I" and not "We".

"Two," he says. "We've been here in Samos eighteen days; we can't make it more than twenty. Have the ships ready for sailing at first light, two days from now." And then he sets down his wine cup and looks at me. "I'm leaving you in command here, Antiochus. From the moment the squadron sails, you take over."

That has me out of my seat as though it had suddenly sprouted nettles, and we stands facing each other across the wine. "You're drunker than I thought," I says.

"No, I'm not drunk, only desperate."

"Then you must be more desperate than I thought," I says. "I've been your pilot twenty years, take or leave a few, and never held a command—never the command of one bloody little penteconta, and now you ask me to take command of the whole fleet."

"I'm not asking," Alkibiades says, "I'm ordering." He leans across the table, jutting his beard in my face. "I use men for the tasks that they do best. I've plenty of good troop commanders, and a good troop commander makes a good Trirarch. He doesn't need to know how to handle sea craft, he doesn't need to know much even about his own trireme. His pilot sees to all that for him. Good pilots are harder come by; and you've said it yourself, often enough, you're the best pilot in the fleet. So you've served

268

twenty years as *my* pilot and never had command of one bloody little penteconta. And now I'm ordering you to take command of the fleet while I'm away."

"Why?" I says. My mouth feels dry and my heart's hammering as though I've just run the Stade. "In Poseidon's name, why?"

He says, "Think for yourself. If Konon was here, I'd give the command to him; but it would take too long to get him back from Gaurium; and failing Konon, I've two senior officers with equal claim to the command; and whichever I appoint, they'll be at each other's throats."

"So you'll appoint me, and they'll both be at mine."

He lets out a sudden roar that nearly takes the top off my head. "Will you listen!" And then he goes quiet again. "Furthermore, there's neither one of them I can trust. Think of them, man, Theramenes—Thrassylus—"

And I thinks, and I sees what he means.

"I shall make my decision known to the Council of Trirarchs tomorrow," he says. "And the same moment that I go aboard the *Icarus*, you will take over the *Belerophon*, and assume the command." He reaches out and gets me by the shoulders. I'm strong, but I doubt I could have broken his hold. "And while I'm gone, you'll lay off the drink, and you'll keep the fleet out of trouble; and you'll not engage the enemy, no matter how perfect the chance may seem. You'll not lift a finger against them unless they attack Samos. If there's anything you cannot handle, send word to me by one of the fast scout boats. Understood?"

If ever I'm sober in my life, I'm sober now. Ye Gods! I'm sober, and I'm thinking fast and hard. But there isn't any other way that I can see. And something starts boiling up inside me—much the same as boils up inside me in the last moment before going into action, after I'm past the stage of being cold with fright. "Understood," I says. "But by Blue Haired Poseidon, I can see storm water ahead, when you make it public!"

"You'll ride it," he says.

"Who'll you take for pilot?"

"Meton," he says.

"May his guts rot!" I says.

Next morning Alkibiades calls the Council of Trirarchs, and tells them he's sailing with ten of the fleet for Phocaea and Karia. There's a silence while they waits to hear who's to command in his absence. And then he tells them; and I stands up beside him, and I sees their faces go blank and then bitter angry.

"Sir," says Thrassylus, "with all due respect, have you been bitten by a mad dog?"

And Theramenes puts his oar in: "A mere drunken seaman—"

They says a good deal more, and none of it complimentary, till I'm minded to smash my fist into their fine clean disdainful faces. Alkibiades hears them out. Then he says, "Gentlemen, may I remind you that you are speaking of your temporary Commander?" and turns on his heel and walks out, trailing that damned cloak along the floor behind him. I stays behind long enough to look a few of them in the eye and show them I'm not hurrying; and then I strolls out after him.

They've been gone a month and more. And name of the Dog! What a month! Left to command this bunch of landcrabs that call themselves a fleet!

The flag squadron hasn't been a day and a night over the skyline before I finds that the whole fleet from the Admirals to the seediest slave rower thinks it hasn't got a Commander at all, and can take life easy. So I calls a Trirarchs' Council—it does me a power of good to see them come in answer to the summons, and know how much they hates it—and I tells them, "Gentlemen, we shall get soft, sitting here on our backsides in this nice comfortable port. From tomorrow we shall take the squadrons out on manœuvres daily, just so's we don't forget how to use an oar or keep station, or which end of a galley the ram is—"

"I'm damned if we do," says one of the Samian Trirarchs, and looks at me through narrow eyes; and adds *"Pilot"* for good measure. And there's a murmur of agreement among the rest.

So then I lets them have it. I've tried to do it friendly-wise, without ill-feeling, but if they don't want it that way . . . "You'll be damned if you *don't!*" I says. "Or are you all safely in the pay of Sparta?"

"You'll pay for that when Alkibiades gets back," someone says. And I looks at him good and hard, and he doesn't say any more.

"You can put that to the test when he does get back! Meanwhile you can remember that it was Alkibiades that put me in command here. And while we're all here I'll tell you something—he's maybe told you already but it won't harm you to hear it again; for whatever reason, or for no reason except that we've all been campaigning a long time, and the first flush of it has worn off with victories coming too early and too easy—we're letting the mastery of the seas, which we had fast in our hands this time last year, dribble through our fingers. Half you rowers, those who haven't deserted, have forgotten how to keep time; your ships are dirty, your seamen and marines go whoring in the daytime for lack of anything else to do. Tomorrow at first light, we put to sea for squadron manœuvres, except for the ships actually undergoing refit, and for ten triremes left on guard."

And we did.

That was more than a month ago. And I've kept them at it, except in the very foulest weather. Some of the young Trirarchs are all right, quite keen in fact; it's the senior men that make the trouble. I heard one of them say to another only yesterday, "It is all very well for the young bloods who have stepped into dead men's shoes. If they lose a ship, unless they go with her they've lost nothing of their own. But it's a different matter for you and me and the rest of us who have furnished our own triremes, to be asked to have them out day after day in these seas, suffering all the wear and tear of a winter campaign for nothing; let alone the risk of losing them."

Well, I suppose nobody likes risking what came out of his own purse; but it'll be a sight more risky to go into battle when the day comes, with ill-trained crews and rowers who've grown rusty for lack of practice. Can't the stupid bastards see even that far beyond their own noses? It's enough to drive a man to drink.

Mustn't think about drink. I've obeyed orders and kept off it since Alkibiades sailed—well almost off it. And Gods! I feel as though Night's Daughters had me by the throat.

I've moved half the fleet up to Cape Rain; keep a better eye on Ephesus from here. From the terrace of the little farmhouse where I make my quarters when I'm up here, I can see the town clear across the straits; a white stain of town climbing up the dark of the hills behind. It would be so easy, when the fleet is out one morning to take them over—an hour would do it. A good fight might even clear the black rot that holds the fleet like a plague . . . No, it wouldn't. Thrassylus and Theramenes would see to that. They hate my guts, the sons of bitches, and they hate Alkibiades worse than before, for giving me the command over them; and they'll see to it that the fleet feels the same, at least so far as I'm concerned. It would take more than those two to turn them against Alkibiades, once he's back among them. But at least the rowers are keeping better time, and the crews are beginning to remember how to handle a ship again. If only it wasn't for those cursed desertions—and there's nothing I can do about them; not when the rowers are bought men.

Hades! I want a drink!

# The Soldier

We made Phocaea, and found Thrasybulus there, busy with his blockade; and after a Council of ways and means with him, put out again in a vicious north-easterly squall, and headed for the coastwise towns of Karia.

We collected a certain amount of tribute; not as much as we'd hoped, but enough to keep the fleet in pay for a few months more. It was wonderful, the effect our triremes beating in out of the winter murk had on the merchants of the Karian cities, sadly though they protested that they had paid one year's tribute, and could not pay another until the next year's merchandise came in when spring opened up the caravan route from the East.

After the payment was made, things generally got more friendly. "Never grudge a cup of wine to the man who's purse you've just slit," Alkibiades said to me on one such friendly evening. It was at Mylasa on the way north again. He seemed full of the old lazy insolent laughter, but there was an ugly twist of his mouth as he said it. And I think the mood he was in accounted for the kind of night we all spent afterwards. Alkibiades and three of the Trirarchs, including myself, and a couple of Syrian merchants. It began in the house of one of the merchants—a small rich house, with the kind of statues one generally only sees in a high class brothel standing gracefully in every niche. Later, under Alkibiades' leadership, it spilled out into the nearest wine-shop, and then into another. Our General-in-Chief was received like a long-lost brother in each one, and anxious enquiries made for Antiochus. I fancy there weren't many wine-shops or pleasure houses among the coastwise cities that hadn't seen those two at one time or another.

"Antiochus has got promotion," Alkibiades told the wine-shopkeeper, flinging an arm across his shoulders. (It was one of those nights when he chose to be blood brothers with the gutter.) "Drinking like his can't go unrewarded for ever. He's in command of the Samos fleet, while I come to disport myself among you."

The other Trirarchs and I exchanged a quick glance; and Telamon's mouth tightened. Even among those of us in Alkibiades' own squadron, there was a good deal of feeling as to his choice of the Commander we left behind on Samos.

"Where's Arsinoe?" Alkibiades was asking. "Her door was shut when I passed."

The shopkeeper said, "Arsinoe?"

"The whore who lives by the East Gate."

"Oh, that one. She's got a rich client who likes her to go to his own house, I believe. She's probably there tonight."

"The bitch! She should have waited for me."

"Maybe she has waited before now, and you have not always come," said the merchant who had been our host earlier.

"Well a man must have some variety!" said Alkibiades. "This is cursed bad wine; haven't you anything better?"

That night grows increasingly blurred in my memory. I think we tumbled into and out of a couple more wine-shops; and I have a confused impression that at one point, Alkibiades demanded my dagger to add to his own, and danced a sword dance alone in the moonlit agora. Any other man as drunk as he was would have killed himself or someone else with the whirling blades. We had collected a few hangers-on by that time, and were making enough noise to alert the very fleet in the harbour. And then at a later time, as we wavered, arms linked and clinging to each other's shoulders, up a narrow street, a woman flitted out of a doorway and on ahead of us—but glancing back. She wasn't the first we had seen that night, but the drink had still held us. I suppose by that time the drink had begun to pall. We all gave chase as well as we could, uttering hunting calls; but it was she who chose, when she turned in the end. And she chose Alkibiades; well, any woman would, I suppose, who had once seen him in the moonlight, even steaming drunk as he was. She managed to elude all our clutching outstretched hands, and let him be the one to catch her. She put her arms round his neck and her mouth to his; and laid herself all along him; she was naked under her mantle, and I saw—I did not seem able to stop watching—how she writhed her body into his, fondling his thighs and belly with her own. She was shameless; no decent whore would have behaved so in the open street in the midst of other men.

I suppose it was because I had reached that exact stage of drunkenness—and yet I don't know—maybe it was something more than that—I was as sickened as a well brought up fifteen year old whose pedagogue has guarded him from all undesirable experience—the more so because at the same time there began to be a shrill flickering in my loins and I felt my own manhood lift itself and grow urgent.

And then Alkibiades was no longer with us; and we lurched on leaderless, a hunting pack now, done with wine and out for women.

I don't know how I found mine. I think I merely saw an open

273

door and caught a whiff of musk, and lurched in through it. But somehow I was in a room with a rickety bed and a woman. The woman was no longer young, and her breasts hung down, but her eyes seemed to me extraordinarily beautiful behind the kohl and the green eye-paint.

And I was being suddenly and ignominiously sick on her floor.

She was kind. Kinder than my girl in Piraeus when I was a boy, and not at all what my wanderings in the wake of Alkibiades had taught me to expect from her sort. She held my head and took the shame away. I was distressed for various causes (mainly, I suspect, because I was maudlin drunk, though the vomiting had sobered me a little), for my last sight of Alkibiades, and my sudden loneliness for Astur, who I had scarcely thought of for a year and more; above all, for the loss of what had been, the brotherhood of only a year ago; the watch fires on northern shores and the galleys drawn up on the tide line; and Alkibiades strolling out from the tamarisk scrub. The night we raced for Selymbria an hour before the proper time; the sleet hissing across the sea when we ran the ships down and pushed off for Byzantium. For days when we could not fail because Alkibiades could not fail and we were his.

She made me lie down on the bed, and lay down beside me; and all the while I was pouring things out to her. I think I even told her about Astur; and all the while I kept on apologizing for the mess on her floor. She said, "Never mind, love, you're not the first," and pulled the coverlid up, and I went to sleep with my head between her soft sagging breasts.

When I woke in the morning she was sitting on the edge of the bed in a grubby pink shift, pinning up her hair. She smiled at me and nodded towards the milk and barley cakes she had set beside the bed. My stomach heaved and I turned my head away and groaned.

"You will feel better when you have something inside you," she said.

And I made the effort and got the milk down and a little of the bread, and found that she was right. There was a bird singing in the room, a little painted finch in a cage in the high window. In the daylight the woman looked older still, and the eye-paint had run into the fine wrinkles of her lids, and you could see that her hair was dyed.

She would let me pay only for the milk and bread, saying that there was nothing more.

I was not quite sure what she meant. "Did I not—? Did I—"

274

She said, "No, love, you were too tired." And she took one small coin from what I held in my hand.

I said, "Please take what I owe you. You would have had another customer but for me, I have cost you a night's work."

She said, "This isn't a girls'-house, love; I'm my own mistress and I can take a night off when I want to."

And I saw that to go on pressing the money on her would be to throw her kindness in her face. I could only hope that she would not go hungry that day because of me. Her room looked poor enough, and she was getting past good pay.

I flung on my cloak, then took her face between my hands and kissed her on the forehead. It was all I could think of to do. "Thank you, darling."

"It is a long time since anyone kissed me like that," she said; and she kissed me back, then opened the door for me to go out into the street.

On the way down to the harbour, I overtook Alkibiades, looking like nothing on this earth, and in a foul temper because he had just discovered that he had lost his signet ring.

"The bitch!" he said. "The little whey-faced bitch! And I paid her well enough, too. I should have stuck to Arsinoe."

"Do you want to go back, or send and have the house searched?" I said.

"My dear Arkadius, I don't even know, now, which house it was; and I can scarcely search every brothel in Mylasa." He was suddenly the old nose-in-air drawling Alkibiades again; and I could see that he thought it beneath him to have a tart's belongings rummaged for his lost jewel.

We went on down toward the ships together.


## The Seaman

Three nights ago I came back late to my quarters in Samos—Alkibiades' quarters, that I have moved into while he's away. It's a vile night, with scuds of rain hissing down the alleyways, and a wind to flay the skin off your sodden bones. Just before I gets to the door, I half sees a shadow moving ahead of me, between the pillars of the little Temple of Artemis. But in the murk and the freeezing rain there's no being sure. I feels for my sword, just in case; and when I gets to the house doorway in the high street wall, the shadow's there, hunched against the doorpost, like a man far spent. He says, quick and breathless, "Don't call the slaves. I must speak with you; I'm from Alkibiades."

I stoops and grabs him by the shoulder as he struggles to his feet. He's squelching with icy water; but I feels the hardness of him under the sodden frieze of his cloak, and just for the moment I've a notion I can smell danger. But that's no more than the wild night and finding him there all unexpected; if he'd come to knife me, he'd have tried it before he spoke. "What of Alkibiades?" I says.

"I can't tell it here in the street. Let me in without the slaves seeing me."

"Why?" I says. "I don't like secrets."

He says, "In Poseidon's name, do as I ask, and be quick! I don't think I've been followed, but the Gods alone know for sure."

Well, it doesn't seem I've much choice in the matter. So I don't stop to ask who's like to be following him. "Go on round the corner of the house, there's a side door to the stable, and good cover under some bushes. Wait there, and I'll come and let you in."

I sees him lurch off into the dark, and then begins to thump and shout for the door slave to come and open up. When he comes, rubbing the sleep out of his eyes, I curses him for his slowness, and when he would be rousing the others, bade him bring wine and bread and cheese himself to the winter-chamber (I knew there would be a brazier alight there in case of my coming), and then get back to his snoring. Then, while he shuffles off to get the food, I slips out to the narrow stable court; there's no horses there now, so no groom to wake; and unbars the door on to the street.

He's there waiting, and slips past me as I pulls the door open. I makes it fast behind him, and puts the point of my dagger under his ribs, only just enough to tickle, and pushes him into the old harness room, till old Isodas had had plenty of time to be away back to his own quarters again, before I takes him into the house.

In the winter-chamber he turns to face me, flinging back the head-fold of his cloak. And in the lamplight I sees him for the first time; a square-set man with a deep-lined face gone dirty-grey with exhaustion. I pulls off my own dripping cloak and flings it across a chest; neither of us taking our eyes from the other.

"Who are you?" I says.

"Alxenor, lieutenant of marines with the *Boreas*."

I've never seen him before, to my knowing, but there's quick promotion and many strange faces in the fleet these days. "What word from Alkibiades?"

He draws a deep breath, and speaks staring straight ahead of him like one reciting a lesson learned by heart. "Alkibiades sends orders that you are to get Lysander out from Ephesus at all costs."

I catches my breath at that, and lets it go softly. "That's something of a change from his orders before he sailed."

The man nods. "Circumstances have changed, and with them, the orders."

"And how in Typhon's name does he think I'm going to get Lysander out, if he couldn't?"

"He will likely come for you, thinking Alkibiades out of the way. At noon on the day after tomorrow, Alkibiades will have the Karia squadron, together with ships from Phocaea waiting out of sight beyond the southern headland. Take only one squadron yourself out on manœuvres that day; if Lysander sees a larger force, he will certainly not come. Meanwhile, Alkibiades will send ashore his orders to Thrassylus and Theramenes to bring out the rest of the Samos fleet; and as soon as you have drawn the Spartans out of harbour, will himself lead in to the attack."

"That'll take nice timing," I says.

"The timing will be for Alkibiades; for you it is only to take your squadron and draw the Spartans out of Ephesus." He's rocking a bit on his feet, with the blind look of exhaustion closing down on him.

"Here, sit down before you fall down," I says; and I pours some wine into the cup for him; he slumps on to the bench by the brazier, and takes it and tosses it off, and a little life begins to creep back into his face.

"Thanks, I needed that. I've come up by the land road, riding hard; and in the end I almost couldn't get a fishing-boat for the straits crossing in this weather."

"It will have blown itself out by dawn," I says. I've just laid hold of something that's been bothering me all along. "Why no written orders?"

"In case I was stopped by our enemies and searched. I came near to it, as it was," he fishes inside his rough tunic and brings out a little packet folded in a scrap of cloth; and spills out something bright into the palm of his hand. "My Lord Alkibiades bade me show you this, by way of token."

And he holds out to me Alkibiades' great signet ring that I've never seen off his hand. I picks it off his palm, and looks closer, to make sure. But there's no doubting it, even to the scrape mark where he dashed his hand on the balustrade on the night he ordered me to take over the command.

"Does that satisfy you?" the man says.

"I'm satisfied." I gives it back to him; but he still holds out his hand.

"I am ordered to take back one of those famous earrings of yours, for proof that I have reached the right man with my message."

And there's sense in that. I pulls out one of them, and drops it into his palm beside Alkibiades' ring, and he wraps them both in the scrap of cloth and pushes them both back into the breast of his tunic.

After that, he eats the food and drinks the rest of the wine; but he refuses the pile of rugs I would have given him beside the brazier for the night, saying that the fishing-boat is waiting, and he must be away back to rejoin Alkibiades.

So I takes him back to the side door, and opening it, I asks him why all this dead-of-midnight secrecy when he's back in Samos?

He says, "Do you suppose Kritias and his lot didn't plant their own men among us before we sailed from Piraeus? The fleet is riddled with Cleontius' spies."

I suppose I've known that all along. At any rate it makes sense of an ugly kind.

"For the same reason," he says, "keep this whole matter to yourself. Even among the Samian officers there's no knowing for certain who can be trusted. Wait to give the order till you have them actually out on manœuvres, and spring it on them then. Pretend to be drunk and foolhardy—anything you like; *only draw Lysander out from Ephesus.*"

And he lurches away into the wind and the drenching darkness.

Well, it's thanks to me that Alkibiades will find the Samos fleet ready for action when he sends in the order to those two comic Admirals tomorrow at noon.

# 21

## The Soldier

The sea was still running a swell from the gale of three nights before, when we arrived back at Samos; but the weather had turned cold and blue, with a brittle clearness in the air that brought the far hills close and made all things seem sharp edged as though they had been cut with a sword blade.

And as we rounded the mole, the sight of the harbour broke on us like a blow between the eyes. For it was clogged with crippled ships. Everywhere, everywhere, hauled up on the slipways, made fast to the mooring posts, splintered woodwork, outriggers torn away; one galley lay on her side on the landing beach with a gaping hole at her water-line, like a stranded sea creature that had got its death wound. Another had as good as broken her back. And over everything, tangible as smoke, lay the smell of disaster.

I asked of the world the stupid, useless question one asks at such times, "What in the name of all the Gods has happened here?"

And my pilot said dully, "We'll know soon enough."

We were next in line behind the flagship; and as the *Icarus* came alongside the wooden sheathed jetty, and the landing bridge was run out, I saw Alkibiades stand for a moment, rigid, as though he could not force himself to move, and then walk stiffly across it to where Thrassylus was waiting for him in the midst of a little knot of stiff-faced officers. There was still an arm's length of open water between the *Pegasus* and jetty when it seemed to me suddenly that my place was at his back—I don't know why; he could have had his own staff with him if he'd wanted a man to his back—and I scrambled over the rail and sprang ashore as the bows came in to the fender-timbers, and strode after him.

"Where is Antiochus, who I left in command here?" he was saying as I came up.

Thrassylus said, "Dead."

"So. What has happened?"

"Come up to your quarters, where we can talk in private."

"I'll have an answer to my question, and I'll have it now," Alkibiades said.

The other shrugged. "What you might have expected when you left such a man in command here, has happened." For an instant they looked at each other like two hounds about to spring for each other's throats. Then Thrassylus let his eyes flicker away from Alkibiades' furious stare. "Antiochus became quite insufferable; mad with a little power. He had the fleet out on manœuvres almost every day, in the foulest weather—"

"A course of action which has my fullest approval," Alkibiades cut in.

"No doubt. Yesterday when he had a squadron of ten out under his own command, he suddenly ordered them to alter course and stand away for Ephesus. He cruised across the harbour mouth under the very prows of the Spartan galleys, shouting obscene jokes and taunting Lysander to come out and fight him." (I had the feeling that Thrassylus was almost pleased at the horrible and pitiful story he had to tell.) "He was drunk, of course."

"Lysander would not come out for any insult, unless it suited him," Alkibiades said.

"Of course it suited him—he must have seen a fine chance to capture ten of our galleys with no risk to himself. A squadron put out in pursuit; and seeing our galleys hard-pressed and out-numbered, I had no choice but to take out a further detachment of our own to try to bring them off. Knowing that you were away on your own affairs and a large part of the fleet with you, Lysander took his chance when it offered; and Gods! How he must have laughed! He brought out the whole fleet, upward of a hundred triremes in line of battle. Theramenes brought out our remaining squadrons, and there was a general action. The Spartan fleet was in good order, whereas we had put out piecemeal, our ships were scattered units and we had no overall command; we never stood a chance. We've lost twenty-two ships."

"Admirably concise," said Alkibiades. "How do you know the part about the obscene jests?"

"Two of the original ten were among those that got back. Antiochus' so-called flagship was one of them."

"Where is she?"

For answer, Thrassylus pointed towards the landing beach, where several galleys lay with their crews and the shipwrights at work on them.

Alkibiades began to walk that way without a word. He must have heard me, or seen my shadow a little behind his on the cobbles, for he looked round, becoming aware of me for the moment, and said, "Coming too, Arkadius?"

"With your permission, sir."

"You have my permission, for what it's worth now," he said, and walked on, looking straight ahead of him. I think he had forgotten me again.

We found the *Belerophon* chocked up even-keel on the sands, her deck almost level with the sea wall. Her sides were gashed and splintered, her rowing benches a shambles stained with blood and ordure. The few survivors of her crew were on board or working along her sides; and the little crowd that had been standing round her melted away as we drew near. The dead, as usual in action, must have been flung overboard to keep the decks clear for the feet of the living, and only the stains on the salt-scoured planking told where they had died. But one shape, stark and unmistakable under a piece of sailcloth, lay lonely, on the after-deck.

Alkibiades stood on the sea wall and looked down, with a face carved out of stone. Even his eyes were stone. The bo's'n saw him and came forward. There was a bloody clout round his head, "Sir—" he said, "Sir—" and could get no further.

Alkibiades jerked his head toward the shape under the sailcloth. "Antiochus?"

"Yes, sir. We thought better keep him aboard until they've made his grave, seeing that Admiral Thrassylus has taken over his quarters—your quarters. Do you wish to see him, sir?"

"Yes," said Alkibiades, and climbed stiffly down on to the deck. I hesitated a moment, and then went after him.

The bos'n himself pulled back the piece of sailcloth, and Antiochus lay there; the wreck of Antiochus, hacked and gashed like his ship, with a black hole in the base of his throat and all the front of his jerkin stiff and black with his blood. His eyes were wide open to the winter sky. I have seen many dead men in my time, usually they look curiously empty, often surprised, a few looked as though they had looked on horror, a few as though they saw the face of a friend. But Antiochus had met death snarling like a wild beast, and his face was frozen into an appalling mask of frenzy and despair.

I gave back a step, I could not help it. One of the seamen said. "Cor! I hope I never sees a deader with a face like that again."

Alkibiades never moved. After a long silence, he said, "Was he drunk?" and the hardness of his voice shocked and startled me.

"Drunk or mad," the bos'n said; and I heard him swallow convulsively. "After the Spartan fleet came out on our trail, he shouted back to the look-out was there any sign of the *Icarus*? He did that about three times, and when the look-out shouted back no, for the third time, but that reinforcements were putting out from Samos, he gave a great cry, and shouted out something about being fooled and how he should have sent scouts to make sure, no matter what the orders were—sheer gibberish it was, sir, no man could make head nor tail of it. Then he orders us to put about, and ram the leading Spartan. And the last I saw of him alive he was up with the marines at the bows, fighting like some kind of madman. One of them told me he flung his sword into the sea and fought with his bare hands. It was as though—"

"As though what?" Alkibiades said coldly as the man hesitated.

"As though he wanted to make sure of not living through the fight."

Alkibiades made a sudden strangled sound in his throat; but when I looked round, his face was as still as Antiochus', and as grey. It was like seeing a dead man looking at a dead man. I thought suddenly how they must have looked at each other that first time of all, when the boy Antiochus caught and returned to the boy Alkibiades his escaped fighting quail. And for that one small matter in the midst of this great one of defeat and disaster, I could have howled like a dog.

And being turned to small things, I saw that he had lost one of the heavy silver and coral ornaments from his ears; the other lying still gay and jaunty among his blood-matted hair. And without knowing it until I heard my own voice, I spoke the brief pointless thought aloud.

Alkibiades said, "He has lost more than an earring. He has lost me twenty-two ships, and I rather think my last hope of salvation. Cover him up again."

And he turned away without a backward glance.

Back on the sea wall, he said to me, "Will you see about asking Admiral Thrassylus to move his things back to his old quarters? I shall be needing mine again, for a short while, at least."

That night, back in his own quarters, he sent for me, but when I got up to the house above the town, he seemed to have no particular orders to give me. I think it was only that he did not want to be alone. Maybe there were too many ghosts to squeak and twitter in the dark corners of his mind to make solitude bearable; and because I had been with him earlier, my name came quickest into his head.

282

He gave me wine, and poured some for himself, but left it untouched on the table, and began to walk restlessly up and down. Not the to and fro leopard-pacing that I had seen in him once or twice before, but a patternless ranging about and about the room, pausing a moment to hold his hands to the brazier, then moving on, to the door, to the shuttered window, back to the brazier. "The Gods have forsaken me," he said. "If they had not, I should have returned one day earlier. One day would have been enough."

"When was Alkibiades ever one to care much for any Gods beyond his own luck?" I said.

He swung round on me. His face was not dead any more, but full of a desperate life; "Do you know how much you sounded like Antiochus when you said that? I tell you, Night's Daughters are baying on my trail."

Then he seemed to pull himself together. He went on ranging to and fro, but his voice, when he spoke again, was his own.

"When news of this reaches Athens, I'm done. And I don't doubt there's a report on its way already, painting everything as black against me as maybe. The fleet is crawling with Kritias' and Cleontius' agents; do you think I don't know that?"

"Best get your own report in quickly, then, sir," I said. "You can ride out the loss of twenty-two ships."

"But not the loss of prestige. What good will any report of mine do without a victory to back it? Athens has grown accustomed to victories; she'll accept nothing else from me."

"It wasn't your defeat," I said. "Antiochus took the squadron over to Ephesus, and against your orders."

"It was I who gave him the command in my absence. Most of the senior officers were against me before. Those that weren't, are against me now, because I set a mere seaman over them. The few hours since we landed are enough to show me that the whole fleet is going rancid on me, because I have let them taste defeat."

"Not the whole fleet," I said quickly.

He stopped again in his pacing, and turned to look at me. For a moment something distantly related to a smile flickered at the corners of his mouth. "It has taken quite a lot to make you forgive me for Astur's death, hasn't it, my Arkadius?"

Then he returned again to his ragged pacing. I watched him in silence; and presently I saw his head go up. "I have one chance left—to score out the defeat with a resounding victory. I have called a Council of senior officers for tomorrow. If we can get Lysander out from Ephesus once more—"

He left the sentence hanging in the air; and I heard my own voice saying dully, "Do you think he'll come, now that he must know you're back in command?"

He spoke with his back to me. "No, I don't. He's not a fool; and as for me, my old luck has deserted me. I always said that I should know when it went . . . Nevertheless, it's the one chance, and I must take it; I've no choice."

We took the whole fleet that was still seaworthy, and cruised across and across before Ephesus as we had done when we first returned to Samos. We kept it up for a day, two, three, four—I forget how many. Of course Lysander never came out.

## The Citizen

In Gamalial that year I married off my sister to a master stonemason. It wasn't much of a marriage for her, and certainly my father would not have cared to see it. But Eudemius was a good enough fellow, and I was fortunate to get her a husband at all, in those days when young men were hard to find, and so many girls were having to go without—especially as I could only afford to give her a very small dowry. And she was willing enough, being a sensible girl though given to tears, and asking little of any husband save that he should give her a great many babies.

So it was a cheerful enough wedding in a quiet way—or it would have been, but that one of the groomsmen arrived late, after the bride had been brought from the women's quarters, in her saffron veil and myrtle wreath, by all the women of both families. He seemed to have forgotten for the moment that he had come to a wedding at all, and said had we heard the news? They were talking of it in the Agora as he came through, and he had stopped to get details, that was why he was late. A fight off Ephesus and an Athenian defeat—more than twenty ships lost it was said—

Somebody said stupidly, "But Alkibiades is never defeated."

And somebody else said, "He didn't do too well at Andros."

"It wasn't truly his defeat this time," said the latecomer getting, as it were, his second wind. "Though he must take the blame for it. It seems he got bored and went off raiding, with the joys of the Karian pleasure houses thrown in, leaving that drunken pilot of his in command—Antiochus, isn't it?—and he took the

284

fleet out to bait the Spartans and succeeded better than he'd bargained for."

There was a whole lot more, the wildest, ugliest stuff; and suddenly the bridal garlands and the scent of storax on the family altar seemed a piece of empty play-acting. But my sister was on the edge of tears, and the wedding must be carried through. I caught Eudemius' eye, and the message passed between us; we got the groomsmen and the questioning, exclaiming guests back into order, and the wedding went forward, until all things had been done and we sent the newly-married pair with their guard of groomsmen off to the bridegroom's home under a shower of sugared almonds.

When the last guest had departed, I turned back to the empty room to help Vasso clear up the debris. I picked up one of the comfits and began to eat it, but under the sugar it was a bitter almond.

Next day the Archons summoned the Assembly. I have seldom seen a fuller turn-out than came streaming up from the lower city. No need for the police with their red-painted ropes to get people to attend that day.

And before the full Assembly, the fleet officer who had brought the news—Thasos, his name was; it has had an unpleasant ring in my ears ever since, and I could never call a child by it—stood up on the Speaker's Rostrum and told his story—and a damning story enough.

He told how Alkibiades, into whose hands we had given our whole war effort, our whole future, instead of carrying out his function with a sense of the noble responsibility laid upon him, had let the fleet fall into slack undisciplined ways, despite all that their officers could do to keep control of them; had finally turned them over to the command of a drunken sot who had never even commanded a galley, while he went off to Karia, raiding and whoring. Where now, the man demanded, was Alkibiades' high-flown promises of Persian neutrality, if not a Persian alliance? Had we, the people of Athens, heard of the string of forts that he had built along the Thracian shore of the Propontis? What possible reason could he have had for their building, unless they were for a refuge against the day when Athens finally tired of his treacheries and cast him out—a refuge which would also furnish perfect bases for raiding the corn fleet. Alkibiades had always been half a pirate. The man's voice ranted on and on; it was vile, scurrilous stuff; but looking back on it now, there was probably something of truth in

285

what he said, just enough of truth to make the dirt stick and though his style was appalling, he was one of those crude natural orators who know how to sway a crowd.

And yet I don't think it was because of anything he said, that we voted as we did. I think it was simply because Alkibiades had failed. Our bold and bonnie conqueror who could succeed in anything, lead us anywhere, who had given victory after victory to whichever side he served. And we could not believe that he would have failed if it had been in his whole heart to serve us truly now. We had forgiven him treachery, but we could not forgive him defeat—it had begun when we heard the news from Andros; the news from Ephesus completed it. So we bayed for his blood like a wolf pack. I remembered his riding out by the Piraeus Gate on the morning that the fleet sailed for Sicily; I remembered the instant when his blue gaze had met mine as he rode by; and the Gods help me, I voted with the rest.

We deposed him from his command, and voted three Generals in his place. His new house was ordered to be sold up from the bed linen in the press to the Thessalian horses in the stables. There was even some debate as to whether or not he should be recalled to answer a treason charge; but mercifully that last degrading absurdity was dropped.

And all the while, after the vote was cast, I was remembering another face, the man behind it shining through his ugly and comic flesh, and heard Socrates' deep voice saying, "If he fails, we shall break him."

## The Rower

He went from us on a clear cold morning towards the end of Gamalial. He took his leave of us kindly, like an old friend going on a journey, and we stood by sullenly and let him go. He had failed us, and we wanted no more of him. We had followed him for a God, and he was only a man after all, and we felt ourselves defrauded.

Perhaps under the new Admirals who were coming to take his place, we should get our pay regularly—there were those among us who said so—and maybe a little glory to warm our cold hands at, beside. But as the *Icarus* pulled away from the mole, the morning seemed to turn colder, and dreary, as though the sun had gone in.

We did not know where he was heading, though I think most

of us would have guessed northward toward his old hunting grounds.

We have never seen him again.

## The Whore

I waited for him a year in the fortress of Bisanthe, and there was no comfort in my flute, and the days were long, and the nights lonely when I woke in the dark and flung out an arm and felt the bed cold and empty beside me. I could have had others to warm it, there's more than one of the little garrison; and others from outside the walls, even the village headman, found means to let me know that they were willing. But when the chief's woman pleasures other men, that is when the trouble starts; I have seen it among my own people; and there would have been no pleasure in it for me.

Sometimes I would let down my hair at the New Moon, and make the old singing magic, the Woman Magic, and pour the black dye into the palm of my hand and try to see where he was, and what he was doing, and how things went with him, in the dark shining surface. But though one or twice I saw his face for an instant, and lost it again, I never saw anything that could give me news of him.

Once in the summer a passing ship put in to land a sick man. And he told us when he began to mend, that Alkibiades was in a fair way to becoming Tyrant of Athens.

And I thought, 'If he wins his gamble, I have lost mine.' And then pushed the thought away from me, and when it would not go, put on my riding dress and had out the mare he had given me, and rode hard along the coast, trying to outride it; until two of the rough-riding garrison came after me and headed me off like a break-away colt; asking me what I thought I was doing to be riding alone so far from the fort, and what good it would be if himself came back to find me in the woman's tent of some outland chief. But in my heart, I doubted then if he would ever come back.

The summer passed, and the land between the mountains and the marshes was pale with barley and then brown with sunburned stubble, and then green under the autumn rains. And the winter came again.

And then one day at the time of the year when the light grows longer and the cold more sharp, I heard a great noise of voices and running feet. I ran to the window and forced back the shutters that had been closed against the wind, and looked out. In the westering light I saw the *Icarus* coming in to the long reedy harbour-creek below the fort.

I wanted to fling open the door to the outside stair and run, just as I was, down and down until I fell at his feet, but I knew the foolishness of that. I closed the shutters again and lit another lamp. I stripped off the old tunic I wore, and pulled on the one of fine violet wool with black and crimson borders that I had kept laid by against his coming. I painted my eyes with the green malachite I had not troubled to use since he went away, and put on the jewellery that he had brought me from time to time, the bronze waist-belt all in one piece that must be sprung on as one springs a bracelet, the ropes of coral and amber, the earrings of silver chains and disks that chimed like a flight of bells when I moved my head. If I had been a virtuous Athenian wife, I know that I should have fled first to see what food was in the house, then to spread clean coverings on the bed. But I have never been virtuous, nor Athenian, nor a wife. I was Alkibiades' woman, and my way was the way of the mistress and the companion. I had plenty of time, for he was a long time coming; there must have been many things that he had to see to. And when all was done, I stood waiting by the fire, shivering a little, but not with cold.

I heard his feet on the stair, and the door crashed open letting in a wild buffet of wind that filled the room with smoke. And I saw him standing against the racing sky, with the wind plucking at the muffling folds of his cloak. He forced the door shut behind him and came to the fire. I do not think he was even aware of me until we were within hands' reach. And then he looked at me, and said, "Timandra, you are here." But his eyes were clouded and he made no move to touch me.

"You bade me to come up and wait for you at Bisanthe, did you think I would be still at Pactye?"

He said, "I think I was not sure that you would have waited for me at all. Everything else has deserted me. I am so tired, Timandra, and so cold."

I ran to the chest in the corner and pulled out the new goatskin coat with its border of running stags that I had worked for him in the waiting time, and came back and thrust him into it. It was meant for out of doors, but he was grey with cold—and cold seemed to come out from him as it does from the dead. Then I made him sit down on the cushioned bench by the fire, and piled on more wood; and shouted down the stairway to the slaves to bring up whatever was best of the food we had, and wine.

When I came to him again, he was sitting forward, his hands to the flames, and the flame-light shone through his fingers so that they seemed edged with dim red fire, and I saw the dark shadows of the bones within. I knelt down and began to chafe his hands between my own while I waited for the slaves to bring the food.

He never said another word until it came, and he had eaten and drunk, and presently he was lying all out along the cushioned bench with his head in my lap. And then he said, touching the embroidered sleeve of his coat, "Running stags. Did you copy them from the pair below your breasts, Timandra?"

"They are one of the patterns of my people. All the women of my people are born knowing how to make the running stags."

He said, "But no star-flowers. Why no star-flowers for me, Timandra?"

"The star-flowers are only for the women," I said.

"I am something of a running stag myself, and the hounds are on my heels," he said after a little silence.

Fear stirred in me. "The Spartans?" I said. They had been the enemy so long.

"More like the Athenians. But it was not that kind of hound pack that I meant."

And we were silent for a longer while, and I seemed to hear a distant baying in the wind, and shut my ears to it as to the thing one must not hear. In Bythinia also, we have our hounds that hunt in the winds under the dark of the moon.

Then he said, "But Sparta too; and Athens, and Persia. They have all patted my head and fed me with honey in the comb at one time or another; and now all three of them would be pleased enough to have my guts to girdle their tunics."

But he did not speak it coldly fierce as he would once have done. And I wished that I could kill every Persian and Spartan and Athenian for the fire and fierceness and splendour that they had killed in him.

I said, "I would like to kill them all, and flay them, and tan their hides for saddle leather, as we do with enemies in my own country."

He said, "Little wildcat!" and smiled for the first time; and the smile made black gashes in his firelit face. He turned his face against my belly. "I am finished, Timandra."

"You are not finished!" I said. "I know you. You will never be finished until you are dead!"

And he said, "There are more ways than one of dying."

The fire sank low, and I dared not move to put on more wood, for fear of disturbing him now that he seemed to have fallen asleep. I had quenched the lamps when he had finished eating, for lamp-oil was none so easy to come by in the North. And the light died with the dying fire and the darkness crept in until I could not see his face.

# 22

## The Whore

All through the rest of that wicked winter, it seemed that My Lord was indeed finished. He had said that there were more ways than one of dying, and it was as though something in him had died. He would sit all day long wrapt in furs like an old man by the fire, scarcely walking abroad, even to look to his garrison or visit his ship on her slipway; not even sending for his favourite hounds from Pactye. Once a day the garrison Commander and the master of the *Icarus* (a new man; they told me Antiochus was dead) would come to him for orders, and to report. He never had any orders for them and he scarcely seemed to listen to their reports. Sometimes he would bid me fetch my flute and play, but in a little I would know that he was not even hearing the notes that I made for him like a ship at sea or running deer or a wind in fluttering poplar leaves. Then he would demand drink, the dark heady brew of Thrace, and lie beside me at last, drunk and snoring, not even like an old man, but like an old hound who twitches and starts in his dreams.

Nobody could reach him; certainly not I. After that first evening, though his body lay beside me at nights, my spirit could not touch his, nor even come near enough to call to him across the distance still between. And in the fort, garrison and seamen began to grow restive. Even when news came that the Thracians had raided one of the Athenian settlements, he said only, "Dexippus will have the matter well in hand," and went on sitting by the fire.

It could not go on like that, I knew; it must end some time, in some way. It ended four days later, with a knife fight between two of the *Icarus'* company. Late in the evening, I could hear men's voices from their quarters, and I knew the sharpened note in them, the restlessness that comes when the spring fret wakes in men and horses. They were holding a cockfight down there; one of the seamen had come, somehow, by a big painted game cock of the Persian kind, and I knew had backed it against all comers. I could hear them laying bets, urging on the champions. And then the note began to change and grow ugly.

I was weaving a piece of cloth, the lamp set on a stool beside me, and I remember how the long upward shadow of the shuttle darted to and fro like the darting of a bat across the brindled goathair web. I looked round at Alkibiades sitting beside the fire, to see if he too heard that note of threatening trouble, but he was staring into the flames, a finger-tip rubbing the place where his signet ring used to be that he lost somewhere in Karia. And I thought, 'How far he has gone from his men, that he does not hear. Too far now, ever to come back.'

But I was wrong. Even as I watched. I saw his head go up a little to listen.

Suddenly the sounds of the cockfight swelled up and burst asunder; there was a snarl and a shouted curse, a smother of angry voices, that sharpened as though men were spilling out into the courtyard below. Then unmistakably the clash of blade on blade.

My Lord was up on his feet and reaching for his sword that lay on the chest. He had been so still the moment before, but now that he moved, he had the speed of a hunting leopard. He rasped the blade from the sheath and flung the sheath away, he crossed to the door and wrenched it open, and went down the narrow stairway three at a time.

I followed him. From the turn of the stairway I could see the narrow court in the light of torches, the little crowd ringing two men who crouched with knives in their midst. A loosed game cock was flapping about on cropped wings, spattering blood on the beaten earth from some wound under its breast feathers. From opposite directions, the *Icarus'* pilot, and Heraklides, the garrison Commander, came running; but My Lord was there before them. Or maybe when they saw him on the stairway wisdom came to them and they held back; I do not know. He strode straight into the angry throng, all men parting to let him through, and struck up the locked daggers of the two struggling in their midst. I heard him shouting; and the splurging uproar grew suddenly quiet, but I never heard what he said. One of the men stepped back sullenly, but the other would have still come on, too blind with fury to see who fronted him. My Lord turned on him; there was a flash of torchlight on polished metal, and his sword point was at the man's throat.

They stood like that a long moment, looking at each other, and all the while My Lord's back lay wide open to the dagger of the man behind him. I thought suddenly, 'If they do not kill him now, they are his men again.' And it was as though the heart in my breast forgot to beat.

Then the man dropped his knife. I heard it ring on the iron-hard earth. Alkibiades lowered his blade, and turned slowly to the other man. "Now yours," he said, and the second knife rang as it fell. He looked about him at the rest, and they gave back a little. Then he pointed with his sword at the flapping game cock, and said pleasantly, "Will somebody wring that creature's neck; it quite turns my stomach, and it's making a mess of our nice clean fort."

Then he caught the Captain's eye, and jerked his head toward the stairway.

I slipped back into the keep chamber as he came up, Heraklides at his heels, and sat myself down quietly in the corner by my loom. There was no other way out of the chamber, or I would have taken it; but I do not think either of them were aware of me.

Alkibiades came in, then Heraklides who shut the door behind them, and they stood facing each other. Alkibiades was still holding his sword. He said, "What has happened?"

"I imagine one of the men accused the other of pressing his bird, or something of that sort. You were on the scene as soon as I was."

"I do not mean only what happened tonight," Alkibiades said. "That was no more than a symptom of the disease."

There was a long pause, and then Heraklides straightened his shoulders with a little jerk, and said, "Sir, it has been in my mind for some time that I must speak to you."

"Then why have you not done so?"

"You have not been very—easy of access since your return."

My Lord laid his sword down on the chest, very gently; and very gently said, "Speak to me now."

Heraklides said, "Sir, the garrisons that you left here at Bisanthe and at Pactye and Chrysopolis have held their posts faithfully, waiting for your return. You returned; and they looked to you to set the times stirring again, to lead them out on some venture that would make the long waiting worth while. But it is all of two months since you returned, and there has been nothing but more waiting; so they grow restive, and the seamen with them. Men fret to be up and doing when spring rises in their blood and their leader has come back to them. Failing that, they will fight among themselves. Sir, the men are rotting like the *Icarus* for lack of use."

"You grow poetical," Alkibiades said.

"I speak the commonest of common sense."

"What do they ask, then? That I should lead them out to raid Byzantium for women and loot?"

"The loot might not come amiss!" Heraklides said grimly; and in his urgency he took a pace nearer to Alkibiades. "Sir, the stores that you left with us were gone long ago. We were able to exact a certain amount from the corn ships last autumn, and that yielded us bread through the winter; for the rest, we must buy from the Thracians; and we cannot do that without money or goods to trade with. Our pay is long in arrears—can *you* give us the three obols a day that are due to us over these many months?"

Alkibiades shook his head.

"We are no more a part of the Athenian Army, we are your men, your war bands; you must use us or disband us; we need to eat and we need to follow a leader. In the name of the Thunderer do something with us!"

Alkibiades stood silent a moment, then he said, "Keep your men from killing each other until tomorrow morning, and I'll do something with you."

When Heraklides was gone, My Lord stood for a while with his head bent and the heels of his hands pressed against his eyes as though he would have thrust them back into their sockets. Then he looked up, and stretched until the little muscles cracked between his shoulders, like one waking from sleep with a day's work before him. When he turned back to the fire, his face was still haggard and puffy with much drink and evil dreams, but the clouds had gone from his eyes, something of the old bright purpose was already returned to them.

He said, "Leave that weaving a while, and bring me my harness, Timandra."

And when I brought it, he began to check it over. (I had kept it oiled and burnished as well as any trained armour bearer could have done; left to him the leather would have been dried out, and all as harsh and out of condition as the hide of a sick hound; but I do not think he even noticed that.) He said, "If we can no longer claim tribute from the Propontis cities, it is in my mind that they might pay none so badly for protection from Thracian raids such as Lysimachia suffered four days ago. That will do for a start anyway. But we shall need to turn cavalry—rough-riders of the Thracians' own pattern, so that we can not merely drive them off, but follow them up in retreat—and we shall have to have some show of cavalry before we make our first approach to the settlements . . ."

I knew how few horses there were in the three forts, but I dared not say a word that might quench the life that had only just returned to him.

And then I saw something in his face, a flash of the old devilry that made me catch my breath . . .

That, having no purchase-gold, was how we turned horse-raider.

In the days that followed, My Lord was to and fro between Bisanthe and Chrysopolis and Pactye, and at his coming, the forts shook themselves and gathered life again, and began to build new stabling against the time when there would be horses to put in them. And the next time the Thracians came down on a settlement, the men of Bisanthe captured five horses, and the thing was begun.

From then on, we raided in earnest. And I too; I rode with the raiders. Not many among the Athenian seamen and marines could handle our few little hammer-headed Thracian horses as I could, nor had they any skill in getting into a Thracian camp and cutting the picket lines. But they were new to it, and I was old; for among my own people horse-raiding between tribe and tribe is like hunting, a ploy for the young men, and often the girls ride with them if they have enough skill to keep up. So to me it was like my own springtime and the springtime of the world came back to me again; and I do not think that I have ever been more happy than I was riding with Alkibiades on those wild nights!

Some times we got other things, too; cattle and corn; but for the most part it was just the horses that we were after.

But we did not raid all runs at random; My Lord had old links of friendship with certain of the chiefs; some had even helped, I learned, in the building of the forts; and these never lost a horse to us. And there were two great chiefs of Chersonese Thrace, Medacus and Seuthes, whose tribal horse-runs we left alone. I think even My Lord knew that he was not strong enough to handle them—for the present time.

A little while after we started the new way of things, two young brothers, Boiscus and Terdes, driven out of their tribe for fighting at the Spring Gathering came in to join us, bringing their horses with them; then a man from one of the Athenian settlements, then a whole bunch of seamen from a wrecked trading vessel; and so it went on. The time might yet come for turning to the horse-runs of Medacus and Seuthes after all.

Maybe Seuthes thought so also; for one day in early summer the look-outs on the walls came running with word that a small company of Thracians were coming towards the fort. "Raiders?"

Alkibiades said. He and I and Heraklides were in the stable court looking to some of the newly captured beasts.

The man shook his head. "Not enough of them, sir; and they have led horses with them."

Alkibiades frowned, and strode off toward the gate. I followed him and he did not order me back. I had taken altogether to man's dress and was with him at all times, in those days; and the cuckoo never sang so warmly and the oleanders along the streamsides never showed such colours to me in any other summer.

At the gate, the guards were standing by; the man in charge said, "Shall we let them in?"

Alkibiades said, "The Propontis is too near to Troy. Send up a few javelin men to keep us covered, and we'll go out to them."

So the gates were pulled open just enough to let a man pass through, and he went out, I and Heraklides following. Outside, a knot of horsemen had just drawn rein and the leader had swung down from his high embroidered saddle, while behind him his men still sat their fidgeting horses. The little wind parted the fur of their tall foxskin hats and ruffled the horses' manes and set the coloured harness-tassels swinging.

The leader glanced up at the javelins on the wall, and down again to Alkibiades. "A warm welcome you make ready, Lord, for those who come to your camp in friendship." His eyes were a curious rain grey in a lean red face.

"Surely I make ready the warmest of welcomes, for do I not come out myself to greet my guests?"

The man's eyes gave a little flicker, as though at some small hidden jest, some enjoyment of a situation that I *think* Alkibiades shared. He said, "That is true. I will say that those are seagulls sitting on your gate-wall, with rushes in their beaks . . . We bring you a gift from Seuthes, Chief of his Tribe."

I caught my breath, wondering what that meant for good or ill; then the man gestured with a hand behind him, and two of his followers dropped from their mounts and came forward, one leading a big raking stallion with a black mane and tail and tiger-spot markings at the shoulder; a riding rug of fine brown bearskin strapped upon him, and his harness hung with small copper bells; the other with a young unsaddled roan mare dancing at the end of a plaited blue and crimson halter. They brought them forward to Alkibiades and made them stand, turning them this way and that, while the tall leader stood looking on, and playing with the silver and turquoise hilt of his dagger.

"This is your gift?" Alkibiades said after a moment.

"This is the gift of Seuthes, Lord of his Tribe."

"It is a fine gift," said My Lord, and smiled. "But why does Seuthes send such a gift to me? I have been wont to take the horses that I need, without waiting for a giving."

"Seuthes bade me to say this," the man said, smiling also, and the men behind him glanced at each other. "That he sends you a stallion and a mare from his own herd, that you may breed your own horses from them and not need to come raiding in his grazing lands; and that therefore he may not need to kill you."

I remember they stood and looked at each other a long moment, and the air seemed to crackle between them as my hair does if I comb it before a thunderstorm. Then Alkibiades said, his smile broadening, "My thanks for a gift worthy of a King, Seuthes, Chief of your Tribe."

He moved forward, and laid his hand first on the stallion's neck, and then on the mare's in token of acceptance. Then turning he gestured for the gates to be set wide. "Or of a friend to a friend. Enter now and drink with me—your men also." And taking the reins from the man who held them, he set his hands on the stallion's withers and made the steed leap and brought him trampling round as the others also re-mounted; and I, as the red mare came by me, I ran and vaulted on to her bare back. She was newly broken, from the feel of her, and she danced under me, but not too wildly, more playing at fright than anything else.

"Give me—" I said to the man who held the plaited halter. He looked round and saw that I was a woman, and grinned at me, but loosed the halter into my hand; and we swept in through the gates of Bisanthe. Alkibiades and Seuthes leaning from their horses to grip each other's shoulders, as men do in friendship among the Horse Peoples.

Medacus must have thought that there was danger in Alkibiades and Seuthes together.

Not many days later was the Festival of Epona, the Lady of the Foals. It is a season of giving; and then there came another gift to Alkibiades at Bisanthe. A smaller gift; a Scythian gyrfalcon, with bells of gilded silver on her jesses, and a hood tufted with heron hackles, and her own glove of white mare's hide. And I remember when My Lord pulled on the glove and took her on his fist and unhooded her to gentle her neck-feathers (I have learned that the Greeks do not know how to handle a falcon; but he had been long enough among the Persians and in the North to learn the trick of it), how her eyes were proud and dark and webbed with a golden lustre, like strange jewels that narrowed and dilated in the sunlight.

Alkibiades accepted the gift with grave courtesy, but when the noble and his falconers were gone, he stood there holding the re-hooded falcon on his fist, seeming lost in his own thoughts.

Heraklides said, "Medacus does not pay so well as Seuthes."

Alkibiades smiled into the sun. "My dear Heraklides, don't be so crude. One does not compare the size of gift with gift; and I have no doubt that Medacus is too proud a man to seem to compete with his brother king for the favour of an Athenian adventurer."

For almost a year I rode with the young men behind My Lord; and there were more and always more of the young men. They came in from all the quarters from which the winds blow, for the booty and adventure and the leader to follow, until all the tongues that I have ever heard, even the Persian, sounded round our watch fires, and we had become a little army spread among the three forts from Pactye to Chrysopolis along the Propontis shore. Joined with Seuthes or Medacus it would have been not such a little army. But it never came to joining the three together. There was a bond between them, an alliance, My Lord called it, and for the rest, I think he chose rather to be free than to be bound in with either too closely.

The coastwise cities and settlements had long since thankfully accepted Alkibiades' protection, and paid a fair price for it, though seldom without grumbling; and so we did not need to raid for our horses any more.

And then, when we were driving off an attack of inland Thracians on Perinthos, I took an arrow-gash in the fleshy part of my arm. It was only a little wound, though jagged where the arrow had torn through. I remember the smart of it, not much worse than a hornet sting. I looked down at it, seeing the torn sleeve of my jacket, and the red dripping through. But we were hot in pursuit, and the speed and the triumph of our going was sharper than the smart of the wound. And I rode on, keeping as close as I could to the big tiger-spot horse that My Lord always rode since Seuthes had given it to him.

But after a time, suddenly the snow-puddled slopes began to darken and swim on my sight, and I found myself falling forward on my horse's neck, and tried to pull myself back; and then the white-streaked backward-flying ground was rushing up to meet me; there was a thunder of horses' hooves around and over me, and then only the dark.

The darkness ebbed a little, and there were horses' hooves again; but under me, the hooves of only one horse, and I knew vaguely that I was being carried across somebody's saddle; and that my arm was on fire, with little flames that jumped as a forge fire does under the bellows, with every beat of the hooves. And then there was darkness again.

And then lamplight; and I was lying under a rug in a little room that I did not know, with an old woman, who I did not know either, bending over me. I tried to ask where I was, and I suppose I must have managed it after a fashion, for she cried a little and kissed me with old soft sour-smelling lips like withered leaves, and told me, "Perinthos," and said that I was one of those brave ones who had saved them. But I was too tired to listen to her properly; and she brought me warm milk with herbs in it, and I slept, despite the throbbing of my arm.

When I woke again, it was a full, daylight waking. And I lay for a while staring up at the rafters and feeling the smart of my wound and the rough warmth of the blanket, and wondering what it was that hurt me so, far down in my dark inmost places where I could not quite remember. And then I remembered; and knew that the hurt was because they had not carried me back as we always carried our wounded, to the fort, but abandoned me at Perinthos like a mere broken chattel.

I did not even trouble to ask the woman stirring something in a crock over the fire, whether Alkibiades had brought me; I knew well enough that he would not turn back from his hunting on my account.

But when the woman brought fresh rags to replace the fouled ones on my arm, I saw that they had been torn from Alkibiades' tunic—I knew the pattern well enough, for I had worked the border myself. I said, "Old Mother, where did you get these?"

She must have thought that I was complaining, for she said sharply, "They were round your arm when the young man brought you in; and I washed them for use again. Do you think that I can be tearing up my best linen to keep you in fresh bandages?"

"No, it is that I recognized the tunic it was torn from," I said; and I remember fumbling out the hand of my sound arm, surprised that I was so weak, and touching the tattered embroidery at one end, because it seemed to ease the ache of being abandoned.

I said, "Was there any word as to my staying here? Any word of sending for me?"

"The man who brought you gave me gold, and bade me keep you until one came to fetch you again. I know no more," she said. And then (for the crying and kissing mood was quite gone from her), "What a woman who's known your kind of life—Oh, I know your sort, my girl—should be doing riding with the Lord Alkibiades' men for our saving, I'd not be knowing. Not that I'm thinking it's for us, you'd do it. But he'll come for you, whoever he is. You're not the kind that every man finds to his taste, but you're the kind that gets into the blood of one here and there."

I laughed, and asked her how she knew, and she said, "I was such another, before you were born."

But I waited so long, and my arm was healed, all but a little place at one end of the tear. And still nobody came, nobody, nobody . . .

And then one day, standing in the doorway of the little house, I saw some of the Bisanthe men clattering up the street—there was much coming and going between the settlements and the forts, by that time. They passed without knowing me, for I was in the shadow of the door; and I stood and watched them until they were gone from sight; and then I went back into the house—the old woman was out at the market—and laid a little gold brooch that Alkibiades had given me, on the bed-place for her to find. Then I went out into the city, to the Temple of the Dioscurii, which was always the gathering place for our horse bands in Perinthos.

They were there; but at first they did not want to take me back, saying that they had no orders concerning me, that my wound could scarcely be healed yet, and if I foundered on the way there would be bad trouble for them.

"This is a new thing!" I said. "Since when have you treated me as though I were something tender out of the women's quarters? Then, if you will not let me ride with you, turn your backs, and let me steal a horse, and I'll ride after in your dust." And when they still raised difficulties, I said, "This is not the only place in Perinthos where there are horses for stealing; but if I can steal no other horse, I swear that when you are gone, I will walk every foot of the way, and take my chance of falling into the hands of the tribesmen!"

So in the end they let me have one of the re-mounts and a corner to myself to sleep in, and I rode back with them next morning.

The man on the gate said that Alkibiades was down at the landing beach. I was past remembering, by then, the behaviour fitting to Alkibiades' woman, and I went down the sloping path to the creek, not caring for the glances that I knew men were casting to each other behind my back. There was no snow here, and the water was deeply green as beryl against the pale winter reeds, the newly-painted sides of the *Icarus* staining it with reflected crimson. My Lord was watching the men at work lashing a new hull cable about her. He turned round when he heard my footsteps, and his brows drew together.

He said, "Timandra! I bade the old hag keep you in Perinthos until I sent for you."

And I said, "I waited long and long, and it seemed to me that I was forgotten and that maybe you would never send."

His eyes moved over me and slowly the frown cleared a little. He said, "I would have sent when I judged that it was time . . . How did you get here?"

"I made your men who rode into Perinthos yesterday bring me back with them—they did not want to, but I made them. It is no blame of theirs."

"That, I do not doubt, for I know your ways, Timandra." He gave some orders to the men at work on the lashing, then turned back to me and said, "Go up to the keep chamber."

I did not move. "Because you are angry that I disobeyed you?"

"Partly. But also because you look like a ghost."

"I am well enough," I said.

He made a sound between laughter and exasperation, and stooped and caught me up and turned back to the path to the water gate. I put my sound arm round his neck, and the dryness of his hair was under my hand, harsh and living like a horse's mane, and the slow strong beating of his heart was against me, and my own heart said, 'I am home! I am home! What are my father's hunting runs to me?'

He carried me through the water gate and across the court and up to the great chamber, and laid me on the bed-place.

I wondered if he would make love to me then. I was spent with the long ride and the ache of the half-healed wound; but I had never had mercy from Alkibiades; I did not expect it. I did not even want it.

But he only said, "Show me your arm."

I held it out, pulling up the sleeve of my tunic; and he drew his finger down the puckered reddish scar with the little crusted bit at one end. "That was a gash!" he said. "But it has almost healed. It was as well we left you with the wise woman at Perinthos."

"I had rather you brought me back here, as we have always done with our wounded," I said.

301

He smiled at me suddenly. "There's a difference. Little bitch-wolf, don't turn into an Amazon; I like you best with both breasts, and this soft brown hide of yours patterned only with stags and star-flowers and crimson-tipped lilies."

"It is only a little scar. Soon it will fade to nothing," I said, seizing on the thing that was quickest understood and countered.

"That one, yes. Nevertheless, you'll not ride with the war band again," he said.

I felt as though he had hit me; but I could not quite believe it, not yet. "I thought it seemed good to you, that I should ride with you," I said in a little.

He put his hands over my breasts, and I felt the dark shadows of the bones at his finger-tips, as I had seen them with the firelight shining through; and he leaned forward and kissed me, hot and fierce but quickly over, his mouth still half laughing over mine. "I've held to you through five summers; and I've a wish to keep you a few summers more. Next time you stop an arrow, it may not be in the arm."

"And because of that, you will leave me behind like some stupid Athenian woman, and ride without me?"

"Not like an Athenian woman, stupid or otherwise," he said, and I knew that he was laughing at me. "Never like an Athenian woman, fox-haired Timandra." And then he ceased the laughter, and said, "Listen, when first you rode with us we needed every spear. Now, we have many spears. We are an army—a mongrel host, I grant you, but an army. It is only when men are at their wits' end for horses, that they risk their mares in battle."

He got off the bed, and stood looking down at me. I wanted to reach up and cling to him, and plead. But it was never any use to plead with Alkibiades; he would do of his own will, or he would not do at all.

"Remember the years of the great campaign here in the North," he said. "You did not help to fight the galleys. How then, is it different now?"

But it was different now. I had been his woman then, nothing more, nothing less, and had asked only what a woman asks. And My Lord had loved me in his way. But he was of his own people, as I am of mine, and a woman had small place in his world, outside the women's quarters. For a while I had been set free of that, I had stepped forward into his world, beside him, and had learned to ask for other things. And now I was to be thrust back into the women's quarters again.

I shook my head; I could not speak, and turned my face away

from him. I knew that if I tried to tell him, he would not understand. It was not in him to understand.

"I'll send one of the slaves to bring you some food," he said. "Then you must sleep."

And he went out, rattling the door to behind him. I heard his feet on the stair, and a gull swept past the window, calling like a lost soul, against the cold blown winter blue.

I pulled the wolfskin rug over me and rolled on to my side, curling up over the pain that was like a stone in my belly; the empty ache of loss for things that would not come again.

Once, I had thought that I might be with child; and I had made ready the herbs to kill the babe before it knew life. I had thought that I would do even that, to keep my freedom of his world, where I could not ride, burdened with women's business. But there had been no need. It had been only the cold and the hard riding binding up my flow, and the next moon all had been as usual. And I had been half glad that I had not needed the herbs, yet half torn with grief that there was no child of My Lord's sowing in my body after all. Maybe I would not have used the herbs. I do not know. I think that for that one gain, I could have lost My Lord's world and not grieved over much.

But to have lost it all for a little gash in the arm . . .

I have cried only a few times in my life, and that was not one of them. I lay hunched over the pain, with my knees drawn up, as a child lies in its mother's body; and dragged my nails across and across my breasts and throat and cheeks, until, when I put my fingers to my mouth, I could taste the blood on them, salt as tears.

# 23

## The Soldier

The autumn after Alkibiades left us, the Spartans caught Konon with his squadron at sea, captured several of his ships and chased him into Mitylene on Lesbos and blockaded him there. The news came to Samos, but there was nothing we could do. We, the fleet, agreed with our new Admirals on that. It was about the only time we ever did agree with them.

The great days of the Samos fleet were past, and quite frankly, even if we left Samos an open door for the Spartans to walk in through, we could not muster enough ships to stand a hope of being able to break the blockade. For a while it looked as if we must lose the rest of the squadron, and Lesbos itself, and have the Aegean torn wide open again.

But again Athens put out one of those superb efforts that still, in those days, sometimes made us proud to call ourselves Athenians. Somehow, yet again—we gathered the story little by little—she was conjuring a makeshift fleet out of nowhere. Every citizen fit to bear arms or stand on a heaving deck was being pressed into service, slaves were being offered their freedom to serve as rowers aboard the hundred or so triremes. They were stripping the temples of gold and silver to furnish new rams and patch up old ships better fitted to the breaker's yard—said the reports that reached us—than to the open seas. The only thing they seemed well supplied with was Admirals; Charminius and Thrasybulus and Theramenes among them.

Just at the beginning of spring we heard that they were coming —a gallant fleet of lame ducks, coming to drive the fine new Navy of Sparta from the seas.

Every ship that could be spared from the safekeeping of Samos put out to join them; my own *Pegasus*, the *Clyte*, the *Halkyone* . . .

But the Spartans were out from Mitylene and making south to head us off. When we anchored in the lee of Arginussae, the White

Islands, that night, the weather was foul, and even in the shelter of the land the short choppy seas made half the crews sick. We could make out, when the seas lifted us high enough, the stern cressets of the Spartan fleet about five miles away.

The weather worsened in the night, with sleet driving before a gale from the gulf, and the curdled green seas running in a short murderous swell. "They'll never attack in this Typhon's brew," my pilot said to me, when we made the morning sacrifice as best we could in the shelter of our spread cloaks. And had scarcely said it when the first of the Spartan galleys appeared out of the murk.

No ordered battle line was possible, for them or for us; and they came down on us like a gale-sped skein of wild geese. We fought them all that morning; and Poseidon may know how it came about that we beat them in the end, but assuredly I don't. Quite suddenly they were falling back on Chios; and we knew that the victory was ours. But there was no heart in us to cheer; and it had not been a victory gained without paying its full price. Sparta lost seventy ships that day; but twelve of ours were sunk, and as many more in a sinking condition, with no hope in those seas and the weather still worsening, of making land. At the time of course we knew nothing of numbers, nothing clearly; we knew only that there were drowned men and floating wreckage in the sea about us; and a trireme with half her outrigger smashed away and her side ripped open below the rowing benches staggered across our bows. But the hissing spray was in our faces, and we were blind with it, and dead tired, and wracked with seasickness though we had long since thrown up all that was in us. And when the orders came, passed back by flag and trumpet from Charminius' flagship, the Gods forgive us, we obeyed them and headed back for Arginussae. It is hard to see what else we could have done; but the Gods forgive us, none the less.

Once back on dry land, thawing out before great fires lit on the beach, and the first of the drowned, Spartan and Athenian alike, beginning to be washed up at our feet, something of a sense of duty returned to us; there was very nearly a mutiny, and in the end the Admirals gave Thrasybulus grudging leave to take forty ships out again to see what could be done. But by then it was too late, and the seas running too high. We got back empty-handed.

From Samos, when we returned to refit, the Admirals sent home a long and glowing account of the victory—they had had it read publicly to the fleet, I suppose for the good of our morale, which was stinking like stale fish by that time. Seventy of the Spartan

League fleet had been sunk, the blockade of Mitylene lifted, freeing Konon and his squadrons to rejoin the main fleet. Athens was again mistress of the Eastern Aegean. They forgot to mention that we had lost more than five thousand men.

## The Citizen

In summer we got late news of the Athenian victory at Arginussae, and for days all Athens was drunk with the taste of it. The great statue of Athene of the Spear in the High City was hung with garlands of myrtle. It seemed a long time since we had tasted victory, and I think to many of us, the knowledge that we, the Athenian people, could gain a victory without Alkibiades brought an almost superstitious relief.

Then rumours of a darker and more ugly side to things, which had not been in the General's report, began to drift in, tarnishing the brightness. Some seamen from the ship that had brought the report, drunk and talkative in the Piraeus wine-shops, started it; the stories of heavy Athenian losses, men left to drown who could have been saved, sinking ships left to their fate in bad weather, in the haste of the commanding officers to get the victorious fleet back to harbour . . . But it was Theramenes, returning in haste, and alone, who brought the full account, and laid formal accusations against his fellow commanders. I suppose he saw what was coming to them, once the story got out, and that seemed to him his best chance of saving his own skin.

It was after Theramenes' return that the names of the lost ships were known for certain. And among them was the *Halkyone*. When I heard it, I wished that I could have known, could have taken my leave of Theron in a different way, said something, perhaps, set their full value on those last moments before he went on board. It is a foolish wish, but most of us have wished it, at one time or another . . .

One day as I was making up the day's accounts before closing the shop, a man stepped in the doorway. I looked up to tell him that I was just about to close; and it was Theron! Theron or his tattered ghost; his face haggard, his hair that I had known bleached with sun and salt streaked now with grey. Having said goodbye to him in my heart, I thought for an instant that it *was* his ghost; and I suppose he must have seen the look in my face, for his own cracked into a travesty of the old grin, and he said, "No, only from Samos."

306

But the grin slipped awry, and I thought he swayed a little as he spoke. Something that had held me for the instant frozen loosed its hold, and I was round the end of the serving table and had my arms about him. I think I was near to crying. "Theron! You're back! I'll never believe another General! Theramenes said the *Halkyone* was sunk!"

"You can believe him in that, anyway," he said, and began to cough a little on my shoulder.

I hauled him through into the chamber behind the shop, and sat him on the bench where once I had sat another ghost, the Arkadian, home from Syracuse. I splashed raw wine into a cup, and made him drink it before I would let him say any more. When he had drunk, and looked a little less grey, I remember sitting down beside him and saying carefully, "The stories are true then?"

"Mostly they're true," he said.

"How did you get away? Were you not on board?"

"I was on board all right," he said, and leaned back against the wall. "So far as I know I was the only man on board to get ashore."

I was silent a little, then I asked what brought him back to Athens.

"The voices of drowned men crying out to me to tell the Athenian people how they died," he said. "But it seems that story is here before me." And he turned his head against the wall and coughed again, and suddenly my hand on his shoulder was flecked with blood.

"You're ill," I said, "wait while I call Vasso; she's the only house slave I have now, but she'll look after you."

"I'm well enough," he said impatiently. "I got smashed against the ship's gunwale when she sank, and broke something inside. It's mending now. Give me some more wine and let me clean up a bit, and then I must be getting on home."

"You have not been home yet?"

"No. Your door comes before mine on the way up from Piraeus; and I thought maybe you'd send word to my sister for me, so that she won't think I'm a ghost, too."

But I think he wanted the excuse to rest, among other things.

So I gave him more wine and called for Vasso to fill the bath-tub with hot water, and helped him to clean up. His breast and belly were a mass of livid bruises, with a half-healed, crusted place under the ribs that he would not let me touch, but salved himself with the ointment I gave him. I pretended that Vasso's legs were no longer up to the trot and I was too busy to warn his sister at once, and so made him rest a little longer. By the time I let him go

307

he looked a little less like a ghost, but not much; a clean ghost at all events, wearing my best tunic, which was ridiculously too small for him.

The Archons sent to recall the Generals who had been in command at Arginussae, to answer to the Athenian people for leaving their men to drown. They came—all save Thrassylus, who wisely made his escape when the summons reached them—and were called to appear before the Assembly.

I went round that evening, as I had often done since his return, to spend a while after supper with Theron. But his sister Myrrhine met me in the outer doorway and drew me aside. "I hoped that you would come," she said. "He will not listen to anything I say." She had long ago given up keeping her veil close with me, and I could see the trouble in her face.

"What is amiss?" I said.

"He says he will go to the Assembly tomorrow to give evidence —and he's ill."

"Is it the damage he had from the wreck? He says that's mending."

She shook her head. "It is not. Oh, he'd say anything rather than trouble to have it seen to, rather than trouble about anything but his revenge on those men up there tomorrow—may they all rot—"

"They probably will," I said. "I'll do what I can, but I never yet came out the victor in any battle with Theron."

And of course I did not that time either, when I went through into the little courtyard, and found him huddled in the last of the sun like an old man. "What is this I hear about your going up to the Assembly tomorrow?" I said, sounding like a mother hen in my own ears; and in his too, I think, for he looked up at me and laughed, and said, "Dear clucking Timotheus. Has Myrrhine been filling you up with her own fears?"

"Yes," I said. "But I can see without help from Myrrhine that you're about as fit as a newborn babe to go up to the Pnyx and stand all day in that crowd."

"I've given in my name as a witness," he said. The laughter went out of his mouth, and I saw by the set of it that nothing I could say or do would shift him a hair's breadth from his purpose.

I changed my ground. "Have you been to the Priests of Esculapius, yet?"

"Why should I? It's mending, I tell you."

308

"It's not," I said flatly, "and you know it's not."

He shrugged impatiently. "It's this cursed cold wind; it catches me across the ribs, that's all. Oh, for Poseidon's sake, Timotheus, stop buzzing round me like a bluebottle round a stranded fish!"

"I'll make a bargain with you," I said. "I'll leave off buzzing; I'll stand by and let you do your best to kill yourself tomorrow—though I'm not vouching for Myrrhine—if you'll promise to come to the Esculapian with me the day after if you haven't succeeded."

He was silent a moment. Then he said wearily, "Have it your own way."

The next day we went up together to the Assembly, and when he took up his position in the clear space before the Speaker's Rostrum left for witnesses and those who had some part to play in the days proceedings, I kept as near to him as I could. But he seemed to have cast off the old man of yesterday, and stood rock-steady on his feet again; so that I hoped it had been only the east wind after all.

The great space was filling up as the crowd gathered; the Generals were brought up through a lane kept open for them by the police with their red-painted ropes, the Archons and magistrates took their places. One can see the Assembly gather so often that it ceases to make much mark on one's mind and passes almost unnoticed across eye and ear, especially if one has other things to think about. And so it was with me that day; chiefly concerned with Theron, I took in little of what went on around me until the Generals were brought in. Then the sudden uproar breaking through the ordinary formless voice of a great crowd brought me to sudden awareness of what was going on about me. Half the crowd seemed to be shouting for blood and the other half for fair play, until all fell quiet as the herald raised his trumpet and the Priests stepped forward to make the opening sacrifice.

It was the day of the Feast of Families, and wherever one looked in Athens, one saw women in mourning for husbands and fathers and sons lost at Arginussae; and that, working on the grief and anger of the people, weighted the scales against the Generals from the first. (I have heard it said that the amount of mourners in the streets was Theramenes' doing, but that's as maybe.) None the less, there was a time during the trial, when the verdict might have gone either way.

The Senior Archon opened the proceedings as President of the Assembly, and Theramenes' charges were read out. Damning enough, they sounded, while the hard, heavy phrases fell into the listening silence. Then one by one, the Generals stood forward to speak in their own defence; Charminius, young Pericles . . . Thrasybulus made the best job of it, forging a most convincing defence from the weather conditions and the necessity for getting the rest of the fleet back to safety before they lost still more ships. Only when he told how, on reaching land, he had instantly taken the most seaworthy galleys out again on an attempted rescue operation, he spoiled it somewhat by trying to throw the blame back on to Theramenes, and on to Thrassylus, who of course was safely out of it anyway.

I saw several of the Trirarchs and pilots, waiting to be called, exchange glances; but when they came to give evidence they bore him out, at least as to the worsening weather and the state of the fleet making it imperative to get the rest into shelter. It may even have been true for anything I know, I who am no seaman.

The trial dragged on, with long speeches from the Councils for Prosecution and Defence, while the crowd grew more and more restive, and the sun was well over towards the west, when Thrasybulus, who as Senior General had at most times acted as spokesman for the rest, was asked if he had anything more to say. He stood forward once more on the Speaker's Rostrum, and I thought, as well as I could see from where I stood, that for the first time that day he looked like a man who had begun to hope. For the first time, too, his voice had an almost confident ring. "Citizens of Athens, you have summoned myself and my fellow Generals to stand before you on trial for our lives, charged with our failure to save drowning men who the seas made it impossible for any mortal power to save; but there is one thing that has found no mention in all this day. I would ask you to remember it, when you come to vote us life or death: that in the hours before the failure of which we are accused, we sank you seventy Spartan League ships, and once more broke for you the power of Sparta in the Aegean."

I remember the silence after he had spoken. In the uproar about the drownings I think a good many people had forgotten the victory. It is often so, with a crowd. I felt them stir about me; I felt doubt growing, and opinion begin to swing. That was the moment when the trial might have gone either way.

And then Theron stood forward, claiming the right to speak.

He mounted the steps to the Rostrum, and stood there with his sandy, grey-streaked head braced high; and on being asked his name and for whom he spoke, replied steadily as though answering some kind of roll-call, "Theron, Son of Menander, starboard side bow oar of the *Halkyone*, sunk at Arginussae." Then, turning to the crowd, he cried out in a voice I had never heard him use before, and hoped never to hear him use again, "I speak for the drowned!"

Quite briefly, his harsh voice cracked and straining, but making himself heard—certainly he had all the silence that any orator could ask for, he told the story again, from the viewpoint of the men left to drown. Told how he himself had got ashore clinging to a bit of deck planking, and how men he knew had cried out to him, if he made the shore, to take word back to Athens, of how they had died.

When he had done, the Council for the Defence protested that sad as was the fate of those drowned, such things happened in war, and that nothing was altered of the Generals' defence. "It was a choice between sacrificing the few or risking sacrificing the many." He submitted that for the men they now saw before them on trial for their lives the choice had been hard, but they had heard expert witnesses give their opinion that it had been right.

But the mood of the crowd was swinging again.

And then Theron, still standing on the Rostrum though drawn to one side, shouted out in that hoarse dreadful voice, "Alkibiades would have turned back for us!"

And that did it. There was a moment's utter silence. I have never heard such a silence in a great crowd; and I saw the confidence and the hope go out of Thrasybulus. And then there was a roar—"Kill them! Kill the swine! They left our lads to drown, give them a taste of their own physic!"

The President of the Assembly made no attempt to control the situation; I imagine he had too much respect for his own skin. Only one of the Senators held out against this mockery of justice. I knew the voice, though I could not see the speaker. It was Socrates.

And suddenly I felt sick at what we were doing.

There must have been many in that vast crowd who felt the same sudden shock of self-disgust; but many and many more were beyond the reach of Socrates' stand for justice; too many who had lost sons and brothers. They shouted and cat-called, yelling to the man who was holding up proceedings to get back to his stone-cutting which was the trade he understood; and in the end, finding that there was no shaking him, they overruled him and it was proclaimed that the vote would be taken as though in his absence.

Theron had come down from the Rostrum; and I had worked my way through to him again by that time, where he stood in the midst of the knot that had gathered round him to ply him with questions, now that they knew him for a survivor. He looked round at me, his face heavy and almost stupid with the effort that he had called out of himself; and I looked back. Neither of us said anything, but he knew what I thought. And when the voting time came, he dropped in his black pebble and I my white one into the pot next to each other.

The death sentence was duly passed, and ordered to be carried out the same day. I did not look at the men who had suddenly no more future than a little bowl of hemlock. They were led away under guard, among the howling of the mob; and the heralds, when they could make themselves heard, announced the next business of the Assembly; the election of the Generals to succeed them.

Theron was rocking on his feet, with a dirty greyness stealing over his face. I said, "Come away. You've helped to kill five men, that's enough for one day."

He nodded, and let me take his arm and thrust a way for both of us through the crowd; the clotted mass of faces and faces and faces that had the stupid, avid look of those who have eaten and drunk too well, and then found a bloody street accident to stare at.

We got clear at last, and headed for Theron's house, that being the nearest. His sister was there in the courtyard, preparing the evening meal. She looked at our faces and asked no questions. Theron went straight to the brazier and crouched over it, he seemed always to be cold, these days. Myrrhine brought a little well-watered wine for us; and we sat for a while in silence. At last I said, "We have done an evil thing. We have made a mockery of Athenian justice."

He said, "It's not the first time," and took a drink and set the cup down, wiping the back of his hand across his mouth. "When anybody says Athenian justice, I want to vomit. I suppose there was such a thing once, maybe in our fathers' day."

"One of those men we condemned today had his own galley wrecked under him," I said.

"He was saved."

"Maybe he wishes he hadn't been, now; maybe the name of Athenian justice makes him want to vomit, too."

Theron looked up at me slowly. "You needn't drink with me, if you'd rather not."

"We're all guilty, come to that," I said.

"You cast a white pebble. You can stand back and say, 'I'm clean'."

"It isn't so easy to escape the guilt of one's city."

"I'll put up with a little guilt for the sake of my mates that I saw drown," Theron said, and he began to cough, pressing his hands over the left side of his ribs. A shallow, dry cough that left blood on his lips.

I stayed on, partly with the instinct one has to be with a friend who is sick, partly because in our differing ways we were both waiting for the same thing, and though neither of us said so, we were bound up in some way to wait for it together.

Myrrhine called us indoors and fed us both, and lit the lamp, then went to her loom. Theron had a little money from the government while he was sick, since the injury had been got on fighting service; but for a rower it was very little, and Myrrhine as good as kept the household going by selling her weaving—for which reason I had taken care not to eat with them before.

It was soon after the lamp was lit, and while the window still showed green with the last of the daylight in the dim lamp-tawny wall, that we heard the voices in the street—the sound that news makes when it runs from tongue to tongue, and men gather at corners and women come to doorways to hear it and pass it on.

We looked at each other, then Theron called his sister, and bade her go out and bring back word. She took up a pitcher as though going to the well, and drew her veil across her face—in that one thing she held to the old days when she had been the daughter of a well-to-do merchant, not the sister of a fleet rower—and slipped out.

We waited, both looking at the door; and in a little she came back, closed the door behind her, and put aside her veil.

"Well?" Theron said.

"The executions have been carried out." She set down the dripping jar. "But they say that one has escaped."

"Which one?" Theron demanded.

She looked from one to the other of us, frowning a little. "It sounded like Thrasybulus—was there one called Thrasybulus?"

Theron nodded. "There was," he said. "That makes three, with Theramenes and Thrassylus."

"They are speaking the names of the new Generals out there in the street, too."

"Who?" I said quickly.

"Adeimantus, Menander, and Tydius the Son of Lamachus."

Theron and I looked at each other, sharing the same thought, wondering at the significance behind the choice of at least two of

313

Alkibiades' most deadly enemies. "I wonder who was behind that selection?" I said.

He shrugged. "The Assembly."

"Behind the Assembly, then."

"The Gods know—Cleontius and Kritias, maybe."

"We really must get out of this way of relating everything to Alkibiades in one way or another," I said. "It's a bad habit."

"It's one shared by most of Athens." Theron said.


## The Whore

We seldom heard anything of the outside world. For myself, it did not matter. I did not care what men did in Athens or Sardis, or whether Spartan or Athenian fleets held power over the sea; and sometimes it seemed to me that Alkibiades did not either. And then I was glad, for the outside world was always a threat that might call him away from me. While his whole heart was turned to spreading and strengthening his hold on the Chersonese, he was part of the world I knew—even, I sometimes thought, playing a game that I knew; for what chief of a hundred horses in Thrace and Bithynia does not seek to make himself greater than another chief? In that world, my spirit could understand and follow him, even though I no longer rode at his side. But when his thoughts turned away to his old world, then I was lost, and left too far behind even to call to him to wait for me.

But from time to time, news did come, brought by a merchant on his way to Byzantium, or a ship's captain putting in for water. So we knew of a great sea fight off some islands called Arginussae, and an Athenian victory, and of many Athenian ships sunk in a storm afterwards. I was sorry about that. I belong to the great plains and the horseherds and the hills of summer pasture; the sea is strange and terrible to me, and I do not like to think of men, so long as they are not enemies of My Lord's, choking out their lives in it. And no matter what Athens had done to him, the men of the Athenian fleet were not My Lord's enemies. That was in his face when the news came.

One day in high summer—it was two years and the half of a year since My Lord came back to the North, and the olives were ripening and the barley in the coastwise terraces white for the sickle against the darkening of the sea—a ship put in in passing, and the rich merchant she carried came up to eat with Alkibiades, for seemingly they had known each other well in the past. They ate on the roof of the great chamber, under the pot-grown shade-vines that I had tended and trained with such care. Just the two of them, while I waited on them myself as I generally did when strangers came. It was better that way, lest they had private things to speak of, not for the ears of the slaves. It was beginning to be cool after the blazing heat of the day, and over the walls of the fort the sea was the colour of pearl. They had eaten kid seethed in milk, and black figs, and I had mixed the second krater full of water and dark Thracian wine; and they sat at ease, both turned to look seaward.

Then the merchant said in his soft deep voice, "You are, as you always were, a host without equal, Alkibiades."

"I fear this does not quite reach the standards of the old days," Alkibiades said. "Next time you must give me notice of your coming, my dear Polytion, and I will have a few score Thracian sword dancers to entertain you while you eat, and three virgins in fox-skin hats to help you while the night away."

"It is pleasant enough without," the merchant said.

"So, then now you shall pay for your supper by telling me the news of the world beyond Cape Helles."

The merchant looked round at him. "Are you interested?"

"That's a strange question. What makes you ask it?"

"I am not sure. You have the air of having all the world that concerns you here under your hand. Your forts and your tribes-men . . . You know they say in the world beyond Cape Helles that you plan to make yourself King of the Chersonese?"

"It serves to pass the time," Alkibiades said after a moment, and took another mouthful of wine.

"It is true, then?"

"It depends on what you mean by King. Two paramount chiefs of my acquaintance both call themselves Kings."

There was a silence, and I heard the sounds of the fort, men's voices and the stamping of horses in the stables and the never ceasing crying of the gulls. Then the merchant said softly, "Of course if you were to become, shall we say, Lord of these parts, including the cities and the settlements—and it seems you're not far off that, now—"

"Not far," Alkibiades said.

"There might be some possibility of a Thracian alliance with Athens—given time."

I saw My Lord's face as he played with the wine in his cup; and I thought, 'It is still Athens—still Athens with you—and the

315

Great Mother have pity on all others who tear out their hearts for you!'

Then My Lord said, "This news of the outer world that you owe me?"

The merchant Polytion made a small lazy gesture with his hands, and leaned back.

"Lysander has command of the Spartan fleet again."

Alkibiades sat up straight. "*Lysander?*"

"Kalitikades who took over from him was killed at Arginussae."

"That I had heard, even in the wilderness," My Lord said. "But *Lysander*! Are you sure? No man can hold the Fleet Command twice by Spartan law."

"Yet most assuredly Sparta had to find a way of getting Lysander back a second time. He's too useful to be wasted at home; all that influence with young Cyrus . . . They have got over the difficulty by making him Vice-Admiral, under an Admiral who counts for no more than a straw in the wind—I can't even remember his name."

"That's unusually intelligent, for the Spartan government," Alkibiades said. "So there is dear friend Lysander back at Ephesus again."

"And acting as deputy Satrap at Lydia, while Cyrus rushes off like a dutiful son to his father's deathbed—and I imagine to make his own claim to the Sun throne before his brother Artaxerxes gets it."

"So, the old Lion is dying at last, is he? If Cyrus gets the throne, life will be magnificent for Lysander. Think of having the King of Kings in your bed, Polytion!"

"It is no laughing matter," said the merchant.

"No, Polytion. It is no laughing matter. But it is not without its amusing side, all the same."

"As deputy Satrap, he has control of the Lydian revenues," Polytion said abruptly.

Alkibiades sat very still for a moment. "Hades! I'd not thought of that. He'll have less cause than ever to worry over the pay for his fleet; while we—while the Athenians—I suppose are in the same old straits, pushed for every obol."

"So it seems, as far as one can say without being in the Councils of the State."

"It is a pity there are no true pirates left in the Navy," Alkibiades said. "They lost the last of the breed in myself and in Antiochus. They could have done with us now." It was the first time I had heard him speak Antiochus' name since he came North again;

and he laughed, but the laughter was twisted inside him. "The present breed are poor stuff—Adeimantus, Menander, Tydius. Three of them to do my work; and they cannot do it."

"Perhaps they are not—overstraining themselves to do it."

Alkibiades looked round at him quickly. "What do you mean?"

And Polytion smiled down his long nose. "I have heard it whispered—we merchants hear the oddest things, you know, and it is probably no more than the tales women tell to a child at bedtime—that however short the fleet may be, the Admirals' coffers are not altogether strangers to Persian gold."

Alkibiades' hand clenched round his wine cup until I saw the knuckles shine white as bone. And his eyes opened with a cold blue light. "If I thought that," he said, "by the Gods! If I thought that—"

"Yes?" said Polytion, and then, "What could you do?"

"Nothing," said My Lord, and dropped his face into his hands.

But when, just after harvest time, word came that this Lysander was busy in the Hellespont and had taken Lampsakus, My Lord shifted his headquarters back to Pactye; I think to be close on hand when the fighting came, though I never heard him say so. Maybe he hoped that there might still be some part that he could play. I do not know. He let me go south to Pactye with him, and I had learned again to ask no more than that.

## The Soldier

We had been saying all that year among ourselves that it was madness to leave the Hellespont unguarded, with the fleet scattered from Samos half across the south Aegean, as we were by then. A few of us even tried to put it to our new Admirals, but only got cursed for our pains. I suppose that the Spartans having refused us fight so long—ever since Arginussae—the High Command thought that they had learned their lesson. It is always a pity when the High Command starts to underestimate the enemy. Alkibiades would have known better.

About harvest time we got word—the *Pegasus* was at Chios with Konon's squadron—that the Spartan fleet were out from Ephesus and heading north. Lysander, who was in command again, must have known as well as we did that the Hellespont was unguarded, and soon the corn ships would be coming through.

We put out from Chios, joining the rest of the fleet off Mitylene and gave chase. But he had the wind of us, and off Cape Helles our scouting vessel met us with the news that he had taken Lampsakus two days ago and made his headquarters there. It was the perfect base from which to cut off the corn fleet.

We put in at Sestos to re-victual—it seemed strange to be back there again—then held on north, maybe two miles farther up the coast, and took up our position almost opposite Lampsakus, at, of all God-forsaken places, Aegospotami! Goats' Creek—only no self-respecting goat would have lived there. What possessed our Commanders to take up such an idiot position is beyond knowing. Or if I have sometimes had a suspicion that it was worse than idiocy, I have thrust it away. They were fools, stiff-necked in their folly; surely it must be unjust to suspect them of more than that . . .

But certainly to have chosen Aegospotami for a fleet base was foolish past belief, and most of us knew it. With no proper harbour but an open and unprotected shore-line, and no nearer source of supplies, once the two days' rations that we carried had given out, than Sestos, two miles down the coast.

Every morning we manned ship and sailed across toward the Spartan base, trying as we had tried so often before, to draw the Spartans out to battle. But Lysander was too wily for that; as he had refused to be drawn from Ephesus until the moment of his own choosing, so he refused to be drawn from Lampsakus. Only every day when we returned, a couple of their light reconnaissance galleys would follow us at a respectful distance—we thought it was a respectful distance—and hang about in mid-stream till we had disembarked; then return to their own side of the straits.

It seemed as though it might go on like that for ever. It went on for six days. On the fifth day, Ariston who was also with Konon's squadron, and I, sick of the disorderly camp, and the mud flats through which the Goats' Creek looped out to the straits, strolled northward into the rising ground, and sat ourselves down on the edge of a derelict olive garden. All round us the cut barley stubble stretched between the straits and the hills, lion tawny in the evening light; southward the tents of the camp sprawled along the shore; the black shapes of the triremes drawn up on the mud, the smoke of camp fires lying low in the air. And beyond, across Goats' Creek, the desolate country was flecked with moving black fly-specks, men off to Sestos for supplies, or for the evening pleasures of the town.

318

And across the straits, the buildings of Lampsakus showed up, acid white, with the Spartan fleet lying below its walls.

"Gods! What a camp!" I said. "Alkibiades would weep to see us!"

"Maybe he does see us," Ariston said quietly. "I can't imagine he'd have a Spartan and an Athenian fleet sitting on his threshold and take no interest."

"If I was him, after the treatment he's had from us, I'd go as far away as possible and take no interest at all."

"Would you? I wonder."

"No, I suppose not," I said.

We sat in silence for a while. I was watching the swallows dart above the stubble. All this was haunted country for us, haunted by those three years when we had followed him from victory to victory; the old feeling themselves young, and the young feeling themselves Gods. And Alkibiades came often to our minds, the drawling voice, the insolent sunny gaze, the flame to warm one's hands at . . . I turned my head and looked northward, wondering if he was indeed watching us from the hills; and saw a horseman coming down through the lower slopes of the cornland.

One cannot look in any direction in Thrace without seeing a horseman, where there are men at all; so I thought little of this one, and did not even mention him to Ariston, who was lying with his head on his arms and his face turned towards the straits.

The man was nearer now, you could hear the beat of his horse's hooves and see the little puffs of dust rising round them; his shadow was lance-long in the sunset light, and I thought it was a fine horse, and the fellow did not ride like a Thracian. Ariston, hearing the hooves also, turned his head and sat up. And in the same instant it was as though some film of unknowing peeled away from my eyes.

"It *is*!" said Ariston. "Zeus! It's Alkibiades!" and began to scramble to his feet.

For a moment longer I did not move, held by some feeling that he was not real, that my own thoughts had conjured him up. Then I was on my feet too, and running, overtaking Ariston, so that we reached him together. We came up on either side of the raking tiger-spot stallion, and he had a hand for each of us—only his hair was grey, not streaked among the gold as it had been when I saw him last, but quite grey.

"Arkadius! Ariston!" (They said he never forgot a face or a name.) "I did not think to find two old friends and such a welcome, before I even reached the Athenian camp!"

"Alkibiades! We were talking of you just a while since. Have you come to join us?"

"I, that am a declared fugitive? Hardly. But I must speak with your Generals none the less."

We turned back beside him, both full of questions that it did not seem to be the moment to ask; neither, I think, quite sure even now that we were not walking beside a dream. I kept my hand on his horse's shoulder as we walked, as though without that link to hold him, he might be gone from us like a breaking wave. And we brought him back to the camp without another word between the three of us.

On the fringe of the camp, others recognized him and came running; shouting, catching at his feet, at his horse, thrusting round him. The old bos'n of the *Marathon* was almost crying, so was a young lieutenant of marines who had barely joined before he left us. Suddenly the dream was gone, and we knew that we had him with us, Alkibiades in the flesh.

He looked round him, greeting this man and that, and then without the least change of manner, demanded, "Since when have the Athenians given up posting sentries or digging covering dykes for the galleys when they make camp?"

"There are no Spartans this side of the straits, My Lord Alkibiades," someone said.

"And they have no ships to ferry them over? Gods! You're enough to break a Commander's heart! Where are your Generals' headquarters?"

Ariston pointed out the tents of our three beauties, pitched in the lee of a thorn thicket. Alkibiades dismounted. Someone took his horse, and he strode off towards them. A good many of us followed him, glancing at each other. There might well be trouble when he and his successors met, and if there was, better that we were on hand.

The Generals and senior officers had gathered for the evening meal before Adeimantus' tent; and they rose from the table, somewhat startled men, when they saw who they had for company.

Alkibiades came straight to the point. "In the name of the Dog, what do you think you're doing here?"

Tydius said harshly, "Surely it is we who should be asking that of you?"

"I've come to give you good advice. Cut out of here and back to Sestos tonight."

"The days when you gave the orders here are past," Menander

said. He was always a vulgar brute, and Alkibiades let him see what he thought of him. He flushed red as a pomegranate in the fading light.

"I said advice, not orders." Alkibiades was obviously longing to blast them all to Tartarus, but trying to keep things cool and reasonable. "I've been sitting up in the hills watching you these five days past, and scarcely able to believe my eyes that you are here at all—on an open coastline, no harbour, no base for provisions nearer than Sestos. Great Gods, gentlemen, *why?*"

"I see no reason why we should account to you for our choice of position," said Tydius. "But since you ask it—we happen to be desirous of bringing Lysander to action. I think you found yourself faced with the same need at one time—"

I saw Alkibiades' eyes and his nostrils widen, but he said nothing; and Tydius went on, "From here, we have a perfect quoin of vantage for watching Lampsakus."

"And Lampsakus has a perfect quoin of vantage for watching you!" Alkibiades' voice cut now like a whiplash. "Lysander has his fleet under perfect discipline—you can see that, even from this side of the straits if you had cared to place look-outs on higher ground. His ships are manned and ready all day to put out at the word of command; and his troops ready to embark. Have you not noticed the Spartan picket-boats that watch you home each day, and hang round till you are disembarked and scattered half over the Chersonese? Do you suppose Lysander doesn't know as well as I do, that your discipline grows worse each day? You post no sentries; at this moment there's scarcely a man aboard your ships; they're all messing about on shore or away after supplies or tumbling the girls in Sestos."

Tydius said icily, "I scarcely think that you, who left the fleet in the hands of a drunken sailing master while you went raiding and whoring in Karia, are the one to talk to my colleagues and myself of discipline."

I thought the trouble was coming then. For a moment I saw bloody murder looking out of Alkibiades' eyes; but he mastered his clear desire to go for Tydius' throat; too much was at stake. He said almost patiently, like a man talking to a half-witted child, "You seek to bring the Spartan fleet to battle, so; but if you lose the battle there will be no chance of another. Lysander will close the Propontis against the corn ships, and it will be the end for Athens as well as for you. Take the fleet to Sestos before it's too late; with the protection of the harbour, you can choose your own time to fight; without it, the enemy can force battle on you at any time, and take you unprepared. Wait for Lysander to tire of the waiting game; he must do that sooner or later; keep scouts posted, and when he sails, intercept him."

"I am sure that my colleagues and I are extremely grateful to you for your—advice in this matter," Tydius began with savage irony; but Alkibiades had other things still to say.

"I have a friend or two, a useful alliance here and there in these parts; I have not altogether wasted these years of exile. Three thousand tribesmen will answer to a trumpet sounding from my keeps. If we ferry them across, we can mount a land attack at the same time—"

"We?" said Adeimantus. "You would join yourself with us?"

"The Thracians are not disciplined troops who will fight under any General set over them. They will follow me because they know me and have followed me before."

Tydius leaned forward, both hands on the trestle table. "But we also know you, Alkibiades. Oh yes, we know you—you come here pretending great concern for Athens—you don't care a feather in the wind for Athens unless you rule her. So you will lead these wild tribesmen of yours, and claim the lion's share in the victory, and Athens will turn to you as her preserver and rush to the Assembly howling for your recall—you who led her young men to disaster at Syracuse for your own glory. (And not only her young men. You killed my father, Alkibiades, as surely as though you did it with your own hands.) You who betrayed her to Sparta. No thank you, Alkibiades; we who are the Generals now, will fight this campaign without your help in the way that we judge best. Now you had better go, before we remember that you are wanted by the Council at home, and feel it our duty to take you prisoner."

Alkibiades drew himself up till suddenly he seemed to dwarf them all; and looked down on them from his immense height. "I regret that I have kept you from your supper so long. One often hears it said that the Spartans, never having had it at home, don't know how to handle money; but Lysander, with the Lydian treasury to draw on, seems to have a remarkable understanding of where it will buy the best results."

And he turned on his heel leaving them speechless—it was almost funny—and strode off to where his horse was waiting for him.

A whole crowd of us saw him off, walking out of the camp with him proud in the knowledge that we were probably wrecking our careers by doing so. Even Konon, who was rather senior for that sort of thing.

It was Konon who asked, "Could you really have produced three thousand tribesmen, or was that just to annoy our beloved Generals?"

"Oh yes, I could have produced them," Alkibiades said. "I could have forced Lysander to break harbour in four days; five at the most. Except for the name, I'm King in these parts; a nice little barbarian Kingdom."

We halted, just clear of the camp, and he sat his horse looking out across the straits a few moments, then round at us. "There's nothing more I can do here. I wish there was for your sakes. As for your three Generals, I'd see them in Tartarus first! Keep your eyes open for trouble, and do what you can about the discipline among your own lads."

He wheeled his horse and dug in his heels with a sudden savagery, and was away northward, lost almost at once in the dust-cloud and the gathering twilight. We stood there as long as we could hear the drum of his horse's hooves, and then turned back towards the camp.

Konon stopped all further shore leave for his squadron that night, and sent a marine company to get back the men already in Sestos; and the Trirarch of the *Paralos* did the same. The rest shrugged their shoulders and went on as before.

It was the next day the Spartans came.

We put out in the morning as usual, to try to draw Lysander from harbour, and as usual we failed. And when we headed back, the two or three picket-boats followed us and hung about in midstream till our crews had disembarked and started cooking the midday meal, or scattered across country bound for Sestos, leaving the ships with only a handful of guards on board. Only aboard the *Paralos* and the eight triremes of Konon's squadron, which rode at anchor instead of being run up the beach, we continued to man ship; and the few who went ashore to cook the food (there'd be none tomorrow, as far as we could see, unless we could come to some arrangement for getting a party into Sestos to fetch it) kept their weapons handy. The others jeered at us as they set off, asking what they should bring us back from the town, and where we thought tomorrow's dinner was coming from.

But that day the Spartan picket-boats did not turn for home as soon as we were dispersed. We could not see, though we learned of it much later from one of the few escaped prisoners, that aboard one of the picket-boats a bronze shield had been hoisted up in the bows and was flashing the midday sun across the straits to the Spartans waiting for the signal to attack. Nor could we see across the straits from that low shore, with the dazzle of the sun on the water in our eyes, the crimson flutter of the flagship's pennant ordering the ships to sea, and the whole Spartan fleet come racing out of harbour.

They were almost halfway over, coming at racing speed when we saw them; when we saw death bearing down on us, with the foam curling back over the grinning rams, and the spearmen on the fore-deck— and our own ships unmanned and the screws scattered over the countryside.

From Konon's fore-deck the trumpet sounded, and others of the fleet took it up, sounding Alarm and Recall. The squadron's few men ashore came roaring down the beach leaving the half-cooked meal over the fires, and waded out to us, and we dragged them aboard even as the anchors came up. The Generals were yelling orders with nobody to yell to. All across country little dark figures were coming at the run without a hope of making the ships before the Spartans were upon us.

It was not that we lost the battle, and with it our last chance for Athens and ourselves, as Alkibiades had warned our Generals just one day ago. It never came to a battle. It was just a bloody massacre.

A few ships got off the beach—ships with half a crew and no rowers, with one bank of rowers and no troops. It was shrieking chaos. The men streaming back from inland had left their weapons behind in camp; a few got on board but were cut down by the boarding Spartans before they could arm. Others turned and ran—and were hunted down and slaughtered among the mud flats and barley stubble. There was nothing we could do, nothing, nine ships in fighting trim against the whole Spartan fleet. We could have stayed and died with the rest, and added to Athens' loss by just nine ships—we came near to losing the *Marathon* as it was; she was boarded but managed to fling off the Spartans who sprang aboard—but we knew the old seaman's adage, that anything saved from a wreck is gain; and I think we all knew the orders we were going to get from Konon, before he gave them . . .

Two hours after the first shock, we broke off the fight, and headed across to Lampsakus. There, so easily that there was a kind of hideous comedy about it, we picked up the sails of the Spartan fleet. Sails and masts are generally lodged ashore in time of action, but when it comes to a chase, sails and oars have the advantage over oars alone! As it turned out, we need not have troubled, though. For as we staggered south down the Hellespont, with the marks of fighting on us and the evening wind in our captured sails, Lysander made no move to follow us. He was busy along the bloody shores of Goats' Creek. He had a hundred and seventy Athenian ships and could afford to let nine go.

We heard later that the fleet was wiped out—that was never in doubt—and our three Generals and three thousand troops, seamen and rowers, taken captive and executed; the rest were simply dead or missing. But at the time we knew only that the long war with Sparta was over, and Athens was over too.

That night the *Paralos* parted from us and headed for home— you can make Piraeus in two days from Sestos with a crack ship—to carry her the news.

## The Whore

My Lord came back from the hills southward after dark, riding as though the Hounds of Night were after him. He would not eat; but that night he got more drunk than I have ever known him. So drunk that when he slid from the bench he lay where he landed, and slept there, sodden and fouled and uncaring. And I did not call the slaves or one of the garrison to help me get him to bed, for I did not want them to see him so; though in Thrace it is common enough to sleep in one's own muck under the table. Still, he was not of Thrace. So I covered him where he lay, and watched beside him.

When he woke, he went and cleaned himself without a word, and came back, lurching, his eyes like balls of blood in his head, and flung himself down on the bed-place. But almost at once he staggered to his feet again; and all that day he walked up and down the keep chamber, walked and walked, like a wild thing padding to and fro the length of its cage.

I sat huddled in the corner; I dared not leave him, I dared not try to make him rest. I simply crouched there with his hound bitch who he had kicked out of the way, shivering against me, until at last, still huddled there, I slept.

I woke to hear the bitch wining softly. It was long after dark, and the keep chamber was quiet of footsteps for the first time that day. There was a strange red glow in the sky beyond the narrow window, and My Lord was standing there, looking out. And his quiet was as frightening as his pacing had been.

I got up and crept to him, the bitch following me. He never moved, and I did not dare to touch him. The red glow was fierce behind the hills southward. And at last I said, "What is it that is on fire?"

He said quite quietly, in a queer level voice that seemed to have no rise or fall in it at all. "They are burning the Athenian camp. There is no need to be afraid of Athens any more, Timandra. I think she's dead."

# 24

## The Whore

After the Athenian Navy was wiped out at Goats' Creek, there were no Athenian ships left in the Propontis or the Hellespont. And the forts that My Lord had built to be the links in a chain joining the Athenian settlements of the North to their home city, would become only little rocks, sundered from each other, and with the storms beating over them, until at last they must be overwhelmed. So I thought, for one whole night, that he would abandon them and take to the hills. And maybe he would let me ride with him again.

But next day, an Athenian fugitive came stumbling through the gate. First the one man alone, then two together, one supporting the other, who had an arm half hacked through below the shoulder. For many days the trickle went on. "It is for this, that you will not take to the hills, but bide here where the Spartans may be down upon us at any time," I said. "It is for these men, who are not worth it, that you wait in Pactye, that they may know where to find you."

He cocked an eyebrow at me, leaning lazily against the wall, with another man's blood on his hands and forehead. "You have been listening to old seamen talking. You should never believe anything a seaman tells you, it is always coloured by sentiment. I object to being chased from my own hearth by the mere shadow of Lysander."

He kept the land gate of Pactye always open and guarded in those days and nights; and it was well into the winter before the thinning trickle of fugitives dried up altogether. He gave them shelter, money from the gold that the cities had paid for his protection, help to get away into the hills or back to Athens, sometimes a grave. The man with his arm hacked through died next day, and there were others who crawled to Alkibiades as a dying hound crawls to his master's hand.

Once or twice they brought news of the world outside, but not often. Men on the run seldom gather much news. The tribesmen brought news sometimes, as they had always done; and the tunny fishers, once they knew that My Lord would pay for it. And so before long we heard that Lysander was going the round of the regained Athenian settlements, setting up Spartan Governors everywhere, but that he was giving safe-conduct for the journey to every Athenian who chose to return to Athens, rather than remain under Spartan rule.

After that, when fugitives came to us, seeking to get home, we had only to send them to Sestos or Perinthos, with all signs of their fleet service carefully stripped away, and leave the Spartan Governors to do the rest. But My Lord's face grew very grim, and the lines on it seemed more harshly cut than ever.

A little while after the news of Lysander's mercy reached Bisanthe—we had returned to Bisanthe by then; the fugitives came there just the same—Heraklides and the master of the *Icarus* came seeking word with My Lord.

That time he remembered my presence, and bade me go and fetch the last of the Samian wine.

I went out as though to fetch it, but I lingered at the head of the stairway with my ear pressed against the door, for I did not trust them. I've no knowing why, but for the first time, I did not trust them.

My Lord's voice said, "What is it that you come to tell me?"

And there was a small silence; the kind of silence in which men look at each other, unsure who is to speak. Then Heraklides said, "Sir, we come to ask your leave to take advantage of Lysander's safe conduct."

"I thought it might be that," said My Lord. "I have seen it in your eyes for many days. I can only thank you for remaining faithful to me so long."

The master said, "Sir, it is not that we would break faith with you; but many of us have wives and children. We have been long away; and it may be that this is the last chance that we shall have of returning to them."

"You realize, of course, why Lysander is encouraging any stray Athenian to crowd back into the city?" And then he gave a kind of roar, "Great Gods! Are you quite fools? Do you mean to tell me that the most wooden-headed rower doesn't see what is going to happen? Lysander will be blockading Athens before the dark of the year—the more mouths that flock into the city the sooner the stores will give out and the Council be forced to ask for terms."

And again there was silence, and then a sound from the pilot that was like a groan. And then he said, stubbornly, "We still have our wives and children. Athens will need men to fight for her."

I listened for My Lord's voice, it was quiet again, and lazy and warm with the old lisp. "I take it you speak for the garrison also?"

Heraklides said, "Yes, sir."

My Lord said, "So. I have led men in my time, but never against their will. You are free to leave for Sestos tomorrow."

And then he laughed, and the laughter cracked a little in his throat. "Ah now, never wear such funeral faces! I've no wife and—no child to speak of, waiting for me to go and be besieged with them at home, and the Olympian Twelve forbid that I should hold back those that have. We have known good times and bad together, let us drink to the good and drown the memory of the bad, and part friends, as we have been so long."

I ran then, to get the wine; and later, from the little room below that I had made my own, I heard them playing kotabos with the dregs in the cups, very gay; but the gaiety had somewhat the sound of heartbreak in it.

Next morning I woke alone in the great bed-place long before dawn, and saw through the cracks in the shutters the fierce red flicker of fire close at hand. I leapt from under the covers and ran to the window embrasure, thinking of attack, and looked out. I saw the guard turret above the narrow anchorage outlined against a red flare from below, and a flight of sparks leapt into the air and streamed away on the gusting wind. I remember a little cold rain was spitting past between me and the flames, not enough to damp down a fire once it was got going; and realizing suddenly that they were burning the *Icarus* on her slipway.

My heart wept as though it were for some great chief on his funeral pyre, with the jars of oil and wine and honey and his favourite woman at his side, and his slain horses piled about him. The smell of burning was in the air, and I thought once I caught the waft of incense.

The rain had turned to sleet, in the grey light of the morning, when her crew and the Athenians among the garrison straggled out through the gates and headed for Sestos.


The Citizen


We closed the port of Piraeus as soon as we knew that we had no ships to hold it, leaving only the harbour at Munychia without a boom, for the corn ships if any got through to us. A few did; those that had started early and passed down the Hellespont before Goats' Creek; a couple from Cyprus. Then Lysander, fresh from making the rounds of our old colonies and settling his own Governors in them, came down with close on two hundred triremes to blockade us from the sea. King Pausanius had already marched his Spartan troops up over the Isthmus, right to our walls; they camped in the Academy Gardens and closed the road to Megara. Agis was down from Dekalia and had closed the road to Thebes.

It was a strange blockade, for Lysander was giving every Athenian from the old colonies who wished to return to Athens rather than remain under a Spartan Governor, safe conduct to pass in through it.

They poured in with their women and children and hastily gathered bundles, praising the mercy of Lysander—until the reserves of food began to run low. Famine hit us in good earnest after the first month. The markets were eaten bare as a barley field by a swarm of locusts. Soon a loaf cost more than a man could earn in two days with honour. People who had dogs began to eat them, and anyone who possessed a horse or mule was rich and frightened, and kept anxious guard over it.

Theron did not last long into the siege, and after a while I was thinking him lucky.

He could not have lived very long, anyway. Whatever the injury he had suffered in the wreck, it was not the kind that mends. The Priest of Esculapius did not say so, but I saw it in his eyes, and so, I think, did Theron.

Towards the end, I used to go to his house every night—he would not let me bring him to mine—so that Myrrhine, who had tended him all day could get some rest. She used to bring out a little food and try to make me eat, but already no honest house in Athens was rich enough to feed a guest, and there would be no market for her fine weaving now; so I used to take my own with me if I had anything to eat, and tell her that I had eaten already, if I had not.

I do not forget those bitter winter nights. There was no money for a fire, and we piled every covering and garment in the house on to Theron's bed, for though towards the end he began to burn with fever, he shivered always with an inner cold it seemed nothing could warm. There was nothing of him between withered skin and great gaunt bones; his breath stank, and he coughed blood and pus.

One evening Myrrhine met me at the door. She had taken to going out in the evenings as soon as I arrived, saying that she went to sleep with a friend down the street, for in that way Theron could have the covering from her bed as well as his own. I was too tired to notice that the excuse seemed a little thin. One was always tired, in those days.

"How is he?" I asked.

"Much the same, I think. The healer Priest was here this morning. He says that he will last a few days more, but not many. You will find everything to hand." And she was gone past me into the winter dusk.

I went into the inner room that was cold and airless with its sick-man spell. Theron's eyes were open, and he looked at me, not speaking; speaking made him cough; but with a ghost of his old smile, which he never quite lost. I did what I could to make him comfortable, and moved the lamp so that it did not shine in his eyes, and sponged the blood off his mouth when he coughed. Presently he grew very cold, and since there was nothing more to put over him but the cloak I was wearing, I took it off and spread it over all, and then lay down beside him, pulling the mass of coverings over us both, and put my arms round him.

He managed a cracked laugh, and said, "Timotheus, this is somewhat late in the day!" And I laughed too, and held him close, with the stink of his sickness all about me. We had never been lovers, but I seemed to know, then, something of what it might be for two who were lovers a long time ago and could lie together on the eve of parting, with only the shared kindness and closeness of friends, because the old demanding fires are burned out.

I think we both slept a little, and when I woke, I knew even before I looked, that Theron was going. Not in a few days as the Priest had said, but now. He was trying to say something, he spoke his sister's name, and I thought he wanted her, and wondered desperately what I should do, for if I went to her friend's house for her, he might die alone before I could bring her back. But as I stumbled out of bed into the icy air, and turned shading the lamp to look down at him, he seemed to gather up all his strength, and spoke quite clearly, though so faintly that I had to bend close to hear what he said.

"No, don't call her, nothing she could do—give me your hand to the—threshold." I had already set down the lamp again, and his hand was in mine; it felt curiously empty, like a hand that is already dead. "I should have got Myrrhine married long ago," he said. "Too late now—no other male relative—do what you can for her, Timotheus." He smiled as though he was falling asleep. The last thing he said was, "Alkibiades would have turned back for us." Then he began to cough, and a great gush of blood came out

331

of his mouth; and as I raised him and held him against me, his head went back and his eyes set. And I knew that the great bony hand in mine was a dead man's indeed.

I laid him down and set to clearing up the mess.

I had barely got him decent when I heard running footsteps outside and then crossing the outer room, and the door burst open and Myrrhine stood there. "Theron—"

"He's dead," I told her.

"I know. Suddenly I knew, and I ran all the way."

She came forward into the lamplight, and I saw that there was green eye-paint on her eyes, and her cheeks and mouth were rouged, and long cheap earrings dangled foolishly gay against her neck. She had forgotten in her speed to rub off the harlot's paint that she must have put on somewhere each evening after she was clear of the house.

She was kneeling beside the bed, looking down at Theron. She stooped a moment and laid her painted cheek against his grey one; and the earrings tinkled prettily. Then she looked up and saw me staring at her, and put her hands to her face. She got up and looked at me quite steadily. "How else do you suppose I kept him fed?"

"I wish I had known," I said.

She made a small weary gesture. "What could you have done? No one buys perfumes nowadays, you told me so yourself. You were doing all you could, and more."

It was cheaper at that time to bury the dead than to buy food for the living, and I managed to bury Theron respectably, by selling the wine krater that had been my father's pride, the red one with the athletes round it, and his armour, which was one of the few things that would still fetch a little money at that time. I would have sold them long before, but that I had always felt that they were his and not mine to sell.

When the funeral was over, I brought Myrrhine back to my own house. I had meant to sell Vasso or give her away to someone who would feed her, as I could no longer afford to do; but I could not have Myrrhine in the house without another woman there. I would have asked my sister to take her, but more than ever, now, no household except for the really well-to-do could afford another mouth.

So she had the women's chambers that had been empty since my sister married. She seemed like one walking in her sleep, and I thought, 'I will give her time to wake up before I talk to her about the future.'

But on the first evening, it was she and not old Vasso, who brought in the bean broth for my supper. "That's Vasso's work," I said.

"Does it matter? I had to talk to you."

I said, "Later. We only buried Theron today. You're tired."

"Now," she said gently; but I saw there was no moving her. "Is it the future you are troubled about?"

"It was very kind of you to bring me back to your house. But I think I ought not to stay here. Only I do not quite know what to do."

"Theron asked me to find you a husband," I said, and felt an oaf for speaking it to her so soon.

"He was too sick to know what he asked," she said. "Even if I had not—done what I did to buy food for us, I know that I have no beauty, and no dowry save what the house will fetch if ever I can sell it. And even for those who have both—" She hesitated a moment. "The men we should have married died at Syracuse or Goats' Creek. There's a whole generation of us will never find husbands nor bear children, now."

"That is true," I said. "And for that reason, if you do not dislike the idea too much, the best way out of the difficulty would be if I were to marry you myself, when the time of your mourning is over."

She stood quite still, with a strange look on her face; and I got awkwardly to my feet. "I would not have spoken of this to you so soon," I said apologetically. "It was you who would have the decision-making on this first evening."

She said, "I know you loved Theron, but—"

"I need a wife."

"One with neither looks nor dowry, and who you have seen with harlot's paint on her face?" she said. I never heard any woman speak so proudly.

"My father tried to make a match for me once," I said. "He told me later, when he was angry with me about something else, that the girl's father said young men weren't so hard come by that his daughter need marry a cripple."

She was silent again, and I waited. Then she said, "It is different, now."

"Not for me," I said. "But we will only do it if you want to. Think it over, Myrrhine."

"I do not need to think it over. When the time of my mourning is over, if we both live so long—I will marry you."

·    ·    ·    ·    ·

333

When the daily corn ration, given out by the government and collected by the head of each household, was down to less than half a measure per head, we sent envoys to the Spartan Kings asking for terms of peace. (After Cyzicus, and again after Arginussae, we could have had peace, each side keeping what we then held; but that would not have suited some in power— Cleontius had roused up the people to fight to a victorious finish. They got him on a charge of evading military service, and executed him.) The Kings said it was a matter for the Ephors; so we sent the envoys off to Lacedaemon, empowered to make the offer that the Spartans had made to us before; each side to keep what we held, only now we held nothing but the city and Piraeus and the Long Walls between.

The Spartans turned our envoys back on the frontier. Let Athens agree to become "subject allies" of Sparta, and pull down a mile of the Long Walls, and it might be worth their coming again.

We said, "That is that," and held on for a while. But towards winter's end, with the old and the sick mostly dead—and the very young too, for many families were driven by then to exposing their newborn children—we went another mission, with Theramenes at its head.

He was gone three months on a task that we had expected to be over one way or the other in a week. Men said that he had grown to like the taste of black broth; and since the Oligarchs in the city had for the most part been the rich men, and the Democrats the poor, the longer he waited, the fewer Democrats there would be to blame him afterwards for the harsh terms he brought back with him.

And they *were* harsh, when at last he did bring them; though they could have been harsher. For, added to the old demand to recognize Sparta's overlordship and pull down a mile of the Long Walls, were new ones. We were to hand over all our remaining ships but twelve, and in those twelve we were to bring back our political exiles—all the rabid Oligarchs that we had got rid of when the Four Hundred were overthrown and we had become free once more.

So we yielded and ceased again to be free. A few voices still cried out against surrender; but most of us were simply too tired to care either way. Five months of famine has that effect.

Lysander rode in triumph from Piraeus up into the city in the hard spring sunlight, with a body of picked Spartan troops marching behind him. There had been quite a few corpses lying around in the streets he was to pass through. The poorest people

334

had developed an unfortunate habit during the last days of the siege, of dropping dead in the streets; and as by common consent, the city had left the last-fallen to lie there for a greeting to the conquerors. But Lysander had thought of that, and the evening before, he sent prisoners of war to collect the dead and tip them into a communal grave-pit. Also he was taking no chances, and the streets were lined with Spartan guards as he passed through.

He rode up to the High City, and sacrificed and gave thanks for his victory in the Temple of Athene Parthenos. I think that was when I really knew that we were defeated.

After that he presided over the beginning of pulling down the Long Walls.

The Spartans had rounded up all the flute girls in the city to play while the task was carried out; and as the great stones of Themistocles came crashing down, the flutes twittered like little birds. (But it must have been the Corinthians who thought of that; it was not the sort of idea that would occur to the Spartan mind.)

There were agitators among the crowds and troops too, paid to fling up their helmets and shout as the stones fell, that this was the beginning of freedom.


## The Soldier

We parted from Konon and returned to Samos while he took his own squadron to Cyprus.

Samos fell a short while before Athens. We rigged a boom across the harbour, and held out as long as we could—all the longer for half expecting that when we *did* fall, those of us still left would get the same treatment as our comrades taken at Goats' Creek. But by the time our losses had made us too weak to hold them off, and they took the boom by storm, negotiations for the surrender of Athens were already under way; and Sparta's terms included the yielding up of the whole remaining Navy save for twelve ships to be used for bringing back Athenian political exiles. There were nothing like twelve triremes at Piraeus, and so the number was made up from Samos. There were just about enough of us left to man the five triremes needed.

My good old *Pegasus* was one of the chosen five; and so I had the honour of bringing Kritias back from Thessaly, where he had been banished after the Four Hundred were thrown out. His courteous, well-modulated voice and cold seagull's eye make me sick to think of, even now; and I got the decks scrubbed as soon as he had stepped ashore at Piraeus into the welcoming arms of a Spartan guard of honour.

I had had long enough to get used to the idea that Athens had fallen, but still it came as something of a surprise to see the Spartan blood-red tunics and grim looks on the Munychian quayside.

Afterwards I was ordered off on a sort of round trip, collecting lesser beauties from up and down the Ionian shore; and by the time I made Athens again it was high summer, and the Spartans, or their creatures, had been in power for more than two months.

Entering harbour I looked up as somehow one always does, to catch the sun-flash from the High City on the great spear of Athene. And I felt a great desire to go up to Athens and see how it was with the city now. I got my exiles ashore, saw to the berthing of the ship, and turned over to my pilot. I had received no orders, and so assumed that I was on leave; and set out for the city, on foot because after so much sea-going, I needed to stretch my legs.

For three miles the road looked much as it always had done; and then suddenly the great defensive walls came to a jagged end, and across the tumble of cast down stones, one could see the marshes and the open country on either side. I was prepared for that; but I was not prepared for the *feel* of the city when I came in through the Piraeus Gate. It did not look so very different from the Athens I remembered. Two months had gone by since the surrender, and there were things to buy in the shops and the market stalls; the streets had been cleaned up, and the people had a little flesh on their bones, though they still wore the sharpened and sunk-eyed look that comes of recent famine. But over everything, there hung a shadow—I do not know how to describe it; it was not only the shadow of defeat but something more. Men glanced at each other overlong in passing, or else took care not to look at all, and between each man and man, was the shadow . . .

I turned my steps towards the High City with something of the same instinct that makes a man head for high ground in the hope of getting out of a fever-fog. But when it stood clear above me at the head of the Panathenic Way, I thought for a moment that something was wrong with my eyes, for there seemed to be smoke, and not the thin smoke of sacrifice, up there against the evening sky. I blinked to clear them, but when I looked again, the smoke was still there.

I remember grabbing a passer-by, and pointing. "Am I mad, or are there fires up there?"

He looked at me, and said, "Where are you from, soldier? Those are cooking fires; there's the Spartan garrison up there!"

"A Spartan garrison—in the High City?" I said stupidly.

"Aye, all among the Gods. They've made their latrines behind the Temple of the Maiden, and you have to ask their leave if you want to go up there to sacrifice, now."

Then he looked at me again, and the thing in his eyes was the same as the thing in the streets. He muttered, "I never said nothing, mind." And wrenched himself from my grasp and half ran away down the street. I knew then that the shadow was fear. The whole city reeked of it.

I decided not to go up to the High City and ask some Spartan bully's leave to sacrifice on Athene's altars. But I did not know where else to go. I had no friends in Athens now; it was suddenly a strange city. In the end, I did as I had done before, when I came back from Syracuse to find my mother dead and our house sold up. I went to Timotheus at the perfume shop.

I don't know why I was so sure this time, that in a changing world, one quiet little man with a game leg would still be there and still unchanged.

He was; and serving a customer. I waited, while the man debated the relative merits of oil of rosemary and almond oil scented with amber. Clearly there was money about again, for such rubbing oil was never cheap, and he bought a good-sized flask of it. But both men had the same famine-traces in gaunt wrists and hollow eyes that I had seen all over the city.

When the customer had gone, Timotheus turned enquiringly to me.

"It's the Arkadian again," I said.

But already he knew me, this time; and greeted me with the friendly respect one finds in the very best of the merchant shop-keepers; men with a quiet dignity of their own, far too proud to lay any claim to being the equals of their customers. It seemed odd to find the old good manners still surviving when the world had fallen to pieces.

"I am glad you did not come a little earlier," he said with a somewhat wry smile. "You would have found me serving an officer from the Spartan garrison."

"I don't imagine that a man can choose his customers," I said.

"Not if he wishes to go on living. Will you come through into the house. Vasso will make you comfortable, and I will join you as soon as I can close the shop."

In the inner room where he had fed me before, there was a woman's veil lying on the end of the cushioned bench, and

I thought I heard a woman singing somewhere in the back regions. His sister, I supposed.

Vasso took my cloak and helped me slack off the straps of my breastplate, and brought me warm water to wash my feet. She snatched up the veil and took it away with her; but when Timotheus came in, the soft singing still came and went in the inner part of the house.

"That's an unexpected sound to hear in this city now," I said.

"It is my wife."

So naturally I asked no more. But after a moment, he said, "We were married at the end of the siege. It is foolish, I suppose, to worry about one's sons having the lawful citizenship of a city that has ceased to exist, but . . . Her brother was my friend and left her in my care since she had no other male kin. This seemed the best way, to both of us."

"She sounds happy," I said. "The brother, he was killed? Died in the siege?"

Timotheus was silent a while, and his face went tight. "He was a fleet rower. One of the few survivors of the wrecks at Arginussae. He died in the siege, but he would have died anyway."

We looked at each other a long moment, in a suddenly brittle silence. Then I said, "I was at Arginussae, but my ship was not wrecked." And after the silence had dragged on a little longer, "I was her Trirarch. I expect now you would like me to leave your house."

"No," he said. "If a shopkeeper cannot choose his customers, I am not such a fool as to think that a Trirarch can disobey the orders of the fleet Commanders—or hold him accountable for not having done so. My wife and Vasso are preparing supper, and of course you will stay and eat it with me. Among all the bad things, it is good to be able to offer hospitality to a guest again."

The old slave came in and set the food on the table. It was not a meal to grow fat on, even now. And neither of us said any more until she had departed and we had taken our places at the table.

Then I said, "I am only just up from Piraeus, where I landed my cargo of recalled traitors this noon."

"Ah, you are one of our twelve," he said. "I wondered."

"I had the doubtful honour of bringing Kritias home from Thessaly; but that time I did not come up to the city. This time I was fool enough to want to see how it was with Athens. There's a Spartan garrison, and the streets smell of fear. In Zeus' name, what has been happening, Timotheus?"

"Athens has been defeated," he said.

338

"It's more than defeat."

He broke off a bit of bread and crumbled it in his fingers, staring straight in front of him; then abruptly he began to talk. "When Lysander went, he left the government in the hands of thirty Senators. Theramenes is one of them, but he stands for the moderates. He was always very prone to moderation—the people call him buskin, now, after those high boots actors wear, that will fit either foot."

I savoured the jest. It was good to know that the people of Athens could still make a jest, even if it was a bitter one.

"Who are the rest?"

"Your charming Kritias is the leading spirit among them. All the most rabid of the Oligarchs that we freed Athens from, five years ago. They are supposed to be only an interim government; but they've no intention of handing over, and they've taken steps to make sure that their fellow citizens are helpless to do a thing about it. You were quite right to say there's a smell of fear in the streets; in less than two months, the Thirty have worked up a reign of terror that does them credit! They started mass trials and executions quite a while ago. First they made a clean sweep of all the informers and sycophants they could lay their hands on—that gained them a certain popularity, until the people realized that it was only a beginning. They have started on personal enemies now; no man is safe if one of the Thirty or a friend of one of the Thirty happens to dislike him, or if he stands between them and something they wish for. No one is safe anyway. Theramenes did bleat a few protests, but he is only one, and his own position none too secure. Sometimes now they don't even bother with a trial—a man is arrested, and later one hears that conscious of his guilt, he took poison in prison. Not that that's new; it's an old trick of the Four Hundred, revived." An added bleakness came over his face . . . Even in his own house, I noticed how he kept his voice down. After a moment, he went on. "But you were speaking of the Spartans in the High City; that's another benefit we owe to Kritias; he sent word to Lysander that a Spartan garrison was needed to make the city safe from 'subversive elements', so now a Spartan watch patrols the streets, and people are beginning to be fetched out of their houses again, as they were—as my father was—in the days of the Four Hundred. The city is dead and stinking."

"We thought that once before," I said.

"And we were not so far wrong. Something at the heart went then, that did not return even in the years of Alkibiades' victories."

I remember we were both silent a short while, and Alkibiades' name seemed to hang in the silence when the other words were gone into the past.

"How that man's name crops up," I said.

Timotheus nodded. "The last thing that Theron said before he died was, 'Alkibiades would have turned back for us'."

And we were silent again.

Later, he pressed me to spend the night, but I had no wish to sleep in Athens. Piraeus seemed clean and decent by comparison, with its seamen and the nearness of the ships. I thought of the girl I used to go to in the street behind the Great Harbour, who might still be there and free that night. So I excused myself, and we parted, without any pretence that I would ever come back.

Once I had to draw aside as the Spartan watch came tramping up the street. And when I looked up to the High City and saw the temple roof of the Maiden outlined against the stars, I saw also the Spartan watch fires. From a house near the Piraeus Gate came the desolate weeping of a woman; and I wondered whether the dreaded night-time beating had come on her door, and son or husband had gone away to drink hemlock untried in prison.

I went out through the Gate with no more trouble than telling the guard who I was and the name of my ship. But once clear of the shadowed tombstones and the oleanders, I turned aside into open country. I knew suddenly that I was not going back to Piraeus, nor to my ship. Whatever plans the Oligarchs had for the *Pegasus*, they could carry them out with a new Trirarch.

I was thankful I had not wasted any of my small stock of money on horse hire earlier in the day. I should have a better use for it now, with a long journey ahead of me. I had gathered from Timotheus while we ate our neglected supper, that Thrasybulus had escaped to Thebes, and I knew that tough cold-eyed little fighting man well enough to be reasonably sure he was not just sitting on his arse there. But magnificently though he had saved the situation when the Samos fleet was on the edge of revolt, I remembered too many other things about him. He was not the leader for my money. And when I left my helmet and breastplate in a ditch, and struck out across country from the back of the Long Walls, my nose was towards Thrace, and I was going back to the one leader left who seemed to me worth following.

# 25

## The Whore

When the Athenians were gone I thought that he would leave the
forts at last, and take to the hills, but he said, "Why should I go
now, when Lysander has gone south and will soon have all the
interest in life he needs in beating Athens to her knees? Besides—
have you noticed something? We don't have as many dealings
with the tribesmen as we used to do. I doubt if my welcome in
the hills would be very warm. You can't blame them; I'm no great
prize as an ally now—not worth a stallion or a trained hawk any
more."

I *had* noticed, and had been telling myself that I was starting
at shadows.

"It is better to hole up within my own walls, at least for the
winter."

"And when the winter is over?" I said.

"How should I know? Perhaps I shall go and offer my sword
to the Great King," said My Lord, and I thought that he was
jesting.

A few days later he called in to Bisanthe what was left of the
garrisons at Pactye and Chrysopolis ordering that both should burn
their forts behind them.

Then truly I thought that the madness of the Gods, of the
Lord Dionysus himself, had come upon him, that he should
beacon it forth to the world that he was in Bisanthe. But he said,
"Alkibiades never yet made a secret of where men could find him,
and it is overlate to begin now." And his mouth was smiling-
insolent, but his eyes were bleak as the winter skies that drove
overhead.

So he sat close in Bisanthe through the winter storms. No more
men from Goats' Creek came. They had got away, or they were
dead. No news came, with the seaways closed by winter. And
My Lord sat by the fire in the keep chamber, wrapped in his

wolfskin robe, and sometimes read in the few books that he had brought with him from the South in the old days, but for the most part just sat, and played with the ears of the hound bitch, and stared into the fire, and bade me bring up more wine. He was as he had been before, but deeper sunk now in his grey fog, like a man without hope.

He went the rounds of the fort, and looked to his men as a leader should; there were fewer and fewer of them, for almost every day the mercenaries slipped away. He seemed not to care, but drank to them and let them go. Even when they took the horses he only said, "That will be fewer to find corn for."—And indeed, with the stores sinking lower and the tribes turning unfriendly and the cities with their markets in Spartan hands, that was worth thinking of.

Spring came, and the alders where the stream came down to the marshes were red with rising sap, and the wind blew from the north-west again. And still he would not leave Bisanthe.

"Why, why, why?" I screamed at him one day; and he said, "Because before I make any move, I must know the fate of Athens; and it is here and only here that news knows where to find me."

"And when you know that Athens has fallen, what will you do then?"

"I don't know," he said. "I don't know," and poured more of the rough Thracian wine into his cup.

I said, "You told me, on the night they burned the Athenian camp, that I need not be afraid of Athens any more, for Athens was dead."

He said, "Be a little careful, Timandra," and his voice warned me that I had gone to the farthest limit that I might go.

And yet I think it was not only because he waited for news of Athens; there was a kind of sickness upon him, not of his body, but of his mind and spirit, and he could no more shake himself free of it and move out to meet the time to come, than a man sick to death can shake off his sickness and rise from his bed and ride to war.

No news came all that spring and into the edge of summer. And then one evening he had gone up to the roof where the gourds growing in pots made a shade and a dancing of leaves when the air stirred. I and the old hound bitch were with him—I do not think he noticed one of us more than the other. And I saw a trading vessel standing in towards the anchorage.

"Maybe here's your news," I said.

My Lord looked up from watching his own hands, then returned to them again.

"Are you not going down to the landing beach?"

He said, "The news will come soon enough. Why should I run wide-armed to meet it?"

I could have battered at him with my fists, screamed at him, clawed his face, anything to rouse him from the grey quagmire that held him captive. But instead I got up, suddenly mad with impatience to have the news and drag it to him, once and for all; and ran down the stair and across the fort and out by the shore gate. Some of our few remaining men were there already.

The ship came in to the little timber jetty that ran out into deeper water; and there was the usual shouting of orders and making fast of ropes. And in the midst of it a man who was not one of the seamen, scrambled ashore.

It was Polytion.

I said, "What news do you bring this time?" not remembering to greet him. But I do not think he noticed. His dark face seemed darker than I remembered it, and the plump lines had fallen slack where the rounded flesh had gone from over his bones.

He said, "News that I've no wish to tell more than once. Where is Alkibiades?"

"On the roof," I said. "Come."

He glanced at the empty slipway. "I thought he might be elsewhere, when I saw the *Icarus* gone."

"They burned her when the crew and most of the garrison left for Athens," I said.

When we reached the roof-top, Alkibiades was sitting as though he had not moved since I left him, the old bitch sprawled at his feet. He looked up past me, and saw Polytion, and said, "Athens has fallen? She must have fallen by now."

"Athens fell almost two months ago," Polytion said.

"Then why in the name of the Dog has no word of it reached me until now?"

"I would have come a good while before this; but I was forced to put in at Samos; we had sickness on board and had to land some men; and the Spartan Governor held me for some time, before I could get leave to go up to Byzantium on the old trading run."

"So you trade with the Spartans now, do you?" said My Lord.

"I trade with whoever has money to buy or goods to trade with, just as I always have done. The amber road still runs to Byzantium, and the rugs of Daskylon are still worth their price."

"I don't doubt it. Tell me of Athens." My Lord pushed the wine cup over to Polytion.

I went to see what I could find for them to eat, and did not hurry too much.

When I got back with some bread and dried olives and goat's cheese, it seemed that Polytion had told all that there was to tell of the fall of Athens, for they were speaking of other matters; other news that he brought with him. The Great King was dead, and Artaxerxes was Son of the Sun in his place. And looking at My Lord as I set out the food before them, I saw for the first time in many months, the life stirring behind his eyes. And I knew that while I was below in the store-room, Polytion and his news had done what I could not.

He said thoughtfully, spitting olive-stones into the palm of his hand, "I have heard it said—when I last wore Persian trousers—that there was not much love lost between Artaxerxes and his golden lily of a brother. That could mean that because Cyrus is so devoted to all things Spartan—especially Lysander—Artaxerxes is the more disposed to be friendly towards Athens."

"So?" said Polytion.

"I was wondering," said My Lord, "just wondering, as to the chances of getting through to Susa."

I remember the silence in the shadow of the gourd leaves, and a swallow hawking across the roof-top after the dancing flies.

"Were you indeed," said Polytion. "No one could say you lacked enterprise, my friend."

"Nobody ever could. Themistocles did it, when Athens booted him out for the crime of having won Salamis for her—and was received with honour and made Governor of Magnesia."

"You have ambitions that way?" said Polytion, arching his brows.

"Certainly the Governorship of Magnesia or some other equally fat province is as good a way as any other, to pass the time in exile. You have no notion, Polytion, how much of a problem it is for an exile to find some way of filling the time. That's why most of us drink ourselves to death; not despair or anything decent and suitable of that sort—just boredom, my dear. No, in going to Susa, I should, in the first place anyway, be seeking nothing more than a little serious conversation with the Great King. There are certain aspects that I could—suggest to him. Little points that may not come to his mind unaided."

"Such as?" said Polytion.

"Such as: that now Athens is crushed, Sparta becomes dangerously strong, and may even, given time, grow to be a menace to the Empire of the Sun. All Greece will be combined under

Sparta's rule, and the Great King might be very tactfully reminded that when the Greeks combine, it is a bad day for Persia, as it was in his grandfather's time. I think he might be brought to realize that to break with Sparta and give a certain amount of aid to Athens would neatly divide the powers again."

"Large ideas, you have, as well as enterprise," said Polytion. "How do you propose to get to Susa?"

"By way of Daskylon. There's an old bond of friendship between Pharnobazus and myself. With luck, he'll give me the necessary letters, and safe conduct for the Royal Road."

"To say nothing of journey gold."

"How well you know me. But I've something left from the gold that the cities hereabouts paid me for my protection these past few years." He got up and stretched. "Gold for the Royal Road, and to appear before the Great King as befits Alkibiades."

Polytion slept on board that night and sailed in the morning.

I lay against My Lord's hard body on piled rugs on the roof, the stars circling overhead beyond the gourd leaves. His hands were strong behind my back and his hair tickled my face. I said, "This time you will not leave me."

And he said, "Last time I knew that I should come back. Not this time—not back down the Royal Road."

"And so you will not leave me," I insisted.

His mouth fumbled for mine in the darkness. Then he rolled away from me and lay on his back, lazy and laughing. "What should I do without my flute girl against the nights when I cannot sleep?"

I have wondered since if any seeds of the sickness still lingered aboard Polytion's ship, for two days later My Lord came in at evening from seeing to the sale of the remaining horses, with a dark flush on his cheeks, and eyes that looked hot enough to burn out their sockets. And by midnight he was tossing and half off his head with fever.

He lay ill for many days, raging through all of them at the sickness that had dared to strike him down and hold him from his plans. I gathered such herbs as I could from the marsh and the edges of the barley land and the woods along the stream, without getting too far from the fort, and made something like the fever medicine that the women of Bithynia brew at such times. And the fever never mounted high enough to send his wits clean away. Only he complained that I was forever playing my flute and the sound of it made bright patterns in his head that he grew tired of

345

watching. I brewed the sleep drink also, so that at least his nights were quiet and dark; and the brewing and everything else, once I had gathered the herbs, I did in the keep chamber, so that I need never leave him alone and defenceless.

Myself, I gave the few slaves their freedom and bade them go, thinking that My Lord was safest without them. Then the few remaining mercenaries left, fearing that the sickness was catching, they said, or that there were devils behind it. Only, for some reason, the two brothers, Terdes and Boiscus, who had been the first to come, still remained. And for some reason I trusted them enough to leave My Lord in their care, while I dealt with the rest.

One morning My Lord woke and looked at me with clear eyes again, and demanded milk. I brought him the mare's milk that I had set by, for the roan mare had lately foaled; and he drank it and tried to get up, then fell back cursing. "Typhon! I am as weak as a half-drowned puppy!"

"Lie still," I said, "and you will grow strong again."

He lay still for a while, watching me as I went about the room. I had taken to men's dress again, it seemed better in those days. Presently he said, "It is very quiet. No sound of the men."

"There are no men save Terdes and Boiscus," I said. "They went while you lay sick. They feared that the sickness was catching."

"Well, we should all be gone by now, if I hadn't taken the cursed fever," he said, and then suddenly strained up on one elbow. "The horses!"

"Antares and the mare with her foal are still in the stable," I said. "And three more against need. Every horse that was in the stable when you fell ill."

"With the men leaving, how did you manage that?" he said.

"I told them that if they took so much as a hair from the tail of a horse, I would make a magic to set the sickness upon them."

"And they believed you?"

"The women of my people, the women of all these coasts, have had something of a reputation since Medea."

He looked at me strangely. "Could you have done it?"

"I do not know," I said. "But I would have tried."

Later, when he had had more milk and slept again, he grew troubled about the unguarded gates, and I told him that I had made the men barricade the land gate for me and narrow the other before they left.

"What did you threaten that time?" he said.

I was putting back my hair which had fallen loose, and did not answer for a moment. It was a hot night, and I had stripped down to my loose under-tunic. The past days had not been easy and I was very tired, so that I forgot he would be able to see the ritual cuts of the moon on my breast and arms. "The same threat did for both," I said.

He watched me and let go a long breath between his teeth. "I am not surprised those poor devils were afraid of you. When you look like *that* I'm not sure I couldn't be afraid of you myself."

"You only once had cause to be afraid of me. And then you never knew it until the time was past."

"I read your message," he said.

It was three days before he could crawl out of his bed and sit in the late summer sunshine; and almost a moon had passed since Polytion's visit, before all things were ready for setting out on the road to Susa. And all that time it had been still, golden weather, the barley stubble pale and shining between the hills and the sea, and the grasslands tawny as a hound's coat; and the heat seemed to beat like a gong out of a fierce empty blueness of sky. But the very night before we were to set out, the weather broke in a great thunderstorm. It grew dark before its time, and the thunder woke among the hills and went booming out to sea; and then came the rain. Big drops that made dark lozenges of wet on the parched ground, then hissing swathes of it that sluiced against the shutters and beat through into the keep chamber on the dark wings of the wind.

And at the height of the storm, the Arkadian came.

At first, when the door burst open and he came stumbling in like something born of the thunder and wind and rain, I did not know him—but indeed his face meant little to me then, in any case—and I remember how My Lord sprang up, reaching for his sword, and the old bitch crouched snarling, waiting only for a word, to fly at the stranger's throat. And then he said, "Your two rascals on the gate knew me from the old days, and passed me through."

And Alkibiades tossed his sword aside, and cried out, "The Arkadian! Great Gods, man! You must be tired of life, that you come bursting in like that!" and strode forward, holding out his hands. The Arkadian took them, and I saw how they gripped together. Then My Lord said, "What have you done to your hands?" and turned them over, and I saw that the palms and insides of the fingers were covered with dried cuts and blisters, and some that had broken and become crusted sores.

"I would never have said that I had soft hands," Arkadius said

347

ruefully, "but I fear they are not as hard as a seaman's should be—or not so hard in the right places."

"A seaman's?" My Lord said.

"I hadn't the passage money on me, so I had to work it from Euboea—they were short of a topman—" he said. And then suddenly, "May I explain all that later, and—may I sit down?"

## The Soldier

I felt all at once as though my legs were going to give under me, and had to ask if I might sit down. Then everything went a bit hazy, and when they became clear again, I was sitting on the piled skins of what I suppose was the bed-place, and Alkibiades' woman was kneeling beside me, holding to my mouth a cup of the sweet heady drink they make from fermented mare's milk in those parts.

Then they gave me food; coarse stuff and not too much of it. I thought vaguely that their stores were probably running low. And when I had eaten, Alkibiades who had been lounging on a carved chest and watching me the while, demanded the latest news of Athens. I told him what I had seen for myself, and all that Timotheus had told me in the little room behind the perfume shop; the whole dirty, damnable story. When I had finished he sat for a while with his elbows on his knees and his head in his hands, staring at the floor. His eyes were narrowed, and the frown-line between them deeper than I had ever seen it; and I saw the sweat prick on his forehead, shining in the lamplight. I saw too, how ill he looked, the great gaunt bones thrusting against the discoloured skin, with no flesh between. I said, "Are you ill, sir?"

"No," he said. "I have been—a stinking fever, but it's gone now. But for that, you would have been almost a month too late to find me here," and jerked his thumb in the direction of the embroidered saddle-bags, clearly packed for a journey, which I had not noticed before in the corner of the room. I looked back at him, startled, but before I could ask the question, he added, "And if you had got here one day later, you would still have come too late."

"The Gods meant that I should come in time."

"Why did you come?"

"To set my sword at your service," I said, and heard the words hanging in the shell of quiet that the great stone chamber made about us in the dying storm.

He raised his head and looked at me with an odd smile, bitter and sweet together. "So one man out of Athens remembers me;

and a man who at one time I should not have thought the most likely."

"All Athens remembers you," I said. "Thrasybulus is in Thebes, and knowing him, he'll be making plans and gathering men; but it's you they still look to, to come again and help them."

"The fools," he said. "Why should they imagine that I would lift a finger to help them, after the second time they threw me out? Only one greater fool, and that is myself, for having much the same idea."

"You mean—?" I glanced eagerly toward the saddle-bags. And he laughed.

"Oh no, I leave it to Thrasybulus to lead a valiant rabble into Athens and overthrow the Thirty. I'm away eastward for Susa, and the ear of the new Great King. There may be other ways of helping Athens than fighting through the city's streets."

I waited for him to go on, but he seemed to have no wish to speak more of his plans; and I was content to follow him blind. To me the chances of ever getting to Susa seemed fairly remote; but of course Themistocles did it in our grandsire's day . . . I said, "Well, you'll have that famous luck of yours to see you through."

He shook his head. "My luck is gone from me—I always said I should know when it left me. I must do without it now, as other men do." He rose and took a turn up and down the room, then checked and set an arm about my shoulders (I have seen him do that to many men, and never one, I think, who did not feel in that moment that he was the chosen brother) and said, "Men used to follow me for my luck—amongst other things—do you still want to follow me without it? Thrasybulus might offer the better chance to see Athens again."

I said, "It's when a man has lost his luck that he needs another to cover his back for him."

I remember how his woman whirled round from her place in the corner of the room, showing her teeth like a vixen. "My Lord has me to cover his back for him," she said. "I am good with a knife, yes!"

Alkibiades said nothing, but looked on as a man may look on at two in the wrestling pit.

And I thought, 'I must go carefully here,' realizing suddenly that of all the women he had had, this bird-boned flute girl with the crooked front teeth and enormous eyes had been with him many times longer than he had ever held to one woman before. I said as though he were not there, and it was just her and me,

349

"Timandra, is there not room for both of us?" and let her see that it was for my need and not for his.

She looked at me a moment, and the vixen went out of her face. She said unsmiling—she very seldom smiles; she laughs or she is grave—"There is room for both of us."

Next morning early, we set out; Alkibiades leading on a magnificent tiger-spot stallion, Timandra on a mare with a three-month foal running at heel, and myself on a sturdy dun with a cast-iron mouth and the sure feet of a mountain goat, as most Thracian horses have. The rear brought up by two enormous tribesmen on the two remaining horses. I felt the laughter suddenly whimper in my throat as I thought of the whole fighting strength of Athens that Alkibiades was used to lead, and what they would say at the state he rode in now. I must have made a strangled sound, for he looked round and caught my eye—and I remember the amusement kindling for an instant in his own, before he set his face again to the North.

The last thing he had done, while the horses waited, fidgeting in the courtyard, was to cut his old bitch's throat. She came up to him, pleased at the horses, thinking I suppose that they meant a day's hunting; and he bent to play with her ears as I had seen him do the night before; and I do not think she felt the knife at all.

"The pups will do well enough, but she was too old to learn to follow another master," he said, cleaning his dagger blade.

I wondered if the man who had once cut off his hound's tail to give Athens something to talk about, would have troubled himself for an old bitch, when his own life lay in ruins about him, and thought not.

So we rode North, into the hills. There were drifts of little bright cyclamen among the stone pines and the scent of the world was like cool incense after the rain. I looked back once and saw fire licking up red in the morning light. Bisanthe was burning. The past was the past.

Four days later we came down to the appointed place on the Black Sea Straits, north of Byzantium, and found a boat waiting for us. Alkibiades dismounted, Timandra and I after him, and handed the horses over to the two Thracians who had ridden with us. "Remember," he said, with one hand on the colt's neck, "remember my message to Seuthes; that I send back to him his gifts, with my thanks, having no further use for them, and that I send with them a small gift of my own, in return. Also, two who have no Tribe of their own, but are worth their bread and salt to any King."

We waited, all together by the boatman's fire, the horses tethered among a clump of plane trees, while the boat was run down into the water and the saddle-bags loaded in; then the three of us climbed aboard, and the boatman pushed out into the narrows. There was no moon and the night was so dark that we might have been crossing the Styx, and our boatman Charon himself.

I looked back, and saw the firelight gleam from a fisherman's hut, and against it, the shapes of the two tribesmen standing to watch us go. They would make camp there for the night, and next day they would be away back with the horses, to the chieftain Alkibiades had called Seuthes. I seemed to remember the name from the old days. And I seemed to hear again, Alkibiades saying, "Three thousand men will answer to a trumpet call from my keep." All that was gone now, and the two men standing on the shore were all that was left of Alkibiades' kingdom in Thrace. And already they were too far off for me to make them out any more.

"Never look back," said Alkibiades' voice beside me. "It only makes you the more liable to fall and break your neck."

A little later the boat grounded on the beach, and he sprang ashore.

We headed inland and slept in a thicket of juniper and wild pistachio bushes and next morning, after eating some of the food that we had bought from the boatman, shouldered the saddle-bags and riding rugs and set off southward for Chalcedon and its horse market.

I wanted Alkibiades to lie up outside the city with Timandra, and let me go in alone. But he would have none of that, saying that he preferred to choose his own horses, when he did not breed them. So the three of us went in together.

In her embroidered leather tunic and Scythian trews, with her hair bundled inside her cap, Timandra is one of the few women I have ever seen who could pass for a boy; she has the flat rump and narrow flanks, and when she binds her breasts there is nothing at all to lift the front of her tunic. She walks and rides like a man, too, but I think, from signs and portents, that she is woman enough in the dark. Alkibiades treated her in an odd way I noticed, almost, at times, as though she *were* a boy. Indeed, throughout the journey it seemed to me that he expected her to be many things at once. His woman and his Erômenos, sometimes his casual friend, sometimes his slave and occasionally his dog. An Athenian woman would have been out of her depth, knowing possibly how to be his dog, but not how to be his Erômenos. But Bithynian girls, Timandra has since told me, ride hunting and horse-herding with their brothers and their men, and even at times go to war with them. And I suppose that is the difference. I know that during all those days of journeying, she had a gay and gallant look about her—a young man's look. And I think that she was very happy.

But I wander down side-tracks as one does when one is tired. I am so tired . . .

We hid the saddle-bags and the riding rugs—there was a small bag of gold-dust and a good store of Persian darics stowed away among the other things in them, so they needed careful hiding—and went into Chalcedon and bought three horses and a pack-mule under the noses of the Spartan garrison. They almost emptied the bag of darics that I carried next my skin, but My Lord Alkibiades said that he had never yet ridden a bad horse and had not the faintest intention of beginning now.

It has always seemed to me unlikely that anyone, having once seen Alkibiades, even before his hair turned grey, can see him again and not know him; and there must have been many in the streets of Chalcedon who had seen him during the siege and after. It was for that reason I had begged him not to go himself into the city, now that it was under Spartan rule; and Timandra had added her voice to mine.

And we were right. Someone did recognize him, though it was not to the Spartans that they betrayed him, which I suppose was something.

Two nights later, as we sat with some shepherds, sharing the wolf fire in the entrance to their fold, the dogs sprang up baying and bristling, wrinkled muzzles raised into the night; and a moment later we heard horses' hooves on the bare hillside, sweeping nearer at full gallop. The shepherds were on their feet. The dogs leapt yelling into the darkness. Then a voice shouted, "Call in your dogs!" And there was a swirling and snarling of shadows, as the horses were brought to a trampling halt on the edge of the dark. "Call them off, or we'll see what a few cuts with the bull-whip will do to teach them better manners."

"It's the Chieftain!" someone said, and after a few moments of whistling and cursing the dogs lowered their hackles and shrunk back to the fire. Alkibiades and I had sprung up with the rest, Timandra still sat beside the fire, but with her little dagger naked across her knee.

Men were swinging down from the horses, closing in to the firelight. There were maybe ten or twelve of them. I saw fringed tunics and fox-skin caps or flapped Phrygian bonnets; and the firelight chinked on curved blades, and a jewel here and there of gold and lapis or coral. My first thoughts had been that we were beset by robbers, but at sight of the men in the leaping firelight, I changed my mind.

He who seemed to be the leader of the party, a big man with lank reddish hair hanging in elf locks from under the goldwork on his cap, said, "You can put up your sword, My Lord Alkibiades, we are twelve to your three, and you need not look to these shepherds to help even the score; they have too much good sense."

Alkibiades made a little bow, and sheathed his blade. I did the same, but like him, and deliberately in full view of the strangers, I made sure that it was loose in the sheath. "You have some business with me?" Alkibiades said coolly. "It seems you know my name."

"It is a name well known in these parts," said the Chieftain. "And there are those in Chalcedon who know the face that goes with it. You have been watched for and expected, as honoured guests." He gestured with his dagger, turning to his own men. "You three search the horses, saddle-bags, everything, don't forget the linings of the riding rugs. Teresh, Samba, Molossus, you search our three guests."

"This," said Alkibiades softly, "is an outrage."

"Throw your sword towards me—no, keep it in its sheath— I've no wish to lose a foot. You also." (This to me.) "And you, boy, set that pretty little dagger in the turf and step back from it."

I shut my teeth and flung my sheathed sword at his feet. He sprang clear just in time, and said, "That was unwise, but maybe understandable. Now your daggers."

"I thought one of these shepherds spoke of you as a chieftain," Alkibiades said, "but I see I misheard him—unless indeed you take the name as being chief of a robber band."

A shout from one of the men told that they had found the gold hidden in the riding rugs. "Ah, so," said the man with red hair. "We reckoned that when the great Alkibiades bought horses, and good horses at that, there was likely to be more gold where their price came from."

The man told off to search Timandra had approached her rather warily, as she backed, showing her teeth, against the thorn hedge of the fold. I had half an eye on him, ready to do the best I could with my hands if need be. "Well man, what are you waiting for?" said the leader; and he reached out, and for a beginning, snatched the cap from her head. Her hair, that had been piled up under it, fell loose about her shoulders; and he gave a startled shout. "A woman! Lord Seitelkas, this one's a woman!"

Alkibiades never turned his head, but he said very softly, his lisp much in evidence, "Lord Seitelkas, if your man touches her, I will find means to kill you with my naked hands before you or your cut-throats can kill me."

They looked at each other a long moment in the firelight; and in the silence the uneasy stirring of the fold flock and the cough of an old ewe sounded very loud. Then the chief turned his head and spoke quickly to the man holding Timandra's cap in his hand. "Search her—but only for the gold. No fumbling at her breasts or the like."

When the searching was done, and they had found every scrap of gold from the darics in the riding rug to Timandra's bracelets, they piled all together on a spread cloak beside the fire, and the chieftain, Seitelkas, looked at it with satisfaction. "Not a bad kill, with the horses added to it. Bundle it up, and their weapons with it." He turned back to Alkibiades. "Those, you shall have restored to you tomorrow when you go your way."

"You are most kind," said Alkibiades. "You do intend to set us free, then?"

"Of course. Did you think I meant to kill you?"

"The thought did cross my mind."

"The Chief Seitelkas does not often slay the strangers in his hunting runs."

"Does he often rob them?" Alkibiades enquired pleasantly.

Seitelkas' sandy brows drew together and his hand tightened on the hilt of his sword, and there was a wolf-growl from the men round him. "Be very careful, Lord Alkibiades, or I might break my usual custom . . . Do you remember, when you laid siege to Chalcedon, the city sent us their riches to carry away and hide? You sent soldiers after us, and heralds who promised evil things if we did not give up the gold. And some of our people grew afraid, so that we gave up to you the gold as you demanded."

"So this is merely—a return bout?"

"You could call it so."

"May I point out," said Alkibiades, "that the gold was Chalcedon's and not yours?"

"It was our honour that was touched, and for the hurt to our honour, we take payment now."

"And Chalcedon, I take it, will never see so much as a grain of gold-dust?"

"No," said Seitelkas, flinging up his head and grinning down that great beaked nose. And I realized suddenly that he was much younger than I had thought, probably a year or two younger than myself, which seemed to add to the sheer insult of our position.

All the while, his henchmen had been gathering up the gold and valuables and strapping the bundle on to the baggage-mule, and now they stood ready to depart. He gestured, and our own three horses were brought up. "And now, since our piece of business has been so much to my advantage, the least I can do is to provide you with better fare and less draughty quarters for the night than you have here. You shall come back with me to the camp."

"And how if I refuse?" Alkibiades said.

"Oh, you will not refuse."

The tribesmen stood round us with drawn swords; one, already mounted, had slipped his bow from his shoulders and notched an arrow to the string. We mounted, and the rest closed up around us; and we rode into the dark. At least they did not tie our hands.

The Chief's summer camp was not far off, and showed a certain amount of disorder. He apologized like the most courteous of hosts, saying that he was on the beginning of the long horse-drove back to his Hall and home runs for the winter; and fed us on barley cakes and honey and baked boar, washed down with the everlasting fermented mare's milk, in a great tent, with carpets such as we seldom see in the warehouses of Piraeus lining the walls and spread on the ground. Timandra ate with the women of the household at the back of the tent; and I wondered how all this seemed to her, remembering that these were her own people.

When the meal was done, Seitelkas stretched himself and belched. "You'll not object to sleeping tied to the tent-poles?" he said affably. "I would never forgive myself if I turned you out into the hills in the dark and you were to fall in with robbers, and you on foot with no chance of escape. But you will see that I cannot have you roaming loose round the camp."

Alkibiades grinned. "I do indeed see your difficulty, and speaking for myself I shall be delighted to sleep tethered to a tent-pole." Then he leaned forward, his hands on the low table before him, "But as to this other matter of taking to the hills on foot—"

"Yes?" said Seitelkas, cocking his eyebrow.

"We shall have a long walk."

"As far as Daskylon, I was thinking?"

355

"As far as Daskylon in the first place. And quite frankly, my kind host, I have the strongest objection to walking."

"You surprise me. Everyone knows that we of the Tribes never walk a step when we can ride, but I understand that the Athenians are great foot soldiers."

"Oh we have cavalry, too," Alkibiades said modestly. "I also never walk when I can ride."

"It is most unfortunate," said Seitelkas. "What do you suggest we can do?"

"You could, of course, return our horses."

Seitelkas shook his head. "We could not be doing that."

"It seemed worth mentioning," Alkibiades apparently yielded the point. He got up and stretched, then looked towards the opening of the tent, where several of the younger men had started a game of knucklebones. "May I? I used to be rather good with the bones."

We gathered round to watch; Seitelkas with us. The young men made room for Alkibiades instantly; it was amusing to see how even then, the famous charm did its work. They played off, started a new game, and played for a while, Alkibiades with fair skill, but not, I knew, so well as he could play when he chose. After a while he looked up at Seitelkas and said, "Join us." The Thracians and men of Bithynia are all gamblers, even when there's no stake; Seitelkas squatted down and joined in, playing against Alkibiades himself.

Presently Alkibiades said, "It is dull playing for no stakes. Can we play for beans or suchlike?" So they played for beans.

I had begun to be fairly sure that there was something more than idle whim behind this sudden passion for knucklebones.

Then Alkibiades said, "I will play you for the horses."

I caught my breath in sudden delight at the old Alkibiades; while our noble host flung up his head with a bellow of laughter, and the tribesmen grinned at each other and slapped their neighbours' shoulders and their own thighs. Timandra had left the women's end of the tent, two or three of the younger women with her; and stood among us in her boy's clothes, with her hair still hanging loose about her shoulders, and her great eyes fixed on Alkibiades' face.

Seitelkas said, "What will you wager? Beans?"

"No wager," Alkibiades said. "Just a straight toss-up with the horses going to the winner."

"But the horses are already mine," Seitelkas pointed out kindly.

There was a pause. Then Alkibiades said, "On foot, in unknown

356

country and among stranger tribes, we shall not get through to
Daskylon alive, and you know it. I'll wager our three lives against
your three horses."

No one moved in the group about them; the young men looked
at each other again, but not grinning this time. Seitelkas and
Alkibiades confronted each other. Then as though making up his
mind, the Chief nodded. "So. That is a reasonable stake. Will you
throw for each horse and life separately?"

"The Goddess of Luck never yet smiled on those who gamble
by halves. One bout of six casts each, and winner take all."

"As you choose." Seitelkas, as the one who had received the
challenge, held out his hand for the knucklebones to make the
first cast.

So Timandra and I stood watching among the tribesmen, while
Alkibiades with a small east-wind smile curving the corners of his
mouth, played for all our lives.

We watched the white cubes flash up in the torchlight, the
quick sure movements of hands catching them on backs or sides;
and I saw that I had been right, Alkibiades had not been playing
his best before. The play was so fast that one could hardly follow
it. But it seemed a long time all the same, before Alkibiades made
the final cast, and sat back, and said, "Seitelkas, you owe me three
horses."

I saw the frown gather on the Chieftain's face, and his jaw begin
to jut, and waited for the storm to break. Then slowly his whole face
cracked open into the broadest of grins. "If ever I see you again,
I'll remember not to play knucklebones with you. So, so, the horses
are yours; now sleep."

We slept tethered to the tent-poles; and we slept well, knowing
ourselves safe under the shield of Seitelkas' somewhat primitive
laws of hospitality. And in the morning our weapons and the
horses were returned to us, and we took to the hill trail that led
south. We were stripped of every coin and grain of gold-dust, even
Timandra's earrings; but at least, we had each a horse between our
knees. "Seitelkas is a man after my own heart," Alkibiades said
thoughtfully to the empty air behind his horse's ears. "He and
Antiochus and I together, what pirates we would have made."

We worked our way round the Propontis, keeping well back into
the hills now that it was a Spartan sea with Spartan garrison in its
coastwise cities. We lived on the country as well as we could, but
pot hunting as we went made for slow travelling, and it was almost
the edge of autumn when we came down towards the Phrygian
border.

That night we found shelter—the first for many nights—in a farmhouse lost in the hills, with the sheep folded in one half of it and the family huddled together in the other. And going out early next morning into the clear cold of the sunrise, to make water, I found Timandra standing under a wild cherry tree whose leaves were already turning coral red, and looking back the way we had come.

She looked round when she heard my footstep, and said, "If we hold on towards the noon sun, we shall strike the road from Gurion in two days. It's a little out of our way, but it will be much better travelling."

"Of course, this is your country," I said. I had gathered something of her story long ago, it was fairly well known in the fleet, anyway.

"Not so far south," she said. "But I know the border country a little. Five days since, we passed within a day's trail of my father's horse runs."

I thought for a moment that something ached in her voice, and I said without meaning to, "Would you be glad to go home to your own people?"

She shook her head. "I have no people, neither father nor mother nor brother nor sister. I have no home but in My Lord's shadow."

We managed to sell one of the horses in Gurion, fairly well, considering the poor brute's half-starved state; and from there on, Alkibiades and I took it in turns to carry Timandra up behind us. It seemed fairer on the two remaining horses that way. At any rate we had some money for the last stage of the journey, and the road made for swifter travelling; and one evening we saw the pale terraces of Daskylon clinging one above the other to its hill slopes, among chestnut and plane trees, with the high snows of the Phrygian Olympus beyond, and knew that we had come to the end of the first stage of the journey,

# 26

## The Satrap

My heart was glad to see that big insolent Athenian, but my head foresaw trouble.

I had been half expecting he might come to me, now that Sparta was the Lord of all that had been Athens. But I had scarcely thought that he would come quite so tattered. Sarbaces, my steward, told me that he arrived without escort or retinue but one down-at-heel Athenian soldier and a woman in boy's clothes, and only two half-starved horses between the three of them.

I sent them fresh garments and a jar of attar of roses, that he might not be shamed by having to come before me in such beggarly guise. But I must have forgotten what he was like, for when he came, it was quite obvious that he would not have been in the least ashamed to come before me stark naked and lousy; he would merely have thought that he was Alkibiades and that was enough.

I gave him all the welcome that was in my heart; for truly there was a brotherhood between us . . . I made him sit beside me and sent for wine and camel's-milk curds. But I could not speak to him brotherly of his loss of the Northern colonies; and that made a barrier between us that I think I felt more than he did. To cover it, I took my falcon from her perch at the end of the couch, and began to gentle the feathers at the back of her neck.

He said, "Pharnobazus, will you do something for me?"

"If it is in my power," I said.

"Give me fresh horses and journey gold and the necessary passes and safe conduct to Susa."

I pretended to find a mite among Istar's neck feathers. It gave me time to think. Then I said, "What business calls you to Susa?"

"To get the ear of the Great King, and point out to him certain matters that it may be he has overlooked."

359

"Such matters as?" I said.

"That with Sparta playing overlord to all Hellas, he may well find himself confronted with all our states welded into one, and that such a united Hellas—admittedly a free alliance—was too much for his great-grandfather before him."

I had supposed it would be something like that, from the moment he mentioned Sparta. "I do not think that the Son of the Sun will take kindly to that reminder!" I said.

"It would of course have to be put more delicately than I have put it to you."

I went on playing with Istar. "This would be for Athens, or for Alkibiades?" I said, for I still needed time to think.

"At one time Athens and Alkibiades were in some sort the same thing."

"And now?"

"I doubt if the severing can be made complete, save by my death. Maybe not even then."

I had come near to loving him once. And even now—as I have said, there was a brotherhood between us, and I would have saved him if I could.

I said, "Athens is finished, a carcass with the flies on it, and the Great King will not listen to you. Let the dead bury the dead. Stay here in Phrygia; and no one need ever know what has become of you. You could have a good life here, money to live well enough, if not quite in your old style—"

"Whose money?" he demanded.

"Mine, gladly given; I do not forget the oath of friendship that we swore at supper, the day that we signed the treaty for Chalcedon. Money to live at least like a gentleman—horses and hounds and flute girls, and honour."

"Honour?" he said; and then, "I came to you remembering that oath of friendship indeed, but not that I might become your pensioner. I came for the things for which I have asked already; for passes and safe conduct on the Royal Road. And for enough gold to carry me as far as Susa, since what I had I—carelessly mislaid in Bithynia." He smiled, the old warm lazy smile. "Do I get it, sworn friend of mine?"

"No," I said after a moment. And I knew from that time on, that in the end I would not be able to save him.

"Name of the Dog! Why not?" he demanded.

The truth was really rather embarrassing, but nothing else would serve. "The Spartan victory has restored to Persia all the Ionian coastal towns which were ours before they became part of your Empire. The Great King is pleased. He will scarcely listen with favour to an anti-Spartan policy."

"Not even though his brother Cyrus is Spartan from the heart up?"

I felt my face tighten in spite of myself. He had struck too near the quick for comfort. "The talk of a struggle for the throne brewing between the Great King and his brother, is no more than the chatter of magpies."

"So?" he said. And I knew that he did not believe me.

The falcon bated at that moment, hanging head downwards from my fist and wildly flapping her wings; and all the while I righted and reassured her, I was aware of those bright blue eyes of his, a little desperate, but mostly mocking. When I had her quiet again and returned to her block, I said, "You must believe what I tell you. The Great King will not look with favour on any plan for the downfall of Sparta."

"Nor on the Satrap who gave safe conduct and journey gold to the man who brings it," Alkibiades said, bitterly amused.

"If you like to put it that way, no."

We had both risen, and stood confronting each other. I felt as though I were trying to break through that insolent blue gaze of his and beat it down as though it were a weapon. But I could not.

He did not lower it even when he broke the silence and said, "So you will not help me."

"Not forward to Susa. Not for the present, at all events."

"For the present?" he said quickly.

And I was weak, I wanted to keep him quiet. "The situation may change—even by the spring," I said.

"And meanwhile?"

"I offered you hospitality just now, and the offer still stands. However, it may seem to you, I have not forgotten our old bond."

I saw refusal in his face, but I pressed on. (Blackness of Ahrimon! I still cared what happened to him!) "Stay here—not in Daskylon but out in one of the villages, where no one will know you, and in the spring, it may be that there will be something we can do. Only keep quiet if it is in you—for your own sake and in fairness to me. You will not be without enemies, and I cannot risk falling foul of the Spartans or of the Great King for your sake."

"In other words, if I accept your hospitality and bide here, I must look out for myself and take my chance."

"Yes," I said. It was better to have that clear between us.

Alkibiades smiled, breaking off a piece of curd from the dish. "Nobody can say you haven't warned me, friend of mine."

# The Whore

The Satrap gave to My Lord a house on the outskirts of Melissa, and the revenues of the little fortified town in the lower valley.

It was a galleried timber hall with its stables and barns behind it, much like my grandfather's hall when I had been a child. A terrace had been built on to it, shaded with old vines, and the spears of next spring's irises showing through the deepening drifts of leaves. Almond trees grew about it, and there was a garden that was almost a paradise in the Persian style. I could have been happy there, if My Lord could have been happy; but from the first day he was fretting to be off up the Royal Road, like a hound on too short a chain. And the Arkadian was not much better.

We had set out on a desperate venture, and they were wild to carry it through. But for me, my womanhood had returned upon me. Perhaps the Great Mother was kind, knowing how little time was left . . .

I put away my man's riding dress for a straight tunic, and bound my hair in a crimson and violet net, reddened my lips and painted malachite on my eyelids; and wanted nothing but to be My Lord's woman, and feed him and be there for him, and lie quiet beside him in the autumn nights when he was satisfied with my body and fell asleep, with Arkadius lying as he did every night, on cushions across the doorway of the chamber; and hear the rain beating against the shutters or watch the white bars of the moonlight searching through, and know him safe within my arms. I felt as though I could hold him safe for ever, within my arms.

But there can never be safety for his kind, because they do not want it. To be safe is to be penned, and at any moment they may break out, because of the fire within them. From the first he would not make any secret of who he was—or of where he was. A lion roaring defiance to the hunters to come and slay him. And one day they would come.

One day a merchant in precious things came, and unfolded his bale cloths on the terrace, and brought out silver and amber and lapis and raw turquoise veined like an iris petal.

My Lord called me to come and look, and choose. I chose a forehead ornament of turquoise, but he brushed my choice aside, and picked out a pair of bracelets, silver hung with great smoky golden teardrops of amber. "These for you," he said. "Honey-in-the-comb. You should always have the warm colours, Timandra," and himself opened the soft silver and sprang them on to my wrists.

And then he asked the trader if there was any news from Athens. "Not that I've heard lately, Lord," the man said. "I'm heading back that way now, if I can get a ship before the year closes in. I'm not one for a winter crossing."

My Lord said, "So—then in lieu of bringing me news, will you take a letter from me to someone in the city?"

"I couldn't do it for nothing," said the trader. "I'm a busy man."

"Two golden darics," My Lord said. "Take it to the house of Socrates; anyone will tell you where it is if you do not already know. The slaves shall give you something to eat, while I write the letter."

"Socrates?" the man seemed doubtful. "Well now, that makes a difference. Anyone that gets mixed up in his affairs is liable to end in trouble."

"They always were," My Lord said.

"And I don't like running into the risk of trouble blindfold. Who's letter will I be carrying?"

"Alkibiades."

The man's mouth and eyes flew open. "Alkibiades! That could be dangerous. I'd say it was worth at least another daric."

"I think perhaps you're right," My Lord said. "Three darics, then. But you will not ask for so much as an obol from Socrates."

"He wouldn't have it; everybody knows that. No, three darics it is, My Lord." But he stared as though his eyes would never come back into his head.

When he had eaten, and gone, bearing the letter with him, and the three of us had gathered to the evening meal, Arkadius said, "Sir, was it needful to write to Socrates just now?"

"Yes," My Lord said. "It may very well be that this is the last chance that ever I shall have of writing. And a letter from me is somewhat overdue."

There was a silence between him and Arkadius that I did not know the meaning of. I know nothing of this friend of My Lord's called Socrates; but I thought it an ill thing that he should write to anyone in Athens now.

Then Arkadius said, "That man will talk."

"I expect so. Being talked about is an old habit of mine."

"But *now*!" Arkadius was suddenly exasperated. "In Typhon's name, man—sir—do you want all Athens and probably all Sparta to know where you are?"

Alkibiades sprang to his feet and strode up and down the room;

then he turned on Arkadius, who had risen and was standing stubbornly four-square by the table. "Yes!" he roared, "Yes and yes and yes! Do you dare to think that I will lair up here in hiding like some sick and outworn beast, swallowing my name and starting at shadows, for fear of a knife between my shoulders?"

Arkadius looked very white, and a muscle flickered in his cheek. "There is no shame in the use of a little common caution."

"Caution is for little men," My Lord said. "I doubt if the Gods have much use for it." He sat down again, quiet now, and looked at Arkadius across the table, his chin in his cupped hands. "If you are afraid to stand too near me, lest I draw the lightning flash, take back your sword and go. No hard feelings, Arkadius."

Arkadius sat down also, stretching out his legs with a sigh as though he were very tired. And after a little, My Lord said, "Well, if you're not leaving, let us begin supper."

## The Citizen

Early in Gammalial, the Thirty got Theramenes. He had stuck to the moderate course, and even dared to argue against some of the Thirty's rulings; that was common knowledge, and I suppose his fellows could not be sure of him. They got him on a charge of evading military service, just as the people had got Cleontius, hustled him through a travesty of a trial, and executed him the same day. We had called him "The Buskin" and had, truth to say, little respect for him. But we had, I think, forgiven him his meals of black broth in Sparta while we starved, and we knew that he had tried to hold his fellows of the Thirty back from some of their most foul injustices. He was the last shred of moderation left in the government; and on the day that began with the rumour of his arrest and ended with the news that he had drunk the hemlock, we felt dazed. This was the first time the Thirty had turned on one of themselves—a new sickening dread woke in us for what might be waiting in the coming days.

In those dark winter days, people began still more helplessly to regret the second time that we had driven Alkibiades into the wilderness. We began to whisper to each other. "He never lost a battle for us when he was in command. He won us back our Empire, and where is it now?" And when we heard the mailed step of the Spartan Watch go by, or heard of someone we knew having been sent for to the Painted Porch, from which those who walked in by daylight were carried out feet first in the dark, "If

364

only those *fools* had listened to him at Goats' Creek, all this would never have come about."

We had never needed him more than we needed him now; and we did not even know where he was.

And then suddenly there was word in the city that Alkibiades was in Phrygia with Pharnobazus—or as some said, biding his time in some hill village of those parts. Men were even putting a name to the village—Melissa.

And a little breath of something that was almost hope ran through the city. The mere fact that we knew where he was seemed to bring him nearer. I for one felt that because he was alive, and I knew where he was, everything was not lost. He might yet come back to us and drive out our Spartan overlords and the Oligarchs who were their jackals. All Athens felt it, like a little wind stirring in long grass—and not only the Democrats, not only the poor and many-mouthed and unwashed, whose darling he had generally been; the Oligarchs must have felt it too. But what to us was a faint and forlorn whisper of hope, to them was the stirring of the dust before the feet of the Furies. They must have seen uncomfortable visions in the night, of Alkibiades returning to set himself at the head of the Athenian people.

## The Queen

Agis the King came back from Attica last year. He watches me still like a hound with a bone that he does not want, but will let no other hound come near. He watches the child, too. Every time I see his little red eyes on the boy, I read in them that he is thinking of the man who fathered him; and then he lifts his eyes and looks at me. He hates me; but not much more, I think, than I hate him.

And now they will take the child from me because he is seven years old, and set him in the Boys' House to train him into a soldier of Sparta; and I shall have nothing left. It is more than seven years since I was with a man; and my breasts ache with emptiness and my flanks grow lean, though my hair is still bright when I bind it up under the Queen's diadem. I am empty. Great Mother, your pity upon women! Spring will not come again, nor the golden flash of the oriole into the shadows of the olive trees . . .

Sparta has conquered Athens and hammered her to her knees. But what is Athens to me?

Yesterday Agis came to my chamber in the women's court. His

eyes were not even cruel, only curious. He said, "I have news that may interest you. Alkibiades is in Phrygia, sheltering from his own people under the Satrap's cloak."

"I do not see him sheltering under any man's cloak," I said. "But what is it to me if he labours in the deepest and reddest pit of Tartarus?"

"You know the answer to that, not I," he said. "This news we have received in a letter from Athens, from Kritias, one of the most extreme leaders of our Thirty—a thoroughly reliable man." He sat down on the stool beside my loom, his hands on his spread knees. "He does not feel that our regime in Athens can ever be completely secure while the people know that this traitor still lives."

"How can he threaten it, from Phrygia?" I asked. I could not speak his name.

"Quite simply. He could come back from Phrygia, and the mob would follow him. And even if he does not, it seems that the hope of him is still in men's hearts."

"And you cannot bring all together under the yoke, a people who still have something—someone—to hope for."

"You should have been a man; you have a good understanding of the situation," he said. "Therefore, since Sparta's interests and the Oligarchs' are one in this, the matter has been brought before the Council of Ephors—I am come from them now—and the decision has been reached that this false hope must be destroyed."

I felt a great stillness come over me; and out of it my own voice sounded, much as usual. "So you will have him killed."

"The order goes tomorrow, to Lysander to attend to the matter."

"How you must have enjoyed signing it," I said.

"I have seldom enjoyed anything more." My Lord looked up at me out of his little angry eyes, and gently rubbed his knees, round and round.

"Are you not afraid that now you have told me this, I shall find means to get a warning to him, so that he may escape you again?"

He shook his head. "The first time the order for his death went out, and he escaped us, there was a time when I thought it might be you who warned him. I wonder if you have any idea, My Queen, how near you were to death at that time? But later, you will remember, we found that the crime lay at Endius' door. Exit Endius. If you hated him too well to seek to warn him then, I do not think you will have come to hate him less in the years since."

"Why have you taken such pains to come and tell me all this?"

366

"Idle curiosity," he said. "Mere idle curiosity, My Queen—the wish to probe a little and see if there was any quick left to flinch."

I said, "I hate him almost as much as I hate you, Agis, My Lord. Are you well answered?"

"Well enough," he said. "You bitch on heat."

And he got up and tramped off, with that rigid soldier's walk of his.

So they will kill him. A dagger in the dark, maybe; an arrow flying by day. I wish I could be there to see it done; to see the blade strike home and the light go out of those hateful, mocking, cruel bright eyes.

To run to shield him with my own body, and die too . . .


## The Satrap

Lysander sent me word to meet him in secret at Mitylene; and I went down under guise of inspecting a ship-building project. When Lysander summons, one does not delay—not, at least, so long as he and the Prince Cyrus remain lovers.

I suppose he thought if he merely sent me the orders he had received from Athens, I might not push myself too hard in carrying them out. And I think he's right in that.

He came to my own house in the city, by night, and by way of a side door left open. I gave him wine, and he drank, and came quickly to the point, in the Spartan way. "We know that Alkibiades is in Phrygia."

"I think most of the world knows it by this time," I said.

"Most of it. He blazes like a signal fire." And then after a silence, he said matter-of-factly, "It is time the fire was put out."

"So?" I said. "And what is that to me?"

"It is this to you—that I bring you the orders of the Spartan Ephorate to handle the—putting out."

"If Sparta wants him killed, let Sparta hunt him down and do the killing."

"Sparta has other things to do."

I said, "The man has eaten my bread and salt, and slept beneath my roof. Why should I betray guest-right?"

Lysander looked me straight and cold in the eye. "*Because* he has eaten your bread and salt and slept beneath your roof. Sparta considers that the harbouring of her enemies is a hostile act."

The city seemed to have fallen very quiet. My fingers itched for the little dagger in my waist cloth; but I was afraid. Mithras knows

367

it—I was afraid; and I hated his square bland face until my guts crawled with it.

I said, "And Athens?"

"The Thirty will sit more securely in their places, when men cease to look to Phrygia for a saviour," he said. "But we are chiefly concerned with Sparta, you and I; and with Persia, and we both know how dear to the Prince Cyrus is the Spartan alliance. There are those who believe that in a year or so Cyrus and not Artaxerxes, the golden brother and not the black one, will be the Great King." He did not speak it as a threat, but there was iron in his voice that made a threat of all he said.

We stood looking at each other across the brazier—the nights were still cold—and neither of us lowered our gaze before the other; but nevertheless, I was beaten, and we both knew it. May Ahrimon the Black One eat his soul!

At last he said quite pleasantly (he is the only Spartan I have ever met who can behave, when he chooses, like a gentleman), "Well, there's no need to talk further on this rather distasteful subject. We understand each other, I see. I leave all the details to you, my dear fellow. And rest assured that when the thing is finished, I will take every step to see that Prince Cyrus knows the service that you have done him."

And he took his leave most courteously, and went out into the early spring night. And he'll never know how near he came to taking my dagger under his ribs as he went through the door.

I took ship for Propontis again next day, then rode for Daskylon, my soft-bred officials grumbling at the speed I set, all the way. And all the way, drumming back to Daskylon with the dust-cloud rising white behind me, I thought the same thoughts over and over again, holding to them fast so they could not get away; that if the matter lay with my own Prince, he would give me the same order as Lysander and the Spartan government. That the man was a danger to Persia's ally, and a danger to an ally must also be an enemy to us. And in between, I thought, 'I warned him! I gave him fair warning! But I never warned him it was myself he must be on his guard against!'

When I got back to Daskylon I did not even wait to change out of my dusty riding dress. What I had to do must be done at once. I went straight through my private apartments to the garden court. The early irises and flame-pointed tulips were coming into flower; and I picked one of them and began pulling it to pieces while I sent for my young brother Megaeus, and for Sousamitras, our uncle; both of them court officials. I have not known either of them very well of late years; it is never wise, in court and official circles, to let one's own kin be too near. But I had done my best in getting them rich posts, my uncle as one of the chamberlains, and my brother as an officer of the guard, and I felt that it must be my own kin that I called on now.

They were a long time coming, or they seemed so. And by the time they came, the ground about me was feathered yellow and crimson with torn tulip petals.

Megaeus eyed them, even while he made me the formal salute, and cocked an eyebrow.

I said, "You have been slow in answering my summons."

"I came as soon as it reached me, leaving my supper half eaten on the table," my uncle said. "And met Megaeus hurrying most dutifully on the way."

Then I gave them their orders.

For a moment both their faces went blank, and I wondered if they were going to make trouble, and which would be the best threat to use if they did. But they are both lesser men than I am—and I yielded to the pressure of Lysander. And in the end, with the help of a golden gift, I had little trouble, except that they were nervous as to how best to do the thing.

Then I rounded on them, and they gave back a hurried step before me. "Listen!" I said, "I have bidden you take as many soldiers as you need—mercenaries, not the guards—and kill him. Do it in any way you like; I've paid you to do the job and I'm not asking how—*so long as it is done!*"

"It will take some planning," said my uncle. "He's an ill man to attack—and there'll be slaves in the house—"

"Three days from now, begins the Feast of Attis. If the slaves do not all go down to the Temple, you can take care of them in one way or another, and it will only look as though they have slipped off to take part in the ceremonies. Great Lord Mithras! Use your own head a little, my uncle!"

And my young brother said, "Satrap dear, you are asking a lot of us and offering no more than—adequate pay. If I do my part of this for you, will you give me the black stallion?"

"I have paid you enough to buy a black stallion for yourself and scarce lighten your pouch," I said.

He said, "Yes, but I want Belatrix, I've always wanted him."

"Take him, then," I said. "And I hope he throws you and breaks your neck!"

"But not till the job is done, eh?"

"Not till the job is done," I said. "And now get out, both of you, and start gathering your men."

And they have gone, the little yelping curs, to gather the pack and pull him down.

And presently Prince Cyrus will smile on me and maybe give me a greater Satrapy—unless I decide to tell Artaxerxes, Son of the Sun, the rumours that are going round about that golden bedfellow of Lysander's. In which case it will be Artaxerxes who will smile on me.

Either way I shall have something to show for having delivered my soul to Ahrimon the Black One.

# 27

## The Whore

The winter passed, and the almond trees before the house put out their first pale flowers among the still bare aspens. And then it was seed time; and the first day of the Feast of Attis and Cybele.

I had gone out on to the terrace before the Hall to bring in some newly saffron-dyed wool that I had drying there, when I heard the distant flutes and cymbals. Melissa is only a small town, really only a village; but there is a Temple of the Mother, and Attis has his altar and his priests there, as often in the country places.

My Lord was sitting on the painted wooden bench beside the door, staring moodily at a lizard that lay basking on the sun-warmed flag-stones at his feet. And Arkadius was hovering in the shadows of the vine close by, whittling a bit of stick. He whittled more and more as the days went by, and My Lord spent more and more of his days just sitting, with his hands hanging lax across his knees. We had been four months in the house on the hillside above Melissa, and he was no nearer to Susa. I knew that Pharnobazus had held out hopes for the spring. I do not think that My Lord had believed him, but there was nothing he could do but wait. And to such as my Lord, waiting eats into the soul.

The flutes and cymbals that had been only a thread of sound, were drawing nearer. I went and knelt beside My Lord, and set my hands on his thigh so that he stirred and looked at me. The lizard was gone in a green flicker of movement and the stone was bare where he had been. I said, "They are bringing the Lord Attis to his people, do you not hear them?"

He listened a moment. "That clashing and twittering?"

"It is the Feast of Attis. They will pass along the track under the hill; come with me and watch them go by."

He shook his head. "Not interested."

But I would not give up. If I could get him to come with me it would use a little time, leave a little less of that one day to get through afterwards. I said, pleading, "I have not watched the Sacred Procession since I was a girl in my grandfather's Hall."

"Go and watch it now," he said.

"I do not want to go alone."

He laughed, and bent suddenly and kissed me quick and hard; then he got up and stretched, and held out his hand to me, and said, "Come then, we will go and watch this procession of yours," as though he were humouring a very young girl.

We went down the hillside together, still hand-in-hand—it was good to walk with my hand warm in his, pulled along by his stride—until we came in sight of the village, and the painted walls of the Temple among its sacred pine trees, and the crowd of men and women edging the track that led towards it. The people nearest glanced round as we came among them, and made room for us. But their whole hearts and eyes were turned upon the track, and the procession that had just come into sight.

First came the three eunuch priests, their arms and foreheads tattooed with the sacred ivy leaves, and then, led and followed by its musicians, and by all the young men and maidens of the village, the Pine Tree of Attis, propped upright in its cart drawn by garlanded oxen. The sacred pine who some say is the God in his tree form, felled only that morning; and bound among its lower branches, the figure of the God himself, brought out year after year, swathed in fresh grave bands, and with his face freshly painted as we paint the faces of our dead. And both tree and God-figure wound about with garlands of the little dark woodland violets that sprang from his shed blood.

So they bring the God home every seed time, that the harvest may be good and all living things flourish and increase.

The cart passed us, the tree lurching and swinging, steadied by the stay-ropes in the hands of the men who walked alongside; and the carved wooden figure jerked in its bonds—and for a little space, because I was with My Lord, I saw all things through his eyes; the perilously rocking tree and the roughly carved wooden effigy with the woman's paint staring on the dead face; and I shrank back. But then my own eyes returned to me, and I saw the Dead God hanging on his Tree; and a long dark waft of scent from the violets all about him drifted to me on the little thin spring wind. And the painted eyes looked into mine.

Here and there, a woman began to wail, swaying in ritual grief, "Ai! Ai!" and others and yet others took it up; but there was no great outcry of lamentation. That would come later.

We watched until the dark waving branches disappeared into

the Temple precincts. And then Alkibiades took my hand again, and said, "Well? Have you seen all you came to see?"

I nodded, and we turned away up hill.

After we had walked maybe the length of an arrow's flight, My Lord said, "The Gods of Hellas, I know, and the Gods of Persia, I know. But what God is this Attis? And why is he dead?"

I said, "He was a hunter, and the beloved of Cybele the Mother of all things; and he was killed by a boar he was hunting."

"And Cybele in her grief, caused the violets to spring up from the darkness of his spilled blood," My Lord said.

I looked round at him, startled. "If you did not know Attis, how do you know that?"

"We tell the same story in Athens, but our hunter is called Adonis, the beloved of Aphrodite, and from his blood there sprang up not dark violets but crimson anemones."

There were small flowers growing on the edge of the cornland that we skirted, and among the rocks; bell flowers and vetch and feathery irises that only live a day; and suddenly at the foot of a stone outcrop, a scattering of brilliant red flowers in the grass. My Lord stooped and picked one of them, and held it out to me. "See," he said, "the blood of Adonis."

I took it. The petals were blazing crimson, white where they sprang from the stem, and with a heart as dark as night. It made me ache in my throat, like the ache that comes before weeping. I said in foolish rebellion, "Why should they have to die?"

"Because they were too greatly beloved, and the other Gods grew jealous. Or perhaps love itself can destroy like a lightning flash, when it is too strong for mortal man to bear."

We climbed a few steps farther in silence, I looking at the crimson flower in my hand. And then he said, "In Athens, we hold the Feast of Adonis in the summer—the women hold it; I never knew a man who didn't dislike the whole thing. They carry figures of him dead and decked for burial on his bier through the streets, and lament for their lost darling until the hair rises on the back of your neck; and they scatter little dark red roses before his bier, that were stained from white by his blood ... The streets were scattered so when we marched out for Syracuse, and the women caterwauling at every corner. The feet of the troops mashed the flowers underfoot;—and yet I scarcely noticed it at the time."

We were in sight of the Hall again, and My Lord began to go more slowly. He said, "Zeus! How I hate this place; this waiting— no nearer to Susa than I was last autumn."

I did not answer; there was nothing I could say. And then he said, "I'm getting soft, rooted here. Even my dreams are going soft. Timandra, I had the oddest dream last night; I had almost forgotten it until they carried the Attis past."

"What was it?"

"I dreamed that I was lying with my head in your lap, as I've lain so often, and you were painting my face as though I were a woman."

I felt as though a little cold wind blew on me out of nowhere. Then I laughed and said, "That should not seem strange to you, who have lived in Sardis. Your eyes were rimmed with kohl the first time ever I looked into them, love."

He pulled me to him by my hand that he still held in his, and kissed me so hard that he bruised my lips. "Nikias had all his soothsayers to interpret his dreams for him, but I have you, little vixen, and you are sweeter in the kissing than any soothsayer."

But it was as though a little shadow ran before me on the grass, and lingered to meet me on the threshold, and would not be brushed away.

And then it was the Third Day, when they cut the dead God down from his Tree at early morning, and lay him in his piled rock tomb.


## The Soldier

This evening Alkibiades came in out of the dusk when the lamps were lit and the evening meal on the table. But instead of sitting down to eat, he went to the olivewood chest where his sword lay, and picked it up and turned back to the door with it.

"Where are you going?" Timandra said.

"Only just outside. I thought I saw someone moving among the bushes."

"I'll come with you," I said, getting up. I didn't have to reach for my sword, I've worn it day and night, these past three days. I don't quite know why; probably just the drums and horns in the village, soft with distance, but always there when one listens.

Timandra cried sharply, "Don't go outside!"

And we both looked at her in surprise. "Why not?" Alkibiades said.

She recovered herself and laughed. "Because the fish is getting cold, and I cooked it for you myself. It will have been only the slaves, if you saw anybody at all. They have all gone down to the village for the last of the sacred dancing, and the rejoicing when

374

there is enough blood on the altars, and they open the tomb and find it empty."

But I thought she spoke a little too quickly, a little too urgently.

Alkibiades shrugged. "Maybe. Or maybe it was nothing but the wind swaying the bushes. Those drums and horns are worse than the women wailing for Adonis, for giving a man the twitch." He hesitated a moment, then came and sat down at the table. But I noticed that he kept his sword with him.

Two days ago, Timandra brought in a just-open anemone flower; the one flower, by itself, as though it meant something, and set it in a silver cup on one end of the chest. It was drooping a little now, so wide that the petals were curling back and the blue-black pollen smudging all around its eye; but the petals were still brilliant, and looking at it, suddenly I thought of Astur. I don't think of him very often nowadays. It's not that I have forgotten, one doesn't forget; just that he has sunk into the dark inner places of memory. I suppose it was because I'm so tired. Lord Poseidon! I'm so tired! No sleep for two nights, and not enough to do in the days. Damn those drums! I remembered the crimson anemones breaking out from the bare limestone by the entrance to the quarries; and the sudden blinding pain of knowing that I was leaving Astur behind me, dead and rotting with the maggots in his eyes.

Alkibiades reached for a raisin cake and said, "Arkadius? You look as if you were seeing ghosts."

I looked round, and the old pain went back to where it belonged. "Did I? It was the drums."

He nodded. "They have a way of waking things better left sleeping. We all have our ghosts, of one kind or another. Gods! what old-woman's talk! I said I was getting soft, mewed up here. Soon I shall begin to grow fat."

"You've a way to go yet," I said, looking at his big lean body and the harsh bones of his face. His eyes were sunk back into their sockets, but they were as blue in the lamplight as I have ever seen them. And then he saw me looking, and smiled, the old lazy smile that could charm a finch out of an arbutus tree.

We sat a good while over the meal, talking of plans for reaching Susa and gaining the ear of the Great King, which I think we both know now will never come to anything. And then suddenly he said, "If the whispers are true, and Cyrus means to make a bid for the Sun Throne, there'll be hard fighting before all's over; and there was never yet fighting without a handful of Greek mercenaries mixed up in it somewhere. If it comes, shall we take our swords and head for active service again, Arkadius?"

"On which side?" I said, grinning.

"Black King or Golden Prince? Who cares, Arkadius? That's the glory of it, who cares?"

And then I saw Timandra's face, and felt that I was an intruder. Anyway, it was late, and time to break up for the night. Alkibiades got up and stretched, then strolled off to the inner chamber, still carrying his sword with him. Timandra lingered a moment, filling a last cup with wine to take in to him as she generally does; and I whispered to her, "Why did you let all the slaves go into Melissa?"

"I did not," she whispered back. "Suddenly they were gone. It makes no difference, there is not one of them that we can trust."

Then she went after Alkibiades into the inner room.

I spread my rugs before the door and sat down on them for a while; hearing the murmur of their voices and a smothered laugh, and then only the faint throbbing of the drums and horns and cymbals from the village, coming and going on the little wind that rose at twilight. The rhythm grows faster and more wild; it seems inside my head, beating with the beat of my blood. Down there in the Temple precincts the priests will be whirling into their final frenzy, gashing themselves so that their blood spatters the altar—I have heard this kind of rhythm before, it always means blood; I have seen the rites of Dionysus in my time.

It might be as well to take a look round. Quietly with the door bar in case they're asleep. How white the moonlight is—a white fire of moonlight; and the wind brushing the bushes up the wrong way.—If they were a cat's fur they'd give off sparks. You can hear the drums more clearly out here, but there's the wind and the moonlight—easier to keep awake.

If I sit down with my back against the door, I can stay out here for a while. The moon makes a rippling like water on my sword-blade laid across my knees. Mustn't look at the bright web of it, or I'll get sleepy. Look into the dark places under the bushes; the places that might cover a crouching man . . .

It is good out here—no lurking figures, nothing moving but the wind; no reason to be so jumpy—jumpy as a cat—it's just lack of sleep, and those accursed drums. The wind sounds like the sea—hushing on the shore where the galleys are dragged safe above the tide-line and the cooking fires of dead tamarisk scrub burn before the tents . . .

Must get up and walk about a bit or I shall go to sleep. Must get—up—

Astur! What are you doing here? Do you remember the night we took Selymbria? No you weren't there, you were dead. Funny, I thought you were dead; I thought you were—dead—Astur . . .


## The Whore

I woke to feel the bed-rugs being flung back and My Lord leaping up from beside me; and the room full of smoke eddying in through the doorway hangings. For an instant, seeming still caught in some dream, I saw him standing naked in the slow swirls of it that the night lamp turned to amber. Then he swept the curtain aside and plunged out into the main hall. I was on my feet too, by that time; I snatched the coverlid from the bed and flung it round myself and went after him. I cried out to him, "Don't open the door!" But he was already flinging it back. Someone had unbarred it; but I suppose they were afraid to come in and kill him, hand to hand. He hurled it wide, and a sheet of flame poured in from the blazing brushwood that had been piled against it. He leapt back and ran to gather up the bed-rugs. I helped him fling rugs and cushions on the flames, damping them down, though the red tongues licked through and crackling brushwood sparks flew up in showers.

He darted back once more, snatched up his cloak and wrapped it round his left arm for a shield. "Keep close behind me," he said, "and the instant we are through, jump aside and run for the darkness; it's me they're after, not you." He caught up his sword.

I cried to him, "Wait! There may be a whole pack of them outside—"

He shouted at me almost exultantly, "Do you think they'd dare come against Alkibiades except in a pack?" I must have been clinging to him, for I felt him shake me off. The flames were eating through the bedding and beginning already to roar up again.

He drew back to gain speed, and ran for the doorway and the curtain of fire.

I was close behind him as he sprang through. The flames burned my feet, sparks clung to me, and the heat was like a blow, searing and choking me. All the world was flame. And then there was a moment of darkness; and against the dark, men outlined in the glare of the fire. They scattered and fell back as he leapt among them, as I have seen hunters scatter before a charging boar. He gave a great war-cry as though to burst the heart out of his breast, and sprang forward to kill and be killed. But they dared not come at him, they dared not stand to his rush; they scattered farther into the dark, and swerving aside as he had bade me, I heard the twang of a bowstring. The fire in the doorway behind him gave them shooting light.

They brought him down as men bring down a lion they do not dare to close with; while I fell headlong over something that caught my feet, and lay all asprawl. One of the arrows grazed my bare shoulder, but I did not know it until afterwards. They brought him down to his knees, to his face. At the last instant he twisted over and lay with his face to the sky.

I was struggling to get up, but something clogged my feet as happens in a nightmare, and brought me down again, driving all the wind from my body, and a wave of darkness rose and swept across me and passed on. Someone was standing over me; the fire shone on the blade in his hand; someone said, "It's only his harlot—let her be."

I saw between the waves of darkness, how they all came in out of the moon-shadows and stood round My Lord, men in rough sheepskin garments. But I had known Persian soldiers and court officials, and I knew them now, the two leaders; the rest were of another kind.

One of them, one of the lesser kind, said, "The corn harvest will be good this year."

And the next wave swept me away with it into a great blackness.

When I woke, the first green light of morning was washing cool down the hillside. The fire had burned out and last night's wind had died away. The morning star that the Persians call Astarte was pale among the branches of the almond trees; and the drums from the village were still. They must have broken the faded violet garlands long ago, and opened the tomb and found the dead God risen.

I lay still, because I knew that when I moved, the dreadful thing would begin. At last I dragged myself to my knees, and crouched there, knowing for the first time that I was hurt in the shoulder. And I saw what I had fallen over. It was Arkadius' body with its throat cut.

I disentangled my feet from the folds of his chlamys, and the coverlid that I had flung round me when I ran out, and got up and went to My Lord. He lay rent and hacked in a score of places. The killers had dragged out their spears, but three arrows still stood in him. His face stared up with wide eyes, his lips drawn back from

378

the clenched teeth. His arms were flung wide, his sword still in his hand and the cloak tangled round his shield arm. The marks of fire were on him, and blood—blood everywhere, the grass under him sodden with it. But there was no more blood coming now.

I knelt, and bent over him and kissed his dead mouth; there was still a little warmth in it, a little warmth left of all that blaze of life. I kissed his throat and belly and thighs, and the strong manhood between them; and held him in my arms. He had not yet begun to stiffen. I knew that once he did, I would not be able to move him. I put out all my strength and managed a little at a time to drag him clear of the blood-soaked ground where he had fallen.

I got up and dragged myself into what is left of the house. Little of the main hall but the scorched mud-brick walls still standing; and inside the door I had to crawl over fallen roof timbers and charred thatch still smoking in places; but the wind blew the wrong way for the flames last night; at the back of the hall the roof-beams still stood, and when I reached the inner chamber it was scarcely touched, by fire or men. They must have gone straight back to tell their master that they had done his bidding. Even my tunic that I had stripped off last night still lay where I had left it, across the clothes' chest. It was only when I saw it that I knew I was naked. I dragged it on. I took a mantle of my own—one of the Greek kind, of soft fine stuff that one winds again and again round the body and flings over one shoulder. It was the best thing I could think of for the purpose it must serve. I took the little ivory box in which I keep my pots and sticks of cosmetic, from the table beside the stripped bed-place. I pricked up the wick of the little lamp that still burned—it seemed strange that it still burned—that I might have light to work by, for the full daylight would not come for a while yet. I took clean linen, and went outside and drew water from the well.

Then I went back to him, bearing all things needful. The last warmth had gone from him in the little time that I had been away.

I set the lamp at his head. I dared not pull out the arrows for fear of what more damage I should do; so I broke them off as close to the heads as I could. I washed the blood from him and combed his beard and his grey-gold lion's mane of hair; and swathed him in the soft folds of my mantle—crimson as the dark-hearted anemones, whose name, men say, means Darling, purple-bordered for the flowers of Attis. In Melissa they would be rejoicing in the Risen Lord. The daylight was growing, but it was not yet strong enough for the thing that I must do next; I moved the lamp to cast its light more clearly on his face, and the flame leapt an instant and cast a flicker of movement over it as though he, too, were about to wake . . .

I took his head in my lap, and began to paint his face with red and saffron pigment and green malachite on his lids, and rimmed his eyes with kohl. And when I had finished it was full daylight, and the flame of the lamp was thin and colourless as though it too were dead. And My Lord's face was as the face of the Attis bound to his Tree.

And now I must go down to the village and find those who will bury him. I must remember the things that I must buy, the people I must pay. The grave and the wine and the honey, the incense to burn; the priests to make the offerings. He was Lord of Athens and Lord of Timandra; he shall not be thrown into a ditch like a dog.

There are the bracelets he gave me; the warm amber. Honey-in-the-comb. They will fetch enough to see him decently buried.


## The Citizen

A little over a year after the Spartans became our overlords, Myrrhine bore me a child.

When the women's chambers had been purified and they let me in to her, she was lying very narrow and flat under the coverlid, with the little thing naked but for the strip of linen where its life had been cut from hers, curled in the hollow of her arm; and the midwife and our old slave standing by as pleased as though they had done the whole thing themselves.

I had meant to kiss her before I looked at the baby, for it has always seemed to me that a man should be grateful when a woman carries his burden for nine months and goes through many hours of pain and the risk of her life to bear him a child. Even if it was a girl, I do not think I would have exposed it—that must be very hard on a woman. But she opened her arm for me to see, and said, "Here is your son," very softly; and I did not even answer her. I looked first at the baby's legs, which was foolish, for one does not pass on to a child the mere mischance of falling out of an olive tree. His legs were reddish and mottled, and had little bracelets of fat at the ankles. I touched the sole of one foot. It was the smoothest and softest thing I have ever felt, and it curled over my finger almost as if it were another hand.

And then I looked at Myrrhine. She smiled at me and reached

out her free hand to touch my face. "Maybe he'll be an Olympic runner," she said; and I knew that she had seen what I was thinking.

"Maybe," I said, "but he doesn't have to make up for anything, to me, Myrrhine."

Her hand went farther round my neck, and she drew my head down until my cheek was against hers. "I used to wonder, when I was young and stupid, why Theron chose to be your friend before anyone else's. The night he died, and you saw me with the harlot's paint on my face, I think I knew." She was growing very sleepy. She said, so low that I do not think the other women heard, for they had moved ostentatiously to the other end of the room and were nodding and whispering together, "I love you, kind, lame Timotheus." Then she gave me a little push and said, "Go now and hang the olive garland on the door."

The olive garland for a boy and the hank of wool for a girl had been lying ready in the room behind the shop, since the night before. I picked up the garland, proud as a boy myself, and went to hang it on the shop door, thinking how pleasant it would be when the day's customers started coming, and saw it hanging there, and the good wishes and foolish jokes that there would be. For the odd thing was that we still laughed sometimes, just as we still begot and bore children, under the Spartans and the Thirty.

And as I opened the door and stepped out into the street, I heard the women wailing against the wailing of the flutes:

"A tamarisk that in the garden has drunk no water,
Whose crown in the field has brought forth no blossom—"

In the midst of the other things that I had had to think of, I had forgotten that it was the Feast of Adonis.

I shut my ears to the sound, and made a great issue of testing the nail that I had driven into the door-post yesterday, to be sure that it was secure, and hung the garland on it, and stepped back to admire the result.

A man I knew was coming up the street; and I waited for him to come up so that he might notice the garland and congratulate me. But he only jerked his chin towards it, and said, "A boy, then." And before I could answer, "Have you heard the news?"

"What news?" I said, somewhat put out, for it seemed to me that mine must be the only news in Athens that morning; but also anxious, for in those days news generally meant word of somebody's arrest by the Thirty. Then as he did not answer at once, I said, "Who is it this time?"

He said, "They're saying down at Piraeus that Alkibiades is dead."

And the brightness fell from the morning.

"It's not true," I said.

"It seems well vouched for. A ship master from Myteline brought it. A reliable man, I'd say."

"How did it happen?"

"Differing stories apparently. The favourite one is that he carried off a girl from her father's house. Wait a moment, the man said her name—Timandra, that was it—and her father and brothers came after him and fired the house where they were, and shot him down as he broke out through the flames."

But I remembered things that Theron had told me, in the long talks we had had during his illness. "No, oh no," I said. "Timandra was with him at Sestos—right from the start of the Propontis campaign. She was a Bithynian flute girl, and if he carried her off from anyone it was from Tissaphernes."

"You seem to know a lot," he said.

"My friend—my wife's brother saw her more than once, and the fleet talked."

We stood and looked at each other in the early morning street, with the flutes wailing for Adonis at the far end of it. He was the kind that takes his time about getting round to an idea, but I saw the understanding grow slowly behind his eyes. "Who, then?" he said at last.

"Spartan or Persian or Athenian Oligarch—we shall never know. But I reckon Kritias and the Thirty will sleep more easily in their beds tonight."

He glanced round as though to make sure no one was standing behind him, and said quickly, "Yes, well—the blessing of the Gods on your son, neighbour." And went his way.

The little knot of mourning women with the dead Adonis in their midst were coming up the street.

"At his vanishing away she lifts up a lament,
    Oh my child! At his vanishing away she lifts up a lament,
Oh my Enchanter and Priest!
Like the lament that a house lifts up for its master, lifts she
    up a lament,
Like the lament that a city lifts up for its Lord, lifts she up a
    lament.

Her lament is for the corn that grows not in the ear,
Her lament is for woods where no tamarisks grow,
Her lament is for a garden of trees where honey and wine
    grow not.
A weary woman, a weary child, forespent . . ."

A girl ran out of a nearby house with an armful of little dark red roses, and scattered them before the bier.

And I remembered, Apollo Far-shooter! How I remembered, the red roses mashed under the feet of the young men marching out for Syracuse. And the young man riding alone with only a groom to carry his great shield; head up in the early sunshine, and the wide gaze that seemed to look on all Athens as lover looks on lover.

I went in and shut the door behind me.

And I thought, 'Our last hope is gone from us now.'

There were many who did not—would not might be more like it—believe that Alkibiades was dead. "It's a trick to make us lose heart," they said. "They couldn't kill Alkibiades as easily as that." A year later there were still rumours that he was alive and had been seen somewhere, in Persia, in Thrace, even lying hidden in Piraeus. "He'll come back," people said. "He'll come back, and save us. He'll come back, and then we'll see—"

In the end it was Thrasybulus who saved us, coming down from Thebes with his following, to make his headquarters in the old mountain fortress of Phyle and gather more—old seamen and soldiers, young hotheads eager to die for the freedom of their city; they got away to him despite the Thirty and the Spartan guards. And when the time came they swept back and set us free. Kritias was killed in the fighting. He made, I'm told, a surprisingly good end.

So we were free, and rebuilt the mile-wide breach in the Long Walls, and said, "We are Athens again."

But we are not. Something that was Athens when I was a boy will not be there for my sons. This is a world that Thrasybulus has coloured like himself, a grey world that does not like ideas any more. It has banned the plays of Euripides because they made men think. It's the kind of world that would like to give Socrates the hemlock bowl.

And there is no Alkibiades to come back and save us from ourselves.

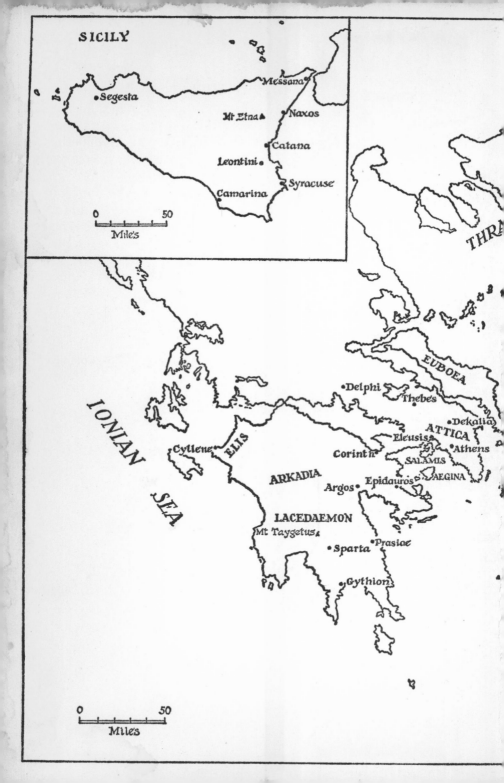